Praise for Michael Cochrane's
Night Soil: A Novel

". . . one smart, wild and supercharged ride from the start to its shocking finish."
> — *Tim Wolochatiuk, Producer/Director of* We Were Children,
> Jonestown Paradise Lost *and* Storming Juno

"Beautifully written, wonderfully funny . . . cannot recommend it enough."
> — *Bill Rogers, Divorce Lawyer*

"Climax is a blast!"
> — *Marcel Strigberger, Author of* Boomers,
> Zoomers and other Oomers

"Incredible, realistic and wild ride through some dark places in our court system . . . but with a great sense of humour."
> — *Lorne Honickman, Lawyer and Legal Affairs Commentator*

"Like a string of pearls . . . Terrific read."
> — *Joel Miller, Divorce Lawyer*

Other Books by Michael Cochrane

NONFICTION

Surviving Your Divorce: A Guide
to Canadian Family Law (6th edition)

Surviving Your Parents' Divorce

Do We Need a Marriage Contract? How a Legal
Contract Can Strengthen Your Marriage

Do We Need a Cohabitation Agreement? How an
Agreement Can Strengthen Your Relationship

Class Actions: A Guide to the Class Proceedings Act

Strictly Legal: A Guide to Canadian Law

Family Law in Ontario for Lawyers and Law Clerks

FICTION

Night Soil: A Novel

Olympic Lyon: The Untold Story
of the First Gold Medal for Golf (2nd edition)

NIGHT SOIL II INFERNO

A Novel

Michael Cochrane

Legal Intel

ISBN 978-1-988344-46-1 (paperback)
ISBN 978-1-988344-47-8 (e-book)

Production Credits
Editor, proofreader, project manager: Karen Milner
Interior design and typesetting: Adrian So, Adrian So Design
Cover design: Adrian So, Adrian So Design
Cover illustration: Huzaifa Mohamedbhai

Published by Milner & Associates Inc.
www.milnerassociates.ca

This work is dedicated to my growing flock of grandchildren:
Luca, Leo, Isabel and the little one we are waiting for as
I write this. We all have stories to tell, and your day will come.
There is only one guide for what you write: be honest.

It is also dedicated to my wife, Rita, who understands
my need to slip away when the story calls.

I also want to acknowledge the inspiration I have received from those Canadian
artists, musical and otherwise, that I mention from time to time, but partic-
ularly for this book, Tony Dekker and the Great Lake Swimmers. Stealing
tomorrow from today. Indeed.

Contents

*Midway in our life's journey, I went astray from the straight road
and woke to find myself alone in a dark wood.
How shall I say what wood that was! I never saw so drear, so rank,
so arduous a wilderness! Its very memory gives a shape to fear.*

—Dante Alighieri, *The Inferno*

1

PTSD

Wednesday July 13

AS A GENERAL RULE divorce lawyers don't make very good psychiatric patients. Alienists ourselves, we've seen too much, been forced to diagnose too many people and then watch them endure the heartbreak of a change that never materializes. I learned early on, people don't change. They simply do–not–change. But, I have to say, it's amusing, in a perverse sort of way, watching them pretend they are, if not better, then at least different. Ultimately, though, it's just sad.

And yet, notwithstanding that very profound insight into mental health, here I sit in a worn knock-off of an Eames lounger, across from *my* psychiatrist, Dr. Sheila Rubin. She has been trying desperately for months now to get me to swallow her so called "analysis" of my situation. "You have suffered a trauma," she opined. Brilliant.

Full disclosure: I'm only here because the Law Society made me commit to a series of counselling sessions as a condition of getting my ticket back after months of suspension. Lucky for me, I guess, that COVID turned out to be a blessing of sorts when it shut down the courts and most law offices for a stretch. I can't say I put the downtime to good use. I didn't speak to my brother, Sean, for months. God, maybe a year. I have no idea how he managed to get through those strange days. And then there was the weight gain and of course the alcohol. Not good.

Dr. Rubin's office is situated on the lower level (read in the basement) of her home in West Toronto, grim Parkdale to be exact. It's mid-July, and hot and sticky, so she has one of those tiny so-called miracle air conditioners from Canadian Tire struggling to cool the room. Like so many miracles, it's not quite as advertised.

Due to the COVID plague, all of our previous counselling sessions had to be awkward Zoom meetings so this is the first time I've actually seen her face to face. Again, not as advertised on her website where, like the stereotypical real estate agent, she appears to be twenty years younger, well-coiffed and simply thrilled to be alive.

Despite the mugginess of this musty little room, she has a large frothy teal wool scarf wrapped around her neck like a monk's cowl. Apparently, her middle-aged neck, and just her neck, is cold. However, the rest of her body must be toasty because she's wearing a floral-patterned cotton sundress, more suited to a day at the beach than any so-called professional encounter. Unfortunately, her frock is also sleeveless. As she leans back in her chair, hands locked behind her head, and swivels her considerable girth from side to side, I must bear witness to her drooping crepey arms and lightly powdered armpits. Dear God in heaven. What did I do to deserve this form of punishment? I yearn for our talking-head Zoom meetings if only to avoid the gale force of her perfume. She smells like a teenage girl who has tried every single sample at Shoppers.

As she droned on, I discreetly admired my Grand Seiko watch and estimated that she had been talking—non-stop—for about ten minutes. Without even looking at me she has just recited the tragic events around Lester Donald's death, forgetting, I assume, that *I was fucking there* when Paul Campbell shot him in the throat. She has also felt compelled to remind me—yet again—that being suspended from practice these long months has given me a wonderful opportunity for personal something *blah blah blah blah blah*. Thank God this is the final session. Next week the suspension ends and I can get back to the office and what's left of my law practice.

But then she suddenly stopped her swivelling monologue, leaned forward, elbows on her knees (which were spread a little too wide for my comfort, I mean talk about manspreading), planted her large bare feet in front of me—clad in worn troll-like sandals no less—and looked right into my eyes. I prayed this was a sign she was wrapping up the session because I had parked on Queen Street and the ruthless towing enforcement was going to start any minute.

Dr. Sheila reached out and took my hands as if we were about to begin a seance. "Andrew, it has been a real pleasure getting to know you these last few months. I've seen tremendous growth in your personal insight. People can change. We can change. It takes work but personal growth is possible . . . you suffered a trauma . . . but you are living proof," *blah blah blah*. The only thing I'm living proof of is that a man can keep a straight face under just about any circumstances if he simply thinks about the implications of the proposed new rules in baseball for a ban on defensive shifts and the introduction of a pitch clock.

As I struggled to avoid looking at, well honestly, the dark grotto between her knees, my eyes landed instead on her monstrous unpainted toes now displayed before me. "Dr. Rubin, Sheila, I appreciate your help. It's been wonderful. Really. You're right, people can change." Trauma? You want trauma? I vowed silently to stop at The Dakota on the way back downtown for something strong enough to wash the PTSD (Pits and Toes Stress Disorder) of those armpits and thick yellow toenails from my memory.

"Andrew, I'm so glad we met." She clapped her hands and, with some effort, rose from her chair and handed me her business card. It was cheap, a blend of soft blues and greens with an image of a wave cresting behind her name. It reminded me of something a hungry timeshare salesman might hand out. "And please feel free to check in with me from time to time. I want to know how things go."

"I appreciate your offer and I'll stay in touch. I promise . . ." *to never set foot in this part of Toronto again.*

I made my way up the narrow creaky wooden stairs and out the side door into the sunshine. Free, free, free at last of this perfumery, I fired up a quality cigar and made my way down the block to the comfort of my new Porsche Taycan (GTS Sport Turismo no less) only to find it covered in flyers for some damn rally about homelessness, rent control and God knows what else is crumbling in this city. Jesus Christ, show some respect for the vehicle.

I pulled a handful of the crap off my windshield and tossed it onto the sidewalk, where it blew past piles of unscooped dog shit, over to a homeless man lying nearby. He was exercising his constitutional right under the Charter of Rights and Freedoms to die of exposure on the streets of Toronto. Tattered and shoeless, the rain dog was staring skyward. I glanced up to see what had garnered his undivided attention. There, dangling on the wires overhead, was what appeared to be a perfectly good pair of running shoes. Why, I have no idea.

As he rocked back and forth on a cardboard quilt consisting of a dozen or so abandoned Amazon boxes he turned to me and slurred, "Not good." He pointed at the shoes. "That's a threat, that someone gonna get murdered here."

In a flash, Lester's face was in front of me along with the memory of his gurgling throat wound and stale menthol breath. Stunned and shaking, I fumbled my keys and cigar to the filthy sidewalk. As I bent down to get my fob he pointed at the remains of my cigar, a twenty-dollar Cohiba. "You done with that?"

It had rolled into a soggy crack running between the curb and one of Toronto's standard tire-rim-destroying sewage grates (three inches too high or three inches too low, sometimes both). With a grimace I gestured to it. "Be my guest."

"Thanks, brother." He reached under the car, grabbed the cigar, took a couple of strong draws to keep it going, tucked his bare feet underneath himself, leaned back, and no doubt began to pine for the running shoes that swayed overhead.

No sooner had I climbed into the safety of the car to calm down, than my phone pulsed. It was Hopeless Helen, the new law clerk I'd been using since Bonnie quit to work at some animal sanctuary or immigrant shelter, never sure which. On paper Helen looked good: law clerk degree from Seneca, some experience, decent references, married, no kids (*Our Shih Tzus are our children!* she gushed) and she did not live in the boondocks. Plus, since I was suspended, all she had to do was answer the phone, open the mail and keep the lights on at my office. What could possibly go wrong? Well, a lot actually.

A little desperate with Bonnie gone, and frankly quite hungover, I unfortunately ignored two red flags during Helen's interview.

Professing to be a fitness nut, she said she aspired to being on some TV show where contestants race across Canada for a prize. (Where people find the time for this nonsense I have no idea. Don't they have jobs? Families? Self-respect?) But I thought, okay, fine, sure, great, what she dreamt of on her own time was none of my business.

Except . . .

I soon discovered that she actually needs hip surgery because of an alleged *sports injury* and she uses a cane. I don't recall seeing any cane during our Zoom interview. When she showed up at my office on her first day—during COVID and maskless—she assured me her three-pronged "HurryCane" was just temporary. I took her at her word, that is until I overheard her arguing with her husband on the phone one afternoon. Apparently, her so called *sports injury* was incurred falling down the stairs as she rushed to a beginners pickleball lesson at the Y. She had been using this cane for no less than two *years* and may soon need a motorized scooter to get around. I can't have her banging into my priceless furniture in a Fortress 500 scooter for Christsakes. Strike one, Helen.

Second red flag? COVID. I assumed she was normal, that is, vaccinated. Nope. And not just a non-vaxxer, but a *virulent* anti-vaxxer. (Virulent is from the Latin, *virus*. How one can be virulently opposed to stopping a deadly virus is a mystery.) Her resistance to wearing a mask should have been a dead giveaway but I was not thinking clearly then.

Instead of reaping the benefits of society's multibillion-dollar investment in science, she has on her desk, beside a half-dozen pictures of her beloved dogs, a foot-long tray of colourful vitamins and supplements resembling a full Lego set. On one side rests a glass jug of her special filtered "smart water" (now there are two words I never thought could be paired) and on the other side a perpetual pot of tea brewing some kind of Asian vine that even Carl Linnaeus surely classified as a weed. When steeped it smells like that toxic shampoo you use to get rid of head lice. Brutal. I've been forced to shut my door as she slurps this brew all day long. Strike two, Helen.

One afternoon I overheard her engaged in a conspiratorial *tête-à-tête* with an anti-vax fellow traveller. They were planning protests at City Hall and she was outraged—*outraged! I say*—that the so-called left-wing media was not reporting *the truth*. She hissed into the phone, "Undertakers are finding string-like creatures in the bodies of people who have died from being vaccinated. *They've never seen anything like it!*"

I was already in a pissy mood and couldn't resist so I muttered under my breath, "I'm not sure why more people aren't using *phenol*."

Like a hungry sucker (the fish and well, yes, the other kind too) she leapt at the bait. "Phenol? What's that?"

I turned to her as if surprised that she hadn't heard about the miracle treatment. "You know, *phenol*. You take a rubber bulb filled with phenol, put the attached tube in your nose and squeeze the bulb to release the vapours. It's *guaranteed* to block the virus."

Her eyes were as big as saucers, thrilled at the possibility that here, at last, was a reliable alternative to the dreaded vaccine. In a hoarse voice akin to someone addicted to meth she whispered, "Where can I get it?"

I looked from side to side to make sure no one would overhear my hush-hush secret and whispered, "It's called a Carbolic Smoke Ball."

Before I could finish, she turned to her computer and morphed into that tech nerd we see in every action movie, the one who, with a flurry of keystrokes, quickly hacks into a major metropolitan traffic control system, and begins turning traffic lights off and on and shutting down nuclear power stations. I prayed she was sharing the phenol scoop with her anti-vax network.

I waited a few beats as she searched the world wide web before adding, "If it helps, the legal search citation is EWCA Civ 1, 1892."

Her fingers were on fire now as she unwittingly hunted for the infamous Carbolic Smoke Ball—the advertised "cure" for the flu, which had killed a million people between 1889 and 1890. The bizarre legal case is every first-year law student's introduction to contract law and false advertising. Sweet justice.

After that incident she didn't speak to me for two days, other than to say, "Very funny." And muttering, without a hint of irony, *"People are dying."*

And that's not even why I call her Hopeless Helen. It will become clearer.

Without a minute to regain my composure after my encounter with the homeless cigar-smoker, I picked up the call from Helen. "Hi, Helen, what's up?' I asked, bracing for her latest screwup.

"There's a client here waiting for you."

Here we go.

"No, Helen, I don't think so. No one is booked for today. It's Wednesday. I'm not seeing clients until Monday next week when the suspension ends, remember?"

As I spoke, a young female traffic enforcement officer—with massive gravity-defying eyelashes (she looked like two black moths had landed on her eyes)—tapped on my car window. I glanced at my watch and held up one finger. No, not that finger. I simply indicated to her that I needed one minute.

Helen was babbling now. "Wednesday? Isn't it Thursday? I thought today's Thursday. Oh goodness. Well, she's here today."

What is she talking about? Wednesday? Thursday? It doesn't matter. I'm not seeing clients until next week. "Who? Who's there, Helen?"

"Hang on." I could hear her asking the person their name. "It's a Ms. Rin . . . Rimins?" I have no idea who she's talking about but before I can say anything she blurts out, "Hang on. Here she is, she can tell you yourself." Oh. My. God. She has handed the phone to the person. No conflict check has been done. No retainer in trust. No intake form. And I'm suspended and cannot give advice. She's going to need more than a HurryCane when I get back to the office.

There was another tap at the window and a firm waving gesture from Ms. Moth Eyes to move my car. In the rearview mirror I could see a fucking tow truck. I looked at my watch, nodded to the officer and mouthed, *"One minute."*

"Hello. Mr. Bierce? Francesca Rimini here. Can you hear me?"

"Yes, I'm sorry but I . . ." Then another tap at the window. No more than ten seconds had passed. I looked at the officer and held up my hands, puzzled at her haste. I mean, I need one minute.

"Mr. Bierce I was referred to you by your colleague Mr. Zanutto. I'm in a very difficult situation. He assured me that you, only you, could help."

Rick Z, King of the Bs. B-list, that is. I would never call him that to his face but that's how I think of him. I mean he's a good lawyer, knows his stuff, straight shooter, common sense, never spreads himself too thin and settles a file when the time's right. Clients are apparently happy and pay their bills. He's just a few years younger than me, dresses reasonably well (due to the Bay's annual suit sale I assume), married to the same woman since law school, kids, grandkids, house in the Beach, cottage in Muskoka, and a solid practice. There were always rumours that he was going to be appointed to the bench. Sounds good, I know, but he just never took his practice to the high-conflict level, the get-down-and-dirty expensive Total War, *à l'outrance*, as we say. I never understood it, but I like him anyway.

Bonnie met him at a couple of her charity events and swooned of course. When I started calling him her "boyfriend" she threw an absolute shit fit and told me that I "could learn a thing or two from him." She could be cold, but I still miss her. Especially on days like this.

"Ms. Rimini, I'm sorry but . . ." I watched as the tow truck pulled around in front of my car and dropped its hitch and the officer started filling out a ticket. The homeless man had risen from his cardboard carpet and was pointing out the shoes swaying above to the officer.

"You fucking idiot . . ."

"I'm sorry? What?"

"No, I'm sorry. Uhh. Not you . . . I just saw someone . . . uhh . . . almost run over a dog . . . Driving too fast . . . poor thing . . ."

"Oh, that's terrible. Mr. Bierce, I'm desperate and need your help. I'm married to Justice Singh and . . ."

Whoa, whoa, whoa. Pump brakes. Come to full stop. "Can I just put you on hold for one second? Thanks." Representing the wife of a judge in a divorce? Good Lord, I need clients right now but there's simply no upside to that kind of file.

The tow truck driver, who looked like a short fat tattooed member of a motorcycle gang, now stood in front of my car. The rain dog, still puffing on my cigar, had moved to the centre of Queen Street and was gracefully dancing and directing traffic. For some reason acid reflux suddenly bit into my chest as I lowered the window and shouted to the traffic flunky. "Listen you piece of shit, if you touch this fucking car . . . so help me God . . . I will sue your fucking ass . . . I need one fucking minute. I'm a doctor . . . I'm dealing with a *medical* emergency. A child's life is at risk!"

She looked genuinely stunned at my toxic tone, flapped her eyelashes, backed away from the car and waved off the truck. Regaining her composure, she held up a finger and mouthed, "One minute."

I popped in a couple of chewable Gaviscon tablets and held up a finger too. Yeah, that one.

I needed to think for a second. Since Lester's shooting I had lost most of my clients and COVID didn't help. I couldn't accept referrals because of the suspension so my practice was pretty much on life support. Was this risky retainer worth it? Take a chance? Rice is rice.

"Ms. Rimini, thank you for reaching out to me. I can be there in about thirty minutes. I'm just finishing up a meeting in the west end on an *emergency* matter." (I know, I know, emergency covers a lot of ground.)

"Oh, I'm sorry, I must have misunderstood, your clerk said you were meeting with your psychiatrist."

Holy fuck. Strike three, Helen. Both my hands were shaking now as I put the car in drive, hit the gas, pulled out, knocking over some idiot on a unicycle (Really? A unicycle. In city traffic.), and left Ms. Moth Eyes in the dust. In my rearview mirror I could see her and the homeless guy helping the stunned clown cyclist to his feet.

I laughed nervously. "Ha, uh . . . yes . . . I think what she meant was I'm meeting with *a* psychiatrist, an important witness on another matter. I look forward to meeting with you shortly. Would you be so kind and put my clerk back on the phone?"

It's a good thing we can't be convicted for our thoughts. Yet.

"Certainly, here she is."

"Helen, Helen?" I could hear her saying something about the hold button and how my phone system was new and difficult. I assure you, it is neither. Then the line went dead.

Forty minutes later—after following a cadre of pseudo-*Tour de France* bicyclists exercising their constitutional right to block a main city street at midday, and then unable to pass a streetcar despite repeated attempts—I finally parked in the underground beneath my office tower. (More on parking issues later. Honestly, it just never ends.)

As I stormed down the hall to my office, a wave of fetid tea fumes filled my nostrils. And if that wasn't enough of a shock to my senses, Helen suddenly came rolling around the corner with one leg in a boot cast balanced on a knee rover, one of those medical scooter boards for the lame. What the F.

"Ms. Rim . . . Rimin . . . the client's in the boardroom. I'm bringing her some more of my tea." She said this with an air of great confidence, as if she had everything under perfect control and the tea was somehow a bonus for that poor unsuspecting woman. I bit my tongue, chewed another Gaviscon tablet, took a deep breath and resolved to deal with Sk8er Grl later.

Striding into my boardroom, I had no idea about the forces I was about to unleash.

2

The Gates of Hell

Wednesday July 13

I HAVE STOOD BEFORE Rodin's sculpture, *La Porte de l'Enfer*, in Paris several times, in awe of his vision of the entrance to Dante's Inferno and his Circles of Hell. I have pondered whether his nightmarish imagining befits what would become of my clients, those who have sinned in the flesh, the lusty who have betrayed reason to their appetite. Would their carnal souls really spin forever in a hellish whirlwind?

Seems a little harsh.

Based on my initial assessment of Ms. Rimini's appearance in my office that afternoon, she did not seem to be in any danger of giving in to such appetites. At my boardroom table sat what appeared to be a fortyish "librarian" straight out of central casting. Plain brown shoulder-length hair, modest beige skirt with matching jacket and a white blouse, buttoned to the top. Even with her Smart Set fashion sense, something felt a little off, but I couldn't quite put my finger on it. Bonnie would have known in an instant; she had a sixth sense for such things. Mind you, even I know that classic Plain Janes don't usually have multiple piercings in both ears and, as I looked even more closely—discreetly of course—I could see a dark lavender lace balconette bra through her sheer white blouse. Interesting fashion choice for a librarian. Hmmm, what lies beneath? The slim tattoos of vines just visible on the inside of her wrists suggested she might also bear the proverbial tramp stamp on her lower back. It was probably a large butterfly, a souvenir she wore home from Las Vegas a few years ago when one of her girlfriends turned forty. Unfortunately, not everything stays in Vegas.

Notwithstanding these seeming contradictions and with no intake form—or retainer for that matter—I pressed on. "I'm sorry to hear that you and Justice Singh are having marital problems. I assume he's also consulting with counsel? Do you have any idea who he will be dealing with?" I prayed it was not one of the top five divorce pyromaniacs around Toronto. Surely as a judge he would have more sense, but you never know what has brought spouses to this point. Marital misconduct can lead to powerful reactions. Corrosion. Combustion. Explosion. Or worse.

"First, Mr. Bierce, I want to thank you for seeing me. I don't know what I'm going to do if you can't help me. So many lawyers have told me they have a conflict and can't help. I don't understand it."

Conflict? I suspected that this was probably not a case of the judge sprinkling small retainers around Toronto to conflict out the top divorce lawyers. The lawyers she would have consulted had a different kind of conflict, a conflict with potential professional suicide. Surely she understood the sensitivity of divorcing a judge.

"Well, I hope I can help. Let's talk a little bit about what has been going on, what led to your separation—and I should clarify that this is just a preliminary meeting. I cannot give any advice or be retained until next week. It's complicated."

"I understand your situation. Mr. Zanutto explained. We're not separated yet but . . ."

Ahh, she is seeking a little strategic advice before pulling the plug. Good for her. You would be surprised how much can be accomplished with a little well-timed pre-separation financial planning. (Advice for which a spouse pays a premium. Honey, I think we should use your inheritance to pay off the mortgage. Once the discharge is registered, wait a year then pull marital plug. Inheritance now gone.) "Okay, so let's take a look at the situation *as if* you were separating tomorrow. We can do some rough calculations . . ."

"I'm sorry, Mr. Bierce, I should've been clearer. I don't want to separate. I need your help to *prevent* a separation. Jay, my husband, doesn't agree with me taking certain steps. I assume you've heard the rumours, from Provincial Court, 1000 Finch Avenue, about what happened a few Christmases ago, before COVID?"

"I've heard no rumours. I'm sorry, but I don't move in the legal circles at criminal court and especially the court on Finch."

There's a court on Finch? I wasn't prepared to admit that I didn't know there was one way up there. And Finch Avenue? Good Lord, it's impossible to use those two words in a positive sentence unless it also concludes ". . . and a suspect has been taken into custody."

I noticed that with my plea of ignorance her demeanor changed and she leaned back in her chair, seemingly resigned to having to tell her story one more time. It was as if she knew she would tell it, get it over with and leave disappointed once again. Interesting.

"I work—worked—at that court. I'm a court clerk."

Oh-oh. Shit. "I see." I cannot imagine a clerk making more than forty or fifty thousand a year. She's not even close to my fee wheelhouse. Bonnie would have intercepted this rice deficiency in a minute. Crap, now I'm stuck talking to her for an hour, and for free. *Fuuuck.*

"I was working for Judge Glinka, in his court. Do you know him?"

Glinka? I think he might have been at Keg's celebration of life at Burdettes Funeral Home a couple or three years or so ago. Admittedly, it's all a somewhat fuzzy recollection given my state of considerable inebriation that evening. "I'm not really familiar with the judge."

"He's been a judge for years. He was appointed at a young age, in his late forties, I think, but he's coming up to his mandatory retirement age soon."

"Wow, that's a long time. Good judge?"

The way she dropped her jaw, raised an eyebrow and scowled at me suggested a certain skepticism. "You really don't know anything about him or this situation at the courthouse, do you?"

"No. I don't."

She let out a long sigh.

"Why don't you fill me in?"

And with my invitation she threw open the Gates of Hell.

3

A Dark Wood

Wednesday July 13

BEFORE MS. RIMINI began her tale I had to ask a quick question. "The tea, from my clerk, I see that you're not drinking it. Do you mind if I move it out of here?"

"Oh God, please. I didn't want to hurt her feelings, her being injured and unable to participate in *The Great Race* TV show. How tragic. But, yes, please. Take it away, it's horrible."

Thank God. I slipped into the hall and dumped two full cups of tea into a planter.

With the toxic stench fading she began her tale of woe. "Back in the fall of 2019, well before COVID, I was asked to organize the courthouse's annual December year-end celebration."

"That's a while back. Christmas party?"

"We're not allowed to call it that. We call it the Festival of Seasons. It used to be a relatively small affair in previous years, sell a few tickets to cover costs, book a room somewhere, drinks, snacks, a little music, drop in, have a drink, then get to the GO train . . . you know." As she said "you know" she shrugged her shoulders as if to say "you understand." "But this particular year it got out of control."

"Out of control how?"

"I had booked the upstairs room at Bandidos on Finch, across from the courthouse. Make it easy for people. You know (shrug). Everyone is invited but you never know who will show. Depends on the weather, you know (shrug), most people either go directly home or they go off to the real parties, you know (shrug), but word gets around to Crowns, court staff, lawyers, some cops . . . spouses are invited but . . . you know (shrug)."

"They're invited but no one wants their spouse around because there's monkey business. I get it." Unconsciously, I started to shrug too.

"No, no, it's because people don't want to spend the whole evening introducing their spouse to every second person, you know (shrug). Anyway, as I said, we sell tickets to offset the costs; $15.00 gets you in, a couple of drink tickets, some apps, you know (shrug)."

"So what went wrong?" Oh God, now I was shrugging after each sentence.

The boardroom door opened and Hopeless Helen stuck her head in. "Mr. Bierce, I'm getting ready to leave a little early if you don't mind. I have a sports medicine clinic."

I let out a sigh. *Right. Sure you do.*

"And it takes me a while to get there." She looked down at her rover scooter as if to say, *here is my cross to bear.* "I see you finished the tea, would you like a little more before I go?"

Francesca and I fairly shouted in unison, "No, no, no, thank you. No tea."

"Helen. We need to talk tomorrow . . ." *about your two weeks' notice.*

"I left that file of the new client contacts on your desk and a note from that doctor who called again."

I paused and closed my eyes. Acid reflux started gnawing at me again. *What is she talking about?* "Helen, wait. What do you mean, new client contacts? And what doctor?"

"The doctor wouldn't leave a name."

"How do you know it was a doctor?"

"I could see the name on the caller ID."

"Why didn't you write it down?"

"Because they said they would call back, so I didn't write it down, but they have called a few times, it sounded urgent."

I didn't know what to say to this idiot.

"I'm sorry, Ms. Rimini, I just need to clarify something else before we continue. Helen, what do you mean there is a file with new client contacts?"

"It's the blue file folder I left on your windowsill. I'm sorry, I really need to get going, my husband's waiting for me downstairs. He doesn't like to leave his truck parked too long. Can we discuss it tomorrow? Look on the windowsill."

I turned to Ms. Rimini, shook my head and asked her to continue, and with another shrug she carried on. "So anyway, this particular year my friend, Dave Goodwin, offered to help with ticket sales. Do you know Dave?"

"Yes. I do."

Do I know Dave Goodwin (aka The Major)? I do indeed. Not just from our days playing hockey together at law school but also from the early days of practice. We had shared chambers for a couple of years. I'm not sure why we fell out of touch but I knew he had gone on to a successful personal injury practice. The past few years, his cheesy ads seemed to be on CP24 TV non-stop. You've seen them. Dave skates up to an old Leaf enforcer, some goon who played half a season, Dave knocks him into the boards, then turns to the camera and says, "Tough? You don't know tough. Been injured? Call 416-HIT-HARD."

I know. Ridiculous but fitting, I guess. Dave's nickname had nothing to do with the military. It was because he was always in the penalty box serving a five-minute major for his cheap shots.

But how was Dave involved in this Christmas crap?

With a shrug she carried on. "Dave offered to sell tickets. We were having problems, no one seemed to want to go."

"Why was that?" (And let me just say at this point that I am now leaving out references to shrugging. Just understand that at the end of every sentence each of us is now shrugging as a new form of physical punctuation. It's exhausting.)

She hesitated. "The year before, there had been some trouble at the Christmas party, a judge got a little tipsy and was being too 'friendly,'" the dreaded air quotes were tossed on, "with some of the younger female Crowns and court reporters."

"Friendly how?"

"Kissing them, patting them on the ass, making comments, pestering them to dance. Some of them were upset and said they were taking a pass on the party in 2019. There have been other complaints about that judge."

"Like?"

"One of the new court reporters was called into his chambers one day. She came in, lights were low, just a lamp on, and he started giving her his usual BS about how beautiful she looked. He did that to all the young women, then he asked her to turn on the lights. She reached over and flicked the office light switch, which he said was a gift from his wife. When the light came on, she could see that the plastic frame around the light switch was an image of a man with his pants down and the switch was his . . . you know . . ." she gestured by pointing with her index finger, "erect penis, and then he said, 'You can flick my switch any time you want.' He was standing there in his underwear in the middle of changing from his judicial gowns."

"This is the same judge we're talking about?"

She took a sip of water and a breath. "Judge Glinka."

"As I said, don't know him."

"You will." She said this now as if disgusted.

"How old is this Glinka character supposed to be? This light switch stuff sounds like a horny teenager."

"It's not! It's serious!" She snapped. "Everyone minimizes his behaviour. The reporter was traumatized!"

Traumatized? By a light switch? That seemed a little much. "But please, continue." And yes, I shrugged.

"He's a seventy-year-old man now but when this happened a few years ago he was in his late sixties. He's married, has a family, grown children, grandchildren. He says he's just being 'friendly.' *It's my Russian background. I love people.* He's been hugging, grabbing ass and kissing any woman he can get his hands on at the courthouse for years. No one did anything."

"Did that reporter complain to anyone?"

"No, some reporters are freelance. Make trouble and you don't get called into work. So she just turned around, walked out, and had a good cry in the hall."

Had a good cry? Come on, she sounded a little thin-skinned to me. Surely as a court reporter she'd seen and heard far worse things than a plastic boner light switch? Christ, people bear witness to the real thing on the subway, in the middle of the afternoon. A light switch? Jesus.

"She wasn't the only one who had issues with him. So that was part of the reason ticket sales were slow. That's when Dave stepped in and offered to speak to a few of his contacts about coming and having a bit of, you know, fun." (Don't forget, we are still shrugging.)

"Knowing Dave, I assume he had some success."

"Oh yeah, too much success. He was selling tickets to lawyers, cops, detectives, process servers, everyone. He even started a 50/50 and the pot got up over a thousand dollars. The other people on the committee were upset with me for getting him involved."

Classic Dave, The Major. He ran 50/50 draws all through law school to raise money for our hockey team's year-end dinner. We never knew how much was actually raised or who won. Interest fell off after we discovered that his brother won—twice in a row. I think that's how they paid their rent.

"So many tickets were sold I was worried that we wouldn't have enough food or drinks, or even that the hall might not be big enough. Boy, was I wrong."

"What happened?"

"Our party would typically have fifty people, max, spread over a few hours. By seven o'clock there were over 100. The place was packed. A bar was stocked. There were Grey Goose vodka bottles in ice buckets on each table. A caterer arrived with food. I said to Dave, we can't have outside food in here, extra liquor, we have to order from Bandidos. He waved me off and said not to worry. It had been 'taken care of.'" More air quotes. "Committee members were furious with me."

Sounded like an awesome party to me. "Was it okay with Bandidos?"

"No one said anything. And more people began to arrive, women who didn't seem to be guests of anyone. A DJ started and people were dancing. It was a party but it was too much, it wasn't our party anymore."

"Judges there?"

"Yeah, about four or five."

"Glinka?"

"In the thick of it."

"Why would any of this cause trouble for you and Justice Singh?"

She shrugged and took a deep breath. "When we arrived at the party, early, to do set up, lots was going on. Jay headed off to sit in the corner and discuss the latest Supreme Court of Canada decision with his government-paid French-language instructor." She rolled her eyes as if to say, nerd alert. "He's trying to become bilingual. He's like that, not a party type. He only went because I was on the committee. I grabbed a drink at the bar, chatted a bit, mingled. Had a few more drinks. You know," uh huh, shrug, "circulated."

"Okay."

"Eventually I had to push through a crowd to get to the ladies' room. As I headed down the hall Justice Glinka grabbed me by the hand and said, 'Give me a Christmas kiss.' Before I could say anything, he pulled me in and gave me a full kiss right on the lips." She paused. "And he shoved his tongue in my mouth. I pulled away, I could see my lipstick all over his face and he was smiling. I dove into the bathroom. It was packed. I brushed my teeth as best I could, rinsed my mouth out and locked myself in a stall for a few minutes. I straightened up, put on fresh lipstick, you know." (Yup, shrug.)

I was stunned. "Was Glinka drunk?"

"I think so. On my way back from the washroom he tried to grab me again, but I slipped by. Once I got back out to the main party area, I could see that things were getting out of control, *drunk and drugs out of control.* There were a lot of people there that I didn't know. I saw a couple in the cloakroom. A cop was getting a . . . you know," she moved her head in a bobbing motion, ". . . a . . . a blow job, right there. The DJ was blasting music and the dance floor was packed. A few women were, like, half-naked, dancing."

"Okay." *Why didn't Dave invite me to these parties?* "There were drugs?"

"I saw in the ladies' room that something was being passed around. Coke. Ecstasy. I don't know. I'm not into that. Anyway, as I stood there looking at this raging party, you know, suddenly Glinka grabbed my hand and dragged me onto the packed dance floor. He pulled me up against himself in a slow dance and started rubbing against my breasts and grinding against me. He said, 'Jay's too busy to take care of you? That's not a roll of quarters you're feeling,' . . . or, 'that's not a roll of lifesavers.' It was disgusting. And then all of a sudden, he reached around and grabbed both cheeks of my ass." She stretched out her arms in a bear hug, took a deep breath. "He grabbed me so tight that his fingers . . ." She looked at the ceiling.

"What?"

"His fingers slipped into my vagina." She cried softly into her hand and whispered, "He said 'Francesca, you're not wearing any panties tonight.'"

Jesus Christ. What the hell. "Why would he say that you're not wearing panties?" I was so shocked, I didn't even shrug.

"Because I wasn't wearing any." She snapped at me.

I wasn't ready for that answer. "Okay, I don't want to pry here but is that normal for you? No panties at parties?"

"No, it's not normal! That's what the doctor recommended because I had a yeast infection."

Oh, gross. I hoped she didn't notice my grimace.

"Where was Jay when this happened?"

"Still *parlez-vous-ing* the latest Supreme Court of Canada appeal cases with his French instructor. I pushed Glinka away from me and ran over to Jay, and as soon as he looked at me he knew something was wrong. I told him what had happened, and he lost it. He ran out on the dance floor looking for Glinka but he was gone. I guess he knew he had gone too far and got out of there."

"What happened after that? Did you tell anybody, report it to the police? A colleague?"

She looked at me like I was crazy. "Report it to who? To the drunk police officers beside me on the dance floor? To the committee members who blamed me for the party being hijacked? The other judges? His buddies? Dave? He'd already left anyway. Tell them that I didn't have panties on? Jay just grabbed our coats and we went home. When we got there, we had a hell of a fight. Jay said I should let it go but I wanted him to do something. I felt he was blaming me. We were up all night. It was horrible."

"That's terrible. But Jay wanted you to let it go? He blamed you?" That seemed odd.

"It gets worse."

"Worse?" I was having trouble imagining something that could top this shitshow.

"The next morning, I demanded Jay do something. At the very least I said that Glinka should admit what he did and apologize. I didn't want to be in his courtroom anymore. So Jay reluctantly went to the Finch courthouse even though he doesn't sit there. He used his pass to get into the judges' chambers, found Glinka in his office, confronted him, and they had words. Glinka said something awful to Jay and then Jay pushed him. Glinka fell, hit a filing cabinet and broke his collarbone. He had to be taken to the hospital."

"Oh my God. How did they keep this out of the news?"

"It may not be in the news, but it has been the talk of the courts for over two years. Everything was put on hold during COVID but now it's finally coming to a head. There is talk of a judicial discipline inquiry or something, maybe criminal charges against Jay, against Glinka too. There's a police report but it says that there was nothing more than two people arguing. Nothing about me. In the meantime, they moved me to Old City Hall. Jay has been moved way out to Milton. We live in Ajax, so it has been a logistical nightmare getting to and from work. During COVID we had to work from home a lot and the tension was unbearable. We barely see each other even when we are at home together. Mr. Bierce, I want justice. I want something to be done about Glinka. Mr. Zanutto said you knew how to get results, that you didn't care who got in the way. I need that kind of help. I need to deal with this even if Jay just wants the whole thing to go away."

I'm not sure I liked what I was hearing about Rick Z. Why was he pushing this case at me? I'm not St. Jude for Christsakes. I don't even know how to handle a judicial inquiry. Or criminal charges. Divorce? She doesn't even seem to want one.

I decided to proceed carefully. No commitments. And let's not forget—no retainer yet. Who's going to pay for this? Not her on a clerk's salary. "Where's Judge Glinka now?"

"On leave. At home. Writing decisions and doing research on a law book supposedly. As if." Her words were dripping in sarcasm. "Full pay too. They say he's going to retire but only on certain conditions."

"I see."

"The worst part is no one speaks to us at either court. We're being shunned."

"You and Jay are being shunned?" That seemed odd.

"Yes. Shunned." She just shrugged (of course) and groped around for her purse. "I'm sorry, I have to get back to work."

Since when are victims shunned? "Wait, Francesca, why would you and Jay be shunned?"

She simply shrugged again. "I have no idea."

That strange word, *shunned*, brought to mind something I'd heard my father say, a long time ago when a fellow in his workplace was causing a lot of trouble for him. He always seemed to have the right quote on the tip of his tongue.

"Warn a divisive person once, and then warn them a second time. After that, have nothing to do with them. Shun them. You may be sure that such people are warped and sinful; they are self-condemned." Titus 3:9-11

Shunned? Self-condemned? Why?

I must watch where I go in this camp of woe.

4

Didn't See That Coming
Friday July 22

I'M GOING TO BE HONEST, having heard that story I realized that if I was going to take this on, I would need some help. Everything Francesca had told me—the assault, the fighting in chambers, the possibility of a judicial inquiry and criminal charges—was right out of my league. I needed advice from someone who moved in this criminal-law world, in these courts. Desperate, I thought of Alvin.

We had not been in touch for several months as he seemed to have taken Randall Williams's *lay down with dogs, wake up with fleas* advice to heart and kept a safe distance from me as the shit rained down after Lester's death. Text messages went unanswered, calls were not returned. After a while I just gave up. I mean, after all, he owed me nothing. Sure, I got his precious engagement ring back for him but that was now well over two years ago and, seriously, I had dragged him into some dangerous shit with Paul and Chloe. Unwittingly, mind you, but still, it was bad.

Anyway, I thought I would give it another shot, so late afternoon I parked myself on the steps in front of Old City Hall with an ice cream cone, hoping to bump into him.

I wasn't there thirty minutes and it paid off. But I had to do a double take as Alvin came through the massive wooden front doors and skipped down the steps. His Dockers and worn corduroy sports jacket were gone, replaced with a stylish summer-weight grey suit of what I assumed was Third World origin (i.e., Banana Republic), a simple dress shirt and a slim blue tie. Of particular note, his battered Blundstones were gone. In their place were contemporary light-brown leather dress shoes. Unfortunately, I also spied flashes of pink human flesh between his pant leg and shoe. Oh God, he had fallen for the dreaded no-sock look, so 2009. At least he had not been drawn into the craze of flamboyant jester-like coloured socks. He was still bald, of course, but now he was sporting a well-groomed scruff-look beard and sideburns. Well, well, well. What's got into you, Alvin? You metrosexual, you.

I dumped the remains of my cone and moved to intercept him. "Hey, hey, my friend. What a *co-inky-dink*. Long time no see. You are obviously keeping well. Looking good, very stylish, very *GQ*." With a generous smile, I quickly grabbed his hand for a shake so he couldn't get away.

I could see that my firm grip caught him a little off guard. "Hey, Andrew. Yeah, life's been busy but good. Hope you're doing okay. Look I'm on my way to . . ." I held on limpet-tight. You're not going anywhere, my friend.

"No problem. I'm on my way to something too, but when I saw you I had to say hi. So great to see you. Hey, but now that I bumped into you can I ask you for some quick advice?" I tightened my grip.

I could feel him stiffen. "Advice? If you need a criminal lawyer, I can refer you . . ."

"No, no. It's about 1000 Finch and all the *shenanigans* going on up there."

That stopped him in his tracks. His hand suddenly felt like it had been pulled out of a neglected aquarium, wet and slimy. "If what you're talking about is what I think you're talking about, I have advice alright—run and keep running. That situation isn't some joke like, you know, that judge wearing a Make America Great Again hat into court. This could be serious shit for a few people."

I'd forgotten about that Hamilton judge who thought that wearing his MAGA hat in a Canadian courtroom the day after Trump became President would be funny. *Funny? Funny like how? Like, I'm a clown?* Not so funny after a judicial inquiry slapped him down.

But before Alvin could say another word, I stopped him and pulled him close and whispered, "Whoa, whoa, whoa. Alvin. Incoming. Ten o'clock. Ms. Novak." I could see the unmistakable Lorelei steaming down the steps of Old City Hall on a direct collision course with us. "Don't look. She's right behind us." No sooner had I said those words, than she sidled up beside Alvin and with a smirk threaded her arm through his.

I was *mutus*, but I wasn't about to give up on his now very sticky hand.

"Ms. Novak." I gave her a thin smile.

Without so much as a hello she turned to Alvin. "Why are you talking to this a-hole?"

Now Alvin was *mutus*. Pussycat had his tongue?

I broke the silence. "Well, this is awkward. I see you two crazy kids seem to have worked things out. How adorable."

Sidebar. I have to say Ms. Novak was dressed to kill, and not in something she would wear to court. I'd seen this black lace minidress before. I distinctly recalled unzipping an identical one off the back of that Muskoka client I had been seeing (which did not end well). I vaguely recalled that party frock was a Monique Lhuillier. Ms. Muskoka's clothing business made them for the designer label. Very nice. In the crook of Novak's arm dangled a beautiful red vintage Hermes purse. Based on her income as a Crown it had to be a knock off. Or maybe her whole look was a rental from The Fitzroy. Probably. That made more sense. Regardless, I have to admit, she looked gorgeous.

And on her hand I could see Alvin's grandma's infamous ring, rubies glittering in the afternoon sun. Well, well, well.

"Alvin, we're going to be late, it starts in thirty minutes." She tugged at his arm.

"Bro, thanks for the advice about Finch." I released his slippery hand from my grip.

Her face flashed anger. "You're not talking to him about that, are you? Oh my God, Alvin. We're trying to build a law practice, not ruin it. And *bro*? Really? Seriously?"

Well, this was getting interesting. "Have you left the Crown? You two building a firm together? Congratulations. Shank and Novak LLP. Has a nice *ring* to it." I put a little extra sauce on the word *ring*. "Welcome to private practice."

"Novak *and* Shank. Not that it's any of your business," she sneered.

Alvin, after giving his face a standard rub, finally regained control of his tongue. "Andrew, we have to go, but for your own sake don't poke that bear. Stick to divorces. He's a good judge, not perfect but good. Never been appealed. He's about to retire. His wife is sick. Let him ride off into the sunset."

"Alvin, shut up." She was furious.

Clearly Alvin knew all about Justice Glinka and 1000 Finch. "What about the things he's done? All that crap? The assault at the party? He's an embarrassment. No?"

Ms. Novak stage-hissed to Alvin, "I thought you said he was smart." And then nearly spat at me, "Francesca should know better and no one believes her bullshit."

"That's a little harsh coming from a sister, isn't it?"

"Don't give me any of that sister 'I am woman hear *Metoo* roar' shit. Women like her are part of the problem. I feel sorry for Jay." Jay? She said that with a little too much familiarity, I thought. "He didn't know what he was getting into when he married her." I glanced at Alvin to see if any of that sounded familiar. Nothing? "She'd been trying to line up a judge or well-to-do lawyer to marry for years."

"She never hit on me," Alvin volunteered weakly.

"I said *well-to-do*. And stop rubbing your face."

It appeared that Alvin's balls were now in that Hermes purse.

"Well, your advice has been invaluable. I appreciate it. Where're you lovebirds off to in such a rush?"

"I assume, being *suspended*," she ladled some of her own special sauce on the word, "you were not invited, but today is Randall Williams's swearing in."

Oh. My. God. Don't say it.

"He's been appointed to the Ontario Superior Court, or didn't you know?" She smiled as she pushed in the dagger.

Randall Williams, the man who did the confidential fact-finder for the Law Society about my alleged misconduct, the man principally responsible for my humiliating suspension, had been appointed a judge. I felt sick.

"Alvin, we're now definitely going to be late. Let's go." She tugged on his arm.

But as they headed away in lockstep, Alvin stopped and turned back to me. "Andrew, Finch, seriously, run."

5

Taking Silk

Thursday July 28

THE VIEW FROM my condo down onto College Street just west of Bathurst can be pretty entertaining. My unit, which I prize as a refuge from the world, is on the third level of what was once an old Baptist Church. The original structure was massive and the top-drawer architects who designed the reno managed to carve a dozen large units into it. I was able to scoop the largest unit on the top level when my client, the developer, got in too deep on his legal fees.

His divorce had been a very unpleasant and expensive uncoupling. He, sixtyish, very successful but already twice divorced, needed to rid himself of a twenty-seven-year-old woman named Marcella who fancied herself a social media "influencer."

As far as I could tell, the only people she seemed to influence were women who were prepared to commit atrocities to their eyebrows and lips, thereby giving themselves a look that was at once pouty, yet also surprised. I have seen her handiwork up close, and it can be confusing upon meeting her clients. What just happened? Is this woman upset or shocked?

Notwithstanding my client's financial investment in his young wife's business and her promises of huge returns, her influencer enterprise did not thrive. The last thing my client needed was a comped stay at a nice hotel or dinner at a restaurant in exchange for his wife giving it a post on her Instagram. Actual cash rarely appeared. However, her lack of success did not diminish her appetite for the good life, a very good life.

There was tension. Arguments. And then threats. The final straw landed on the sixty-year-old camel's back over dinner at Canoe one evening while my client was entertaining a very wealthy potential investor. The well-heeled gentleman was interested in his next Toronto church-to-condo development.

Marcella, my client's bride of less than three years, decided this would be the perfect moment to insist she needed a Mercedes G-Wagon, the AMG G 63 4x4. (About $350,000 loaded and I know for a fact that you have to wait a year.) She had done her research on the vehicle and wanted it—immediately—for her business as an influencer. My client waved her suggestion off and suggested politely that they should discuss it later. She persisted. He deferred. Awkward silence ensued. She persisted. He patiently deferred again. The potential investor's head swivelled between them like he was at a tennis match. And she, incapable of reading the now chilly room, persisted one more time. Enough was enough, and let's just say that when my client gave his next answer she looked both pouty and surprised. An expensive and bitter divorce followed and she's driving a used KIA now.

So, one man's loss . . . another man's condo.

My main living room window gives me a direct view to the nightly shenanigans on the street below. Too many homeless, lots of students, nurses coming home late and dozens of people out walking their dogs which have been barking while locked up in 700-square-foot condos and apartments all day long. (No such issues in my building as I single-handedly ensured our condo bylaws declared it a pet-free zone in per*pet*uity.) Tonight, drink in one hand, I have been watching a group of scooter riders gather near the Vespa shop. Sometimes I actually miss riding around downtown on Novak's Pussycat, especially at night, when the catcalls and homophobic slurs weren't as common. The impending fun on the street below, though, could not distract me from the one-page letter in my other hand. I was not taking its contents very well.

The Toronto Police had not returned my robes in the many months since Lester's shooting. Why? Because, as this letter explained bluntly, they had destroyed them. Correct. Destroyed them. During COVID some idiot in evidence storage decided that, since Paul's trial for murder was over, this blood-soaked pile of black cloth—the silk reserved for Q.C. robes, no less—was "unsanitary and unsalvageable." Out with the garbage went my precious gown. I'd had it for over thirty years. I sat in my bay window stewing about this total malfeasance, conjuring some form of lawsuit. Surely there is someone I can sue.

I stared at the remaining parts of my court gear laid out on my white leather Fendi couch: one red velvet barrister's bag (only Q.C.s get red bags) with my initials *A.M.B.* embroidered on the side, one well-worn white (sort of) court shirt, one set of white tabs (admittedly also showing their age), one flat black leather case for storing my tabs (a little battered but still doing its job), my black waistcoat (thank God the police didn't try to snatch that as evidence), my box of silver cufflinks (two pairs, equally lucky) and one pair of double-pin-striped court pants with cuffs (recently dry cleaned). The only thing missing was my beautiful silk robe that for decades I had draped over my shoulders, feeling like a superhero. If I wasn't so furious I would cry. Instead, I poured another generous glass of sorrow-dampening Irish.

Obviously, I had to replace the robe. There was no question. I grabbed my laptop and logged into Harcourts, (monopoly provider of legal gowns in Canada since Before Christ) to see what was available. I was justifiably worried. With the Q.C. designation having been abolished for years and no longer handed out, were they even making silk gowns anymore? This could take a while, so I topped up with more Irish.

As I scrolled around their website, I decided that while I was ordering a new robe, I might as well freshen up my total look with a couple of new shirts and some crisp new tabs. I would get back on the litigation warhorse looking like a new man.

I kept scrolling. Shirts. Shirts. Shirts. Good Lord. Premium Cotton Court shirt, $245.00? That's ridiculous. I recalled that my first court shirt—granted it was a poly—had cost just $35.00. But if, as expected, business returned to normal, I would need two. So I found my size and hit Add to Cart. I scrolled to another page. Tabs. Fresh Q.C. tabs, a modest $18.00 each. That's more like it. Again, I would need two. Add to Cart. I scrolled further. Gowns, gowns, wool gowns, wool gowns . . . and then, finally, silk gowns. My jaw dropped—$1,500.00. Add to Fucking Cart.

Oh, I am definitely suing someone.

6

Penrose Stairs
Wednesday August 10

THE NEWS ABOUT Williams's judicial appointment had really shaken me up. As I sat, head in hands, in the Barristers' Lounge at Osgoode Hall a few weeks later, my mind was spinning nightmare scenarios. Would I have to appear before him, here, in these beautiful, rich, wood-panelled courtrooms? It would be torture looking up at his smug shit-eating smile leering at me from the ornate wood dais, his special red judge's sash draped over his shoulder, a flaming reminder of his new-found power. And let's face it, judges gossip in the washroom and over lunch too. Was he going to bad mouth me to other judges? I would never know what they had heard from him. Prick. Returning to active duty on the frontlines was going to be tough enough post-COVID but now I would need to worry that every case I had could wind up in front of him or some other now-tainted judge. Shit. Shit. Shit.

My growing paranoia was interrupted by a cheery voice. "Looking glum, Mr. Bierce. I thought you'd be happy to be back at it."

It was Rick Z. "Hey, Rick. Getting back in the saddle has had its challenges. And I had to order new gowns . . . By the way I meant to send you a bottle of something as a thank you for the referral of Ms. Rimini. What's your drink?" I lied. At this point I had no intention of sending him anything other than maybe a Tim Hortons card. If that.

"Are you taking it on?" He seemed surprised.

I decided not to ask why he had referred her to me. A referral is a referral. "Still thinking about it. I'm not retained yet. Not really my area but she needs help. She needs, you know, . . ." I paused for effect and looked at him, ". . . *access to justice.*"

We both burst out laughing.

"Right, right, of course, *access to justice*, well, good luck with that." He just shook his head. "I'm glad to see you're back from the suspension, though. Not everyone can handle that bullshit. Look at Blair Colette, what a shitshow that was."

"I heard he was suspended for misappropriation of some fees."

"Some fees? Three million. Spent it all. After they suspended him, I think he knew it was just interim, you know. The full disbarment axe had to follow. Three mil's a lot of money. Compensation Fund had to eat it."

"What's he doing now?"

"No one knows. He just walked away from everything—practice, family—got on his motorcycle and fucked off. That was a year or so ago."

"Brutal."

"You said it."

Brutal indeed but Rick Z had no idea just how brutal. And I wasn't about to breach solicitor-client privilege by letting him know that I was, in fact, very much aware of what had gone down with Mr. Blair Colette. His wife, Maggie, had been in to see me for a consultation about four or five years ago. Bonnie had cleared the decks for what Ms. Maggie Colette insisted was an *emergency* consultation. With a proper conflict check done and $10,000 in trust I, eventually, spent an afternoon with her discussing the approaching shitstorm.

Short version? The Colettes were like many other Oakville, Ontario, families (average household income over $200,000, near the highest in Canada). Blair had a successful law practice in Toronto. Maggie (an OWL—Oakville Woman of Leisure) worked as a volunteer at the Oakville "Art Gallery." (Trust me, as a member of the AGO Curators' Circle, I can tell you to save your time, nothing of note. Sure, there was that Curzec exhibit in 2013 but really, nothing else.)

This family was living the good life—beautiful 4,000-square-foot home with a pool, expensive cars (one Tesla SUV, one BMW X6, plus one Harley Fat Boy S motorcycle that Maggie had bought Blair for his fiftieth), kids had been in local private schools and then went off to McGill and Dalhousie. Family had a nice year-round chalet up at Beaver Valley, a ski club membership, Burlington Golf Course membership, took high-end vacations every year with friends and they had a very well-appointed cellar stocked with the best wines to toast—nightly—their good fortune. That was all on the plus side of the ledger.

However . . .

On the other side of the ledger, they had something else, a HELOC, or Home Equity Line of Credit (HELOC actually stands for How Everyone Lives on Credit). The equity in their home was being regularly drawn down to pretty much vapours. Blair would throw lump sums at the LOC every couple of months to keep their boat (dare I say yacht) afloat and then the family would draw it down again. And again.

There was also the money Blair had borrowed from his law partners, which he assured them would be repaid from his deferred year-end draw. Except, as is wont to happen, he got in over his head with a couple of clients, lost a winnable case and was stiffed on fees. (Client went bankrupt, turns out he'd been living on credit too.) Unfortunately, there would be no year-end bonus draw for Blair and in fact he now owed the firm money. That's when he told Maggie that some belt-tightening for the family would need to start. And that's when she set up the appointment for the so-called *emergency* consultation.

Unfortunately, that consult had to be postponed—along with any belt-tightening—until the family got back from their two-week vacation in Greece with two other couples. On a private yacht. On credit.

We rescheduled the *emergency* meeting. But then it, too, had to be postponed until Maggie returned from a week-long "girls' trip" to Europe, celebrating one of the wives turning fifty-five. On credit. Belt-tightening? What belt?

When she and I finally sat down it was because the next installment on fees for the children's university tuition and residence was overdue, but guess what? The HELOC well had gone dry. Bone dry.

Maggie's response to the family's fiscal crisis? "Should we get divorced?" I didn't know what to say. Divorced? I almost burst out laughing. Why would you get divorced? Half of zero is still zero, actually less than zero when you deduct legal fees. Instead, I sent her home with some advice about protecting herself for the next couple of months. Stash some cash if she could. She needed to be realistic, this family's ship was going down. As she was leaving our meeting, I asked her where she got the $10,000 for my retainer. Yup. That's what had drained the well's last drops, the drops intended for the children's tuition. Oh well.

A few months later I sent her a short email, just to check in, see where things were at, as I'd not heard anything from her. Within the hour she responded, everything was fine. She was in California enjoying a birthday gift, a tour of Napa Valley vineyards with a parliament of OWLs. Blair had turned a corner. Money had come in. University fees were paid in full. HELOC paid down. Life was good again. Belt was no longer in need of tightening. No need to divorce. No need to panic.

However . . .

A few months after that call there was panic, a lot of panic, over at Blair's law firm, as his partners discovered that to solve his family's financial problems he had taken three million dollars from a client's settlement funds in an estate case. Shit hit fan. Dominoes began to topple. The Law Society got involved. Auditors swooped in. But all the money was gone. Blair disappeared into the sunset on his Harley Fat Boy. Maggie and kids ended up fine, but Blair was disbarred.

I'm sure they miss him sometimes.

So yeah, brutal.

Rick Z searched for an empty locker. "I don't know about you but getting up to speed on the new technology has been a challenge, Zoom meetings, ChatGPT, AI, Caselines. Some lawyer apparently uploaded over two hundred documents on a motion and some of the docs were over five hundred pages with exhibits. Can you imagine a judge dealing with that pile of crap? In the old days they would have just rejected that pile of shit at the counter. Upload, download, e-signatures, Docusign, I'm not good at that stuff. I finally just gave up and hired a young techie lawyer to deal with it. You know these new grads, seriously, who cares if they know any law, as long as they can work the computer. She's the most expensive law clerk I ever had but I'm too old for this shit."

As I watched Z pull his gowns out of his blue velvet barrister's bag to get dressed for court, I wondered what on earth he was talking about. I knew how to do a Zoom call but Caselines? Docusign? Chat? What the fuck was he talking about? I decided to change the subject.

"Bummer that I missed getting to Williams's swearing in," I lied. There was no way Rick Z could know whether I was invited or not. "I'm looking forward to my first appearance before him," I lied again, and let that statement hang out there to see what Z's reaction was to his appointment.

My comments barely seemed to register as he stripped down to his boxers and socks and began stuffing a locker with his generic Brooks Brothers brass-button navy blazer, white button-down shirt, striped tie, grey flannel slacks and—Oh God—penny loafers. What next, white tube socks? A Catholic high school grad, he was apparently still dressing like he did in Grade 12.

"You may have to wait awhile. You don't appear much in Barrie Superior Court, do you?"

"Barrie? Seriously?"

"Yup and word is he ain't very happy up there." He laid out his court shirt, pants, tabs and waistcoat. As I watched, I prayed my new silks would arrive soon.

"Barrie? Dear God." That was like being sent to the judicial salt mines.

Standing there in dreadful boxer shorts patterned in Peanuts characters and garish matching socks (I assume these were gifts from his kids, surely a grown man would not buy such things for himself), Z turned to me and in a half-whisper said, "I know, I know, and apparently he's taking it out on everyone, court staff, lawyers. He had a self rep in tears over some problem with documents filed late, chewed out some young woman wearing a hijab, nijab or a burka. I can never tell the difference. Absolute shitshow of complaints already."

"Barrie? Barrie?" I just kept saying it over and over, trying to digest this development.

Barrie is possibly the worst courthouse in Ontario. I heard that the court staff were praying they would find mould somewhere and shut it down like they did with Newmarket's equally ghastly courthouse. These structures were surely designed by some frustrated failed "architect" who graduated at the bottom of his class and then applied a bizarre M.C. Escher–like sense of humour to his designs as a form of revenge on the world. I mean Corbusier would have had this architect jailed in one of his own demented structures.

Consider this. Depending on which side you enter these buildings you could be on the same level but a different floor. I once entered an elevator on the second floor, pushed a button to go to the fourth floor but then emerged on a totally different second floor. The Penrose-like stairs are a terrible alternative as they lead you through drab concrete-slab stairwells to locked doors. Halls wind around the building connecting visitors to ancient, painfully slow elevators that go to places you didn't need to go.

Men's washrooms? Don't ask. The stained urinals are no more than eighteen inches from the floor and always surrounded by a veritable moat of errant piss. In the public stalls no one would dare sit down for fear of sponging up the previous occupants' misfires. Toilet paper? Strictly BYOP. Comments on the walls of the stalls range from sexually threatening to downright hilarious. One Latin-literate occupant wrote simply, *Brutum fulmen!* *

The "Barrister's Lounge"? Designed cruelly to discourage anyone from spending time there. I've been in warmer bus stations. The small meeting rooms outside courtrooms, intended for settlement conferences with clients, are always locked to ensure no one can use them. A sinister interior designer had limited the palette of colours for walls, floors, doors and even furniture to an even two: a murky brown no doubt called Elephant's Breath and a pinky beige known as Dead Salmon.

But it occurred to me one day, a few years ago—as I waited three hours to meet with a judge for all of fifteen minutes—that the Barrie courthouse was in fact a brilliant architectural homage to the justice system. There was surely a method to the madness.

And now this real-life version of Escher's *Relativity* is where Randall Williams will spend his days as a Justice of the Superior Court. So, there is a God after all.

---

* Empty noise.

"You'd think he would be grateful for the appointment," continued Z, "I mean, Mr. 'Chapman's Vanilla Ice Cream' Williams doesn't exactly fit the latest flavours of the month for judicial appointments, if you know what I mean."

I tried to appear uninterested and hoped that Z, who was stuffing his Peanuts boxers into his court pants, would just finish getting dressed. On the back of his shorts, Snoopy was saying, "I'm allergic to mornings." Good grief, it's hard to take a person seriously knowing they're wearing such undergarments.

"Still, gratitude has a short half-life. But I heard through the grapevine," Z gestured to indicate that the gossip was obtained over drinks, "something odd happened and Williams somehow got his appointment on very short notice. He apparently thought he would be sitting in Toronto as head of the Commercial List, you know doing the big corporate cases, top lawyers, big-buck, big-dick stuff. Instead, he ended up in Bugtussle doing foreclosures and low-level motions by people who can't afford their mortgage, never mind a lawyer."

"I didn't figure him for someone who would leave private practice and the money, you know."

"Yeah, I guess he had his reasons. Anyway, birds gotta fly, fish gotta fry. And I gotta scoot. I'm in Divisional Court on an appeal."

And with that pronouncement he threw his black wool gown over his shoulders, fastened its two long ties behind his back to keep it in place, grabbed the handle of his big black briefcase and dashed off to court.

I was consumed by a wave of envy.

7

Wetting My Silk
Thursday August 11

I WAS REALLY STRUGGLING with what to do with Hopeless Helen. Help was scarce. Good help was nonexistent and everyone I ran into had the same complaint. Where were all the staff? I had a headhunter searching for a replacement, but so far she had not come up with anything. Not even interviews. Helen was better than nothing but, not only had three strikes crossed her plate, she had whiffed on so many other things, it was pathetic. If I let her go maybe she could find a job doing something less complicated, less important, no phones involved, a greeter somewhere perhaps—as long as she wasn't forced by *the vaccine Gestapo* to get a vaccination shot or wear a mask, of course. That would be too much to bear.

Bonnie and I had exchanged a few texts over the last year, just staying in touch. She said she wanted to make sure I was okay but was always too busy to go for lunch or, God forbid, drinks. Same excuse. No staff to cover for her. Surely the animal sanctuary could spare her for a couple of hours.

If I could just get her to meet, I planned to lure her back with a generous package: more money, more benefits, five weeks' vacation (she would never use it) and a parking space in the building *plus* a gas allowance. No one wants to mask up and take the GO train or subway anymore. She could get to and from the office in the comfort of her own car (one of the less than three hundred sad little Honda Insights sold that year, I believe). How could she say no?

There was a knock at my office door. As it opened, Helen's face poked in followed by a wave of toxic tea fumes. She wheeled forward a little on her scooter. "Mr. Bierce, can we speak for a minute?"

Oh shit. What has she done now? I didn't like the tone of her voice. "Sure, what's up? Everything okay?" I braced myself.

"Well, I have some good news and some bad news."

Oh God. Oh God. "Okay." My nails dug into the padded arms of my Aeron chair.

"First, your new gowns have arrived from Harcourts. The box is on the boardroom table." Before I could leap out of my chair and rush to them, the other shoe dropped (at least not the one bent up on her scooter). "And I have to give you my two weeks' notice. I have accepted a job at another firm. I'm sorry."

I looked at her, stunned. "What's the bad news?"

With Helen leaving in two weeks, I now had a perfect excuse to lobby Bonnie—intensely—to come back. I immediately texted her. *What's up? Keeping well? Work at the animal sanctuary going well?*

It took a few minutes for her answer to pop up. *I work at the Immigrant Welcome Centre and have for the last twelve months since leaving your office.*

Shit. I was sure it was some kind of an animal thing.

Then more. *I see your listening skills have not improved while suspended.*

This was not getting off to a good start.

Sorry. I was hoping you would join me in celebrating an old legal tradition called "Wetting the Silks." The police threw away my silk robe and the replacement just arrived. I need to christen it now that my suspension is over.

Wetting the silks? I've never heard of that.

Very old tradition. A bunch of us are gathering at The Vatican Gift Shop restaurant over on Gerrard to break in our gowns. I would really like it if you joined us.

I was lying, of course. The only known reference to *wetting* any legal gowns was about 150 years ago in Goderich, Ontario, when, rumour had it, a new lawyer was required to buy rounds of drinks for everyone when he got his gowns. So, while not entirely truthful it seemed like a great tactic to lure Bonnie in from the boondocks for a face to face.

Long pause. I watched my phone.

Where and when?

Yes. She's in. *Thursday September 15, 7 p.m. The Vatican. I'll text you the co-ordinates. Your presence is my present. LOL. Oysters on the half shell.*

Long pause. *I'm allergic to oysters.* With a throw-up emoji.

Shit. *I will cancel the oyster bar immediately.*

I'll try to make it.

I called The Vatican and reserved a table—for two.

I'll get you yet, Bonnie.

8

Justice Delayed
Monday August 29

I HAD TO MAKE a quick appearance at 393 University on one of my new files, the Marrs case. To be honest I had not really read the file in detail, nor even met the client yet, but it sounded like a horrible situation, a custody dispute—over twins, no less—which frankly I have not had much appetite for. As I was just coming on board, I needed to get the matter adjourned until I could (maybe) get Bonnie back in the saddle. A delay of a few weeks would not hurt anybody so I was pretty confident the adjournment would be granted by the court. The lawyer on the other side—my nemesis Fernstein—naturally opposed it.

Why oppose the adjournment? So he could run up some fees and hope his client saw him as their fearless advocate, of course. Fernstein knew it was a waste of his time and my client's money, so he sent a fresh-faced junior up as a sacrificial lamb. He ordered this little fellow (I'm not kidding, he was so small he could have been a charter member of the Lollipop Guild) to try to get me to commit to some terms for the adjournment, visiting with the twins or something, to lock me into a timetable. Not likely. I'll dictate the speed at which we move—or don't.

So, already in a very bad mood (more on that in a minute), I torched the kid with an eloquent and passionate request for an adjournment.

It felt great to be back on my feet in a courtroom, so I gave it a really over-the-top performance with all the standard BS about children's best interests. I even got costs against his client for opposing the adjournment. Take that news back to Fernstein and your client.

And why, you ask, was I in a pissy mood? Well, before I even got to court that morning, there was an unfortunate incident in the municipal parking garage beneath Nathan Phillips Square. And by incident, I mean I had to dispense a little justice to some douchebag before I headed up to court.

Background. You may or may not be aware of this issue, but the abuse of parking spaces is not confined to misuse of Small Car Only spots. No, yet another problem is now plaguing Canadian parking lots. The "disabled." They are now apparently among our most active citizens. They go to the office, the mall, arenas, bowling alleys, theatres, sporting events, cycling, fitness centres and parks, to name just a few activities. I even saw disabled parking spots in front of a rock-climbing facility. Seriously. You name the location or event and not only are the disabled there, but they are in desperate need of the most desirable parking. These spots—which are well defined and extra wide—now consume *entire rows* near elevators and entrances. Okay. Fine. I'm sure there are genuinely disabled people. But. It's my considered view that if we, the able-bodied, are denied these choice spaces, then these special parking spots must be used appropriately, and by appropriate I mean by the *actually disabled*. Not the lazy, the simply too fat or those people who are *just going to be a minute*.

Anyway, before I headed up to court on the twins custody matter, I was unloading Black Beauty 2.0 (the replacement for my original legal briefcase, destroyed the day Lester was killed) from my car, and witnessed a Ford F-150 pick-up truck, Agate Black, V-6, 4x4, fully dressed with those large sparkling chrome rims (an option that is clear evidence of a major dick), wheel into a spot clearly marked, **"Disabled Only/Permit Required"** directly in front of the entrance to the infamous PATH underground pedestrian labyrinth. The driver parked at such an angle that the adjacent disabled spot could not be used either, except perhaps by some poor handicapped soul on a motorized scooter.

I waited and watched. On each side of the truck's cab hung Canadian flags on makeshift poles made from hockey sticks. In between the sticks were strung handmade signs, proclaiming "My Body, My Choice," "F*ck Trudeau," "OUR Charter Rights STOLEN!" and "NO JUSTICE!" A bumper sticker proclaimed to the world that up front in the cab sat a "Proud Member of the Fringe Minority with Unacceptable Views." Another sticker affirmed his love of dogs. All overwhelming evidence of a problem.

The driver's door swung open and out hopped an apparently healthy, full-bearded, middle-aged white man in work boots, jeans and the seriously overdone red-and-black checkered flannel work shirt. As I saw him drop the tailgate and with obvious agility unload cases of bottled water onto a dolly, I wondered what his disability—at least physical—could be. I struggled to reconcile what I was witnessing.

With the dolly fully loaded he started to wheel his cargo to the PATH entrance but then, having noticed me watching, began to feign a limp—acting not even worthy of a high school performance of *Richard III*—as if he was truly struggling. Not very convincing, my friend. I watched as he disappeared into the labyrinth beneath the city.

I wandered over to see if he at least had a disabled parking permit. On his dash sat a very poor photocopy of an actual pass with papers strategically arranged so the permit numbers could not be seen. So, here we had not just a disabled parking spot scofflaw, but a permit fraudster to boot. As much as I needed to get to court, this could not be left unaddressed. His sign said, "NO JUSTICE!"? Well, as William Gladstone said, *Justice delayed, is justice denied. And I delivereth.*

I was not about to risk damaging my own new wheels, so I looked around, first for cameras (none) and then some instrument of justice. A couple of electric golf carts (used to ferry around the brain-addled who have forgotten where they parked) were sitting nearby and I was in luck, the keys were in the ignition. I hopped in one and drove it right up against the driver's door of the big Ford, so tight there was no way he could access the vehicle. Unfortunately, there was also considerable scratching of the paint, stretching from the taillights to the front fender. I drove the other cart up against the passenger side in similar fashion. Tight. Very tight. I pulled the keys out of both carts and threw them into the dash of the first one. That big truck was not going anywhere, anytime soon. I guess you could say it was disabled. I really wanted to stick around and watch the fireworks, but having levied a douchebag tax and with real justice calling me to court, I had to go.

Two victorious hours later, as I followed Fernstein's battered junior Munchkin out of the courthouse and onto University Avenue, I saw a Black middle-aged man wearing a sandwich board and carrying a picket sign in front of 393 University. Clearly not one of the Chinese Falun Gong organ-thief protesters who usually gathered there, he paraded back and forth bellowing into a small megaphone, "Stripped of my Charter rights! No justice! No lawyer will take my case!" Over and over. Occasionally he would stop and hand a sheet of paper to a passerby. They in turn would glance at it and immediately throw it into the overflowing waste basket at the corner. I watched as he earnestly exchanged protest paperwork with a few of the Falun Gongers.

I guess somehow he had reached the end of his rope and concluded that the best way to have his legal dispute resolved was simply to yell at ordinary people on the street.

I worked my way a little closer to read his sandwich board message. Ahh, now I could see. He did not like the outcome of his divorce. Get in line my friend, get in line. The front read: "Court Took My HOME! Gave My Wife EVERYTHING! Bankrupted ME!" On the flip side it cried, "My Lawyer ABANDONED ME! Judge BIASED! I Lost EVERYTHING! NO JUSTICE!"

For colour, he had added a picture of the judge who presumably presided over his personal tragic shitstorm, but the photocopy was so bad it was hard to tell if it was a man or a woman. Beneath it was a carefully printed biblical quote.

It is not right to be partial to the wicked or to deprive the righteous of justice!!!!
*Proverbs 18:5 **

I assumed his wife was the *wicked* and he, the *righteous*. As I watched him, I pondered the prevalence of this simple yet helpful demarcation, often used by warring spouses and divorce lawyers. Wicked v. Righteous.

---

* I don't recall the original authors of the Bible using so many exclamation marks, especially since that form of punctuation really only came into use around 1400 AD. What do I know.

Good morning, Your Honour, my name is Bierce, initial A. I appear on be-half of Mr. Righteous. My friend Mr. Bull in a China Shop, initial S., appears on behalf of Ms. Wicked. Shall we proceed?

Yes, Mr. Bierce, please call your first witness.

Thank you, Your Honour, I call to the stand His Lord Jesus Christ. Please take the Bible in your right hand . . .

Should be an interesting cross-examination.

Oh shit. Mr. Sandwichboard saw me staring at him and was now making a beeline toward me. As he approached, I could see that his protest paraphernalia included something stuck in his hatband.

He handed me a sheet of paper. In bold letters at the top it said, *$50,000!!! to an honest lawyer!!! who will take my case!!!* The slip of paper in his hatband was indeed a cheque for $50,000, made out to *An Honest Lawyer!!!* That would be a tidy retainer for any lawyer if he is looking to launch an appeal.

He stared at me for a reaction. "I see you are an unhappy litigant. Going to appeal?"

"I was denied my Charter rights! My lawyer abandoned me in the middle of the trial!" He was angry. And unshaven. He smelled like dirty clothes that had been ironed.

"Well, with a $50,000 retainer you shouldn't have any trouble finding a lawyer to handle your appeal."

His eyes lit up. (Not the Christmas morning kind of lighting up either. More the Halloween kind.) "Are you a lawyer?"

"Yes, but . . ." No way I was going down this rabbit hole.

"Will you take my case?"

"No, I only do real estate." It was the furthest thing from a divorce lawyer I could think of on the spot. "But as I say, you won't have any trouble getting a lawyer if you plunk down $50,000 as a retainer."

"Well, the $50,000 is only payable IF they win."

"Ahh, I see. Then I wish you good luck . . ." *in your hopeless cause.*

As I turned to head back to my car in the underground parking, I saw two police cruisers at the entrance and the Checkered Shirt Undesirable Views Man angrily waving his arms as they took notes. Hmm. Maybe I should hang back a few minutes.

While I waited, a veritable *turba** of Gongers had begun to crowd around me, thinking that here at last was someone prepared to look at their brochure of gory pictures. Now, how the hell do I get out of here? I started to push through the gathering throng but then it occurred to me: Mr. Denied His Charter Rights Sandwich Board Man did indeed have the right to counsel, and I just happened to know the perfect lawyer for him. (Exclamation mark!) I turned back to the sandwich board man. "Have you spoken with Mr. Fernstein? He is one of Canada's top lawyers."

"No, would he take my case?"

"He *specializes* in cases like yours." I pulled out my phone, called up his coordinates, took out my pen and wrote my least favourite lawyer's contact info on a yellow sticky note. "His office is nearby. You should head over there and meet with him. Follow that little fellow over there. He's his associate."

"I can't thank you enough." His eyes were like spinning pinwheels now.

"Don't thank me. It's my duty to make sure you get the right lawyer. Now, I will warn you. He's busy. He's good and he's probably going to say that he can't take your case, but trust me, if you prevail on him, really push, he'll change his mind. He just likes to play hard to get. You follow me? Don't take no for an answer. Just sit in his reception area until he says yes. And tell him to do your appeal ASAP—after all, Justice Delayed, Is Justice Denied."

He nodded earnestly at that famous legal maxim, swung his board around and toddled off up University Avenue.

And I, having this day dispensed justice no less than three times already, headed back to the office with a smile on my face. I'll pick up my car later. Exclamation mark!

------

* mob

9

Cornucopia
Tuesday September 6

THOSE LAST FEW WEEKS with Hopeless Helen were an endurance test. The file of "client contacts" she had left on my windowsill? The ones she had been accumulating while I was suspended but for some unknown reason chose not to share with me? It turns out that the publicity around Paul and Chloe's courtroom meltdown and Lester Donald's shooting had not only *not* hurt my practice, I was in fact being swamped with potential clients looking for precisely that kind of representation—Total War with blank cheques.

As I flipped through the pile I found over a dozen phone messages, emails, even a few handwritten letters, all seeking my war-room advice. I looked at the dates on the messages, many were months old. Mothers and fathers in ugly custody battles, grandparent melees, property conflagrations, support pyrotechnics, people who were arguing about whether they were even married. It was a veritable cornucopia of conflict, a feast of fisticuffs, a holiday hamper of hostilities . . . okay, enough. But it was good, very good. The only problem was, would any of this potent pot of pestilence (one more) still be stewing for me now that I was finally back?

Through my door, which barely blocked out the stench of her tea, I called out, firmly, "Helen!"

Gingerly, she rolled into my office. "Yes . . .?" She looked worried.

"All these messages from potential new clients, why didn't you tell me about them?"

"I thought I did. Remember? And you were suspended. That's what I told them. You couldn't act for them, so I just put them in that file until you got back." She had the look on her face of a child who had done something really stupid, like put a toy in the toilet.

"Have any of them called back?"

"A few." She went pale.

"What did you tell them?" I'm not sure why I even asked this question because I knew the answer. "You didn't tell them that I was seeing a psychiatrist, did you?" I rose from my chair.

"A few . . . sometimes . . ." She started to edge her rover out of my office and said defensively, "Well, they wanted to know why you hadn't called them back. Like that doctor who kept calling."

"The one who wouldn't leave his name?"

"Her name. It was a woman doctor, but I finally got her to tell me. She called again this morning." She smiled as if this tidbit might deflect our conversation down a more positive path.

"But I'm here. Why didn't you put the call through?"

"I've been having trouble with the phones again. They're very complicated and when I got up to knock on your door, I spilled my tea." There likely goes a large slice of expensive carpet. Possibly a hole has burned through to the floor below. "And then the phone rang again with Mr. Shank. You should call him. He has called a few times. You know it hasn't been easy lately. The world has gone crazy." She started crying and blubbering. "Some psycho damaged my husband's truck over at the Nathan Phillips Square parking lot. He was just dropping off water for our rally against vaccines . . . the police are trying to find out who did it . . ."

Oh-oh. "That's terrible." Who knew that I had unknowingly dispensed a little justice to her husband. Sweet.

"And then Mr. Shank called again."

"Alvin Shank has called?"

"A few times."

I was bewildered by this woman. "Where's the message from this doctor?"

"I have it here." She inched toward my desk, reached into the little basket on the front of her rover and handed me a pink message slip.

I read the name, and the remains of my day came crashing down.

10

Count Your Blessings
Meanwhile back on February 8 . . .

Early on in the counselling, during our Zoom sessions, Dr. Sheila wanted to get into a discussion about my own divorce. A regular Inspector Clouseau, she thought it might have something to do with the zeal with which I represented my clients.

"Andrew, let's talk a little about your marriage. What was that like? It ended badly?"

Ended badly? This was akin to asking Germany if WWII had ended on a sour note. "Yeah, it ended badly."

"What happened?"

Funny that talking about how it ended made me recall how things began.

"I had been out in practice about two years, an associate in a small firm, working for three real pricks who thought they were doing me a big favour. There was a recession on—again—and I was supposed to 'count my blessings,' they said, because I had a job, so I resolved to make the best of it. They treated me like shit. No office. No support. No mentoring. I had a crappy desk crammed in beside their expensive new photocopier. But I sucked it up. Kept my mouth shut. Did what I was told—and some of that wasn't pretty. Borderline criminal, unethical stuff. My compensation arrangement was 'eat what you kill' so I put my head down and I killed."

"An eat and what kill?" She looked at me puzzled.

"Eat what you kill." I mean, how hard is that to understand? She still stared at me, clueless. "It's simple. No clients? No collections? Then no money that month. If you don't kill, you don't eat."

"But how would you live if there were no collections one month? Pay rent? Eat? Buy clothes? That seems like a hard way for a young lawyer to start out."

"Well, it sure focuses your attention on getting the job done and the money collected. I was hungry many months, in every sense of the word. One time I asked for a small advance, my rent was overdue. Their answer? No, sorry, can't swing it. It would set a bad precedent. That was the same month the managing partner bought a Porsche 959. So, if it came in the door and the client had money, I did it. It was collect, collect, collect. And you know what? I collected. I became a fucking machine. Sorry. I worked seven days a week. No holidays. But within two years I wasn't hungry anymore. I'd bought a fixer-upper house in Leaside, put a good tenant on the main level while I lived in the basement and carried a *ridiculous* mortgage. I was doing alright. I mean, I was doing alright compared to some of my former classmates who were packing up and moving to bust-and-boom town to get work. Not me."

"Bust-and-boom town?"

"Calgary. I was going to make it in Toronto. Period. Eventually the partners in another firm noticed my kill-to-eat ratio, what I was taking home, and they asked me to join them, you know, become a partner with them, co-sign the lease on this shitty little office they had over on Parliament, help pay off their new photocopier and fax-telephone system. Suddenly I was the golden billing boy. Come on aboard partner."

"What happened?"

"I told them to fuck off and found a spot over on Adelaide in Chambers—a bunch of sole practitioners sharing space and overhead. I moved out—with all my clients I might add—and opened my own shop, hung out my own shingle as we say. There was a clerk working for some old-timer. I would get her to do stuff for me from time to time. Pay her on the side. It worked out well."

"Was that around the time you met your wife?" She said this cheerfully, as if the clouds had opened up and a beautiful angel descended.

"Please don't ask if it was love at first sight. I can't take that corny shit."

"So you don't believe in that?"

"You do know what I do for a living? Love at first sight? Come on. Please. People *convince themselves* it happened, but no, truth is, there is no such thing. So jot that insight down. And . . ." I raised a finger.

"And?"

"And I should just mention that I have amassed many other valuable insights or relationship truths, if you like, about so-called love that may be of benefit to your work and patients." I mean I might as well help her out. Public service if you will.

"But first you were going to tell me about your wife."

"Ahh, yes, meeting my wife-to-be. Case in point. One night I was substituting for a friend at a community college. He was teaching an introductory course to a bunch of law clerks. He couldn't make it, so I stepped in and gave a lecture, killed time, told a bunch of war stories. That's actually where I first met Bonnie."

"You mention her a lot."

"Yeah. Anyway, on a break I went to get a coffee and there was this young woman in front of me. She was struggling with English and trying to pay for something."

"Where was she from?"

"The Soviet Union. Well, East Germany to be exact. She had come to Canada about a year after the wall came down in '89. She was in her twenties. Blonde. Beautiful. Dressed well, all things considered . . ."

"What do you mean?"

"I could tell that she was on a tight budget but making the most of what she had. No makeup but beautiful, a real natural beauty. You couldn't help but notice her. She knew how to present herself. Skin-tight Armani jeans, tucked into thigh-high black leather boots, heels of course. She had on a beautiful white poncho, Dior, I think—I mean, obviously everything was a knockoff, but really smart looking. She knew what she wanted. And she was hungry. I guess I liked that. We got to chatting about her courses (she was taking an introductory health science course), her impressions of the West, how rich our lives were here compared to what they had in East Germany, life in Toronto."

"And . . ."

"Short version? She was actually already living with some guy, a business guy, but we started seeing each other on the side. A few months later she moved into my place. We got married. I got her started studying at University of Toronto, pre-med. That's where she met the next rung on the *ladder to excess* in one of her classes, a younger fellow, a doctor, guest lecturing, a man with more promise, I guess. We had troubles, we separated. Got divorced."

"That feels like you skipped over a lot . . ."

"Yeah, I suppose, but those are the important parts. We fought in court. Settled on the third day of trial. I had to settle, I was out of money. The judge told me how wonderful it was that we'd settled, to *count my blessings* and appreciate how lucky I was to get a spousal support release from her. *A clean break is good*, he said."

"From what I've heard that is valuable, isn't it? A spousal support release?"

"It is. But in order to get that settlement and the release I had to give her my house, the equity in it, and pay her legal fees. Her new partner was helping her out financially. My lawyer was, shall we say, *weak and getting weaker as I ran out of rice*."

"Rice?"

"Money."

"I see." Sheila pursed her lips a little at that tidbit. "And that's why things ended badly." She had a real gift for understatement.

"That and because after it settled I would still drive by *my* house from time to time and get pretty fucking angry. Sorry. One day she happened to be out on the front lawn with her new partner, tending to *my* garden. I'd been drinking . . . quite a bit . . . and I stopped and got out to talk to him."

"Talk? About what?"

"It was a little one-sided but I told him to watch out for this little bloodsucking fucking Soviet parasite who had ice water in her veins, or words to that effect. Police were called. Cop gave me a break because he had been through the same kind of shit. I had to park my car and take a cab home, though. As I left, the cop said I should *count my blessings* and be glad there weren't kids involved."

"No charges. That was lucky."

"Yeah, but you know, I had another insight that day."

"What's that?"

"You can get tired of counting your fucking blessings. Pardon my French." I could tell she didn't like that kind of language.

"You said you know other truths about love, relationships."

"Many."

"Such as?"

"Are you married?" I assumed she was because I could see that the walls of her office were plastered with pictures of her and some large, bearded fellow.

"I get asked that a lot by patients and, yes, I'm married."

"Do you think you have 100 percent of your husband?"

That caught her off guard. "What do you mean, have 100 percent?" She glanced at one of the pictures on her wall.

"Do you have *all* of him? Or is it possible he has been withholding a piece of himself from you?"

"I . . . I . . ." She didn't know what to say. "I don't know. I don't think so."

"Well, here is something you of all people should know, must know. You *never* get 100 percent of your supposed loved one. There is always a piece, could be big, could be small, but it's not yours. Ever. It could be someone from their past, a former lover, a missed opportunity perhaps, or it could be grief, or even a child who will always take priority over you, a destructive parent, abuse, scars . . . I could go on. But that piece is withheld, and it's withheld for a reason. People say, 'Oh. I'm an open book.' Really? You should read the prequel."

"Well, we've been married for thirty-one years. So far, so good." She seemed a little nervous and actually knocked for luck on the veneer of the budget, modular particleboard desk I expect she ordered through Wayfair.

"Well, that's just great. I guess you should *count your fu . . . your blessings.*"

I think she didn't like my tone because I noticed her glance at her watch and decide to wrap up our session. "So, Andrew, progress." She clapped her hands and said this excitedly, likely to reassure herself more than me. "I think we—you and I—we're beginning to understand, I see how your marriage ended so badly, what it has meant to you."

"That's part of it. Of course there was also the bolt cutter, blood and tears incident." I had to laugh. "That pretty much capped things off."

Even on Zoom I could tell that shook her up.

11

Love Unlocked
Meanwhile, back on Tuesday March 8

IT WASN'T UNTIL our next Zoom meeting the following month that I had a chance to share with Dr. Sheila the incident that really brought my whole marriage debacle crashing down. Seriously, I couldn't wait to tell her.

"So, Andrew, we were talking about your marriage ending badly. You said there were tears. And blood?" I could tell she dreaded hearing what may have happened.

"And let's not forget the bolt cutters." I jumped in with a smile.

"Yes, of course." She looked ashen even with one of those fancy video-conference ring lights illuminating her puffy face.

"We honeymooned in Greece. Have you been?"

"No, but it's been on our bucket list. I hear it's beautiful." She cheered up briefly. Maybe a happy story would unfold.

Bucket list. Jesus Christ. I hate that expression.

"I've been twice. For our honeymoon we stayed on the island of Santorini. I booked a suite on the west side of Oia, looking out over the caldera, this huge underwater basin that was caused by a volcanic eruption a long time ago, quite something. We toasted the sunset every night from our private infinity pool."

"Sounds lovely." She was taking the bait.

"From our VIP suite we would walk down narrow stone paths and explore the village. At this one spot there is a rocky point that looks out over the caldera from the ruins of an old fort that was used as a lookout for pirates. You can climb up the steps to a vantage spot and look out over the Mediterranean. We went up there on our last night and put a love lock on the fence. You know about love locks?"

"Yes, lovely act of devotion."

"Act? Yes, interesting choice of words. I had found an old vintage lock, copper, green with age, very expensive too. I had it engraved with our names."

"I don't think you've ever told me her name."

"I promised myself that I would never again let her name pass my lips."

"How long have you been separated, divorced?"

"Since 1998."

"That's a long time to carry around that promise, that kind of bitter promise. Don't you think it's time to let it go? It must be hard."

"So far, so good." I knocked on my Airia office desktop. (Which I assure you is real wood, solid American black walnut, French polish.) "You know, as they say, *Love is patient, love is kind blah blah blah, it keeps no record of wrongs, blah blah blah, it rejoices with the truth.*"

"Andrew . . ."

"Anyway, I'd had our names engraved on this gorgeous lock along with the date of our marriage. As the sun was setting, I surprised her when I pulled it out of my knapsack, and together we locked it on this ancient fence that's a part of the ruins. We placed it there along with hundreds of other locks to the applause of the people who were there watching the sunset. I gave her the key to the old lock and to the cheers of the crowd she threw it over the cliff into the ocean. Quite a night."

Dr. Sheila stared at me. I could tell she was puzzled about where this was going. What did this have to do with blood and tears?

"After the divorce I got it in my head that the lock shouldn't stay on that fence."

"Oh, Andrew, you didn't?"

"Oh, I did. I flew to Santorini on what would have been our wedding anniversary, booked the same suite, ate a big dinner of fried octopus, had a couple of bottles of wine at the same restaurant and then I went up to the *ruins*—how fitting—at sunset. Do you know how hard it was to find bolt cutters in that little village? Anyway, I brought along the remains of a bottle of ouzo for a toast, granted I'd already had a bit to drink and, as the sun got ready to slip below the horizon, I set about cutting that fucking love lock off the fence . . ."

"Oh, Andrew, I'm so sorry."

"It was a real mother too, because there was no place to really get these old dull bolt cutters wrapped around the loop that slides into the base." I demonstrated like I was cutting a bush with hedge clippers. "You know what I mean? I pried and twisted and cut but it was hard, it wouldn't come off, so I just hammered the son of a bitch with the bolt cutters until I knocked it off the fence. I had a guy film it so I could show her."

There was silence as the image of that scene sank in.

"And the tears? I hope you had a good cry after this, let it all come out."

Was she crazy? "No fucking way. Sorry. Me? Tears? I was ecstatic, drunk, but ecstatic. Unfortunately, there was also a bridal party up there taking pictures. When the bride saw me flipping out on the fence and the love lock, she burst into tears and cancelled their shoot. Collateral damage, I guess."

More silence.

"And blood? You mentioned blood." She really dreaded that question.

I took a few seconds to fully conjure up the memory of my final moments that evening.

"I decided it would be fitting to toss the broken lock over the cliff into the sea, where the key is, very dramatic. No?"

She just stared at me blankly in the glow of her video ring.

"Unfortunately, my awkward cutting and twisting of the lock had made such a mess of it that when I picked it up and went to toss it, a jagged piece of old copper snagged my finger and palm, sliced my hand open like a razor blade. There was blood everywhere. I rinsed my hand off with the rest of the ouzo and then my camera guy took me to a clinic."

I pulled back my sleeve and held my hand up to the Zoom camera to show her the still visible, ragged scar. "Quite a mess. Twenty stitches."

Worth every one of them.

12

Spiral
Tuesday September 6

I TUCKED THE telephone message from the doctor into my pocket and went for a mental health march. *Salvitur ambulando.** Nothing could prepare me for returning that call. On that thin slip of paper was the name I had vowed never to speak. Why was she reaching out to me? Over and over again? It had been years but the thought of her still made my skin crawl with pins and needles. She was going to give me shingles from all the stress. Again.

Head down, I proceeded up York Street to Osgoode Hall. There used to be no better place to sit and think than on a bench in front of that beautiful old building, but the racket of construction had ruined my outdoor oasis. After I slipped through the black iron cow gates, I headed inside to the refuge of the Great Library. No one does research in the library anymore, so I climbed up the cast-iron spiral staircase into the stacks, to a stool near dusty old volumes of the *Modern Law Review*. Here, I could try to sort this out.

If I returned the call, I would have to speak to her. If I didn't return the call, she would likely just keep calling. Would I be able to keep it together? Something must be up. Did she want money? Impossible after all these years. We were *a vinculo matrimonii*. I was free of this *adultera*.

––––––

* Walk to solve it.

Maybe I could get someone to return the call for me and find out what she wanted. But who could I stick with that task? Hopeless Helen? No, she'd probably just blurt out some nonsense.

I paced the narrow passage until I pulled a thick green *Black's Law Dictionary* from the shelf and leafed through it. The smell of its fine old pages brought back memories of law school, of better times, when the law was just stories in books, not real people. Not awful people, like her. My hand landed on an old expression, *per Angusta ad Augusta.** Indeed.

Inspired by those words, I resolved to call her.

I wound my way down the stairs and stepped out of the Great Library onto the magnificent mosaic floor of the upper rotunda. Gazing down from the top of the great staircase into the main rotunda, it reminded me of the interior of a Genoese palace. How beautiful, even as lawyers in their black robes scurried back and forth, pulling their big black brief-cases to the courtrooms below. Strange, but being there was suddenly a great comfort.

I took a breath and dialled.

My call was answered on one ring. "Sunnybrook Hospital. How may I direct your call?"

Sunnybrook? "Uh . . . Hello . . ."

"How may I direct your call?"

My mouth was dry, my tongue was paralyzed. I would need to speak her name.

"Hello, can I help you?"

I looked at the pink slip in my hand. "Yes, I'm sorry, can you connect me with . . . Dr. Daria Volkov?" There, I had said it, but I felt like rinsing out my mouth.

"Yes, Oncology. One moment please."

Oncology? Odd. The connection began to ring. Once, twice, three times. No answer. Good. Maybe I could just leave a message and be done with it. I could feel myself sweating through my suit as pins and needles rippled across my shoulders.

"Hello, Dr. Volkov." Her voice had not changed in all the years. "Hello . . . Hello."

---

* Through difficulties to honours.

"It's Andrew."

"Oh, Andrew. Thank you for calling me back. It's been so long. I left messages. I know you have had your hands full recently. It sounds like you've had a difficult couple of years. I'm so sorry."

Sure you are. "What do you want? If it's money, the release was quite comprehensive."

"Oh, Andrew, of course not. It's not about money."

"Then what?" My stomach twisted into a knot.

"It's about your brother, Sean. He's here, at Sunnybrook, in Oncology. He's my patient. He asked me to contact you. I've been trying to reach you for weeks."

It's amazing how many distinct shards of thought can be jammed into a fraction of a second. Sean. Oncology. Her. Now a doctor. Santorini. Both times. Lester. All flashed by in an instant. I looked at my scarred hand. Now my chest was in a vise too.

"Andrew? Are you still there?"

"Oncology?" I had to think for a moment. I had not heard that word for years, not since our mom passed after her battle with cancer. And hers was not one of those battles that cliché-filled obits describe as "courageous" either. It hit her hard, fast and with no mercy. Courage? There was no time for courage.

"Yes, Sean has been treated here for a few months now. It's prostate cancer."

"Our uncle died from that . . ." I whispered it to no one in particular.

"Yes, Sean mentioned that. He would like to see you. You should come soon."

I was stunned. "It's not a great time."

"Andrew, when I say soon, I mean you have to come now."

"Oh."

13

Sunnybrook T-Wing
Thursday September 8

I've never liked visiting a hospital. In fact I hate it, almost as much as visiting what is often the next stop, a funeral home.

How well can a blue surgical mask stop COVID when it does nothing to block the stench of sickness, of worry, of urine, of all the smells of a hospital? After a visit those odours cling to me for hours. I delayed so I could summon the strength to go see Sean. I had lots of good excuses too. Fernstein was all over me about those twins. The week since the adjournment had flown by. He was trying to arrange visits, but I could not get my client, Ms. Marrs, to respond. Now he was threatening to return it to court. I would need to call her again. I wish Bonnie was here to help.

Having downed a generous drink in the car, I took a deep breath, spun through the revolving doors of Sunnybrook and headed to T-Wing. As I followed the Oncology signs down smelly corridors and past waiting rooms filled with anxious families, my mind, as it is wont to do, began to break it down. *Onco*, Latin for tumour. Even the Ancient Greeks had a word for these deadly lumps. *Logy*, the study of something. *Oncology*, the study of deadly lumps. My skin crawled at the thought of being near people filled with such loathsome growths.

Outside Sean's room, I paused for a moment to steel myself and pop in a handful of Tic Tacs. It had been nearly a year since we last spoke.

Pushing the door open a few inches, I peered in to see if he was awake. That unmistakable pungent hospital smell of urine soaked with meds swamped my nose. I reeled and felt like throwing up.

But. Oh God. I was too late. His bed was surrounded by a half-dozen priests all standing in silent prayer. Pins and needles gripped my shoulders again. He's gone. I should have come when Daria told me to come. I'd waited and now it was too late. *Coward.* My eyes began to well up. *Coward. Coward.*

The elderly priests turned to me in unison. Each was clutching a long strand of thick black beads. I recognized them immediately as five-decade rosaries, a loop of five sets of Hail Mary beads, each group of ten separated by a medallion—the punctuation of an Our Father—and then, the dangling climax, a silver crucifix. Each bead touched was supposed to be a prayer, a presentation to the Virgin Mary of a rose from the Crown of Roses. Such an imaginative faith. Those simple black beads were magical enough to transport me back to our days as altar boys at our parish, St. Gertrude's, uttering her special prayer, "*. . . for all the souls in purgatory, for sinners everywhere, those in my own home and within my family. Amen.*" The words came back so easily.

A short heavy-set priest with bushy silver hair, in full garb including a long black cassock, walked over, pressed himself close to me and took my hand. Like many men of a certain age, he had small bits of food still on his face from his last meal. Oatmeal or scrambled egg (or both) was my guess. On his clerical vest I could see what appeared to be traces of yesterday's mushroom soup and that his armpits were ringed with salt stains. His breath was so foul it momentarily overpowered the scent of urine. I was not grateful for the exchange. I know priests take a vow of poverty but even the poor wash their clothes and brush their teeth from time to time.

Notwithstanding my obvious recoiling from him, he leaned in. "You must be Andrew. Come in. Come in." He turned back to the group, "Let's give these brothers some privacy." The priests took turns mumbling something to Sean, squeezing his hands, and then filed out of the room. The bushy-haired guy handed me a small rosary, patted me on the shoulder and left. I stood there alone, silently, not six feet from Sean. Relieved that he was at least still alive, I couldn't move as my mind flashed back and forth from the foot of the altar at St. Gertrude's to the foot of his bed.

"Hey, Buddy Boy, get over here so we can talk." Sean's voice was weak. I'd never heard it like that before. His had always been the voice of confidence. Even when at rock bottom—and he had certainly spelunked there many a time—he sounded hopeful, as if things would turn around. He would be back, not necessarily on top, but back. He didn't sound that way now.

"What the hell? What happened?" Stupid questions. I know.

"I guess Daria told you. Prostate cancer. Stage 4. I had a prostatectomy a few weeks ago—robotic, no less—but it seems it was too late. Ignored a few symptoms, sort of like Uncle Willie, I guess." He was whispering to himself. "Then COVID meant delays, and I guess that vasectomy the archdiocese made me get years ago probably didn't help either." He actually started to laugh at the thought that as a priest he had been forced to get one. "Not much to be done but manage this last stretch. It's spread. Daria has me on some heavy-duty stuff for pain."

"Daria. How did she get involved? I haven't seen or heard from her in years and then all of a sudden she's calling me. I should have got back to her sooner . . . my idiot law clerk."

"Bonnie's no idiot. Come on, Andrew. Don't blame her." He still could summon the tone of older brother.

"No, Bonnie's gone. She left to go do charity work for some immigrant place. I have this replacement, an idiot on a skateboard." I was babbling. "It doesn't matter. But Daria? How?"

"She's one of the best oncologists in Canada. Funny how these things turn out. She's been fantastic."

I said nothing.

"I know how you feel about her, but a lot of time has passed, Andrew."

"Give it another century. I might come around."

"God, you're a hard-ass. Come and sit." Even drawn and pale, he still had that killer smile.

As I pulled up a chair, I found myself unconsciously fingering the rosary beads the priest had given me. One man's rosary, another man's worry beads, I guess. We talked and got caught up like we hadn't in a long, long time. I was surprised how much he knew about the shitstorm I'd been through, my suspension and even my visits with Dr. Sheila. His year had been bad too, worse. And yet we still managed to laugh about our troubles. Brothers. Like the old days.

Everything was going great until Daria stuck her head in the room. "You fellows getting caught up?"

I let out a deep sigh and said nothing, but Sean leaned forward and smiled. "We're good, Daria. Just need a few more minutes to discuss a little business." Sean did his best to sound upbeat, but I could tell he was exhausted.

"You've been pushing it today. Let's think about getting some rest soon."

She was gone before the door closed. Good. I didn't even have to look at her.

I turned to Sean. "Business?"

"Yeah, listen. It's complicated. You know about my issues with the archdiocese, the threat to defrock me."

"They've backed off I assume?"

"Not exactly. Don't think for a minute that these fellows don't play hardball. That group of crusty old farts that just left, they were praying for me to live a little longer for a reason."

"What are you talking about?"

"Look, bottom line. I don't want to be defrocked. If I was, I wouldn't be allowed to be buried at St. Augustine's, the cemetery for priests out near the Scarborough Bluffs. I'd never even thought of that but suddenly, you know, it matters. Defrocked, I would have been on the street, no income, no prospects at my age, nothing. I was desperate, I needed money and I needed some medical expense coverage. A lot of this stuff is not free. The archdiocese was picking up the tab for anything not covered by OHIP."

"That's generous."

"Not really. There have been, there are, conditions."

"Like what?"

"That's what we need to discuss."

I pulled my chair a little closer, gripped the worry beads and braced myself to hear what Sean was being asked to do in order to remain a priest and be buried properly.

Holy Mother of Jesus.

14

A Deal with the Devil
Thursday September 8

SEAN WAS WORN out, but I could tell he was determined to finish the business end of our meeting.

"There's going to be a provincial election in early November."

"Okay. Did not know that. I haven't been following politics, you know me. I didn't even know an election had been called."

"Yeah, I know what you always say, *there's no money in politics.* An election has not been called, yet. Here's the deal. Ordinarily the election would have been the first Thursday in June next year, but Premier Palmer—he's a Liberal . . ."

"Very funny. I know that much. Remember, I was there picking you up off the floor after he won the Liberal leadership."

"Good memory, if not good memories. Well, he's going to dissolve the Provincial Legislature early and call a snap election."

"How do you know?"

Sean just looked at me as if to say, *Please. Trust me. This is my world.* "There's a candidate named McKay who will be running in Parkdale–High Park. Conservative. Now, the riding is not typically what you would consider promising territory for a Tory. Neighbourhood is poor, lots of tenants, shelters, halfway houses, you know . . ."

Poor? He was being generous with that description. That part of town is crap, plain and simple. Always has been.

". . . but McKay and his family live in a tony corner of the riding, up on Riverside Drive so he has a foot in the riding."

"Sean, what's this got to do with you getting better? Why waste your time on an election months from now?"

"Andrew, come on. I'm not going to get better. I'm just hanging on here so I can try to hold up my end of a bargain and I'm going to need your help."

"Okay. But what can I possibly do to help?" I had not said those words to Sean in years but whenever I had said them, I always lived to regret it. "And what bargain?"

"In Parkdale–High Park, in the last election, the NDP ran a young guy, a newbie, international relations/Red Cross stuff, lives in the south—poorer—end of the riding, could be a strong candidate but sort of a woolly head-in-the-clouds-on-policy-stuff kinda guy. No political instincts. But he'll run again."

"Sounds familiar. NDP. Not Dependable People."

"Tell me about it. Anyway, this guy's name is, wait for it, Bierce—Aaron Bierce."

"Sean, seriously? Come on, first of all, I thought you were working for the Liberals to get Palmer elected last time, and secondly, if you think I'm going to help some Dipper get elected just because he has the same last name, it's not happening."

"No, no. You don't understand. The archdiocese wants McKay to win in Parkdale–High Park. He's Conservative and hardcore Catholic. They're backing him to eventually become PC leader. The current leader, Corbin, is in trouble, he's going to have to step down. The story has to break at some point. Palmer knows about it and wants to take advantage of the PCs being in disarray when the news comes out. Hence the early call. Archdiocese figures they will then have the premier *and* the leader of the opposition in the bag, no matter how the election turns out. Win-win. But no one knows."

"How do you know all this?"

Again with the *don't ask* look. "So, anyway, some early polling and potential number splits suggest McKay has a modest but tight shot at winning in Parkdale–High Park. There's a Liberal running, of course, probably this Polish guy, Kaminski, he'll draw a lot of votes but not enough to win. It's going to be a tight three-way race. Here's where we come in."

"What do you mean *we*?"

He took a shallow breath. "I had agreed to run as an Independent in the election in Parkdale–High Park using my last name, Bierce. The thinking is that two Bierces on the ballot will confuse NDP voters and draw enough votes away from Aaron Bierce to help McKay edge by both Bierce and the Liberal guy, Kaminski."

I sat back in my chair and stared at him. "This is how Conservatives think they will win elections? Hoping voters are dumb enough to vote for the wrong Bierce?"

"Actually, yes. It has worked before. In the last election up north there were two Crawfords on a ballot to try to split votes. But it's not very often that the riding situation, the names and numbers align, you know, two Bierces and one—me—willing to play ball. Well, actually, being forced to play ball."

"Where're you supposed to get the energy to run in an election? How do you campaign? You can't even get out of bed. You're crazy. Your meds are messing you up. Does Daria know about this?"

Lupus in fabula. Speak of the devil and the devil appears. She stuck her head in again. "Guys, you're going to have to wrap this up. Sean, you're due for a bath and the nurses need to get started."

"Okay. Okay. Give us two minutes." She let out a sigh and left. I still had not looked at her.

"Sean, you can't do this." It was just another mad scheme.

"I know I can't. I may not even be alive come election day. But I told the archdiocese that you would do it for me, that you would put your name on the ballot, campaign a bit and help to split the NDP vote."

I was gobsmacked. "What!? Why would you do that? Why would I do that? Without speaking to me? Sean, it's crazy. I've got a practice to rebuild. I know nothing about politics and what I do know, I hate. I can't do it. I can't. I won't."

"Andrew, they're going to proceed with the defrocking, pull my medical support, everything, the medical coverage, a proper funeral, the burial, the cemetery. Everything." *My God.* I thought, *he's going to cry.* Unprecedented. "I asked Daria to reach out to you, but we couldn't reach you. She tried for weeks. They gave me an ultimatum. You were my only out."

"It's true, Andrew. I was here the day that priest showed up from the archdiocese." Daria had slipped back into the room and stood not two feet behind me. I was surprised I hadn't detected her toxic presence. I must have been tired, with defence shields down.

I turned to face the devil.

I couldn't speak. My God, she was still beautiful. Her ice-blue eyes exactly as I remembered them. Not a hint of makeup, her natural beauty glowing. Her hair was as blonde as the day I first laid eyes on her. But then an anguished feeling deep inside me surfaced, as I recalled that Satan can disguise himself as an angel of light. This was still the devil.

I turned away from her to Sean. "That old guy who was just here? He threatened you?" I couldn't picture that shabby Friar Tuck being a heavy.

"No," Daria chimed in, "it was a younger priest. More business than church. Arrogant, pushy. He has some connection with St. Michael's Hospital, on the board of some big Catholic foundation. I heard one of the priests say he has friends in Rome." She pointed at the ceiling and said *friends* like it was the Pope himself. "He was awful. I had to throw him out. Sean was having a panic attack. He was so mean, cold."

"Well, I guess you would know." I couldn't resist.

"Whoa, Andrew. There's no need for that. Daria's been a godsend." Sean suddenly had a surge of enough energy to defend her.

"Godsend? In the circumstances, that's an interesting choice of words." I turned back to Daria. "So, you know about this? This blackmail?"

"I tried to reach you. You were not calling me back."

Fucking Hopeless Helen.

"And I've done everything I can to make sure many of Sean's medical bills are covered, so they wouldn't have that leverage over him. But I can't stop them from defrocking him, taking away his entitlement to a proper burial. I don't have that power."

I looked from Daria to Sean. "Who is this guy? This priest?"

"Father Shannon. He's new, came over from Ireland a month ago. Tough. Fixer. If you're going to do this, you'll need to meet with him. I need you, Andrew."

I'd heard that before. It was getting late. The September sun was setting over nearby Mount Hope Cemetery. I looked at Sean. In the failing light, he was gaunt, yellow and weak. He looked afraid. Unprecedented. Standing there, I recalled his youthful face, the face of the laughing altar boy, the one horsing around behind the priest during mass at St. Gertrude's.

"So, you say this Shannon is a tough prick?"

"He is. He's not someone to mess with, Andrew." Sean's voice was hoarse now, exhausted.

I threw the rosary beads in the waste can beside Sean's bed. "We'll see."

15

Behold

Friday September 9

IT HAD BEEN OVER a month since I had met with her, but I was still wavering on whether I would take on Ms. Rimini. She had called a few times, checking in and asking if I had made a decision. I had spent way too much time even thinking about her case without a retainer and money in the bank. The thought of *pro bono* gives me hives. There was no fucking way I was taking on any charity cases at this point. I had to rebuild. Besides, there were a couple of good cases just waiting for me with bags of rice.

So, without committing to take her on, I suggested she make a list of every person she recalled being at the party, put them in categories: judges, lawyers, cops, staff, everyone who was on the Festival of Seasons committee, everyone and anyone. The list would serve three purposes: one, it would help determine if there were any conflicts; two, I could get a good sense about who was there and how deep the shit could go; and three, it would keep her busy for another week while I pondered this situation.

But I needed to know so much more about the judicial inquiry process. Alvin was a level-headed guy on everything—except, of course, Ms. Novak—and he had said clearly that I should run away from the case. I had to admit that advice was persuasive. And then again there was the money. How was she supposed to pay for this? Inquiries can go on for months, years. It could ruin my practice if it dragged on, right when I'm trying to rebuild. Plus, there was the fact that I knew absolutely nothing about judicial inquiries. I'd looked on the Judicial Council website and saw there had been less than a dozen of these things in the last decade. Many of the judges who get into trouble resign before the naughty evidence starts to pour out to the public. Even a Justice of the Supreme Court of Canada had pulled his retirement ripcord rather than face an inquiry over his mischief in a bar down south.

There was not a lot to go on, but my research had uncovered at least this much: if the judicial complaint went ahead, a panel would be appointed to deal with it. The panel would be made up of a Superior Court judge, a judge from the Ontario Court of Justice, a lawyer and a layperson. There would be a presenting counsel, a lawyer who essentially acts like a Crown attorney. That lawyer would present evidence of what the judge supposedly did wrong. The accused judge would have his own lawyers at his own expense but could ask for reimbursement of legal fees in some circumstances. It looked like the judge who was disciplined for wearing the Trump MAGA hat to court had to pay his own lawyers. I bet that hurt. I could find nothing about financial help for the legal bills faced by the person who made the complaint. They're essentially just a witness. It looked like any legal advice they'd get would be on their own dime. Well, that's not good.

Then there was the possibility of criminal charges against each judge. Singh could be charged with assault if Glinka wanted to proceed. Glinka could be charged with sexual assault if Francesca wanted to proceed. Aside from COVID delays, why nothing had happened yet on those counts was a mystery. But again, even in a criminal process Francesca would simply be a witness. No need for a lawyer. And no money to pay for one. It looked worse by the minute.

I could see why other lawyers had steered clear of this snake pit. So why should I take it on? Why did she want me as her lawyer? And where was her husband? His attitude was a bit of a puzzler. Why would Glinka admit to anything? It also sounded like Francesca was on her own in terms of evidence. No one was coming forward to support her version of events. It was turning into a classic her word against his word. The more

I thought about it, the more I realized how bad it could get. This could turn into another Big Ears Teddy Ghomeshi shitshow. A "he said, she said" battle with lawyers trying to weed out the liars.

Even if it got sorted out, how it could address their bizarre shunning was the next mystery. What kind of people were behind the closed doors of the courthouse? Shunning the poor woman. Why? But then again, really not my problem.

To be frank, after turning all of these questions over and over in my mind I was leaning heavily toward telling her I couldn't help. There would be no need for a fuck-off-fee discussion. I would just say, like everyone else, that I was not interested. I'm no social justice warrior. The crazy nightmare with Sean and the supposed election was also going to be taking up my time. I needed to figure something out with the archdiocese and this Father Shannon goon. Could I cut them a cheque? Buy them off? Regardless, I would need to make decisions about both the election and Rimini, one way or the other.

It was getting late. Hopeless Helen was, of course, long gone to her *sports injury clinic*. Her period of notice was ticking down to its final days, and I could see her being less and less engaged with every passing day, and that's saying something. I had no prospects other than somehow luring Bonnie into returning, maybe. Big maybe.

Perhaps a glass of something strong would help me sort these matters out, so I pulled out the remainder of a bottle of Red Breast. Not much there but it would do just fine. Clearly, with everything going on, I needed to restock my dwindling office supply.

With a half tumbler of Irish in hand, I decided to sit down and finally spend some quality time looking through the "Potential Client File" that Helen had amassed over the last several months. First thing I noticed? Not one conflict check had been done. Then, no intake forms had been completed. There was no indication as to whether she had given them information about my retainer and fees. However, to her nominal credit, she did note on a couple of matters the person who had actually referred the client. That might provide some clues about the quality of the lead— and also tell me who I might have to call to apologize for not following up with their referral. Bottom line, though, I would be calling back these potential clients blind.

As I flipped through the memos my mood brightened. There was a name I recognized immediately, my rockstar client Patrick McGovern had a referral for me. He was one of the few people who had reached out to see if I was okay after the shooting. COVID had been tough on a lot of musicians. No touring and no merch sales had hit them hard financially. That had to cause some stresses at home—not to mention two spouses actually being around each other when they're used to one being on the road for months at a time. I hoped he was keeping things together after that close call with the nanny. Based on Helen's chicken scratch it looked like he had called a few times. I would call him first.

There were older notes about a couple of calls from Ms. Marrs. This was the custody dispute over twins that I had adjourned—brilliantly—a few weeks ago. I expected a motion to force something to happen any day. But on the downside, it was a file with fucking Fernstein. He was driving me crazy with demands to arrange visits. Why does everything need to be so hard? And I really need to actually meet her to review the situation and get a further retainer. I resolved to follow up with her after speaking with Patrick.

Before I started dialling anyone, I decided to poke around on the internet to see if there were any clues about some of the other potential clients. One of the names I searched popped up with multiple hits. Morgan. Financial guy. Bay Street. Player. Lots of news items. Spoke to the Chamber of Commerce last year about "Future of Big Cities After COVID." Bunch of charitable stuff. Interesting. Very interesting. Looked like his office was in the same tower. That would make life easy. Message from him was only a week old. I would call him third. There should be lots of rice in that matter.

Another note was from a Ms. Dellwood. Fraud allegations against her soon-to-be-ex spouse of twenty-five years? Hmm. Maybe. Every divorcing woman thinks her spouse has an account in the Caymans because their cruise ship stopped there for a day of shopping. I put it aside. God, I wish Bonnie was here to sort this stuff out.

Things were looking up, especially since I had found a forgotten half-bottle of Johnny Walker Red stashed in a cabinet. So I decided to carry on with some searches of a few names on LinkedIn. I wasn't on there ten minutes and guess who I should behold. None other than Ms. Lindsay

Braun, the Girl in the Tangerine Suit who worked with Randall Williams. The humiliation of our last encounter still hurt. That fucker Williams had really set me up and embarrassed me in front of her. God, that was bad. As I read her profile, I could see that she'd posted an article for the Advocates' Society and had been part of some webinar panel discussion. I hit a link to the article and my head was spinning as I read the title, "Tech innovation, justice evolving, AI issues and learning efficiency . . ." *blah blah*. Wow. Bunch of tech gibberish. Never figured her for such a nerd.

I scrolled to her bio to see which lawyer at Williams's old law firm had scooped her up as an associate after he was appointed to the bench. Well, that's interesting—her bio said that she left the firm and went out on her own. Odd move. Sole practice is not a recommended career path for a young woman of her limited experience.

I took a generous sip of JW, thought a minute and threw a Like on her post with a quick comment, *Great article. In these challenging times technology may be a lifesaver for those seeking access to justice. Well done.*

Fortunately, the internet has not yet developed a sense of smell.

With a toast to her career move I resolved to find a way to cross paths with her again. But any dreamy thoughts of the Tangerine Girl fizzled when my inbox lit up with an email from Ms. Rimini. Oh shit.

Dear Mr. B. I really threw myself at this. I was able to come up with the following list. It's pretty comprehensive. Jay's not happy but it's done.

Oh great, she's done already. So much for delaying things a week.

As I had suggested, she broke party attendees into groups.

Judges: short list and I recognized none of the names. Just great.

Court Staff/Others: again, I recognized none of the dozens of names.

Cops: another half-dozen names. Not one known to me.

Lawyers: God, there must be thirty names. I ran my finger down the list. Dave The Major was there, of course. I got about halfway down the page and came to a screeching halt. Well, well, that little bald eunuch Alvin. Whose name should I behold? One Lorelei Novak.

This is getting interesting.

16

Thank God, I'm a Country Boy
Friday September 9 and Saturday September 10

WITH THE HALF bottle of JW scotch now gone, I pushed the unread memos aside, along with naughty thoughts of the sultry Ms. Novak, softly cursed Hopeless Helen and texted Patrick McGovern.

Hey Rockstar. What's up? Saw a note that your friend might need some advice. Let me know when you're free.

He hit back to me in seconds. *Glad to hear your [sic] OK. You're [sic] clerk said you were in a psych ward or something. LOL*

Fucking Hopeless Helen.

Nope. I'm good. She was a temp. Gone. New one on the way.

Bummer. You need Bonnie man. She was awesome.

Yes, she was. Who's your friend?

Best not to text about it. Can you call me?

Sure. Sit tight.

I still had his number programmed into my phone. Wrapping up his case with that beautiful deal sealed in a marriage contract seemed like it had been only weeks ago, but at least a couple of years had passed. The COVID time warp still rippled.

He answered on one ring. "Yo, bro." Still sounding like Peter Pan.

"Hey, how's life treating you? Things staying settled at home? Get through COVID internment okay?"

"Yeah, we managed. I wasn't on the road at all. We were both hanging out with the kids. It was okay. We'll see. Now that we're setting up some gigs again, I'll be back out there. We'll see." He could not have sounded less enthusiastic about home life.

"Okay. Well, keep me posted." I made a mental note to take a look at his marriage contract to refresh my memory about how I pulled his nuts out of the fire in the middle of that trial up against Leslie Kaplan, after his affair with the nanny. If things went sideways again, we would need to act.

"Will do. Look, I don't know if you're taking on new work but my buddy needs some serious help. There's a shitstorm brewing and he has his head in the sand."

"Not good. Better to be proactive, you know me."

"That's what I said, get ahead of this. But he's been down this road before and hates lawy . . . dislikes talking to lawyers."

"Well, when his predisposition to my tribe improves you know where to find me. Give him my number."

The last thing I'm going to start doing is chasing some client who is up to his neck in the shitsand but cursing the person pulling him out.

"Are you doing anything tomorrow?"

Hmmm. "What's up?"

"I thought maybe we could take a drive out to meet him. I could introduce you, put in a good word, calm him down a bit about lawyers. I already told him what you did for me and Laurie."

Notwithstanding the ongoing effects of COVID, my sense of smell was suddenly activated. "Pat, why are you so concerned about this guy? If he's in trouble but is not willing to pick up the phone then I can't chase him to try to convince him how much he needs me, just so he can call me names and tell me to fuck off." After all, remember, I have that cardinal rule about reaching out to clients. I never make the first call. They need to reach out to me—personally. There was a long pause. "Pat?"

"I hear ya, bro. Okay look, this is solicitor-client privilege, right?"

"It is unless you're about to tell me that you are going to commit a crime."

"Ha, no . . . It's The Coop."

"The what?"

"The Coop . . . Cody Cooper."

"The country singer?" Admittedly, faux country was not my music, but I knew the name because Cody Cooper had been lavished with just about every music industry award over the previous five years. Back and forth to Nashville. Big and getting bigger. Sort of Canada's answer to Chris Stapleton crossed with Garth Brooks, but better looking from what I could tell.

"The one and only."

"You guys buddies?"

"Sorta but looking to make it more than that. We have talked about doing something together."

"I never figured you for a country boy." Although I did recall that Keith Urban had a soul patch at one time. And Billy Ray Cyrus did too. And of course there was the unfortunate Garth Brooks–Chis Gaines fiasco. Curse of the soul patch.

"Gotta go where the fans and money are, bro. At my age the rocker format is wearing a little thin. Even the Stones cannot pull it off. Their last album was shit. Mick's eighty for Christsakes. Time to hang it up. Country's fan base is a little more tolerant, shall we say, especially with male acts. Jesus, no one cares if you look like you just climbed off a tractor as long as you write a good song and wear a big hat. Or even a trucker cap for that matter. I got a couple of tunes in the works, you know, and not the usual dog, truck, farm, tractor, grandpa's advice, she done me wrong, I done her wrong, drinking too much whisky shit either. Good stuff. I gotta tune I wrote called "Hockeytonkin'." You know, instead of "honky-tonkin'." My agent says it's worth a look so we're talking to Coop's people. But I need to get in a little tighter, if you know what I mean. Jam with him a bit. I figure if I can help him solve some personal stuff, it makes life easier for everyone."

"So tomorrow?"

"What if you and I took a drive out to his place in the country, to his compound."

"Compound?"

"Yeah, its awesome. He's invited a few folks, just to hang out, ATV, have a few beers, maybe shoot some guns, listen to music, look at cars.

Why don't you come along? Even if nothing comes of it, at least you got to meet him and see the place."

"I don't know Pat . . ."

"I'll even cover your hourly rate for the day if it doesn't work out . . . and I can pick you up in my new car."

I snapped to attention on that news. "Pat, you do recall that my hourly is a grand."

"How could I forget?"

"New car? What have you got now?" I confess to a weakness for cars. They interest me. A lot. Always have.

"Mercedes AMG GT Roadster, new out of the box."

"Sport with the 590hp?"

"Mmm-hmm"

"Colour?"

"Matte black."

"Foil?"

"Of course. Had to when it can get up to 100 in 3.2 . . . and I'm not talking kilometres." He was practically giggling. "What time can I pick you up?"

"Here's the problem, I have to be back in TO by the evening . . ."

"Not a problem, bro, cuz I have to be back for eight o'clock anyways, it's Laurie's book club night and I've got the kids."

"On your own?" No wonder he wanted to get back on the road.

"No, with the nanny . . ."

Oh shit. Alarm bells started to sound in the distance.

"Pat . . . nanny? Seriously?"

"No, no, no, not to worry. No danger. Laurie made sure of that. This one's a real bruiser. I'm actually afraid of her. Kids are too. However, the cleaning ladies, that's another matter. They're a couple of honeys . . ."

"Pat, please don't. Can you pick me up in front of my office?"

"No problem. Nine o'clock okay?"

"Yup and where're we going? Where's this compound?"

"I'm not allowed to give the address or coordinates for good reason, but it's out near Prince Edward County. We can get there in less than two hours."

"I bet we can in that new rocket."

"See you in the a.m., bro. Oh, and you might want to dress casual. Leave the lawyer look downtown. It can get a little good-ole-boy-like out there. You know what I mean?"

"I get it."

The next morning I put in a few hours at the office and by 9 a.m. I was sitting on the steps in front of my building when the rocket rolled up. Beautiful. Just beautiful. He had finished the Roadster with the large AMP window decal and a yellow racing stripe front to back. The driver's window scrolled down to unleash pounding music, Patrick's beaming smile and, of course, one soul patch. "Good morning, counsel. I wasn't sure you owned a pair of jeans and some boots but you're looking very casual. Well done. Hop in. I grabbed us some Starbucks."

Pat was dressed like he was going to a rodeo, shiny new cowboy boots, plaid western-style shirt, blue jeans and a belt buckle the size of a dinner plate. Our travel soundtrack was all Coop all the way. Patrick was clearly a fan, singing along to every song. Me? Not so much. Jesus, one song was called "Love Poultice" with Coop moaning about an old cowboy's sick horse named Buck that had to be put down. It actually ended with a gunshot. Not exactly line dancing material but then again, I wasn't being paid to be a music critic. "Hockeytonkin'" suddenly sounded like Grammy material beside some of this crap.

We exited the 401 and took a bunch of back roads deep into Prince Edward County. Patrick pulled over abruptly at a battered sign that said, "Big Dog Organic Chicken Farm," climbed out and pushed open a simple wooden gate to a dirt road that had one of those metal cattle guard grates over a small creek.

"The sign is an inside joke. Hank Williams, 'Move It on Over.' Get it?"

"Nope."

He started singing, "You know, 'a big dog's moving in.'"

"Clever. He has chickens?"

"No. It's not really that kind of ranch. But he's country, the real deal."

Patrick gingerly maneuvered the Roadster over the cattle guard and then hopped out to close the gate. It seemed like a pretty common farm setup until we went about 100 yards, through a row of trees and rounded a corner. That's when we hit the real gates, something George Strait would have been proud of, with white stone horses rearing up over ornate iron work and a soaring fountain. Patrick rolled up and gave some sort of password over an intercom.

"Wow."

"Oh, you ain't seen nothing yet." Oh God. Did I just detect Pat suddenly developing a little southern accent?

We wound our way down a kilometre of interlocking stone laneway to a massive post-and-beam lodge-style home perched on a hill overlooking a small lake. There were about a half-dozen cars and trucks in the drive. A security type walked over to greet us. He recognized Patrick and showed us where to park in front of the five-car garage. All the doors were open and I could see a row of high-end vehicles: a Mercedes G-Wagon, a Maserati, a new Porsche 911, a Rivian pickup and, intriguingly, something I didn't recognize. I would need to loop back on that one.

"Mr. Cooper is in the Chevy. You can take an ATV or golf cart if you like, but it's probably just as easy to walk there. Just follow the path down by the lake and around to the fields."

I turned to Patrick. "He's where?"

"You'll see."

We walked along a beautifully landscaped path, past a large dock that stretched out into the small lake. Three or four young women were sunning in lounge chairs. One was strumming a guitar. They gave us not so much as a glance as we passed.

Once past the edge of the lake, I could see what looked like an apple orchard flowing up the side of a small hill. Under a cluster of trees was parked a vintage car. As we got closer, I could see that the car was actually just off the ground on a barely visible concrete platform, more of a display than ready to be driven. Soft music could be heard.

Patrick knocked on the hood and called out, "Coop. You in?"

There was no response but then the music stopped, the passenger door swung open and a very pretty young woman with long blonde hair, in a pink and orange poplin summer dress, stepped out, straightened her clothes and smiled. "Mornin'."

"Good morning."

Without a word she picked up her sandals and walked barefoot down the path toward the dock.

The driver's door swung open and out stepped the man himself, The Coop. Easily six foot four, he could not have weighed more than 170 pounds. He reached back inside the car and pulled out an ash blond–coloured cowboy hat, slapped it on his thigh and parked it on his head. It looked so comfortable he could have slept in that hat. "Hey Pat, what's up?"

I instantly got the vibe that we were not expected and had interrupted something, something intimate. I hate that vibe.

"Hey, Coop. I want ya to meet someone. Remember the stuff you were telling me about and how I mentioned a lawyer buddy who could help? Well, this is the man. Andrew Bierce, Q.C."

Coop looked me up and down. And winced. "I hope you didn't share too much, you know that stuff was private . . . and we had been drinking a little." He didn't look happy.

"No, no. It's cool. I just wanted ya to meet. See if there's a fit. If there is, my man Andy's a problem solver."

Patrick was trying way too hard. *My man Andy?* Come on. He sounded needy. Not a good look for an aging rockstar, especially one dressed like a drugstore cowboy. And he was definitely developing a terrible southern accent.

"Mr. Cooper. Nice to meet you. That's a '47 Chevy if I'm not mistaken."

"You're not mistaken." He looked at it proudly.

"Fleetline, Aerosedan. Fastback. Nice. Not the original paint, though. Good look with the whitewalls." I pointed at the chrome grill. "You salvaged the chrome spears too. Well done." I nodded approvingly.

"I tried to have them match the original paint."

"The best colour, I think, was the deep maroon. It was a popular car in its day. They sold about 150,000 of them that year."

"You don't say? You sound like a man who appreciates a good automobile. Care to take a peek inside?" He gestured to the passenger side.

"Are there any more young ladies in there?"

"No, no more," he laughed at that and looked at Pat with a knowing smile and a wink, "*auditions* are finished, at least for the morning."

I walked over, extended my hand, "Pleasure," but climbed in the driver's side. My attitude? *You may be a big fucking deal to some people, Mr. Love Poultice, but not to me. I'm just interested in your car.*

He leaned in the driver's-side window. As I sat looking at the vintage instrumentation, he bit. "So, you're a lawyer. I've tangled with a few." He said tangle as if he had roped a steer.

I didn't answer. "How did you manage to get the Fleetweave upholstery? This can't be original."

"It's original. I had my guy source it in the States."

"Nice. Radio work?"

"Yup. Give 'er a whirl."

I turned the ivory knob and the sound of music poured out like honey. Beautiful original speakers. I knew the song. "Tennessee Waltz." Classic. "Ahh, Patti Page. Beautiful. The original owner would have heard that song on this very radio. That's perfect. You know that song was No. 1 on the pop, country and R&B charts at the same time? Never been done since." I sat back to listen.

"Sounds like you know yer music too. Patrick says you solved some problems for him and Laurie."

I held up a "let's be respectful" finger to my lips to stop him until the song finished. When it ended, I motioned to him to come around to the passenger side. He climbed in and shut the door. We rolled down the windows and I turned off the radio. I could see Patrick standing in front of the car smoking a cigarette like an expectant father.

"What's a Q.C.? Does that mean you keep everything on the Q.C., you know, quiet?"

"It stands for Queen's Counsel. Actually, with the Queen just having died a couple days ago I guess we're called K.C. now—King's Counsel. Anyway, it's a special designation for senior lawyers. They don't really give it out anymore. Look, before you tell me anything, I want you to know, I'm not here looking for work. I'm very busy these days, working on a big judicial inquiry about some nasty judge . . . But I can tell from what Patrick has said that he cares for you, has a soft spot. Older brother kind of vibe? I don't know. He seems to think you're headed for some trouble. He wants to help keep you from stepping in something. I was able to help him with some similar, shall we say, cow pies."

"He said—and I quote—you're a 'fucking wizard.' I don't usually use that kind of language."

"Me neither. It's vulgar. Toxic. Un-Christian." (I know. Whatever.)

"Exactly."

"Anyway, when someone has personal problems, especially in a marriage, sometimes a little preventative care, sort of a *poultice* if you like," I'm not sure how I pulled that one out of my ass right there on the spot, but I guess I was inspired by the surroundings, "can avoid all or at least some of that trouble. If you ever think you want to chat about that kind of stuff, I'm around. Otherwise, it's been cool meeting you and seeing your place, especially this sweet ride."

He nodded. "Cool. Do you have to leave right away?"

"Not really . . ."

"Time to see another car?"

"Sure. How many have you got?"

"The Compound is three hundred acres. I've situated about a dozen classics around the property, my favourites tucked in here and there. I like to spend time in them. That's where I do my best work."

"Yeah, I saw her . . . cute."

He thought that was pretty funny. "No, no, I mean songwriting. I climb in a car and stuff just comes to me. Neil Young told me he did the same thing . . . but sometimes they're for recreation as well." He popped open the glove box to reveal a handful of condoms. Ahh, to be young and rich. "And call me Coop. Everyone does."

"Anything nearby?"

"Sure, come on." He turned and called to Patrick, "Hey Pat, we're taking a little hike." The three of us headed up a small hill and then stopped on a ridge that looked down into a shady gulley. A small brook flowed through it right beside another classic car that was also up on a poured concrete platform. The sun was shining through the willow trees and reflecting off the water and the car. It was so beautiful, I imagined for a moment being buried in such a place.

"What do you think?"

Patrick was awestruck. "Gorgeous." At least he didn't say, "Real purdy."

It was stunning. "A '53 Plymouth Cambridge? I don't think I've ever seen one in the flesh." It was a buttercream colour with a brown roof. Original paint, no doubt. It looked like a small cabin, a home. I wanted to curl up in the backseat with a bottle of scotch and that young woman who'd just left.

Coop turned to Patrick and suggested he head back to the dock so we could take a few minutes to check out the car and chat some more. He seemed delighted to leave and said he was starving. We climbed into the spacious front bench seat and as we sat in that beautiful car listening to the brook, Coop sketched out his storm clouds. After twenty minutes I felt like I needed a program to keep track of the players: an ex-wife (Caroline); childhood friend from their days in Winnipeg, former band member and now business manager (Brent); the business manager's wife (Kim); and Kim's daughter from a previous marriage (Kayla). Bottom line? Coop and Kim were having an affair and wanted to come clean with Brent.

He stopped his tale of woe. "Well? Is that enough?"

"Enough trouble for a double album, my friend. You really need to be careful with this. This Brent fellow, can he be trusted? I mean, if things go sideways over you and Kim, can he put your business in the ditch?"

"He has control of everything, writes the cheques, pays the bills, keeps the lights on and me on the road."

"That's a lot of power over you. Who're your accountants? Who does the books?"

"He does it all."

"Do you have access to everything?"

"Yup. But I don't pay much attention. Kim does more than me. I just make the music and spend the money. Why?"

"Could you move a copy of all the business records on short notice, discreetly, if you needed to?"

"I suppose. Kim could set it up."

"I'm suggesting you get me a set of your books for the last three years. No need for anyone to know. Do you mind if I get a colleague of mine to take a look at things on the QT? She's a forensic auditor. Just take a peek to make sure everything's in order. She can set it up in case the shit hits the fan, so all you would need to do is throw a switch and block Brent doing any damage. She'll do it for me as a favour. It would be a wise precaution."

I could see him thinking about it. It was big, considering I had not even been retained.

"Confidential? Brent wouldn't know?"

"Nope."

He thought a bit more.

"My concern is if you and Kim announce to him—or worse, your situation is discovered—then he could blow up Cooper Music with a few keystrokes."

"Yeah, I guess. We're being very discreet. There's no way he could know, but sometimes I get the sense he knows and pretends he doesn't. Weird."

Oh God, the naïveté of people who think their indiscretions are not going to be discovered. They are *always* discovered. They *want* to be discovered.

"Well, I'm sure you're right but you never know. Accidents happen. There's no downside to having an emergency switch." I didn't like the sound of Brent possibly suspecting something. He could be burying bombs as we spoke.

"Yeah, I guess you're right. Okay. I'll set it up. Just send the stuff to you?"

"Yup. Here's my card. I'll take it from there. In the meantime, be careful. With a little planning you can avoid a lot of trouble."

"I hear you. That's what Pat said, you're a planner. You know how to get a deal. Strategic. I need that."

We started to walk back to the house along the path near the lake. As we got to the dock, the young women who had been sunning were all gathered around Patrick. As if on springs, they all popped out of their chairs to come and say hello to Coop.

Suddenly, his Nashville twang returned full force. It was pretty good considering he was born in Newmarket. "Hey, pretty ladies. Y'all having a nice time in the sun? Maybe it's time to head up and get us some lunch.

Whaddaya say?" He was so cool. Killer cool. He reminded me of Sean in a way. His invitation was met with a din of giggling, tittering and laughing from these twentysomethings. "This here is a friend of mine, Andy. He's a big-shot lawyer from the city." Oh God, really? *From the city?* Where were we, in the hills of Kentucky? We're two hours from the CN Tower.

One young lady had hung back a bit but then stepped forward. "I believe we've met before, Andy."

It was none other than Ms. Selena Gomez Grande Ariana, Patrick's former nanny, now supposedly a budding image consultant. I turned to Patrick. He looked down at his new cowboy boots and polished them one by one on the back of his blue jeans.

As I said, people–don't–change.

17

The Vatican Gift Shop
Thursday September 15

THE VATICAN is a cool little speakeasy bar over on Gerrard, perfect for wooing Bonnie back. I wanted to wow her a bit with something she had never experienced. It's not over the top in terms of prices and the vibe is cool. Once she saw it, I was sure she'd want to be back downtown instead of stuck in the Scarboonies where she worked now.

I got there a little early, sat at the bar for a bit and had a couple of drinks. By 7:15p.m. I was still at a table alone and getting worried that she was bailing. The "wetting my silks" story? Oh God, so lame. I should have just come out and told her I needed her back. She might walk in here, see me sitting alone, feel totally out of place with the 416 vibe and just turn around and walk out. Who could blame her?

No sooner had I fashioned that nightmare than in she strolled. And not in the usual black from head to toe. She was wearing a beige jumpsuit, green silk scarf, messenger bag over her shoulder and tan boots. Go, Bonnie. As she passed the end of the bar the heavily tattooed bartender (tattoo apparently required in order to graduate from serving school) called out to her, "Hey, Bonnie, *slava boy oofgoaa*" (basically something in a foreign language). She smiled and raised her hand shyly, as if to say, don't make a fuss.

I stood as she got to my table. "Bonnie, I was getting nervous . . . so great to see you." I gave her an awkward kind of post-COVID hug.

"Great to see you too, Andrew. You're looking prosperous." That was her way of saying I had put on weight.

"Yeah, I know. Staying home through COVID, suspended," (whispered), "and not working out cost me big time." I patted by stomach with a grimace.

"You stopped running too? You know people were allowed to keep running outside."

"Very funny. So I got lazy too."

"When do the rest of the lawyers who are wetting their silks arrive? Should we get more chairs?" She raised her arm and signalled to the bartender, "Admir, we'll need more chairs."

I pulled her arm back down. "Bonnie, Bonnie, I confess the wetting of silks was a ruse to get you here." I turned to the bartender. "It's okay, Bashir, we're good." He laughed as if he knew it was all a joke. "Sorry, but I really wanted to get together. I was desperate. You have been a little *remote*, shall we say?"

"So, of course, you make up some silly story."

"I'm sorry. Look, can I get you a drink? What do you like?"

She raised her hand to the bartender and then pointed at my head. "Admir, usual. On his tab. Thanks."

"Okay. I get it. You have been here before. I was hoping to impress you. How do you know Basmair?"

"It's Admir, and he's from Albania. He came through our service and I helped get him settled in Toronto. Back home he was a chemist." As she explained more about his family's arrival, he set down another straight bourbon for me and a Kentucky Mule for Bonnie.

Two hours later, and after two awesome Augustine pizzas, we were laughing about our crazy last year together and what had unfolded after Lester's funeral.

"What happened with Teresa Savoie's claim on the life insurance policy that her husband was supposed to be maintaining?"

"Dismissed with costs. She owes me $35,000 for costs but cannot pay so I'm SOL. Get this, though. Fernstein took her file without a retainer up front and he had to eat his fees. That must have been over seventy grand. Cheers to that fucking prick getting what he deserved." I raised my glass.

She did not. "Still with the language?" She frowned and shook her head.

"Sorry, it's the bourbon talking."

"What happened to the fireman with the condoms blocking his septic, the one who was looking for support from Ms. Wood?"

"Grim. He died from his burns, along with his support claim. Now she's fighting with his estate."

"Sad."

"They're all sad, Bonnie. They're all sad."

"Why did they end up suspending you? It wasn't because of Lester, I hope. You had no way of knowing Paul would do that."

"No, it wasn't because of Lester or Paul, although that didn't help. It was because of my *relationships* with Ms. Lululemon and my client in Muskoka, the irregular billing to her company. That was considered unprofessional, *conduct unbecoming*. That prick—sorry—that *jerk* Randall Williams did a confidential fact-finder for the Law Society that pretty much buried me. There are only three copies of his report: the Law Society has one, he has one and I have a copy locked in a desk at the office. That's why I was suspended. Ten months and I had to go to counselling with a shrink out in Parkdale."

"Andrew, it *was* unbecoming. You knew better. Counselling probably didn't hurt either. Did it help? I ended up talking to someone for a few months about what happened. Angie, Paul, Lester." She stared into her drink. "I still get headaches from the fall."

"Yeah, I guess it helped," *not really*, "but what ever happened to consenting adults?" Bonnie looked at me as if to say *You still don't get it, do you?* What could I say?

"But the suspension's up. You're back in the office?"

"Yup, back at it and . . ." I took a mouthful of bourbon and got ready to pitch Bonnie with more money, more vacation and parking. I wasn't going to fool around with any coy negotiating or back and forth. I would just put the whole package on the table and throw myself on the mercy of the court. "And it's been busy. New clients. Interesting clients." I lowered my voice to a whisper. "Do you know Cody Cooper?"

"Cody Cooper!" Her stage whisper caught even the attention of Admir who probably thought it was a type of car. "Oh my God. I'm a huge fan. I have every CD."

Oh brother, I'm not sure which was worse, she loves his version of country music or that she still buys CDs. "Shh shh, . . . it's just at the front end. He needs advice. You know, the usual."

"Still, that's great. Referred by Patrick McGovern, I assume?"

"Yup. They're buds. Right now, things are on the back burner. I've sent three years' worth of his business books over to Naomi Smart to take a quick and dirty."

"She's good. I liked working with her. Valuation?"

"No, more of a 'what's been going on?' audit. My spidey senses were tingling."

"You and your spidey senses." She smiled and was enjoying the catch-up. Good.

"But you know what surprised me, even after everything that happened with Angie, Lester and Paul? People still want it, you know, Total War, blank cheques. But, Bonnie, . . ." I took a deep breath for my pitch.

She cut me off. "Andrew, I would like to come back to work with you."

I just about fell off my chair. "What?" Was this because of Cody Cooper? I hoped not, because he wasn't actually a client yet.

"I want to come back to work for you. I know you probably have hired someone and they're settled in there now, but I was thinking part-time until you are ramped up again and then maybe return to full-time . . ."

"Bonnie, . . ."

"I know this is out of the blue and I should have given you a heads-up. It's not fair to just drop it on you."

"Bonnie, . . ."

"I'm sure we can work out a salary. I would consider a cut if that was the only way to make it happen . . ."

"Bonnie, . . . stop."

"Don't make me beg. You're a better negotiator than me."

"Bonnie, stop. Yes, you can come back. But . . ."

"But what?"

"No cut in salary. In fact I'm prepared to increase it. Plus, I want you to take more vacation. I have a parking spot for you, and I want to help with your gas . . . and I would want—need—you to start as soon as you can. What do you think?" I hadn't seen a smile like that in a long time. "Is that a yes?" I felt like I was waiting for an answer after proposing marriage.

"Yes, of course. Of course." She was thrilled.

"Great, let's celebrate. Basmier, two more!"

"I have to add just one condition . . ."

Wow. I wished she'd mentioned that sooner.

18

A Voodoo Spell Was Cast
September 15

AS BONNIE BEGAN to explain her one condition for returning to work with me, a familiar thought streamed through my mind: *Why does everyone suddenly lose all common sense as soon as they get involved in politics? Honestly, it's like a magic voodoo spell has been cast over them. They will believe anything.* I did my best to keep a straight face as she began to gush about her latest heartthrob.

She was breathless. "While working at Immigrant Services I met a young man named Mateo Reyes. He's Filipino-Canadian, he and his family have lived in Scarborough for years. Honestly, Andrew, I have *never* met a more devoted, kind-hearted, *caring* person. He helped us so much at the Centre. He is *loved* in the community."

Oh boy. Here we go. Heart-on-her-sleeve Bonnie has fallen for another earthly saint. I smiled weakly as I was not about to blow her potential return to the office by pouring cold water on her new hero. "He sounds pretty special. I'm sure you'll be able to stay in touch."

"Well, it may be a little more than that and this is where the condition comes in. He's going to run in the next provincial election next year, he's getting organized now and has asked me to be on his campaign team, maybe co-chair. It's very exciting." She was clearly thrilled and deeply honoured.

My eyes rolled—discreetly, of course. "Really? How exciting. Which party?" Knowing her penchant for hopeless social causes I prayed it was not some crazy Canadian version of the Filipino New People's Army communist gang of pseudo-society savers.

"The Greens!" She uttered these two words as if the party was clearly the next wellspring of provincial, if not world, salvation. I smiled and let out a small sigh of relief, realizing that sadly she had been sipping the worst flavour of Canadian political Kool-Aid—Green Apple.

I didn't have the heart to tell her that this was a hopeless cause. "Wow. Green Party in Scarborough. Would not have guessed that. I always thought that was pretty solid Liberal, even NDP, turf."

"It has been in the past, but Mateo is going to change all that."

Standard political delusion had already set in.

"He's mobilizing the community like never before."

Never heard of that approach before.

"We have been out knocking on doors, meeting people, having BBQs. People are responding to him."

Wow. Sounded like Trudeaumania (circa '68) all over again.

"Well, that's great, Bonnie. So, you'll need to be away from the office a bit. Is that the condition?"

"Yes, basically. But I promise it will not affect my work."

I decided to reassure her—if that's all it would take to reel her in. "Bonnie, I have no doubt you'll be doing your usual great work. Not a problem."

I figured she would start off strong working for this young fellow, but then about halfway through the campaign she would see his polling peak at 2 percent and dial back her commitment. Political polls can be wildly wrong, unless they are in the 2 to 3 percent range. Those numbers don't lie. I guess she would need to learn the hard way. Oh, Bonnie.

Above all, I dreaded the thought of telling her that I, too, might be a candidate in the next election and that it would be happening a lot sooner than she thought.

19

The Eunuch
Friday September 16

I HAD DELAYED calling Alvin back, in part because I wanted to gather a little more information but also because I had not forgotten how he ignored my calls and texts while I was suspended. I thought he should get a taste of his own medicine. However, seeing Ms. Novak's name on Rimini's potential witness list made returning his calls just too good to resist.

He answered on the first ring. "Novak and Shank."

"Has a nice *ring* to it." Drop of hot sauce on the *ring*.

"Hilarious, but getting tired. Thanks for finally calling me back. I've been trying to reach you for days. Do you know how hard it is to slip away from Lorelei?"

"Trouble in paradise? Leash getting uncomfortable? By the way, if you're looking for your balls, I think they're in her purse."

"Fuck you very much. Look there are things you need to know about the Finch matter and I don't have a lot of time."

"Hang on, I have another call." I didn't but I made him wait on hold for a few minutes. I came back to him cheerfully, "Okay, sorry, I'm all ears."

"Bierce. This is serious."

"I know it is and it's getting more serious by the day because I know exactly who was at that party—one Lorelei Novak. You neglected to mention that she was there. She would make an interesting witness, so I assume there is a good reason you didn't mention her."

"Yes, she was there and yes, she knows what was going on. She's rebuilding a network that you wouldn't believe. She has had a hard time coming back from the gossip about her memoirs."

"Pillow talk network?" Surely, she wasn't keeping up her extracurricular activities now that she was back with Alvin. But then again—people don't change.

"Very funny. Look, obviously she has stayed in touch with Randall Williams. Now that he's a judge it makes sense to maintain that relationship—a *professional* relationship."

"Of course, it's *professional*. What else would it be?"

"Funny. Do you want to talk or not? I'm trying to help you. Anyway, she was speaking with Williams yesterday. He's miserable up in Barrie."

"I heard. Word gets around."

"He told her—on a confidential basis—that he had exciting news. They're going to move him."

"I'm sure the lawyers, court staff and people of Barrie will be grateful."

"Whatever. You'll be interested to know that the attorney general is appointing him to lead a judicial inquiry into the alleged misconduct of a certain Toronto judge. Announcement's in a week or so."

"What?" Williams leading the Glinka Inquiry? This had shitstorm written all over it. How am I supposed to sit in front of him at an inquiry without boiling over?

"Listen, I gotta go. And there's more. I don't think you have a complete list of who was at the party. Oh-oh. Shit. Here she comes. Don't let anyone know where you heard this. Okay? We'll speak later."

I was *mutus*—again.

20

Bless Me, Father

Wednesday September 21

I HAD TRIED to book a face-to-face with this Father Shannon character but the Irish bugger was hard to track down, constantly on the road and not available even for a call. I began to think he was avoiding me. While I waited to hear back I did a little research, but it revealed little more than a few routine facts about him: he was forty-five, well educated, and had virtually no presence on social media.

The first time I reached out I suggested we meet for coffee right in the lion's den, the archdiocese offices at 1155 Yonge, but that was immediately ruled out. That said something. Too close to home. But his secretary eventually called me back with an intriguing alternative—the good Father had tickets to a Blue Jays game. Wednesday 7:07 p.m. Yankees were in town. Could we meet there? Interesting. Why not? I guessed that there was less likelihood of actual fisticuffs if we met in public. Within minutes of accepting his offer an e-ticket popped up on my phone. Section 125, Row 1. Good seats.

The Jays were making a late run for a wild card playoff spot so games at the Rogers Centre were sold out. After another full day at the office with a new client, I fought my way to Gate 4 through insane drumming and a mob of chanting fans. I wish they'd put half as much energy into their own physical fitness as they did drunken bawling at people. If I was a professional athlete, I'd be embarrassed to see my name on the back of these yahoos.

I arrived at my seat fifteen minutes early and was disappointed to see the roof closed. The view of edge walkers on the CN Tower is sometimes more thrilling than the ball game. As I made my way down the aisle, I could see the supposedly formidable priest in a leather Blue Jays collegiate jacket working his way through a bag of popcorn. When he stood to greet me, I wasn't sure if I was shaking hands with a priest or a midsized leprechaun. Father Shannon could not have been more than five foot eight, so I had a good six inches on him. If he weighed 150 pounds after eating the popcorn it would have been a lot. However, despite his diminutive size, I could detect from his handshake that here was a lean, physically powerful man, a fierce leprechaun. But for his otherwise very ordinary haircut, I would have sworn I was shaking hands with that maniac Irishman, MMA fighter Conor McGregor.

"Father, pleasure to meet you. Wonderful idea to watch the Jays. You're a fan?"

"Pleasure is mine. I'm glad you could join me. I come when I can. This game takes some getting used to."

"It's an acquired taste. I like to get here early, see the players warm up, settle in, national anthem, first pitch."

Without asking me whether I wanted a drink, he flagged down the beer guy and paid for four tallboys. (So much for priestly vows of poverty, four beers at a Blue Jay game runs $50.00 with tip.) As he held a cold one to his lips he said, "I understand you're not opposed to having a drink."

Interesting comment. "Thanks." I left my beer untouched. "I never drink till the Jays homer." (Not really, but, you know.)

He smiled and nodded. "Interesting plan. But I hope it's not a thirsty one. Cheers." With his accent he sounded quite harmless, not worried that I might be after his Lucky Charms.

Aside from meaningless chatter about baseball and life in Toronto, he said nothing of Sean, not even a, "I'm sorry he's unwell." But I could wait. I'm used to letting people fill the silence. By the fifth inning my two beers remained untouched and Aaron Judge had struck out twice. Game was tied 3-3.

At one point I was tempted to get into it with a row of woolly-toqued hipster idiots sitting behind me. Non-stop talking, taking pictures of themselves, texting and phoning friends, showing each other texts and TikTok videos, trying to get on the jumbotron, betting online, anything but actually watching the game. And the beer and coolers? I stopped counting after the beer guy made his sixth delivery. I nearly went off when their drunken conversation turned to foulmouthed whining about how they'll never be able to buy an f*ing home in Toronto. Really? I thought of the days I'd spent living in the basement of my old place in Leaside, listening to my tenant enjoying the main level, scrimping on everything to pay that crazy fucking mortgage. Go to a Jays game? I didn't even have cable to watch a game. Fucking Daria. These idiots are sitting in $200 seats and have spent even more than that on beer and coolers *and they're not even watching the game.* Buy a home? You don't deserve to own a home.

But I had to let it go, more important things were afoot. The huge jumbotron scoreboard flashed an invitation to comment on whether fans wanted to bring back *Bark in the Park* night, when fans bring their dogs to a baseball game. Oh Jesus, kill me now. I made a mental note to hire a bot to register fifty thousand negative votes. The only dog that should be at a ball game has mustard on it.

The fans in the cheap seats tried to get a wave going and Shannon began to tiptoe toward the real reason for our meeting. "I've heard that you had a couple of tough years, your partner was killed in a courtroom. Suspension. Difficult times. But you're back at it now?"

"Yeah, getting back at it." Patience. "Yankees are certainly paying Judge an awful lot of money to strike out." Wait. Let the little priest talk.

"Those kinds of things can jump up and bite a candidate for public office. Are you prepared to deal with that?"

Oh, so we're jumping right into it. "Who said I was a candidate for anything yet?"

He smiled and reached under his seat for another tallboy. "Can we speak frankly?"

"Of course." Well, at least you can.

"Andrew, I want you to understand the situation. I'm here in Toronto for what the archdiocese calls special projects. Your brother Sean is one of my special projects. His potential laicization, his care, his commitments, and—if everything unfolds as it should—his being laid to rest at St. Augustine's are all within my hands now."

"You'll forgive me, father, but Sean's commitment, the archdiocese's commitment and the 'unfolding as it should,' where is this understanding, this *simony*,* written down?"

He just laughed. "Simony? You surprise me." He took a long sip of beer. "But you're a lawyer, naturally you would want this to be written down. But that's not something that can or will happen. This will be done on trust, on faith."

"I'm not a big believer in either of those concepts."

He raised his eyebrows as if to say *I'm not surprised*. "And please don't think about sending me any emails or text messages summarizing any *arrangement*. I'll deny everything and it will guarantee that nothing happens for Sean." His tone was cold, matter of fact.

"I see." Patience. I waited.

For someone new to baseball, the good Father certainly knew the "Let's Go Blue Jays" cheer and joined in a full-throated seventh inning stretch rendition of "Take Me Out to the Ball Game," sounding like he thought we was singing "When Irish Eyes Are Smiling."

As we sat to start the bottom of the inning, he spoke again. "Your brother is a lucky man."

I cut him off. "You mean the one with terminal cancer?"

"Yes, that one. He's lucky that the archdiocese protected him as long as they did. Back home that would not have happened."

"No, I suppose in Ireland he would have been a cardinal by now."

He crumpled his beer can and tucked it under the seat. "Andrew, from what I know, from what I've heard, I think we are similar in some ways, so we can speak frankly. We're not people who—forgive my salty language—fuck around. So please don't insult my intelligence by making weak jokes about simony, Ireland and the church. Let me put it this way, either Sean or you will be the Independent candidate in Parkdale–High Park. By doing so, you will split the vote in order to help put our friend Mr. McKay over the top as MPP. That will happen or your brother is on

---

* Sale of ecclesiastical favours.

the street and headed for a grave in parts unknown. I'm not sure I can say it any plainer than that." He was cold. Confident. Mean.

"I see."

Suddenly a roar swept around the stadium as an entirely coincidental fan wave seemed to lift a Jays' homer into the right field upper deck. One swing of the bat and three runs scored. Jays were up 6-3. I reached for a beer. "At last, we have something to toast." I offered my second tallboy to Father Shannon. "It's a little warm, but it's a beer." He took it and we drank quietly to the Jays' expected victory.

As we made our way out of the stadium to Front Street, the little man took my hand in an earnest handshake. "Andrew, do we understand each other?"

"Perfectly."

"We can count on you?"

I nodded. "You can count on me . . ." *to find a way to fuck you over the first chance I get, you smug little leprechaun prick.*

"Excellent. I'm glad we met. My people will be in touch."

We said our goodbyes and I immediately headed back to the office to call Sean. It was late and Daria answered. "Are you his receptionist now?"

"There's no need for that tone with me, Andrew. Can't we move on? For heaven's sake, it's been a long time."

"I need to speak with Sean about Shannon."

"He's sleeping. Did you meet with that priest?"

"I did. I need to ask Sean something."

"What?"

"This doesn't concern you."

"It does if it concerns Sean."

I paused for a second. "Okay. When he wakes, ask him about this. Shannon said Sean is *one* of his special projects while he is in Toronto. I would like to find out what else he's involved in."

"I'll ask him but I overheard the priests talking in the hall after their visit with Sean. Shannon is also here to clean up something involving the Christian Brothers. Abuse at training schools or something, confidential settlements. They seemed worried."

Oh God. Christian Brothers? We're really headed for the gutter now.

21

Tangerine Help
Thursday September 22

IF I DIDN'T NEED help before, I sure needed it now. My practice was loading up, I was on the verge of committing to take on Francesca's case, Cooper's matter was simmering and probably going to pop and these election issues with Sean were about to become a priority. Fernstein had, of course, served me with a motion to allow his client to see those god-damn Marrs twins. The hearing date was approaching and I needed to file responding material or get another adjournment. Could I pull a rabbit out of a hat? It would be tough, especially with no instructions from the client.

Bonnie had come on board and was getting back up to speed. She was clearly thrilled to be back at it but she could only do so much. I needed legal firepower, and technology firepower. It was then that I recalled Ms. Techy Tangerine Dream, Lindsay Braun. Could I lure her into working with me? Surely she couldn't be enjoying sole practice. Money would be a factor I bet. Plus she would be, you know, nice to have around. Maybe possibilities outside the office? Perhaps. *God, what was I thinking? Old fool dreams.*

It wasn't too late, so I poured a tall scotch from my replenished stock, dug up her number and called.

On one ring. "Lindsay Braun."

"Andrew Bierce."

Long pause. Big sigh. "What can I do for you, Mr. Bierce?" She sounded very cautious, downright skeptical.

"I just want to say that I was impressed by your paper for the Advocates' Society panel. I see you're on your own now and I am a little curious if you're taking on referrals. I need some help on a couple of matters." Test waters.

Long pause. Nothing. Then, "I'm not sure it would be a good fit for me given your track . . . your situation . . . well . . . it wouldn't be a good fit. But thank you for your interest."

Hmm. What could I say to tempt her? Get her interested? "In terms of fit I think you should be open to quality work. You know I'm on the verge of a potential judicial inquiry concerning sexual harassment at the Provincial Court up on Finch and I need good support, especially legal technology support. It's confidential right now but your former colleague, Justice Williams, is being tapped for the job and I thought . . ."

"What did you just say?"

"It's a judicial inquiry . . ."

"No, did you say Randall Williams is going to be appointed to lead that Glinka Inquiry?" I couldn't tell if she was thrilled or in shock. I assumed she really enjoyed working with him.

"Yes, that's the rumour. I think the announcement will be made very soon. He's sitting in Barrie right now and word is he's unhappy, so . . ."

"Oh, this is just too rich for words. He's going to lead an inquiry about sexual harassment? This is unbelievable. I can't . . . I can't . . ." She was aghast. And then she hung up.

What the F.

I stared at my phone. What just happened? Then it rang. It was her. "Are you telling me that . . . that . . . I can't believe this . . ." There were several profanities, some of which even I would have been proud to utter and then she hung up again.

I was starting to question her stability. Maybe she was on her own for a reason.

She rang my phone again. "Are you free?"

"You mean now?"

"Yes, now."

"Sure, if you can come to my office. I'm working late. I'm at . . ."

"I'll be there in thirty minutes."

I didn't know what to say. "Sure, absolutely."

I decided to use those thirty minutes to clean up my desk, gobble breath mints to make sure I didn't smell of scotch and prepare to make a better impression on this beautiful young woman this time around. Recollections of her long, thick, auburn hair, gorgeous shy smile, freckled nose and that sharp tangerine suit flowed freely. Sigh. I couldn't wait to see her again.

True to her word she was at the entrance to my office at 8:30 p.m. sharp. As I opened the door, at first glance I thought it was one of Toronto's notorious pothead bike couriers dropping off a package. She was wearing blue jeans tucked into thick red wool socks and wore a lime green bike jacket with one of those yellow glow-in-the-dark road safety vests over top. Her leather gloves were fingerless and her hair was tucked up under a bright orange helmet covered with stickers that declared, "Share the road!" A leather crossbody messenger bag hung over her shoulder and on her feet were those curious cleat-like cycling shoes that click into stirrups. Disturbingly, she also had what appeared to be a large cold sore on her upper lip. *Yech*. Was this even the same person I had seen at Randall Williams's office a couple of years ago? She was a mess.

"Hello, Ms. Braun. Nice to see you again." I did my best to hide my surprise and disappointment at her appearance.

"Are you here alone? Are there any staff still here?" Not even a hello. She sounded paranoid.

"Yes, I'm alone but there's no need to be worried."

"I've heard that before." Her sneering tone didn't sound good.

"Come in. Let's sit in my office." I was sure she would be blown away by my authentic Arne Jacobsen Egg chair. "Honestly, there's no need to worry. Would you like a drink?"

"No. Absolutely nothing to drink. No drinking." That didn't sound good either. Maybe she had a problem with alcohol. That would be a concern. She settled into the Egg with her bike helmet in her lap. She pulled off her gloves to reveal the battered hands and dirty chipped nails of a greasy mechanic. Jesus, I hoped she wouldn't touch anything, especially the chair.

"I meant like a Diet Coke, tea, coffee or something."

"I'm fine." She looked around the office and then nodded toward what had once been a thriving Golden Pothos (Devil's Ivy). It was now a shrivelled stick that looked like it had been caught in a forest fire. "What happened to that plant? And it smells awful."

"Oh that, some idiot dumped a cup of tea into the soil."

"That must have been one shitty cup of tea."

"You have no idea. So listen, I'm glad we can talk. You think you might have some interest in working with me? I'm back from my break," better not to mention the word suspension, "work has been pouring in, there are a few interesting but pretty complicated situations." I was chattering like a schoolboy. "I have an interesting custody file involving twins. You could get involved in that. I could sure use help on it. The hearing date is coming up." I didn't want to get into the Sean problem. "I know you haven't seen me at my best . . . but . . ."

She stopped looking around the room and stared at me, assessing what I was saying, measuring me on some kind of personal BS meter.

Nothing.

I tried to shift the conversation. "That's an authentic Arne Jacobsen Egg chair you're sitting in. What do you think?" She did not seem the least bit interested in my chair. Nothing. How odd. I mean, it's a beautiful chair.

I soldiered on. "Are you enjoying being on your own? How do you like sole practice?" Innocent questions, I thought.

She bit my head off.

"How do I like sole practice? Do I like not being able to get a job in this entire fucking city despite my impeccable qualifications? Have you seen my CV? Have you read it?"

I held my hands up in protest. "Whoa, whoa, whoa. Look, I have no idea what you're talking about. Is the market that tough out there? I thought there was lots of work."

She reached into her messenger bag which I noticed was, while functional, also a little dated. Kate Spade. Outlet mall stuff. Nice but, you know. She handed me a crisp sheet of paper.

"This is the reference letter Mr. Williams gave me when I left his firm."

I read it. Short but fantastic. "Wow. He's a fan. That's quite a reference."

"Read the last few lines."

If you require any further information, do not hesitate to call me personally at . . . Okay. That's standard.

"Anyone who called him was told not to hire me because I was a *problem, difficult, not a team player*." As she spoke her tongue would slip out and flick over her cold sore as if licking it would make it disappear. It was very distracting. And gross. "I have been so stressed out I can't think straight."

I guess that could explain the cold sore but still, not attractive. If ever there was a reason to wear a mask it was staring me in the face.

Based on her attitude so far, Williams's opinion might not be too far off the mark. Frankly, she came off like a bit of a bitch. So I just played along. "How do you know he said that?"

"My first few interviews went well until they made the call to him and then there was no call back. But one day a senior woman lawyer over at McCarthy's, I had just interviewed with her, made the call to Williams. When she hung up, she frowned and told me what he'd said. Oh, she was *very sympathetic, totally understood* but she didn't offer me a position either." Tongue flick. Cringe.

"Why would he do that? You seemed to work well together." The memory of that horrific day, of him dropping the fuck-off fee on me flashed through my mind again.

She looked down. She was angry. "I can't say. I signed an NDA." Tongue flick.

Oh-oh. NDA doesn't just stand for Non-Disclosure Agreement. It also means No Dirt Aired.

"Why an NDA?"

"Obviously I cannot tell you because of the NDA."

"Did you get independent legal advice before you signed?"

"No, I just signed, took the money and got out of there."

"Do you have a loonie?"

"What?" Tongue flick. Please stop.

"Do you have a loonie? Or a toonie. I'm not fussy."

She rummaged around in her Kate Spade and pulled out a toonie, slid it across my desk and looked at me.

"I consider myself now retained to provide you with ILA on your NDA. You can tell me everything. Solicitor-client privilege."

"Seriously?" Tongue flick. If she did it again, I was going to have to say something.

"Seriously. What happened?"

She actually seemed relieved. "I don't know where to begin."

"Take your time." I was tempted to put my feet up, pour myself a drink to hear the story, but thought better of it. *Don't blow it. Don't blow it.*

"The short version is Williams was a well-known sexual harasser within the firm, well known, that is, to everyone but me. Staff, lawyers, students. Everyone knew but I only learned of it after I articled. There was talk, lots of rumours, but nothing happened to me, so I went about my business. I was on a contract and wanted to be hired back."

"What happened?"

"One night we were reviewing your matter, that Savoie insurance case. I thought it looked like a good case. But he really seemed to have it in for you after the Novak grandma's ring–Pussycat memoir debacle." The tongue flicking was now as pronounced as Francesca's shrugging, and I was determined not to start licking my own lips along with Ms. Braun.

"Debacle? Why, what happened after we settled her case?" I was still proud of the horsewhipping I had given Williams, even if the Pussycat scooter in exchange for legal costs was pure revenge and not very good business. I ended up selling it as-is to a pet store in Thornhill for cash. They just parked it in the front window for show with kittens climbing all over it. The revenge on Novak had been sweet but brief.

"Williams let Novak's final account sit around for a while and then said that he couldn't bill her for some '*reason.*'" Oh God, air quotes. "He asked the partners to write off all the time he and associates had spent on her case. No fee. The partners—and associates who got burned on billings—wanted to know why, of course. Then someone passed on the gossip that Novak had been in a *relationship* with Williams and there were questions, lots of questions, about her matter and then there were questions about other files, other write-offs he had put through accounting without partner clearance. Then his wife got wind of their rumoured relationship, the memoirs and suddenly her company, AllPublishing, moved their business to another firm. There was a huge uproar and more complaints started coming out of the woodwork."

"But what's that got to do with you?"

"I was one of the complaints that came out of the woodwork. That night that he and I were supposed to meet to prepare your case? We were alone, late, he said he was tired and needed a drink. He offered me one. I don't drink but I said okay to be sociable. I was working with a *senior partner* after all. *La di da.* He poured me a large vodka and then as we worked he started to complain about how difficult his marriage was, how he didn't want to go home, how their marriage had been dead for a long time, their kids were gone, there was no love, then it turned to how much he enjoyed working with me, how he hoped I would be hired back so we could continue our 'friendship.' He downed his drink and poured another one. I was a bit woozy from just a few sips of the first glass, but he refilled my drink too. The next thing he was all over me, he had me pinned against a wall, tore off my blouse, pushed up my bra, he was grabbing my breasts, kissing them, telling me he loved me. I was in shock . . . I grabbed my blouse and just ran." Her tongue flicking, cold sore licking reached a gut churning frenzy.

She was in shock? I was in shock. "Holy shit. What happened? Did you go to the police?"

She looked at me as if I was crazy. "I said nothing for a few days but then he started sending me texts, awful messages, some with pictures of you know what, touching himself, asking me to meet him, telling me he was in love with me, begging me not to say anything. I tried to avoid him, but other associate lawyers could see that I was not myself. Then he switched, overnight. He started to pretend that nothing had happened. And then it got worse, he started spreading rumours that I'd been coming on to him, flirting, in order to get hired back . . . suggesting that maybe I should be let go."

I suddenly had a flashback to Keg's funeral, when I was drunk, sitting outside in the rain with Lester. I recalled seeing the very pretty Ms. Braun waiting for Williams in the back of the big black Escalade that picked him and Larson up. It was crystal clear (sort of).

"It was a nightmare. A few lawyers, partners, actually believed him at first. But eventually it all came out when I had to report it. The senior partners brought in a confidential fact-finder, senior woman lawyer—you probably know her, Gillian Morris, *supposedly* tough—to see what had been going on with all these staff and lawyer complaints. And then there were complaints from clients. Williams had been pulling the same bull-shit with several female clients, including sending dickpics. His billings were half of what they should have been because he was writing down his time as considerations for his *liaisons with clients*. But then, after a few got angry with him, he started doing it, you know, writing off his fees, just to keep the clients from complaining to the Law Society. It was a disaster. The partners wanted to murder him."

That dirty fucking hypocrite had done a fact-finding report about me and my Muskoka client that buried me at the Law Society and here he was doing the same, if not worse. Bastard.

"How on earth did they keep all this quiet?"

She ignored my question and looked at me. "Don't you remember our meeting in the Algonquin boardroom? You, me, Williams?"

How could I forget that humiliation in front of her as I sat there with a brutal hangover? I felt sick at the memory. What could I say?

"I'm surprised you couldn't tell by the embarrassed look on my face as I sat there that something was clearly wrong."

Huh? Was she hurt by my supposed cluelessness? Was I supposed to be sensitive to her situation? How the hell should I know what's going on in boardrooms at night between her and Williams? They looked pretty cozy as I recalled it.

"No, no, I was caught off guard, I guess. I had no clue." Wow. I realized that I had totally misread her at that meeting and had then tormented myself for months with images of her embarrassed smile. Click. Click. Click. All for nothing.

"You were hungover. We could both smell the booze off you. It was pretty obvious. Randall thought it was hilarious. He was telling everyone after you left about the fuck-off fee plan, and the booze, saying we would need to hang those pine air fresheners they use in taxis to clear the smell. He was afraid that if anyone lit a match the room would go up in flames. He was worried about the artwork. He . . ."

"Okay. I get the picture. I had my reasons for being out late the night before. I'd just been to that child's funeral, the one that was poisoned, the one who died. I took it pretty hard." Oh God, how humiliating. And then she'd seen me puking all over the food court. It was killing me to think of it. I tried to move on. "What happened after the fact-finder's report?"

"The partners thought maybe the best course was to just throw him out of the partnership. Then someone suggested maybe they should try to move him to another firm. Cover it up. That was ruled out because it could come back on the firm. I mean he was a name partner. People would ask questions about the move. But then Larson, you know him, Williams's protégé, he had another brain wave and calls were made by senior partners to the attorney general. The next thing we know, Williams was suddenly put on a fast track to be appointed to the bench. Sickening."

"Not exactly a MeToo shining moment." I suddenly recalled Rick Z's comments that there were staff complaints about him in Barrie. I wondered if the dirty hound had started groping staff up there.

She just rolled her eyes at the mention of MeToo. "Then they had to deal with us, the rest of us, those who came forward. We had met with the fact-finder. We had told our stories. We had a lot of confidence in Ms. Morris. People were getting pretty upset that he might skate away."

"So what did the firm do?"

"With Williams moved out, Larson took over. He told us that our careers were on the line if it became public. The firm might go down. So, we were marched into the Algonquin Room, one by one, presented with three things: a cheque, a so-called reference letter and an NDA. There was a brief mention of ILA but Larson was clear: if you wanted the cheque and the reference letter, it was a one-time offer. Take the money, leave the firm, keep your mouth shut. They cleaned house."

"What about the clients, the Law Society?"

"Let's just say that several clients got their full-blown divorces done free of charge and were refunded their full retainers in exchange for not complaining and signing NDAs. And then the associates who had to work for free mopping up Williams's cases were furious. They got together and demanded the firm pay them their full rates on all the write-offs and bonus them. And there were more NDAs."

"What about the fact-finder? Surely, . . ."

"Ms. MeToo Morris? She got an extra big cheque and signed an NDA."

"Wow. This must have cost the firm a fortune. That's a lot of NDAs. I wonder if it would be worth taking a run at throwing them out. NDAs can help get deals done but they sure cover up a mountain of shit . . . sorry, I don't usually use language like that."

"I've heard worse. Trust me, I've looked into the enforceability of NDAs. Did a lot of research. They're solid, especially if signed by lawyers who should know better. The lawyer associations have talked about supporting legislation to make them unenforceable, especially in cases of sexual harassment, but the bills have gone nowhere."

"I can imagine."

"Those of us who took the cheques and reference letters, we can't get jobs if someone calls Williams. He burns us. Now he has the firm over a barrel because the partners all lied when they gave him glowing references and hid the complaints in order to get him appointed to the bench."

"So, I guess the idea of His Honour dealing with a Glinka inquiry does not sit well with you."

"You have a gift for understatement."

Notwithstanding her grungy courier-like appearance and the irritating tongue flicking, I was starting to like her. Plus, she'd kept her dirty hands in her lap and hadn't touched anything valuable. "Okay, I want to be straight with you. I haven't said yes to the inquiry yet. I'm not sure how the client can pay. That's a big factor. I don't work for free."

"I'm aware."

I ignored her sarcasm. Surely, being on her own, she'd discovered the reality of billing clients. "I may not even have the full story from my client yet either. But, if I took it on, and if Williams was to hear it, would you be interested in working together on it? Now understand, it can't be a personal vendetta. It's about the client who was assaulted."

I lied. Of course she should make it personal. I certainly intended to. Talk about an opportunity for Total War. I was dreaming about breaking out some of my more medieval weapons on His Honour Justice Randall Williams. I just needed an opportunity to roast the bastard.

"However, your strong feelings can be fuel for our client's fight for justice. You know what I mean?" I tried to sound a little more ethical and professional than I actually felt.

"I get it."

"Interested?"

"Depends. First, I'm only interested in working here if you take on the inquiry."

"Okay. Second?"

"I would need to see an offer—in writing."

That was fair. "I can put together a proposal for compensation. I don't think you'll have a problem with it. It'll be generous. I'll cover all your fees, your insurance, your OBA, your LSO fees. Parking . . ."

"I ride a bike."

"You are very brave." Insane actually, but brave sounded better.

"I'm street savvy."

Whatever you say. "Vacation too."

"What's that?"

I began to love her. "Any questions?"

"One."

"Shoot. I'm an open book." Granted, many pages, entire chapters in fact, have been redacted.

"Are you an alcoholic? Your drinking, is that going to be a problem? I can smell it sitting here." Whoa. Talk about blunt. I was not ready for that one and I felt my face flush with embarrassment. It must have been obvious because she immediately added, "I guess, I mean, I don't want that to be a problem."

"No. I'm not an alcoholic. I admit that I have, in the past, sometimes celebrated too much."

"Like after the child's funeral?"

Wow. She could be brutal. I could feel her BS detector scanning me again.

"Alcohol will not be a problem." I decided to change the topic. "And just so we have everything on the table, it's not just the potential inquiry, there are some other things, files, I will need help with."

"Other things? What kinds of other things?" Her caution—and tongue flicking—returned in a flash.

"There has been a flurry of new potential divorce clients, a bitter custody case, for example, and something to do with the Christian Brothers. What do you know about them?"

"Right now? Nothing. But I could know everything there is to know by the end of the week if that is what you needed." She smiled. Such confidence. Shame about the cold sore.

"Welcome aboard." I reached to shake her hand.

Her hands remained in her lap with a firm grip on her orange helmet. "I'll wait to see your offer."

Good answer.

It looked like I was on my way to hiring my first ever associate.

What could possibly go wrong?

22

Ah, Politics
Monday September 26

I WAS SITTING outside Starbucks on a September morning enjoying a rare moment of peace and quiet, and a second latte courtesy of my favourite barista, Daphne, when a troop of a half-dozen older women in pastel MEC clothes and mountain climbing boots passed by the patio. Clearly members of the heroic *fuck you, we've decided to let our hair go grey* demographic, their chattering was punctuated only by the steady *click click click* of their walking sticks on the concrete sidewalk. Yes, walking sticks, the kind so essential for making one's way around the downtown core safely on a sunny September day. I had to laugh, though, when the group collided with a young woman walking a half-dozen dogs. Mayhem of barking, biting and pole jabbing. Hilarious.

My joy was interrupted when my phone pulsed. Oh God, it was Daria again. "I'm hearing your voice way too much these days."

"The feeling's mutual. I spoke with Sean and he says you need to meet with a fellow about your campaign."

"What did he have to say about Shannon and any other so-called special projects?"

"He said the Christian Brothers matter is a serious problem for the archdiocese. There was a lot of physical and sexual abuse at training schools a couple of decades ago. The church has helped cover it up.

Christian Brothers are refusing to work with the archdiocese to help mop up victim claims. They consider themselves on a direct line to the pope and think they have the archdiocese over a barrel because they knew what was going on. They don't want to pony up any money to pay victims. Shannon has come in to deal firmly with the Brothers and the victims. The archdiocese is worried they may end up being stuck with a multimillion-dollar compensation bill from the provincial government. Shannon and a team of lawyers are marching around the province getting confidential settlements with victims for a fraction of what they are entitled to."

"This guy is something else. More fixer than priest."

"Sean says it all has something to do with why they want McKay to get a seat as an MPP. They seem to think he could become premier in the next election. He will keep the abuse matters under wraps and stickhandle the archdiocese out of funding any huge settlements by sticking the province with the bill. He can also deal with some other problems they are having on abortion funding. He wants you to meet with this fellow, hang on, I have his name here. Dikembe. He will start your campaign."

"Dikoobe-who?"

"Dikembe. D-I-K-E-M- . . ."

"Never mind. Tell him to come to my office. I'll meet with him there. Campaign? This is ridiculous."

A few hours later I was back in the office getting ready to return Love Poultice Cooper's urgent call when Bonnie buzzed me to say that a young man was here to meet with me. A *handsome* young man. *Involved in politics. Oh, how thrilling.* Oh boy, here we go with Ms. Swooning Heart-on-Her-Sleeve Bonnie. I must tell her that he works for the archenemy of her precious Greens.

"Put him in the boardroom and I'll be in shortly." I put the finishing touches on an employment offer and emailed the generous proposal to Ms. Braun with a simple, *I look forward to working with you.*

When I finally rolled into the boardroom, I had to admit the young man was indeed handsome. Tall, dark and handsome. Very well dressed too. Upscale casual as they say. And when I say dark, I mean he was as black as any human being I had ever seen. "You must be Dikoobe. Nice to meet you." I stuck out my hand.

"It's Dikembe. I've been waiting nearly forty minutes. And I don't have a lot of time to meet with you. It was a stretch to get away to come downtown. I should be in the riding. I have a lot of work to do."

"Well listen, Dikoobe. Election or not, I don't plan on doing any work just yet, so sit tight."

He laughed. "You don't seem to understand. I'm not talking about your 'campaign.'" He threw the dreaded air quotes on the word campaign. I hated him already. "I work for Mr. McKay. Father Shannon sent me here to get you to complete this paperwork so we can get your name on the ballot as soon as the call happens. You don't need to do anything. Just sign the paperwork and I'll make sure your name is in. After that you're on your own."

"I'm busy too, so why don't you walk me through this? Quickly."

"Big picture? When the premier calls the election the seats stand Libs 68, Cons 40, NDP 15, Greens 1: Total 124. We feel we have a shot at a majority but it is going to be tight."

A majority government? Sixty-three seats minimum? This kid was in dreamland. "Listen, I don't follow this stuff closely but from what I can tell, the Liberals would need to lose a hell of a lot of seats, so brace yourself, they're headed back to power minus a few seats. You're dreaming if you think there is a Conservative majority in the works."

"Well, fortunately you don't need to worry about such *dreams* as you put it. In Parkdale–High Park it's shaping up to be a tight two-way race between us and the NDP. Liberals will drain a few votes, but they are running third. We're expecting that they'll come on a little stronger and that will pull more votes from the NDP, we figure. My job is to get McKay elected. Your job is to play a role in that by simply allowing your name to appear on the ballot, siphon off some votes from the NDP candidate, maybe enough to help put McKay over the top. Every little bit helps."

"I got it." I wondered if he knew about the so-called understanding with Shannon about Sean.

"It's not really for me to say but if I were you—or your brother—I would count my blessings."

Oh boy. I think you know how I feel about someone telling me to count my blessings. My blood started a slow boil. "Really, and why is that?"

"You're needed. If they—Shannon, really—didn't need you, then we wouldn't be having this meeting. It's good to be needed." So, he obviously knew what was going on.

It took another fifteen minutes but it became pretty clear that I didn't have to do a goddamn thing other than sign the nomination papers and appoint a CFO to have my name on a ballot. He was going to take care of everything.

I ran my finger down a list of twenty-five names and signatures. "Who are all these people nominating me?"

"People in the riding. They are all verified local residents. Memberships have been paid."

"No campaigning?"

"None."

"No all-candidates meetings?"

"None."

"No door-to-door meet-and-greet?"

"None."

"No standing on street corners with signs, smiling and waving like an idiot at people driving to and from work?"

"None."

"No money from me?"

"None."

"No fundraisers?"

"None."

"So, no greeting people as they stagger onto the subway early in the morning and crawl home at night?"

"None of those things unless, of course, you decide you want to. Campaigning would be great, but we don't expect it."

"Right." I laughed at that prospect.

"For a guy not interested in politics you seem to know an awful lot about campaigning."

He clearly wasn't aware of how deeply involved in politics Sean had been or how much I had picked up behind the scenes during his various campaigns. I mean, how could I not get steeped in some of this BS when I had to rescue him from his drunken swan dives off the wagon?

"As long as I don't have to do any of those things, I'm a happy camper. I can focus on my practice and ignore the election like I always do. Where do I sign?"

"Sign here. This is good, it will work. Time is very tight and we need to have it filed as soon as the writ drops. It's only a twenty-eight-day campaign so we need to move fast. Once filed, we will get a Certificate of Nomination. After that you're free and clear."

"Great. Thanks, Dikoobe. It was real pleasure meeting with you." I'm confident he knew that could not have been further from the truth.

"Pleasure was all mine. By the way, I hope you realize you won't even be able to vote for yourself, or any candidate, because you don't live in the riding—something that I'm sure will be pointed out eventually. Too bad, though, McKay would certainly appreciate your vote." The sarcasm sauce was dripping from his voice as he left. "Now I know what Father Shannon meant. And by the way, your office has a pretty funky smell going on."

"Thank you. It's being dealt with." *A-hole.*

After he left it seemed like a good time for a big drink and to bring Bonnie up to speed on my upcoming career in politics.

She was not impressed. Furious actually.

23

Surprise
Friday October 7

AGAIN, FOR DAYS, Alvin was not returning my calls or texts. Then out of the blue I got a text.

I'm free to discuss in 5 minutes. I'll call you. Stand by.

Jesus, that poor fucker was whipped. But five minutes later—to the second—my phone pulsed. When I picked up I put on my creepiest *Silence of the Lambs* Buffalo Bill voice, "Put the lotion in the basket."

"What?"

"It does what it's told. Put the lotion in the basket . . ."

"Oh, fuck off. You're such an asshole. I'm trying to help you and I'm taking a big risk doing it, so just listen and stop being a jerk-off."

"You listen, I've been trying to reach you. You're the guy who says he has something important to tell me and then goes into radio silence."

"Whatever, I have my reasons."

"I'm sure you do. Like protecting your lovebird law partner from getting involved in this shit. What has she got to hide anyway? Or do I have to wait for her memoirs?"

There was a long angry pause. "You don't understand. Do you want this information or not?"

"What do you have that I don't?"

"Your list of people at the party, like I said, it's missing a name."

"How do you know who's on my list?"

"That's not important. I just do. There's one name missing, Justice Singh's French instructor."

"Hang on." I called up on my screen the list Francesca had prepared and scrolled down. "Okay, I'm looking at the list of government staff now. What's his name?"

"*Her* name."

Oh-oh. There's a rule about husbands taking private lessons.

"What's *her* name?'

"Pauline Hébert."

I recalled that Francesca had mentioned her nerd judge husband heading off into a corner at the party to *parlez-vous*, as she put it, with his French teacher. And I seemed to recall that she said the teacher was still there when she went to tell him about Glinka's ass grab. Weird, but I had made the assumption that because they were talking about law, the French teacher must be a man. Stupid assumption. But regardless, man or woman, why wasn't the name on this list? That had to be a deliberate omission.

"Okay. You're correct. That name's not on my client's list. Why would she leave it off?"

"I think you need to have a conversation with your client about what really went down at the party, her history with him. Just remember I told you to stay away from this."

Frankly, I was stunned by this bit of news. What was going on here? I retraced my steps: Francesca came to me to chase down the ass-grabbing Justice Glinka for some kind of justice. She said she needed to do it even if her husband wanted to do nothing and let it blow over. It was threatening her own marriage. Why? Why leave out that name?

"Bierce? You still there?" Alvin's voice sounded like it was miles away and in a well.

"Yeah, I'm here."

"I gotta go."

"Yeah. Thanks."

I needed to know more about this party. I decided to go to the source. The Major.

24

The Major
Friday October 7

I HAD NOT SPOKEN to Dave in ten years, maybe more. I resisted simply dialling 416-HIT-HARD and instead a quick Google search tracked down a very cool website for his office in Liberty Village. I pictured Dave, with his high-end-plaintiff personal injury practice, sitting in some cool loft space, surrounded by juniors, clerks doing his bidding and a bank of telephone operators answering calls 24/7.

Within ten minutes of leaving a message on his mobile, my phone rang.

"Biercey Boy. How the fuck are you?"

"Hey, Major. Great. How are you?"

"Hey, hey, no one's called me that in a long time. I'm doin' good man but you, yeah, what a fucking nightmare with that Lester thing. Suspension too. I mean what the fuck?"

"Add COVID and it was my *annus horribilis*."

"Something wrong with your anus too!? Oh shit! I'm so sorry. Can we sue someone?"

"No, I mean *annus hor . . .*"

"I know, man. I'm just shitting you. What's up? What can I do for you?"

"I was hoping to get a little insight into the Glinka matter. They have announced the inquiry."

"What took you so long? When I heard that Francesca was meeting with you I thought you'd call me asap."

"I've been trying to get a handle on this thing. Taking my time. She said you offered to help with the party."

"Uh, well, that's not quite right, but I definitely helped at least get it off the ground. She begged me to get involved. We have a bit of, you know, history. I used to bang her a few years back when she was on the prowl working as a clerk at an insurance defence firm. I was hoping she wanted to resume some of our extracurrics more than actually work on her party."

"She approached you?"

"Oh yeah, but I had no time to spare. I was in the middle of a jury trial, you know the fatal crane accident on Yonge a few years back, but I couldn't really say no with her being married, so to speak, to Jay, Jay Singh."

"So to speak?"

"This is QT, right?"

"Yeah, of course. I'm just trying to understand. You know I don't move in those circles."

"Understood. Look, she and Jay have had their issues. The wrong kind of ups and downs. Not, you know, . . ." I imagined him pumping his fist to indicate intercourse. "I don't think Jay ever really knew how interested she was in landing a partner . . . if you know what I mean. She's a flirt and he's a bit of a *learned lawnerd*. I think rumours eventually filtered up to him that some lawyers had taken her out, that maybe she had been on the prowl for a lawyer or a judge. Have you seen her tats?"

"Just on her arms, the vine things."

"Yeah, well there's more down below." He laughed at some obvious memories. "Are you going to help her get out of this shit?"

"What do you mean get her out? She's the victim, all this crap with Glinka kissing her, grabbing her ass. Why did they tolerate this BS from a judge?"

"Oh boy. Biercey. My man. You need to step back on this. The last thing she or Jay wants is anybody inquiring into what went on at that party or at Finch the next day."

"I heard that Ms. Novak was there. You know her I assume? God knows what she has to say about this." I was fishing. I needed to know why Alvin was warning me away and why Lorelei had such harsh views of Francesca.

There was a long pause. I assumed Dave was taking a long drag on a cigarette. "Lorelei Novak. Now there is a strange situation."

"How so?"

"You of all people know about her so-called *mem*oirs." He leaned heavily on the *mem* as he said it. "That Application about her and Alvin and the ring, the one you filed in Superior Court, it made the rounds. It was a public record and everyone—I mean everyone, lawyers, judges, cops, clerks, everyone—read about her rumoured kiss-and-tell *mem*oirs. *Pussy*cat." Now the emphasis was on the pussy. "There was a lot of speculation, rumours about who might be in it. When people are fucking around there are rules. She was toxic after that. No one wanted to be near her. Why do you think she left the Crown's office? No one would work with her. And the judges? Oh man, I heard you could scrape the frost off the windows when she appeared in court."

"So if she was so toxic why would she be at the party?"

"She has been on the *Lorelei Novak Redemption Tour*, sucking up to lawyers, buying rounds, trying to redeem herself. Especially with the judges. Without them back on side she might as well move to Vancouver. Hence her fervent support of Glinka. And why do you think she hooked up with Alvin?"

My mind flashed back to the summer afternoon when I bumped into Lorelei dressed to kill on her way to Williams's swearing in. It made sense if she was putting on a show for judges and the bar, looking like she was partnered up. Settled down with Alvin. "Do you think Novak and Glinka were, you know?" I unconsciously pumped my fist.

"No idea. But I kinda doubt it. Was he in the *mem*oirs? I doubt it. The other judges and lawyers like Glinka. He can be a little rough around the edges, but they like him. He gets away with a lot of stupid high school stuff and comments. I heard that one day he dry-humped, from behind, one of the women judges in the lunchroom when she bent over to get something from the fridge. They all just rolled their eyes and waved him off, thought it was harmless goofing around. Everyone saw the hump but the humped and humper denied it ever happened. They stick together. What do you expect?"

"So Novak will back up Glinka?"

"To the max. There's no downside. If there's an inquiry, then she stands up for him. If there's no inquiry, everyone knows *she would have stood up* for him. She's telling anyone who'll listen about her support for him. I mean, which side would you rather be on—all the lawyers and judges or the unpopular Ms. Rimini?" He laughed. "Oh right, you picked Rimini. I guess Rick Z was right."

"What do you mean?"

"When everyone was talking about the *incident*, I started one of my pools for who would be crazy enough to represent Francesca. Mr. Z picked you. I think he made a hundred bucks. I came in second."

People. Don't. Change.

"Just out of curiosity, who did you pick?"

"You'd know him to see him, that guy who's always wandering around court with his client's file in a fucking Sobey's shopping bag. Little guy, in running shoes half the time."

A text message popped up on my phone. It was from Daria. *You need to get over to the hospital right away.*

Shit.

"Dave, listen. This has been great. I just got a text about an emergency. I'm gonna have to deal with it. Can I call you back? Later?"

"Sure. No problem, but I'm starting a two-week trial Monday so it may need to be at night. Maybe grab a drink somewhere?"

"Sounds good. Cheers."

I called Daria. "What's up?"

"That priest is back and he has Sean pretty upset."

"That little fucker. Keep him there. I'm on the way."

25

Back to Sunnybrook
Friday October 7

IT TOOK NEARLY two fucking hours to get from University and Adelaide to Sunnybrook. Unbelievable traffic up the DVP on a Friday afternoon as people fought their way out of the city at the start of a long weekend, to enjoy the Thanksgiving holiday and the last few decent days of weather before the cold set in.

By the time I got to Sean's room Shannon was of course long gone. Daria was asleep in a chair in the corner and Sean, looking ghastly, was out cold.

There was a sheaf of paperwork from the archdiocese on the table beside Sean's bed. As I flipped through the documents I thought my head would explode. It looked like Sean was *consenting* to being defrocked. I'd done some research into the process to see if there were any tripwires I could use to mess up Shannon and learned that laicization is generally delivered as a punishment. However, it could also be done on a voluntary basis as a sort of favour to the priest involved if he was seeking an exit. Either way, once done it can be restored only by express rescript from the pope himself. Why had Sean signed these papers?

"Oh, you made it." Daria woke from her sleep. "Shannon's gone."

"I did my best to get here. But the DVP."

"It's okay. I'm not sure you being here would have made any difference." She sounded exhausted.

"What's that supposed to mean?"

"It doesn't mean anything other than what I just said." This was followed by muttering in Russian. Wow. I'd seen that angry face and heard that snarling voice before. She was in a mood and a long-lost rage bubbled up inside my chest.

"Did you see what Sean signed? He's consenting. He's asking to be defrocked. Why? Why would he do that?"

Sean woke. "Andrew, come here. I can explain." He was so weak it sounded like it might be his last sentence. "Shannon told me about your meeting, at the game."

"I told him I would do what they want. I've signed nomination papers. I'm in."

"I know, but he doesn't trust you. He wants to have my consent in his hip pocket as leverage. If you don't look like you're holding up the bargain, he'll use it. I didn't have any choice. I told him he could count on you but . . ." He faded away, into a drug-induced sleep, I assumed.

"I had to give him some sedatives, he was so upset. I'm surprised he even woke up. I was here when Shannon forced Sean to sign. He was awful. He said sign the documents as presented—no changes—or you go to a pauper's grave. He told Sean that he was a delegate direct from the Vatican, that he has absolute authority over the process. Even the archbishop could not intervene. Sean signed three sets of documents, Shannon left this copy and told Sean, *Your brother, the lawyer, says he likes things in writing? Well, tell him here is something in writing.* Then he was gone."

I pondered this turn of events as a slow rage continued to build on top of what Daria had ignited. I don't like being put in a box.

"What are you going to do?"

It started to boil over. "*Tortura pessima.*"

Daria recoiled from me. She'd seen that angry face and heard that snarling voice before.

26

Back to The Major
Friday October 7

I DROVE—IN the reverse fucking traffic—back downtown to find that Bonnie, God bless her, was there working late despite the long weekend. The office was finally returning to some semblance of order. Her desk, as usual, was meticulous, intake forms were being completed, conflict checks done and retainers were being deposited. Things were looking good, very good. I had at least ten quality consultations set up. I just needed time to deal with them.

Between my new commitment to Bonnie and honouring the offer I had made to Ms. Braun, I also needed to start some serious billing. I'd been subsidizing everything through COVID, particularly my office lease. There were no government CERBs for lawyers, I assure you. Since I got my ticket back, I had not sent out one bill and had been basically working for free on Francesca's matter. My personal rice supply was being drawn down. I even paused the AGO art rental rotation for six months. It was humiliating. The Curators' Circle would be asking questions.

But, I was glad to be home at the office and my first thought was to pour a large glass of something strong and spend the evening plotting the takedown of that malicious little leprechaun. I called across the hall, "Bonnie, I can't say how good it is to have you back. I appreciate you spending the extra time to get caught up too. Helen was not, you know, in your league."

"Thanks. It's good to be back. But this is going to take some time to clean up. And I can't figure out what that smell is. There is something around here where the carpet is soiled. Anyway, I don't have time right now, there is a file folder on your desk of a dozen things that need immediate attention, one of which is Naomi Smart called. She wants to meet with you asap. And what the heck is this?" She held aloft a purple file folder wrapped in a piece of duct tape. "It was sitting in a drawer over here. It says LSO."

Holy shit. She was waving around the confidential Williams factfinder. I was sure I'd locked that in my desk. "Oh, thanks. That's mine. I'll take that." I shot out to her desk and grabbed the file. "That smell is Helen's tea. It was her tea. It spilled."

"No, it can't be tea. I know tea. No tea smells like that. It's like a chemical smell but more pungent. I'll figure it out later. We may have to call the landlord. I have to get going, Mr. Reyes has a community meeting tonight and I'm on the advance team. With this traffic it will take me an hour to get out to Scarborough."

"It was brutal coming across town. Do you think this fellow actually has a shot at winning? I mean, seriously?"

"It's not just about winning. Someone needs to hold this government to account for the last several years. Homelessness, infrastructure, immigrant settlement, refugees, . . ." *blah blah blah*. Oh boy. Here she goes. Bonnie was headed off on one of her rants. Sorry I asked.

I thought I'd better pump the brakes. "You're right, Bonnie. There's so much to be done." I tried to sound as if I gave a shit, like anything she or Mr. Green Rebese were doing could possibly make a difference. She looked up with a scowl to see if I was being sarcastic. Of course I was. "No, but seriously. I hear you."

She just shook her head and began to pack up her purse. "You'll never change. Some politician you'll make." Suddenly her head snapped up. "Oh my gosh. I almost forgot. There's someone in the boardroom waiting to meet with you. A Ms. Braun. She's been waiting over an hour."

Oh shit. With the crisis around Sean and Shannon I had forgotten that she'd agreed to stop by to discuss my offer. This was not how I wanted things to begin. As anxious as I was to know whether she was on board, for some reason her grim cold sore popped into my head. It had been a

few days, surely it had cleared up by now. My tongue unconsciously started to search my upper lip for one.

And worse than that, satisfaction of my craving for a tall glass of
something in the whisky family would need to wait. I had vowed to watch
my drinking, well at least while she was around. I mean, let's not get crazy.

"Thanks, Bonnie. Have a good night and seriously, good luck with
Mr. Rebels."

"It's Mr. Reyes. You're something else. Politicians need to remember
names, you know."

"Right, sorry. And I'm not a politician." Whatever. How am I supposed to remember all these crazy new immigrant names?

To my relief, in the boardroom sat the Lindsay Braun of old. Beautiful.
The faux deranged bike courier look was gone. She was in a sharp charcoal business suit and black turtleneck, laptop was out and she appeared
ready to start work. Unfortunately, her cold sore was still quite evident. I
prayed it wasn't going to be a persistent facial feature. I would try to focus
on her hazel eyes. Beautiful.

"Lindsay, great to see you. I'm so sorry for being late. My brother is
very ill. He's in hospital out at Sunnybrook. Traffic was terrible. How are
you? I'm glad you stopped by. Are you ready to join forces?" I was blab-
bering like a teenage boy again and desperately trying not to look at the
now crusty wound on her lip.

"Mr. Bierce, do you have one of these?" She held up her cellphone,
an Android in a bright pink case. More Kate Spade from the looks of it.

My face burned. "Yes, I have one of those. Look, I'm sorry. I want to
be honest with you on everything." *Well, not everything.* "In all of the crisis
around my brother—he has cancer," *Cancer for heaven's sake!* "I forgot we
were meeting. It's as simple as that. I just forgot. I'm sorry. And please,
call me Andrew."

"Just be straight with me. That's all I ask."

"I promise to be straight . . ." *as circumstances require.*

"The offer looks fine. I appreciate it and your generosity. I know
what firms are offering right now and it's a very good offer."

Gulp. "I have the feeling there is a 'but' about to erase everything nice
that you just said."

"I have a couple of questions."

"Shoot. I told you, I'm an open book." Hopefully her BS detector was not working.

"I've been asking questions, looking around. There's a rumour that if an election is called, you're running for office."

Oh God. How did that get out? The election has not even been called. It's supposed to be a secret. Surely Bonnie hadn't said something.

"And I need to know why you're interested in the Christian Brothers. What does it have to do with divorce work? Or the inquiry? I was pretty clear that I'm here to work if—and only if—you're taking on the Williams Inquiry. If you're not taking it on and you're running for office instead, it looks like you're just bringing me in to babysit your practice. I'm not interested in babysitting."

I had to respect her doing some background research on me, but her tone was getting a little pushy. "First, Lindsay, it's not the *Williams* Inquiry. It's the *Justice Glinka* Inquiry." She was clearly looking at this as an opportunity for revenge on her supposed mentor. (*Excellent.*) "Secondly, the Christian Brothers situation may be of concern to a potential client." Okay. That was vague and I stretched the truth a little. "If you're uncomfortable with the subject matter . . ."

She stared at me. "What about the provincial election and the babysitting?"

"Where did you hear that? About the election?"

"Does it matter where I heard, if it's true? I live in Parkdale. I've done work with the Green Party locally. There's talk you're going to run as an Independent simply to split the NDP vote. There are even cheap brochures floating around." She threw one onto the boardroom table. "Pretty cynical, if it's true."

Yikes. She lives in Parkdale? And Green? Oh God, not another dreamweaver. But on the bright side, if she accepts the position she should be able to move to a better part of town.

I looked at the brochure. It was indeed a cheap black and white sheet, a photocopy with an imprecise fold. Very unprofessional. My name was all over it but I'd had absolutely no input. Apparently, I'm against homelessness and the closing of group homes but in support of more food banks and shelters for victims of domestic violence. Interesting. I wonder if I'm in favour of free ice cream too. I was a little curious to see what position I was taking on other local issues. Road repair, people picking up their dog's shit, for example, or banning unicycles.

"It's complicated. It's just something I may have to do. Besides, there is no election." I set it aside for later.

"It's unprincipled."

Wow. She's cheeky. "Really? And whose vote is the Green Party splitting? Aren't you just helping to elect someone you certainly don't approve of? As I said, it's complicated. The only thing you need to worry about is whether this hypothetical election will affect my practice and any work we do together. The answer is no."

Oh-oh. She was staring at me again. The BS scanner had been activated.

"What's the status of the inquiry?"

"Apparently it'll be announced this week. The bureaucracy needs to staff it, find space, Glinka will need to get a lawyer, presenting counsel need to be hired. Knowing the current AG, that little exercise will be a textbook lesson in political correctness, checking all the right boxes."

"I get it." She nodded knowingly. Interesting. "Are you retained yet by Ms. Rimini?"

"No, but I hope to pin that down this week. It's way overdue." I could see her weighing things. "You've met Bonnie?"

"Yes." Her calculations continued. "Impressive."

"You have no idea."

"Green supporter too." She smiled.

I wasn't going to push her on her politics. Dream on. I could see she was uncertain. "Look, if you need more time to think about it, that's not an issue. Think about it. I've got work to do, a pile of new clients, let's talk tomorrow." I stood and extended my hand. "No matter what, it has been a pleasure getting to know you a little bit better." *Except for, you know, the lip thing.*

She took my hand, her grip was firm but frankly ice cold and yet sweaty. What is it with women's hands? "I'll be in touch."

And with that she headed for the front door. At the last second she turned and said, "You know, your office is nice but it smells awful. You should have someone check it out."

"It's tea, someone spilled tea."

She frowned at me. "You blame a lot on tea." Then she was gone.

Did the office really smell that bad? Had I just become accustomed to the stench? Oh my God. *Was I starting to smell?* I gave my suit a sniff. Fucking Hopeless Helen.

First order of business, I sent Naomi an email. *Got your message. What's up? Need to meet?*

Second order of business, I poured a large glass of bourbon, held it to my nose and inhaled deeply. I needed to get back to Dave so I took a mouthful and dialled his cell. Nothing. Another mouthful. I tried his cell again. He answered after three rings and I could hardly hear his voice over the noise. "Dave, I can barely hear you. Where are you?"

"Hey man, I'm at Barb's, the steak house. A bunch of us are having a few drinks and dinner. Come on up. Join us."

"I thought you have a trial on Tuesday?"

"I do, but a man has to eat. Come on up."

He's right, a man does have to eat and I had not been to Barberian's in a few years, since just before COVID. The last time had been for a private party in the Wine Cellar with some fashion partners of my Muskoka client. I recall eating an awesome twenty-four-ounce porterhouse, accompanied by a beautiful wine and then the rest of the evening becoming a tequila blur.

Dinner and drinks? After that session with Sean and Daria, why not? "Okay, I'm on the way." I was also a little curious about seeing the man up close after all these years.

Before I could get out the door, Naomi's response popped up. *Yes, we need to meet asap. What's your day like on Monday? It's Thanksgiving but if you're good, I am.*

Good. How about around 3 p.m.? My office?

Good. See you then.

When I arrived at Barb's, Dave and a half-dozen of his lawyer friends were parked in the private dining room upstairs and well on their way. Dave waved me over. "Hey, Bierce, we're just about to order some food. Come and sit with me. Guys, this is Andrew Bierce. We went to school together. Terrible hockey player. He was in that shitstorm shooting at 361 a year ago. Sit here, we wanna hear all about what went down in court with you and Lester. I want to know what the fuck happened." I could tell Dave had already finished a few vodkas.

I slid in beside my former teammate. That wild, carefree young face I recalled from law school was no more. It was now pale and puffy with a five o'clock shadow that was getting closer to nine o'clock. His hair was bone white. With his sports jacket off, his sleeves rolled up, shirt collar unbuttoned and his tie loosened, he could have been mistaken for the dispatcher at an old taxi stand. He had slipped off a worn shoe and it sat on its side, a hole in the sole. This was not the "you don't know tough" lawyer in the TV ads or on his website. What had happened?

I really didn't want to revisit that day with Lester but from the way the group had now turned to me it was obvious that I may have been invited to this gathering as one of Dave's party favours. "It wasn't pretty. Not much more to say than what was in the news. I've kinda blocked it out. It was pretty scary . . ." I suddenly felt queasy and my heart started pounding. Just the mention of Lester's name brought back the smell of gunfire, wet wool and his final stale menthol breath. I needed a drink and I tried to change the subject. "How's your wife? Kids? You guys still ticking along?"

He just laughed. "Hindenburg #2 went down in flames a long time ago. You know what that shit's like. Still in recovery mode. It busted me. I'll be paying support to two exes and four kids until I die. But, come on man. Details. What happened at 361 Uni?"

"Let me get a drink first." I signalled the waiter. He looked familiar. "Double scotch, Macallan's, the fifteen-year-old if you have it."

With that deflection Dave ordered another round for himself and turned to hear one of his buddies telling the group an indiscreet tale.

"So check this out guys, my client, good guy but bit of a dick, takes his kid to a hockey tourney down in St. Catherines. Kids are coming from all over. These are thirteen- to fifteen-year-olds, boys and girls. They're all staying at the Best Western. Third night the moms and dads get to-gether in the hospitality suite for the usual parental piss up. Pool's closed. All the kids are supposed to be in bed, curfew right? But a few, you know, are running up and down the halls, yelling, sneaking beer around. The usual. Crazy."

As he told his tale I thought I recognized this fellow. He had gone to our law school but a year ahead of Dave and me. Short, now overweight with thinning red hair, his pudgy face flushed pink, I think he used to do family and civil litigation but got lazy and slid over into small-time criminal law, legal aid, children protection shit. I recalled that he shared a crappy street-level office over in Cabbagetown near my old starter firm. Three empty pint beer glasses sat in front of him. He was trying very hard to look young in a tight blue sports jacket with a light purple windowpane pattern. It probably fit when he bought it a few years ago. He wore a floral print shirt, open at the neck, no tie and, of all things, he had a small earring. His sartorial investment was not paying dividends. I was afraid to look under the table for fear he wore no socks.

Digressing for a moment, he slurred out a thought. "I always ask if there're kids staying at the hotel for a tournament, I hate that noise and shit. Anyway . . ."

"So that's why your car's always at the Motel 6 . . ."

"Fuck off. I'm telling a story here." That was a little surly.

Pudgy Red carried on. "Anyway, a couple of the parents start doing a head count but one kid's missing. My guy's kid. But then they can't find my guy either. They're looking all over the fucking place. Where do they find him? In the pool."

"I thought it was closed," Dave chipped in.

"Holy shit. Drowned?" Another lawyer named Bill offered a comment, his wits clearly dulled by wine.

"Drowned? I wouldn't have a fucking client, you idiot."

"Right. I think I've had too much."

"Ya think? No, he's in the pool and he just happens to be sharing his noodle with one of the moms, one who's not his wife."

"I'm pretty sure that's not the first time that's happened at a hockey tourney." Bill was determined to stay in the conversation and with his hands outstretched looked around the table for laughs. "Is that even a crime?"

"No, but it's the first time that a dad's in the pool with a mom, while his fifteen-year-old son's upstairs in bed with that mom's thirteen-year-old daughter. All of them are pissed."

"Fuck me. The kids too?"

"Oh yeah. On coolers. But then, get this, Dad #2 . . ."

Bill drained his glass of wine and held up his hands. "Whoa. Wait, who's Dad #2?"

"Listen, you idiot. Dad #2 is the husband of Pool Mom, he's not even supposed to be at the tourney but he's checking up on her. He found the two drunk kids in Mom's room so he starts storming all over the Best Western looking for you know who. He finally shows up at the pool and finds his wife doing an adult version of the doggie paddle and then there's a fucking donnybrook in the pool! Everyone's in there slugging, hitting each other with chairs, pool skimmers and life savers, trying to drown each other. Cops are called. Anyway, the two dads get charged with assault."

"What a shitshow." I was glad everyone seemed to have forgotten about me.

"Oh yeah. I got retained by Dad #1. His wife has thrown him out." He finished his beer in one gulp and through a belch told me, "Bierce, I should give him your name. You like that shit."

"Thanks. I'll watch for him." Based on what I had heard I seriously doubt he could afford the freight and I was not going to waste one of my business cards on him.

"Happy ending, though."

"How?"

"The kid scored a hat trick the next day and their team won the fucking tourney." He slapped the tabletop so hard his empty glasses toppled over across the table.

"Fifteen-year-old prodigy?"

"No, no, the thirteen-year-old girl! She was lighting it up."

The laughing and hooting and hollering went on for a good five minutes as Pudgy Red filled in even more of the dirty pool details.

After I had picked through a plate of pickled veggies I leaned in to Dave, "So what's the deal, hanging with these guys? You do PI not criminal, right?"

Dave leaned back into me and whispered, "Yup. PI. And only PI. I know enough to stick to my knitting these days. This is about referrals my friend. Referrals."

"Ahh, I see. Makes sense. Can I ask you what's the deal with that Christmas party? Glinka? What am I missing?"

Dave laughed and turned back to the group. So much for confidential advice. "Boys, boys. Listen up. Bierce here is going to take on Francesca as a client for the Glinka Inquiry." That triggered a series of groans and whistles. "He wants to know *what happened* at the party." Oh God, air quotes. "All those present at the party raise your hand." Every hand went up. Oh shit. Was this a setup? Every one of their names must be on Francesca's list.

One middle-aged lawyer, quiet guy, at the end of the table said to his drink, as it disappeared, "I heard a rumour it will take a week to hear evidence about Francesca's escapades. Someone said she and Glinka were going at it off and on for a couple of years before Jay came along. There were others too. Isn't that right?" He elbowed Pudgy Red knowingly.

"Fuck off." More beer-induced surliness. "I'm single, I can fuck who I want."

Another chimed in. "I wouldn't want to tangle with Royce either. Not worth the aggravation, dealing with the second coming of Christ Q.C. . . . er, I guess K.C. now." This produced another knowing laugh from the group.

"Royce Hughes? Is he involved?" Oh. God. No.

One by one, around the table, they began to jump in. Talking over top of each other.

"Glinka retained him for the inquiry. He's not gonna fuck around. He'll tear Francesca a new one. I'm surprised she's going ahead. She'll have to make some kind of deal."

"She doesn't have much choice now. It's too late. They're moving up the day for getting things organized."

"Whoa, whoa. What do you mean they're moving it up?" I put my drink down.

"Man, you better get on board with this if you're going to represent her. They have Williams leading it, plus that old guy from provincial court, what's his name? You know, the guy with the dead-pool eyes."

"Harold."

"Right. Harold."

"Justice Harold is on this thing?"

"Yeah, and some layperson. Black woman, director of some shelter for battered women."

"I believe the new term is *intimate partner violence*," Pudgy chirped sarcastically and triggered a round of laughter.

"Word is Williams couldn't get out of Barrie fast enough, so he pressed the chief judge and the AG to get the presenting lawyers on board and allow some preliminary hearings to begin, set some timetables, discuss witness lists, deal with questions about the scope of evidence. They want to get underway asap."

"Holy shit. I've been so tied up with my brother . . ." I was stunned.

The inquiry starts soon. I have not been retained. I have no money in trust from Francesca. Lindsay will come on board only if I take the file. Cooper's matter is about to go sideways. Sean's fading fast. And I'm supposed to be a candidate in an as-of-yet uncalled election. I felt pins and needles sweep over my shoulders and suddenly remembered I was supposed to get a shingles shot a while ago but couldn't because of fucking COVID.

I finished my drink and fumbled for my wallet. "Sorry guys, I have to go."

The Major raised his glass and looked at me with a drunken smile. "Don't worry. I got it. Careful with this one, Bierce. Someone's gonna get hurt." And then he motioned, like he did in his TV commercial, as if taking someone into the boards—hard.

27

So Arduous a Wilderness
Friday October 7

AS SOON AS I got back to the office I called Lindsay and left a message. "Ms. Braun, Andrew Bierce, there has been a development, a change of plans. I have learned that the inquiry has been moved up. There are going to be organizational meetings next week. If you're on board, I need to know now. Please call me asap."

Next call, Ms. Rimini. She answered. "Mr. Bierce, I was wondering when you were going to call. I heard that the inquiry is starting next week. Organizational stuff. Someone called to ask if I had a lawyer. I didn't know what to say. I said that I had met with you."

"You're right, it has moved up. Not to worry, I've been on top of this pretty much daily. Next week it will be getting off the ground. I know it's Thanksgiving, but I'll need you to be in my office on Monday to sign some paperwork and give me a preliminary retainer of $20,000."

"Twenty thousand." She said it like I had asked for a million dollars. "I can't afford that. There's no way I can get that amount of money. I'll have to talk to Jay, but he doesn't even want this to happen. Shit. Shit. Shit."

"Well, I don't work for free, surely you appreciate that. Everything we have done to date I've done without any retainer from you."

This is the kind of nonsense I would have avoided if Hopeless Helen had done a few simple things like an intake form or shared my retainer agreement. Bonnie would never have let this happen.

"I thought you might take this on *pro bono*."

Pro bono? I almost burst out laughing. "I do not do *pro bono* work. You must have RRSPs? Collapse an RRSP if you need to. I'll leave it with you, but I'll need a retainer ASAP. There's a lot of work to do."

"But . . ."

I could see Lindsay's name on the phone. "Look, I'm sorry. I'm going to have to let you go. I need to take another call. Good night. Let's discuss it tomorrow." I picked up the other line. "Lindsay, you got my message?"

"Yes, you're retained?"

"Yes," *well sort of,* "she will be in on Monday and I would like you here to meet with her. She should take you through the whole story on her own. There is also some other new information we need to review with her. I know it's a holiday but can you come in, and early? Say eight o'clock? And I need you to sign your compensation agreement if we are going to do this."

"I'll be there. I'm looking forward to this." So this is what she sounds like when she's excited. Good, very good.

Before I could dial Bonnie at her community meeting with Mr. Rebees my phone pulsed. I answered. "Andrew Bierce."

"Royce Hughes." His velvety voice transported me back to the nightmare in the courtroom again. My mind reeled. I took a mouthful of bourbon. "Mr. Bierce? Are you there?"

"Yes, sorry. I was expecting a call from my junior."

"How are you? It has been quite a time these last couple of years."

"Yes, true enough. COVID has been a bugger."

"I was thinking more about your own personal situation. I hope everything is settling down for you."

Was this genuine? Was it bullshit? Or was he just being a prick? Stay cool. "I'm good. Thank you for your concern, though. I appreciate it."

"I understand you may be representing Ms. Rimini in the inquiry. I thought it might be useful to touch base about her evidence in advance of meeting next week." His voice was so butterscotch smooth, so confident. Where was he going with this? "Could we speak off the record for a few moments?" He somehow managed to sound open, almost vulnerable. How did he do that?

"Of course. Happy to." Off the record? Sure, but I'm not giving you a fucking thing right now.

"Small world that Judge Harold might sit on the inquiry."

"Yes, small indeed." I thought poor Harold must be pulling out his bone white hair wondering what he had done to deserve this shitshow.

"I've spent quite a bit of time with Justice Glinka over the last week, reviewing his evidence, and I was a little surprised to learn that his relationship with Ms. Rimini had been so *longstanding*." He said it as if he really meant *intimate*. "After speaking with him, frankly I was puzzled about why she wished to proceed. Have you had an opportunity to review her evidence, all of her evidence, with her?" He now sounded genuinely puzzled, totally baffled. How can a voice shift so effortlessly?

"Yes." That was partially true. I'd heard her version of events, but I needed to hear what she had to say about Dave's new alarming insights. Based on what he'd said I was not prepared to send her to slaughter at the hands of Royce Hughes, K.C. "I think the part about him putting his fingers into her vagina on the dance floor soured her on their friendship." Was that understated enough?

He wasn't the least bit fazed. "There was quite a bit more to their relationship than that, though, don't you agree?" Well, that's interesting. He didn't just deny outright that it had happened. "I think you probably know what I'm talking about, you know, their *previous history*. The whole thing made me wonder if there was not some way to spare everyone—the parties, the judges, the public—the agony of the hearing and, of course, the province the expense."

My God, now he sounded like we might be able to perform a public service and receive medals. *Public agony?* The famous Mr. Hughes was looking for a deal. There must be something bothering him if he has put that on the table so soon. Patience.

"Of course, I understand. Since we're speaking off the record, how would you imagine such an outcome evolving?"

"Off the top of my head?" He sounded a little surprised, but gosh, willing to give it a try.

Off the top of your head, my ass. "Sure. I won't hold you to anything. We're just talking."

"Well, I guess one option is everyone could agree there was a terrible misunderstanding, feelings were injured, and they walk away from this precipice." *Praecipitium* indeed. "My client wants to retire. Your client and her husband want to carry on as best they can, professionally at least." *Wow, what does that mean?* "We can probably talk to the chief justice about where Justice Singh wishes to sit going forward and to the AG about where Ms. Rimini will be assigned. I took the liberty of touching base with the presenting counsel, confidentially of course, and they are open to not taking this any further while we talk, and provided all parties agree."

"Interesting option." And pretty fucking good off the top of his head. "But people, the media, the profession, I assume would want to know what happened, why it had settled. How it had settled."

"Good point. I was thinking that we could announce that Justice Williams had met with the parties and counsel, wisely mediated the issues between them and helped everyone reach an amicable agreement about their misunderstandings. Confidentiality agreements, NDAs, would be signed. No one would speak to the media and we would move on. As we both know, the news moves on pretty quickly these days."

My first thought? Lindsay would lose her fucking mind if this was the outcome. NDA? OMG.

He was speaking to me now as if we were colleagues, on the same side. But I needed to stay in my lane for now. "That's very true—and I'm just speaking off the top of my head right now because I have no instructions, of course—but another consideration is my client has incurred very significant legal fees to date. She has dipped into her savings to do this. How would her fees be addressed?"

"Good point. I would need to speak to my client. He, too, has incurred fees, but I could speak to him about your fees if that was all that stood between us resolving the matter and an inquiry."

Well, well, well. Let's go deeper. "Okay, that's one option. And if we were not able to come to such an understanding, a settlement on those terms, how do you imagine the matter unfolding—off the top of your head?"

His voice pivoted to *Death in the Afternoon*. He was now wielding four *banderillas*.

He plunged one in. "I would be forced to explore your client's considerable rumoured sexual history at 1000 Finch and elsewhere, particularly the specifics of her previous sexual relationship with Justice Glinka, the money that changed hands, the reference letters he wrote for her to obtain her position, the letters she wrote him, what actually happened that night at the party. The next day. And previously."

"I see."

Then another. "Unfortunately, I would be forced to raise the real reasons why her husband assaulted my client. I understand he is not supportive of her moving forward with the inquiry."

"I'm not aware of anything in that respect."

Then a third. "I have a witness list that already stands at a dozen, two of whom are judges who sit with Justice Glinka and will support his version of events that evening."

"I see."

"There are also lawyers who will support his version of events. I believe you know one." He had saved his sharpest *banderilla* for last. "Ms. Novak."

Hughes sounded like he knew a hell of a lot more about this than me. Letters? Money? Novak? The real reason Singh assaulted Glinka? What else had Francesca left out?

"Ahh, yes, Ms. Novak. I guess she has her reasons." Did I sound like I knew what I was talking about?

"Nonetheless." With that one word he acknowledged nothing and said everything that needed to be said about why she would support Glinka. Such a perfect answer.

"Understood. Mr. Hughes, . . ."

"Please call me Royce."

"Royce, I appreciate your call. I'll be meeting with my client again on Monday morning. Perhaps we can speak after that? If there is a way to resolve matters to my client's satisfaction, I'm of course in her hands. I appreciate that it's about more than an incident at a party. It's about personal privacy, dignity, not to mention the administration of justice."

Perhaps that little pile of collegial bullshit sandbagging would encourage him to put down his tools, stop working and let me catch up.

"Yes, that would be wonderful. Let's touch base later." He paused. "I suppose if the matter was resolved it would also allow you more time to campaign. I understand you are considering a run in the rumoured provincial election. Very admirable."

How the hell does he know?

"Not everyone is prepared to put themselves out there these days. Politics is a rough business, not unlike the legal game in some respects." He laughed like we were old friends. His voice drenched in honey. I pictured him sitting in his office, in a green leather high-back chair, impeccably dressed even at this hour, perhaps in a burgundy velvet smoking jacket, a brandy in hand, looking out over the city from high atop the downtown towers. I began to adore the man.

"Yes, it can be rough. But at least the law has a few good judges to referee the game."

"Quite right. Enjoy the rest of your evening."

"You too."

With that he was gone.

I proceeded to get very drunk. (In fact, I would end up being drunk pretty much all weekend.)

28

Youth, No Patience
Monday October 10, Thanksgiving Day

LINDSAY WAS SET up at the boardroom table at 8 a.m., ready to go. Even though she was in on a long weekend, she still looked sharp. This time in a navy jacket and matching skirt, but again with the black turtleneck. All business. I gazed at her lip—discreetly, of course—and couldn't make out any telltale signs of you know what. And on another positive note, her fingernails no longer looked like she had worked in a food processing plant deboning chickens. She'd been for a manicure, soft pink dip powder from the looks of it. Nice.

My head was pounding from overdoing it all weekend. After speaking with Royce an entire bottle of the good stuff was gone and I had also put a major dent in my liquor supply at home. And when I saw her, through bleary eyes, sitting there, I suddenly realized—*holy shit*—she's going to need an office. In all the time I had spent on her compensation package, an office had never occurred to me. An office. Of course. Now I would need to brace myself for some pushback. I was sure that, like every typical junior lawyer, she would be all over me about not having *her own space*. I'd heard the talk among colleagues in the Barristers' Lounge that young lawyers these days treat their offices like personal goddamn loft apartments with gym bags, purses, shoes, bags of takeout food, designer water bottles and entire extra wardrobes piled on the floor and draped over chairs. Youth.

However, on the other hand, there was no way I would subject her to the same bullshit I had to accept when I was a junior lawyer, sitting by the fucking photocopier. Something would need to be done. I just wasn't sure what that was.

"Good morning, Lindsay. Listen, for the last few days I have been giving a lot of thought to an office for you, you know, to get you your own space. I have some quality furniture coming for you—it's been delayed by COVID backlogs—and we'll get you set up with a desktop computer, phone, email, business cards, the works. Bonnie will work with you on it. Sound good? I assume you have gowns?" I prayed she couldn't smell the booze off me as I felt it leaching through my shirt.

"Sure. Whatever. I'm fine working off my laptop and phone for now. I have gowns. I guess a business card would be okay but, you know, no one really uses them anymore, so no need right now." She looked at me kind of funny. Suspicious. Oh no, she can smell the bourbon.

No one uses them anymore? What on earth? COVID's been blamed for a lot of shit but surely not the death of the business card. I take great pride in mine: pristine, bone, Garamond Classico SC typeface, good weight, Q.C.–embossed. Perfect. She'll want one eventually. I mean, who wouldn't? Wait. Holy shit, Q.C.? I will need to get new cards with K.C. Another expense I don't need right now.

"Well, we'll get you some anyway. Okay?" No response. She tapped away silently on her laptop.

I wasn't prepared to let her in on my conversations with Royce Hughes. Just yet. She might lose it. "Ms. Rimini is coming in at around eleven o'clock. We need to walk her through not just the events at the Christmas party, but her entire relationship with Glinka. Her history. Their history."

She glanced up but then put her nose right back into her laptop. "Okay, but I came in early to begin work on a strategy for bumping Williams off the inquiry. I'm using OpenAI and ChatGPT to develop a memo setting out a process to expose his harassment history but without breaching the NDA."

She sounded like she was working on a factum for the Supreme Court of Canada. Openay? Chatsomething or other? What the hell was she talking about?

Oh my God. The impatience of youth. This is not some schoolyard skirmish to be carried out in a fit of pique. We're talking war here. "Whoa, whoa, whoa. Bump him off? Why would we do that?"

She seemed stunned by my question. I think I may have shouted a little bit and my head was pounding.

"Uhhh, because he's a pig who assaulted me and is not fit to rule on these issues? I read your memo to file. There's no way he should even be allowed to sit near our client never mind judge her evidence."

"Oh, you have so much to learn, Grasshopper."

"Grasshopper?" She looked at me as if I had started speaking Chinese. "What are you talking about? Have you been drinking?"

"No. For heavens sake. It's eight in the morning. Bear with me. Think it through." I needed to focus. "*Think.*" Maybe I said that a little too loud again.

"What is there to think about? We need to bump him."

I moved to the other side of the office to keep the scent of booze as far away as possible. "*Think* for a minute, *please.*" Oh-oh that was definitely too loud. She looked concerned so I lowered my voice to almost a whisper. "If we bump him off—which would be tough without breaching your NDA—then nothing happens except delay and the AG and chief justice bring in a new judge. Williams denies everything and slides off to fight the allegations in several months, if at all. In the meantime, we are tied up on the Glinka inquiry with a new judge of unknown disposition. In the worst-case scenario, you're now a witness at the new Williams Inquiry and off the Glinka one. How is that a help?"

"But what's the alternative?" She looked very skeptical.

"*Tortura legum pessima.*" Even hungover I pulled that Latin right out of my ass. Not bad.

She stared at me. Surely, she knew some Latin.

"Torture. Patient torture, of course," I explained.

"Torture?"

I stared at her. So much to learn.

"Okay, I'm lost."

I shook my head. Latin may be a dead language but my goodness, it wasn't actively spoken for over a thousand years for nothing. "*The torture of laws is the worst kind of torture.* Don't you relish the prospect of sitting at the counsel table, day in, day out, week after week, looking up at Williams as he listens to our client's evidence of sexual harassment, of sexual assault, while you sit there smiling like a crocodile, waiting for him to come into the water? And with him knowing that he has engaged in the very same odious behaviour—and even worse—with you? That's torture."

I could see her rolling that potential scene around in her mind, frowning a little, but also imagining. "Go on."

Good.

"Every night I can see him there, at home sitting in the dark with a stiff drink wondering, *When is my sordid history going to emerge? Tomorrow? The next day?* Can you imagine the outcry he would face if it was revealed during or even after the inquiry that he was a harasser too? That he had women sign NDAs? And then sat in judgment of another harasser? He would worry that someday he might very well be in Glinka's shoes, or worse. Oh, it's too delicious to pass up."

Frankly, I was thrilling myself just talking about it. At last I could take the sword to that prick Williams. The revenge would be sweet.

A smile crept across her face. "Okay. I think I'm getting it. But won't someone say that we should have spoken up sooner?"

"How could we? You had no choice, you couldn't because of the NDA. It makes it even more delicious."

"Okay. I think." Good. She was coming around. "But it sounds, well, conniving, even . . . well . . . *evil*."

Maligno? She's a babe in the woods if she thinks this is evil. "Williams's dilemma gives us—I mean our client—an advantage over him. Leverage of which only we are aware. Is that evil? No, this is war."

Her shoulders slumped a little as she looked down at her laptop with a frown, seemingly dejected. "Is this how it works? Everything?" Her voice was sullen.

Oh God, don't wimp out on me already.

"Not everything. But this is how it *can work* when you are up against rodents like Randall Williams and the Glinkas of the world. The rules of engagement need to be *broadened* somewhat in their application for Total War."

She stared at her laptop.

"What?" I prodded. Why did she seem to be having such a hard time with this?

"Is this why she was referred to you? Because you know how to *broaden the application* of the rules, for the so-called *Total War*?" She said Total War like it was *maligno*, a dirty thing rather than the sword of justice.

"I prefer to think she was referred to me because of my reputation for the patient but tenacious pursuit of justice through the setting of deadly traps. Sometimes one must wait for the rodent to put his nose right on the cheese." I clapped my hands together so suddenly she nearly jumped from her chair.

She stared at me and her tongue shot out to lick a sore that was no longer there. I said nothing and waited. There was nothing more to say. Would she cross the Rubicon?

"Okay." She paused to give it one last thought. "I'm in."

"*Alea iacta est.*"* My God, the Latin was just rolling off my tongue. I have to drink more of that really good bourbon.

"What does that mean? More grasshopper stuff?"

"Look it up in *Black's Law Dictionary.*"

"I will, if you look up OpenAI and ChatGPT."

I shook my throbbing head and looked at my watch. It was already 9 a.m. "Whatever, but before we bring in Francesca we have another lesson to cover. And I assure you, it is not in *Black's Law Dictionary.*"

---

* The die is cast.

29

The Graph of Gratitude
Monday October 10, Thanksgiving Day

I LOOKED AT my watch. We had about ninety minutes before Francesca arrived. It would be more than enough time to explain one of the most critical concepts any young lawyer in private practice must grasp. It's a lesson best shared early, at the hands of a wise mentor, rather than learned the hard way, stepping on an IED planted by a client.

Even if Francesca showed up a little early it would give Bonnie a chance to gather some more background from her. They had not yet met so it was a good chance for them to get acquainted. Bonnie could give her a smell test.

I opened the doors of my whiteboard, grabbed a fresh marker and drew two lines as the axes for a graph. At the top of the vertical line I wrote one word, *Gratitude*. Across the bottom, under the horizontal line, I wrote one word, *Litigation*. Lindsay turned her chair toward my simple graphic, if not eager, at least curious.

Before I could say a word, Bonnie, early as usual even though it was Thanksgiving, stuck her head into the boardroom. "Good morning, everyone, I just wanted to let you know that Ms. Rimini is here. She has a coffee. What shall I tell her?" She gave Lindsay a broad smile. It was great to see them hitting it off. She had apparently passed Bonnie's smell test with flying colours. Speaking of smell tests, I was still trying to keep a safe distance from Lindsay in case the bourbon seepage continued.

"And did you hear the news? Premier has called the election! Monday November 7."

Oh great. Who calls an election on Thanksgiving weekend? Now I have the election on top of all this nonsense. And Bonnie would be slipping off to more meetings. "Thanks, Bonnie. We're going to be about twenty minutes tops. I asked Ms. Rimini to bring along her résumé. Can you review it with her, so we have a better understanding of her background? She is also supposed to have a bag of rice with her." I rubbed my fingers together.

"Understood." She closed the door.

Lindsay cocked her head to the side. "Rice?"

"That's for another day, Grasshopper."

"Again with the grasshopper?"

"Never mind. Back to our graph. Here is where you meet a client." I pointed to the intersection of the two lines in the bottom left-hand corner of the graph. "The client arrives with their legal problem. As they explain it to you it becomes clear that they feel they don't actually need a lawyer. Perhaps they have a degree from WWWLS and know all the answers."

"WWWLS?"

"World Wide Web Law School."

Ah, at last she cracked that beautiful smile. Progress.

"Their considerable research has revealed that they—the *righteous* in this horribly unfair situation—are a victim of their spouse, the *wicked*. The whole matter should be easy, it's quite straightforward. They just need you to write a few letters to clear things up. It's a pretty basic divorce. They should have sole custody of the children, get generous child support, at least half the family's assets—but assume none of the debt— and receive either full spousal support or a full release of any obligation to pay spousal support. They may even have prepared a detailed Excel spreadsheet for you to, you know, speed things up, save time and costs. At this point their level of gratitude is zero, probably even less than zero."

"Less than zero?"

"Of course. They actually resent even having to meet with you and spend their hard-earned money on a lawyer for such an easy situation. But they will hold their nose—and the purse strings—on any money that needs to be spent. They regret even giving you a retainer and already expect a refund of most of it once you confirm that their careful analysis is accurate. *Lawyers! They're so greedy!*"

"Come on. Not *all* clients?"

"*All* clients." Oops. I was getting loud again. "And the ones who try to pretend that they don't feel that way? They're *the worst*. Bear with me. So, notwithstanding their confidence in their own legal opinion, you—an actual lawyer—begin to probe, ask a few questions, explain that here, in Ontario, we don't actually follow the law of Florida, Utah, the Netherlands or Australia, where most of their online research was focussed. You scan their colour-coded comprehensive spreadsheets and with just a few questions determine that some assets—like their pension, for example—have been left off. *My pension? Why should I have to share my pension?* And what about those debts for which they are jointly liable? They were left off too? *Yes, I co-signed the loan, but I never wanted to buy that boat our family has used for the past ten years.* Suddenly they realize that, while they are still righteous in their cause, of course, they may actually need you. *This is so unfair!* And their level of gratitude climbs a few inches." I drew a line upward on the graph.

"Okay. I get it."

"But no, wait. Their spouse hires a lawyer. Perhaps a good one. The line of gratitude goes higher. Their spouse has hired a terrible lawyer? The line goes even higher. The financial statements prescribed by the Rules of Practice—rather than their selective Excel spreadsheets—reveal more challenges. The line goes higher. *Thank God you are my lawyer!*"

"Okay. I get it." She frowned.

Now I was in full flight, pacing back and forth, arms flailing. "But wait. The judge at the case conference doesn't seem to like our client. It turns out they're not a very good witness. Their victim routine has worn thin. They have made selective disclosure. They come across as angry, selfish. Why won't they share time with the children? Get back to the career they sidelined and earn an income again? *But I can't find work even though I'm a trilingual chemical engineer.*

I had her laughing now. Such a sweet laugh, such a pretty girl. Did my heart just flutter a little? I had almost forgotten about her, you know. I carried on. "*However,* notwithstanding your best efforts, their case has not settled and they must go to trial."

"Of course. Total War."

"You throw yourself into it, work night and day, weekends. A few weeks later the trial is over. And you have delivered. It's a good result. Certainly within your written recommendations for settlement—recommendations that were given but rejected months ago as 'giving in to the wicked.' They weren't going to cave! On to trial and victory! Their appreciation of your work is now at its climax and we enjoy the peak of their gratitude." I moved the line on the graph to the very top. "However, tomorrow is another day."

"What? Surely not . . ."

"Oh yes. They wake up twenty-four hours later and recall their dogged work at law school of the web. *Wasn't this case easy to begin with?*" I drew a line sinking on the graph. "All you've done is deliver the result that was right under our collective noses from the beginning. *Why did this cost so much? This should have been settled without a trial.*" The line approaches the bottom of the graph. "*It was so straightforward. I did all the work myself. Those Excel spreadsheets told the story.* They cannot believe how expensive it was. *I am a victim after all! A victim of lawyers!* Gratitude is again less than zero within forty-eight hours of your good work being completed."

She stared at me.

"And that, Grasshopper, is why the cash-up-front retainer was invented. If you don't have your money in your trust account before that trial, you are probably not getting paid."

Her expression was one of dismay. Perhaps the Grasshopper references were wearing thin.

And, as if right on cue, Bonnie knocked softly and stuck her head into the boardroom. "Andrew, I've finished with her on her résumé." She made a face that I'd seen before. *Oh-oh.* It was the expression Bonnie wore when she had a bad feeling about a client. "And she doesn't have the retainer with her. She says there was a problem." *Oh-oh.* Now I made a face that Bonnie had seen before. It was one of building anger. Hungover anger.

Given my just completed lecture about the Graph of Gratitude, Lindsay chimed in. "This is not good."

"And Cody Cooper has called again. He's very upset and says things are going sideways fast."

"Cody Cooper is your client?" I thought Lindsay was going to jump out of her chair. "I'm a *huge* fan."

"Me too!" Bonnie was thrilled to find a music soulmate. They began to sing "Love Poultice" together and laughed.

"Easy there, partner. He's a client but it's hush-hush. Let's focus on the problem at hand. We have a client who hasn't paid a retainer. We don't work for free and the preliminary hearing on evidence is imminent."

"What are you going to do?" They said it together and then burst out laughing again. At least someone is having fun. My head was pounding and I seriously considered a hair-of-the-dog solution.

"Bonnie, let's get her in here to meet Lindsay and then can I speak to you in my office?"

I guided her out the door toward reception while I headed for my office and some aspirin and some hair. A few minutes later Bonnie slipped into my office and shut the door. I looked at her. "Okay, what's up?"

"You tell me." She walked over, reached into my wastebasket and pulled out the empty bottle of Blanton's. "This was almost full when I left on Friday night."

Here we go. Like a wife at a wedding, she's monitoring my drinks now. "I'm fine."

"You reek of booze. Is this how you want to start with her? With me? You need her. Us. She's good. You're supposed to be rebuilding. You're in an election now too."

I raised my palm to her and hoped she didn't notice that it was trembling a little bit. "I'm fine." I decided my hand was best kept in my pocket.

"Andrew, we need to discuss this." So she did notice.

"Absolutely, but later." *In your dreams.* "Right now, I need to know what's up with Ms. Rimini. I've seen that look on your face before. What was your vibe off her?"

I could tell she was concerned. And disappointed in me. She screwed up her face, let out a deep sigh, reluctant to say anything. "Well, I'm surprised she got this far with you. She has trouble written all over her. Have you seen her résumé?" She held up the pages as if they were garbage.

"No. I was hoping we could discuss it after you had reviewed it with her. Why?"

"She certainly bounced around a lot before she landed at Finch. In and out of jobs. No letters of reference from any of them. She has all kinds of excuses for why she was fired—or quit before being fired. None of her schooling was completed, not even her training as clerk. And you know who gave her references to get the court clerk job?"

"I'm afraid to ask."

"Glinka and your friend Dave Goodwin."

"Oh God. Then why's she pursuing this? I don't get it."

"It's obvious. And while we're at it, the Marrs matter needs attention. It has just been sitting there since the adjournment. The motion is coming up. You haven't even met the client. Could Lindsay take it on? And don't forget to call Cody Cooper. He's left two messages."

"Yes, Lindsay could take on Marrs. I'll brief her on it."

To be honest I had not done a lick of work on the file other than get that adjournment. It looked more and more like an ugly custody fight and since Angie's death I had lost my appetite for that kind of file. I'm sure it will come back, but just not yet.

"I'll call Cooper, but Bonnie, what?"

"What?"

"You said, it's obvious. What's obvious?"

"You'd better have a heart-to-heart conversation with Ms. Rimini—after you call Cooper."

"What's obvious?"

"Andrew, you told me a long time ago that people go to court for one of two reasons." She flicked up her fingers. "Revenge or justice. Which one do you think this is?"

Based on what I had heard so far it was certainly not justice.

30

Missing Pieces
Monday October 10, Thanksgiving Day

BONNIE HEADED BACK to her desk as I grabbed my phone to give Coop a quick call and noticed that it was already 10:30 a.m.

He answered with a terse, "Where the fuck have you been, man? I left messages."

"I'm sorry it's been pretty wild around here. I'm about to start a *huge* judicial inquiry into a judge's misconduct." I tried to make it sound like I was on the trial of the century. My head went to a new level of pounding.

He clearly did not give a shit. "That may be so but if you're gonna help me, I need you when I call, not days after I leave messages. If you can't handle this, man, I'm gonna need to find someone who can." His faux country accent was nowhere to be found. He just sounded like someone from Newmarket who was in deep shit.

"What's up? Did something happen?"

"Fuck, man, I don't know where to begin. Can we meet? Can you come out to the Compound?"

Oh brother. Not really. "Of course, are you around tonight? I'm just wrapping up with my witness for the inquiry."

"Yeah, I guess that'll work but this is serious shit, man."

"What happened? Is everyone okay?"

"Brent, my business manager? He walked in on me and . . ."

"His wife? Oh shit. Are you okay? Is Kim okay?" I knew this would happen.

There was a long pause. "Not Kim. He walked in on . . ."

"Oh shit, one of those groupies?"

"No, he walked in on me and Kayla, his stepdaughter."

"Please tell me you were playing Scrabble."

"Nope."

"I assume Brent lost it."

"Worse than that."

"What could be worse than that?"

"He called her a bunch of names, threw her out and then . . ."

"What?"

"He says he won't tell Kim, he'll keep it a secret, but in return I have to help him."

"What do you mean help him?"

"It's fucked up. He says he wants to record again. He wants us to be a duo again, like when we started out, release an album. He says he's got a whole bunch of new music that he's been writing, saving for the day he could return to performing. And there's more."

"What?"

"He wants me to add his name to some of my older tunes for song-writing credits. He claims he wrote some of those songs with me."

That's not what I would expect a father to say after catching a man in bed with his stepdaughter. "What did you say?"

"What could I say? I told him we needed to sit down and discuss things calmly. This is fucked up. If he tells Kim, she's gonna lose it. We were getting ready to tell him that she's gonna leave him to live with me."

"Okay . . ." I cannot imagine that conversation now. "What about Kayla? Where is she? What if she tells someone?"

"She's not going to say anything. Her mother would kill her. She can keep a secret, plus she's getting ready to leave for school anyway. She's off to university in a few days in B.C. . . . I promised her some stuff to keep quiet."

"Okay. Good." I was afraid to ask what had been promised but that was not the most immediate problem. Brent had Coop over a barrel.

"And I'm not recording with him again. We broke up for a reason. He was a shitty guitarist. And a pothead. He didn't write any of those songs. He was too stoned to play half the time. He's not getting credits."

"Okay. Sit tight. I'll come right after I finish with this witness. I'll be there by five or six o'clock. I'll keep you posted if it's later."

"Okay, but we need to meet. This is a shitshow."

Yes, it was. And it was entirely self-created as usual.

It suddenly occurred to me that I had never actually been retained by Coop. I had no money in trust and had probably logged a few grand of time on him. Bonnie would never have allowed this to happen. I was getting sloppy. I had a flashback to the Law Society audits years ago, when I got sloppy the last time, when I had taken on too much. It was happening again.

I looked at my watch. It was 10:45 a.m. I could spend a couple of hours with Francesca, then spend a few minutes reviewing the Marrs file with Lindsay, hit the road and be at Coop's place by five o'clock if the traffic was okay. Tight, but doable? Not really. I reached into my drawer, took a few sips of the hair of the dog and gave myself a generous spritz of cologne to cover the smell.

Then my phone pulsed. It was Daria. "What's up?"

"Sean needs to meet with you. The election's been called."

Here we go. "I know. Of course."

"Again with the tone? I thought we could move on? Focus on Sean."

"Daria," I hated even saying her name. "I'm very busy with clients. Can't it wait? I mean, it's the first day. I have like a month. And I'm not doing anything anyway."

"Twenty-eight days."

"Okay split hairs. Twenty-eight days."

"Sean says there's something you need to do, a file of new information that you need to review. He wouldn't tell me but something's changed. He said it's urgent."

"Okay, look, I will stop in there on the way to meet my client later today. I can be there at 3:30 if the traffic's okay. But I can only stay for fifteen minutes max. Tell Sean I'll be there." I didn't wait for an answer. Shooting for 3:30 p.m. would make it very tight for getting to Coop by

5 p.m. Impossible in the usual traffic, actually. I'll have to text him and move it to later.

I stopped by Bonnie's workstation. It was, as usual, immaculate but the carpet around her chair had been torn up. The smell of Hopeless Helen's poison tea was still quite strong. Jesus, how can she work here? There was a note on her screen. *Slipped out for a minute to see Mateo about the election.* Oh brother, here we go. She is getting election fever on the first day. Not good. I scribbled a note for her to prepare a retainer for Coop and get $10,000 in trust.

I slipped back into the boardroom where Francesca and Lindsay seemed to be discussing the "fingers in vagina" part of what happened at the party and the "no-panties yeast infection." Still gross.

I could see that Lindsay was clearly horrified. And furious.

Watching them sitting there like two logs burning on the same bonfire, I wasn't about to tell either of them about Royce Hughes's call and his, frankly wise, proposed walk-away settlement. The prospect of settling this Glinka shitstorm, saving Francesca from the trauma and reaping a tidy payment for her legal fees was looking very attractive. Win-win-win. But I have to be honest, as I slid into a chair at the end of the boardroom table the fact that I had absolutely no retainer began to weigh on my bourbon-bruised mind—heavily. And, still, something inside me needed to know what she had to say about her so-called longstanding relationship with Glinka, Dave and even what happened with Pudgy Red. (Based on his beer-fuelled storytelling at Barb's he would, like most lawyers, make the world's worst witness.) Were all her historical escapades going to be thrown in her face? Why would she risk walking into a humiliating potential slaughter? Why wasn't her husband sitting here with her, supporting her? What was I missing?

I sat across from her, Lindsay by my side, as usual ready to blaze notes into her laptop. "Okay, let's begin with a complete review of what happened—from the start." I noticed Lindsay roll her chair about two feet away from me. Hmm, too much cologne perhaps.

Francesca let out a long sigh and gave a bored shrug. "Not again. Honestly, I cannot bear another discussion about that party."

She picked the wrong time to look inconvenienced by my invitation to review the very reason she sat before me. It touched an exposed nerve. *Oh, well isn't that just too bad.* On the eve of the judicial inquiry you can't bear to have *another discussion?* You, who have shown up today without a retainer but expect my high-level legal advice, advice from the one person willing to talk to you?

I looked up and saw the Graph of Gratitude on the whiteboard. How appropriate. I figured I had at least twenty-five grand of my time invested already and *nothing in trust.* I'm so stupid. Maybe it was that graph or the pounding headache, but suddenly I wasn't prepared to waste another second on Ms. Rimini. She needed a reality check for what was coming.

So why not start with a bomb?

"Okay. If you don't want to talk about the party let's start earlier than the party. Let's go back to the first time you and Justice Glinka had consensual sex in his office."

Lindsay gasped. Francesca was, as I like to say, *mutus.*

"Was it before or after he gave you the reference letter to get the job at the courthouse, a job for which you apparently were not qualified? Or both?"

She stared at me. Nothing to say?

"I have spoken with a number of witnesses," *well, I had at least heard about some rumoured witnesses,* "each of whom has confirmed that you and Justice Glinka had a, shall we say, *longstanding* pre-existing sexual relationship. True or false?"

Nothing yet? No comment? Okay, let's keep going.

"You *begged* Dave Goodwin to help you get the party organized. He was in the middle of a big trial, an unwilling volunteer, pressured into helping you because you're married to a judge. You've had a sexual relationship with Dave in the past. True or false?"

Still *mutus?* Really? Okay. Let's go deeper.

"At the inquiry there will be witnesses testifying about your previous active social life and your search for a husband from the ranks of lawyers or judges." I mentioned Pudgy Red. "And lawyers, one of whom, Ms. Lorelei Novak, . . ."

"She should talk . . . Ms. Pussycat Memoirs." And a shrug. Oh, now she has a comment.

"Nonetheless." *Wow, I'm starting to sound like Royce.* "She will testify that you were the initiator of any sexual contact with Glinka—all consensual. Judges—three, in fact—will support Justice Glinka's version of events. Would you care to comment?"

There was no shrugging now. She started to cry. Sob actually.

I pushed a box of tissues across to her, but before she could blow her nose, compose herself and either deny or confirm anything, Lindsay absolutely exploded. "What has any of that got to do with what Francesca says happened at the party? She was assaulted! Plain and simple. I . . . I . . . can't . . . If you were sitting here talking to a man about having an *active* sexual history, you two would be high-fiving each other." She was apoplectic. "Have you even heard of section 276 of the Criminal Code?" As she continued yelling at me, she began furiously tapping the keys of her laptop.

"Of course I've heard of it. What're you suggesting?" *Actually, I had not.* The Criminal Code was not my area. The closest I had come to it was Chloe's criminal charges when she poisoned Angie. Even thinking about that sent a blast of pins and needles across my back. And, hangover aside, I did not like Lindsay's tone one bit. We're supposed to be on the same team.

"Well, then you know that the judge should not consider *any evidence* of Francesca's prior sexual activity. The focus should be on the incident at the party. Did it happen or not? It's insulting to suggest that any of that historical sexual evidence is relevant or will be admissible. It's just designed to smear her."

She looked down at her computer screen, hit a few more keys and the next thing the list of criteria from section 276 of the Criminal Code was being projected onto the TV screen in my boardroom. Damn, I thought it was just a widescreen TV and here it has been an HD monitor all along. Who knew.

Lindsay began to check off the criteria a judge is supposed to consider when looking at sexual assault allegations. As she read them out, visions of the Ghomeshi trial several years ago flashed before my eyes again—a nightmare rehash of who did what to whom—before and after his alleged assaults. I remembered his lawyer being absolutely roasted for even daring to ask questions about the complainants' sexual history.

Groggy Ghomeshi Flashbacks of Witnesses' Testimony
Well-prepared lawyer: He choked you during these sexual encounters?
Hapless complainant: Uhh, yes.
Lawyer, pressing: With his hands?
Now unsuspecting complainant: Of course.
Lawyer, pressing harder: That must have been awful.
Now confident complainant: Uhh, yes, it was.
Lawyer, maintaining grip: Did you send him a message the next day saying, "I love your hands?"
Complainant, feeling floor suddenly give way: Uhhh . . .
Lawyer, calmly: Did you send flowers to him after he allegedly assaulted you?
Now confused complainant: Uhh, yes.
Lawyer, who already knows answer: Did you have another sexual encounter with him—at your own home—after he allegedly assaulted you?
Complainant, now gulping: Uhh, yes, but . . .
Lawyer, holding an exhibit aloft: I'm reading a handwritten letter which says, "You kicked my ass last night and that makes me want to fuck your brains out." Is that your handwriting?
Complainant, wishing she was on Mars: Uh, yes.
Lawyer, pulling something else from her file: Did you send these photos to him . . . one in a bikini and a photo of you fellating a beer bottle?
Complainant, arms flailing: Uh, yes, . . . bu . . . it was . . . bait . . .?
Lawyer, throwing heavy anchor to drowning witness: Was your sexual contact consensual?
Complainant, as she navigates to bottom of cold lake: Uhh . . . no . . . it wasn't . . .
Result? Acquittal and General Societal Mortification.

Snapping back to reality, I scanned the list of factors Lindsay had on the screen. Even as a (somewhat) humble family law lawyer, I immediately saw several gaping holes. In deciding whether to admit evidence of sexual history the judge could consider "the interests of justice, including the right of the accused to make a full answer and defence." _Oh God, that's an_ *open door for evidence.* The last one on a list of eight factors was, "any other factor that the judge, provincial court judge or justice considers relevant." *Seriously? Open door?* That one's a veritable trapdoor that allows a judge to do whatever the hell he or she wants. A good lawyer would have no trouble with these factors. And for Royce? It would be a picnic.

"Okay. I see the list of factors. As I said, I'm familiar with them," *granted for all of three minutes*, "and what if Justice Randall Williams springs the final 'any other factor' trapdoor and decides these historical things are relevant? Don't you think we should know what we're dealing with before we stand Francesca on that trapdoor with a noose around her neck?"

Lindsay calmed down a little. A little. "I guess, especially if the recent Supreme Court decision in *R. v. Hay* is going to be a typical experience, you know, with a review of the twin myths." She started to tap away on her computer.

Hay? Twin myths? I had no idea what court decision she was even referring to. My head was pounding and I seriously thought of popping out for more hair of the dog but I decided to press on.

Francesca stared at Lindsay, clueless. "Twins?"

So did I. I needed to buy time to get my head under control. "I agree, Lindsay. I'm very familiar with the Hay case. Let's review the details. I think it would be helpful."

"Really? In detail?" Lindsay seemed caught off guard.

"Yes, Francesca needs to know what she faces. Put it up on the monitor." I was struggling to create the impression that I was familiar with this case.

"The details? Really?"

"Yes, it's a good case to help us understand what we're up against, what Francesca faces."

I mean, how bad could it be given what we had heard from her? Run of the mill "he said, she said" sexual assault, I assumed.

We all turned to face the monitor as the case suddenly appeared on the screen, *R v. Hay* (2022) SCC 222, and the Alberta Appeal decision beside it. This monitor was great, really paying dividends, and I loved how Lindsay was so smooth with the technology. We made a formidable team.

Lindsay began slowly. "The case of *R. v. Hay* originated in the Alberta Court of Appeal. Their decision is on the left. Mr. Hay had been acquitted of sexual assault at his trial on the basis that there had been an honest mistaken belief that the complainant had consented to . . . um . . . um . . ."

I guessed that she was being a little shy, a little embarrassed about the sexual aspect so I decided to help ease the way. "Lindsay, it's okay, we can be frank. We're all adults."

"Oh, okay . . . there had been an honest mistaken belief that she had consented to anal intercourse."

Whoa. Whoa. Whoa. No way. What have I started?

Lindsay continued, head down, avoiding my eyes.

"Mr. Hay and the complainant had met online. They began to see each other. A few weeks prior to the incident that led to the alleged assault they were having vaginal intercourse on a bed, she was on top. She asked him if he had just put his finger in her anus."

Oh Lindsay, for God's sake. I looked down and covered my eyes.

Bravely, Lindsay carried on with her summary of the facts. "He responded that, no, he had not, but then he asked if she wanted him to put his finger in her anus. She replied that she did. He then put his finger in her anus while they were having vaginal intercourse . . ."

Sweet merciful Lord. Take me now.

Lindsay took a deep breath. "And she, at least according to Mr. Hay's evidence, began to moan and grind against him. He said that she enjoyed it when he put his finger in her anus."

I had an urge to wash my hands.

Lindsay picked up the pace, became quite clinical and actually started reading from the decision. "Three weeks later they were again having vaginal intercourse. The complainant was on top of him and he again inserted his finger into her anus. She apparently told the accused, 'I love it when you play with my ass.'"

Oh my God, where is this going?

Lindsay's pace quickened a little again and became more matter of fact. I think she just wanted to get it over with. "The complainant moved to the end of the bed, where she was kneeling. Vaginal intercourse continued from behind. During this intercourse the accused's penis slipped out of her vagina. Instead of reinserting it into her vagina he then attempted anal intercourse . . ."

Oh, sweet Lindsay. I'm so sorry. What have I done?

Faster now. "The complainant became angry and asked him to leave. He said he misunderstood the situation, apologized and hoped they could carry on their relationship. She disagreed. He was charged with sexual assault. He was acquitted at trial on the basis of an honest misconception of her consent based on the previous conduct of inserting his finger in her anus more than once and her enjoying that during vaginal intercourse."

If I hear finger in anus one more time.

"The Court of Appeal set aside the acquittal, reversed it and convicted him of sexual assault on the basis that there was no honest mistake about consent. Their previous discussions about putting his finger in her anus could not be interpreted as implied consent to anal intercourse. In registering a conviction, the Court of Appeal reviewed the twin myths. The Supreme Court of Canada agreed with the Alberta Court of Appeal and his conviction stood."

Lindsay let out a long sigh, relieved to have gotten through the whole sordid tale.

"And his sentence for this assault?" I have to admit, I was curious.

"I'm not sure what happened to him but the max is fourteen years."

Whoa. Fourteen years? That seemed a little harsh. Especially since I assumed over his grim time in jail someone would return the favour.

Francesca had not said a word during Lindsay's very matter-of-fact overview but she now sat up suddenly interested. "What're the twin myths?" (Yes, with a shrug.)

"The twin myths are that evidence of a complainant's past sexual activity means (1) they are more likely to have consented to the activity in question, and (2) that the complainant's evidence is less likely to be believed."

Francesca looks puzzled. "What does that mean?"

"Basically? It means that her moans and grinding against him in the previous encounter when he inserted his finger in her anus . . ."

Lindsay!

". . . were not enough to allow Mr. Hay to conclude that she would consent to anal intercourse. The more intimate the behaviour, the more time should be spent ensuring through verbal clues—not non-verbal clues like moaning and grinding—that there is consent. Basically, he should have asked if he could put his penis in her anus."

We're done here.

"Okay. I think we have heard enough. Let's move on."

But still puzzled, Francesca shrugged and asked, "No, I meant what does that mean for me? Does it matter if things happened before between Glinka and me?"

Lindsay and I looked at each other. *Oh no. Please no.*

Lindsay spoke up immediately. "Well, *technically* it shouldn't, but someone is going to ask and you may have to answer. The judge would have to rule that the line of questioning about your sexual history violates the twin myths."

I jumped in and asked the obvious. "Had Justice Glinka done this before, . . ." I made a weird gesture with my fingers, ". . . you know, with your consent?" The way Lindsay screwed up her face, it looked like she wondered why I was pretending to play the accordion.

Francesca looked uncomfortable. Like someone had put their finger in her anus. But then she said, "Not exactly . . . but he has hugged me in his office a few times, very tight . . . I couldn't say no . . . I was his clerk . . . it was before I met Jay."

As I watched her flush with embarrassment, I realized that this was the very calculation that Hughes must have already made. If the evidence of her prior activity with Glinka and others is allowed, then she's likely in trouble. There is a risk that no one will believe her in the face of that evidence. No one will *want* to believe her. But if the evidence is not allowed, it could be quite a different story. Therein lay the risk.

I glanced at Lindsay. She looked like smoke was coming off her again. She was boiling over. I think she saw something in Francesca that looked familiar.

I looked at the terms of reference for the inquiry: ". . . inquire into allegations of misconduct by Justice Glinka at a party on December . . ." *Misconduct* was a broad word but it was confined to one day. And it was *his* misconduct that was the focus, so the onus would be on Royce Hughes to convince Williams that the inquiry needed to hear all about the history leading up to the incident on the dance floor. Would the inquiry stick to the narrow question? Would they observe the so-called twin myths? The question would need to be framed tight. Very tight. *Q: Did Glinka grab her ass on the dance floor and put his fingers into her vagina?* Period. Ignore everything else. If the answer is yes, he did it, then he's gone. So what if that had happened before? Why should it matter? Office or dance floor, before or after the party, this was not acceptable conduct for a judge. In fact, I started to think that maybe we wanted all the evidence of previous encounters to be entered as evidence. Let's hear it all. Although that would be a very rough ride for Francesca. And to what end?

It was a lot to consider and I could see the wheels spinning in Lindsay's fuming head. "What's the standard of proof at an inquiry? Is it the same as a criminal trial?"

She posed a good question. In criminal cases the standard of proof is high, beyond a reasonable doubt. In the summaries of previous judicial inquiries that I had read the standard was lower. It was on the balance of probabilities at best. However, notwithstanding the lower standard of evidence required, judges were still being held to a very high standard of conduct. Would the inquiry judges allow as much evidence as possible? That could hurt Francesca. But then any improper behaviour by a judge, regardless of when it happened, would have to be resolved in favour of Francesca. Judges simply can't do this crap, no matter where or when. So it could help. But would it? That would hurt Glinka. Or would the judges cover for each other? Judges were lining up to defend Glinka. These questions must have worried Hughes as they worried me now. No wonder he was looking for a way out for everyone. My head was splitting. I needed a drink.

Lindsay and I both looked at Francesca. Whether she liked it or not, we knew we needed answers. We couldn't go in blind. And if we didn't settle beforehand, could she handle a brutal cross-examination by Hughes?

Lindsay spoke gently to her. "Francesca, where do you want to begin?"

"I don't know," she shrugged.

"Why isn't your husband here?" Lindsay's tone was so warm.

I could tell she was ready to give up and that Lindsay's soft touch had pierced something. "He's totally against this going forward. He will not support me. In fact he's half terrified and half furious."

"But why? Why terrified?"

"He gave up on me a long time ago when he met Pauline. I thought it was about learning French, but it turned into a lot more. He wants a divorce. He wants to be with her. There's no turning back. It's over." She was hopeless.

"So why do this? Why put yourself out there like this? If Glinka's lawyer convinces the inquiry that they need to know about any history between you and Glinka—and others—it will hurt. You will get dragged through the mud. They're lining up to take a swing."

"I know it will hurt. But Glinka did what he did. He had no right to treat me like that. And then to taunt Jay the way he did. He brought that broken collarbone on himself."

Whoa. "What do you mean Glinka taunted Jay?"

"When Jay went to see Glinka the next day, they had words, it wasn't just about me. When Jay confronted him about grabbing me, Glinka admitted it, he said something to the effect that maybe *Francesca wouldn't be out there on the dance floor looking to get her ass squeezed if Jay wasn't so busy squeezing Pauline's ass.* Somehow Glinka knew that Jay and Pauline had been caught screwing on the couch in Jay's office. He told Jay that if I made a complaint then he and Pauline were going to be a part of it and they were going down too. *What's good for the goose.* That's when Jay pushed him and he fell."

The missing piece. Their shunning suddenly made perfect sense.

I looked at my watch. I had to get going. There was no time now to discuss Marrs with Lindsay. It would need to wait. Maybe tonight. "Francesca, there's no upside for you in this inquiry. You could even be 100 percent successful in telling your story, get Glinka disciplined and removed from the bench, and you'll still end up divorced. And let's not forget . . ."

"What?"

I had to be honest with her. "Even if we wanted to go ahead, you have no money to pay us to do the work."

"I know. I'm sorry."

"Has Jay actually talked about getting a divorce?"

"Yes, when this mess has been dealt with. After. It won't be a difficult divorce. Jay made sure of that." She suddenly sounded bitter.

I found that hard to believe after the way this marriage was coming apart at the seams. It had the hallmarks of a Total War now. "Why do you say that?"

"I signed that goddamn marriage contract. I released my claims on his pension and our home—well, his home; he owned it before we got married—basically everything."

"What about support? Did you release that too?" Lindsay jumped in.

"There's some kind of formula that applies if we had children, but we didn't. He changed his mind about that too. I'd have to look at it again. I didn't know what I was doing. I'm really getting screwed now."

Lindsay jumped in again. "Did you get independent legal advice?"

"Yes, Jay insisted. He drafted it himself. I just signed. I just wanted to be married." She shrugged. "He's getting away with everything."

The three of us sat in silence. I looked at my watch again.

"I just want this over. It was a mistake. Can you get me out? Make it end?"

She was quitting. After all the work we had done—for free—she was quitting.

I dropped my wrist to my lap and looked at my watch discreetly. I needed to get to Sean. I still hadn't told Francesca or Lindsay about Royce Hughes's settlement proposal. But suddenly it looked fantastic—if it was still even on the table. But then again, he had not actually committed to anything. Shrewd. Very shrewd. Had he made that call to make me slow down on my prep? Had I fallen for one of my own sandbagging tricks? Was I getting sloppy?

"Francesca, I believe you. I believe Glinka did what you said he did." I felt that needed to be said. "I don't like just walking away from this," *especially unpaid*, "but we need to make some tough decisions. I have to get to another meeting across town. So, let's do this. Let's think about this overnight and meet again tomorrow. Also, can you scan your marriage contract to Lindsay? She can take a look at it. See what's there. You need to be proactive on that no matter what happens."

She shrugged. Of course.

"Lindsay, the other matter, Marrs, will need to wait."

"The motion is in two days and we have no instructions . . ."

What could I do? I shrugged and left.

31

I Don't Have Time for This Shit
Monday October 10, Thanksgiving Day

I WAS HALFWAY down to the parking garage when my phone pulsed. It was Bonnie. "What's up? And where have you been?"

"I had to meet Mateo. He wants me to co-chair his campaign." She sounded thrilled.

"Bonnie, we are pretty busy right now. We need to discuss this."

"I know, but we did discuss this when you hired me. Remember? You do know I'm here on Thanksgiving. And did you tell Naomi Smart to meet you here at the office at three o'clock?"

Shit. Shit. Shit.

"I'm an idiot. I forgot. She has some information on Cooper's situation. Is she there now?"

"She just walked in. I can't believe you asked her to come in on the holiday. She has a family, you know. And don't forget about Marrs. The motion is coming up in two days."

"Tell her to meet me out front. We'll have to talk in the car. Lindsay and I can discuss Marrs tonight."

For someone who is a highly sought-after, respected forensic accountant and an absolute crackerjack with numbers, Naomi took upscale office casual to a whole new level. Tiny little thing, she couldn't weigh more than a hundred pounds. She had perfected her own haute office-soccer-mom look: a combination of perfect blue jeans (I think I spotted the discreet For All Mankind label), immaculate white T-shirt (Guess), navy waffle-stitched ball cap, mocha cashmere cardigan, spotless white Vans sneakers and gold aviator sunglasses that matched her simple, small gold-braid earrings. She had a look that was perfection in both its simplicity and quality. As she walked closer to my car, I saw, perched on her shoulder, a beautiful cream-coloured messenger bag, Lucrin. And it was real.

Married to another accountant, with a couple of kids in private school, she has a very good life. Any file I've ever had with questionable numbers, I sent to her for a quick-and-dirty look-see. More often than not, she was quick and found the dirty. We had both profited handsomely off the arrangement, hence her willingness to just jump into my car on Thanksgiving. She had finished with Coop's books and I wondered if she had something.

When Naomi hopped into the front seat of my Porsche, she was her usual upbeat self. "Hey, handsome, I thought we were meeting at your office. What's up? Where are we off to? And by the way, nice car."

"How would you like to meet The Coop himself? I'm driving to his Compound now."

She laughed. "Andrew, I have kids, you know, and I'm skipping out on them on the long weekend. I can't just drive off to Prince Edward County on the spur of the moment." She thought it was hilarious. "Oh, to be single again."

"You would get a chance to meet the man, the musician, the legend, see the famous Compound. And there are usually other musicians hanging around. You're a Blue Rodeo fan, aren't you? Jim Cuddy?" *Not sure where I came up with that one.*

"Cuddy will be there? I'm in."

"I can't guarantee it but there's always someone like that, you know. Cuddy, even Keelor, could be wandering about just strumming a guitar."

"Hang on, I'll let my husband know I may not make it back in time for Thanksgiving dinner at his parents' place. It's okay, he owes me one." She pulled out her phone and sent a text. "Done."

"First, we need to make a quick stop at Sunnybrook Hospital."

"What's up there? Client?"

"No, my brother is there getting treatment and I just need to pop in to see him. It's on the way if you don't mind waiting in the car for a few minutes. I'll be five minutes. Max."

"You mean Sean?"

"You know Sean?" Does everyone know Sean?

"I was CFO on more than a couple of Liberal campaigns. Sean was always trying to fudge a few expenses past me on behalf of candidates. He spent campaign funds *creatively* shall we say. He was one of the greats."

"That sounds like Sean."

"It was hard to say no to him. Such a charmer." By the sound of her voice I could tell she had fallen under his spell. "What's he in Sunnybrook for? Skin clinic?"

"No, it's worse than that. He has prostate cancer, stage 4. Not looking good."

"Oh, I'm so sorry. I know he had his issues with the archdiocese and other things but he was a delight to work with. I really liked him. Everyone did. I remember him being such a force in Palmer's Liberal leadership run back in . . . oh gosh, what year was that, few years ago? He kinda fell off the radar after that."

Fell off the radar? No, he fell off the wagon and I boosted him back on.

"Why don't you come up and say hi? That would cheer him up. Then we can hit the road."

"If you think it would be okay. I would enjoy seeing him again." Sure, I thought, if you like the sight of grey, dying people.

When we slipped into Sean's room I could see Naomi felt differently. Sean looked terrible. A new deeper shade of grey. Daria was by his side with a row of pills in little paper cups instead of turkey and the fixin's. "Andrew, I'm glad you could make it. Someone's not doing so well and taking it out on his doctor."

I ignored her. "Sean, I hope you don't mind I brought along a visitor. Do you remember Naomi?"

He brightened up immediately. "Naomi, of course. So good to see you. This is my doctor, Daria. Are you giving my little brother a hand with his campaign?"

Naomi looked at me with raised eyebrows as if to say, *You? Politics?* "What campaign?"

"I haven't had a chance to bring her up to date on my so-called political non-aspirations. She's helping me with a client. We're on the way there now and I thought I would stop in. The doctor," I was still trying to say her name as little as possible, "said you had something for me."

"I do. But Naomi, as great as it is to see you, do you mind if Andrew and I speak confidentially for a couple of minutes?" His voice was barely a whisper. The room had a new level of awful smells, so I needed to keep this quick.

"Not at all. I can wait in the hall if you need me to." Naomi started to head for the door.

"No, it's okay. Naomi, you can stay. She knows how to keep a secret. What's up?" I waved her back.

"Besides, I'm not involved in any provincial campaigns this time around, I'm sitting it out, so don't worry about secrets. Frankly, I'm a little curious about what Andrew is up to. I seem to recall that you're not much for politics."

Sean pushed a thick envelope across his bedside tray. "You're going to need this."

"That looks like a lot of reading, reading that I don't have time for."

"Things are shifting a bit in Parkdale–High Park."

"Parkdale? What are you two up to in Parkdale? Everyone's talking about Parkdale." Now Naomi was curious.

I explained the vote-splitting situation as she laughed and shook her head. "I've heard of long shots but that takes the cake. McKay isn't going to need any help winning that riding. Our Liberal will run a distant third."

"The archdiocese disagrees. It's the Dippers. The church is holding us to an agreement to work to split the NDP vote. Sean is counting on it. If we don't help, then he's to be defrocked. It's complicated. They have a sword over our heads."

Naomi's demeanour shifted. She didn't like the sound of that. She was dead serious now. "I heard a rumour that the federal Conservatives are going to provide a lot more help than you would ever be able to give."

"I thought you said you weren't involved in this election."

"I'm not involved in any *campaigns* but that doesn't mean I'm not following the situation closely, very closely. I heard from my colleagues up on the Hill in Ottawa that some Irish fellow was up there asking the feds to grease the wheels in Parkdale. They're working hand in hand with their provincial counterparts."

"To do what?"

"Not sure. But something's up with the candidates."

"Something is up. That's what this envelope is about, Andrew. Once the campaign is underway the federal Conservatives are going to appoint the NDP candidate, Aaron Bierce, to a cushy policy position at the UN in New York. He's dropping out of the campaign. He won't be on the ballot. They're trying to clear the field."

Naomi jumped in. "That would jive with what I heard from the Hill."

"That's great. McKay will win. Now they don't need us." I was thrilled.

"You're half right." Sean looked horrified. "They don't need us."

Oh shit. I recalled Dikoombee's comment: *It's good to be needed. Otherwise, Shannon wouldn't be giving you the time of day.*

Daria moved to the side of Sean's bed. "That priest has Sean's consent to laicization and is not returning phone calls or messages. Neither is Dikembe. I think Shannon is going to hang Sean out to dry."

"Dikembe's involved?" Naomi recognized the name.

"Yeah, he's running McKay's campaign."

"I've crossed paths with him before. Nice looking, young fellow, but he plays rough. Doesn't like to lose. I guess he's taking no chances. Clearing the NDP challenge out of the way is taking a snowplow to it, though."

Suddenly Daria was crying. "What're you going to do, Sean?"

What's she got to cry about? Jesus.

"I don't know. I don't know." Sean sounded hopeless. I couldn't believe it, but in his hands I could see rosary beads. Oh brother.

As I stood there I felt my phone pulse with emails and text messages and stepped over to the window for a quick review.

Bonnie: *Media has been calling here about the inquiry. I haven't given them your number. I told them you are tied up in court. What shall I say?*

Bonnie: *You're invited to participate in an all-candidates debate next week hosted by the West End Poverty Coalition. In your calendar. Details to follow.*

Bonnie: *Another all-candidates debate the following week sponsored by the Parkdale Tenants Association. I have put it in your calendar.*

Bonnie: Toronto Star, National Post, Now *mag and* Globe and Mail *reporters have called for interviews about the election. And the inquiry.*

Bonnie: *A lawyer named Gavin McPhellan called. He says he has been asked to be presenting counsel on the Glinka matter but wants to speak with you about dates as he heard there may be a resolution. I will send you his #*

Royce Hughes: *Can we chat again this evening about a new development?*

Well, even the great man works on Thanksgiving. I sent him a short reply. *Sure. Will call later, 7:30 p.m.?*

Bonnie: *Lindsay said something about an office? And that I was dealing with delivery of her furniture? Care to fill me in?*

Shit.

Lindsay: *Francesca has come up with $5,000. Enough?*

I sent a quick response. *No, not even close. Find out if Judge Singh has a lawyer. Get a name. If so, get him or her to call me.*

Dr. Sheila: *Just checking in. Hope all is well. Heard you are running to be my MPP. Best of luck. Neighbourhood needs help. There was a murder at the corner of my street! Happy Thanksgiving!*

Lindsay: *Forgot to tell you I have an update on Christian Brothers. I tracked down the leader of the group of victims. Lots of settlements, over 150— all confidential.*

Lindsay: *Also, we need to discuss that dog file, the Marrs matter.*
Full stop.

What? Dog file? *Dog file?* What does she think she's calling a *dog file?* I hadn't heard that term, reserved for stinker files, for years. Where does she get off? That Marrs file is a quality referral. That custody dispute has huge potential. We have $10,000 in trust just for the adjournment and the consult. That's not a good start for a junior, hastily judging the quality of a file. That really pissed me off. I decided to ignore her for now, but we needed to talk. That's bullshit.

Cooper: *Hope you're on the way. Crap hit fan.*

I glanced at the thick envelope that Sean had given me and wondered if there was any point now. If they were tossing Sean aside because they didn't need us anymore, then what was the point? He was going to be defrocked and it was over. Period. I could forget about the election and get back to work.

I looked out the window at Mount Hope Cemetery and felt a chill run down my spine. *If it was over, then Sean would need to be buried somewhere. But where?*

I don't have time for this shit.

32

To the Compound
Monday October 10, Thanksgiving Day

I THREW THE thick envelope Sean had given me onto the back seat and Naomi and I rode in silence for a good twenty minutes. She finally broke the ice as I pulled into the En Route for gas. "Do you want a Tim's?"

I winced. "There's a Starbucks in there, you know."

"Starbucks it is. Double shot latte I seem to recall."

"You're good."

I gassed up and wheeled around to pick her up at the entrance. She slid in and asked, "You want to talk about Coop before we get there?"

"Yes, anything's better than all this political BS with Sean and the archdiocese. What a mess. What did you find? Anything interesting?"

"The books for the last three years are pretty straightforward. On the face of it there's nothing unusual."

"But?"

"But that's on the face of it. Now, understand that this is an over-simplification for the lawyer brain . . ."

"I can take it. But . . . go . . . slow . . ."

She laughed. "Good. So when I drilled down in a few areas there were lots of unaccounted-for money transfers leaving a couple of accounts. Modest amounts. One is a monthly transfer to a Newmarket account and then immediately transferred again to a credit union in Banff. Another is to an Aurora account and then again to the Banff credit union."

"Are we talking about a lot of money?"

"Not really, in the scheme of things. I mean Coop's making a fortune. And that's what made it so strange. It's not a lot and it's right there if you look. No attempt to hide it. You know sometimes people get too clever and they raise suspicions by doing crazy pretzel-like financial moves trying to cover up a big fraud? More often it's best just to take the money in small amounts that no one ever pays any attention to."

"So what are we talking about?"

Over the last three years about $500,000 from just those two accounts. There's probably more. If I go back three more years, it could be the same. How many years has Brent been doing the books?"

"I think Coop said from the start, fifteen years?"

"Even with COVID Coop's performance earnings have been biggest in the last few years, but his songwriting credits have been making money long before that. It's the cash cow. That could mean a few million if these small transfers have been happening since day one. And remember that's just based on a quick-and-dirty. If I roll up my sleeves I may find more."

She just loves doing this stuff and said *roll up my sleeves* like she was getting ready for a warm bath.

I decided to fill Naomi in on Coop's full picture and the plan to unveil his relationship with Kim. I left out the stepdaughter incident and his feet of clay.

"I'm not sure what has happened since I spoke to him earlier today, but I assume matters took a turn for the worse. And speaking of turns, the entrance to the Compound is somewhere around here." I slowed down near a six-foot-tall black plywood silhouette of a cowboy leaning against a pole and chewing on a straw. That has to rival those little fake wells on the lawn for country corniness. As I was craning my neck to locate the nondescript gate and the Big Dog Chicken Farm sign, who should I see walking along the road? Coop, with a young woman's arm draped around his waist. She had a big chocolate lab on a leash. Oh God, I could tell that it was not Kim, so I prayed that she was not the stepdaughter.

As we pulled alongside, I lowered my window. "Hey, Coop. Out for an evening stroll?"

"Hey, Andrew. Sweet ride." The lab immediately jumped up and put his filthy paws all over the driver's door. I discreetly tried to push him off. "Aw, don't worry, he won't bite. Willie's a big softy, aren't you?" Coop then began mindless sweet talk to the pooch about *who's a good dog, and who's a good boy?* After a few excruciating minutes of nonsense dog blather, he looked up. "Yeah, I had to get away from the house. It was getting a little heated." He turned to his companion. "I believe you already know Sarah Trager. She's been helping me with shaping my image."

Shaping his image? The only shaping she was doing was helping the bulge in his faded jeans.

His partner for this romantic stroll was none other than Patrick McGovern's girlfriend. So, Ms. Selena Ariana Gomez has a name. Sarah Trager. "I do remember you. We met a few years ago at the courthouse. Nice to see you again."

Note: People don't change.

"Why don't you hop in and I'll drive you back up to the house. We can sit down for a bit with my colleague, Naomi Smart. She's been doing some forensics for us."

Sarah chirped in. "Oh, forensics. I just love *CSI Las Vegas* and all that criminal forensic stuff. It's sooo interesting."

Idiot.

Coop just smiled patiently. "I'm not sure all three of us could squeeze into your fancy car."

I had no intention of squeezing all of them in and there was no way that fucking dog was getting anywhere near the interior of my vehicle.

Sarah gave Coop a kiss on the cheek, stepped back and said, "You go ahead. I'll walk back up with Willie. It's such a nice evening."

Coop patted her on the ass and said, "Thanks, doll. I'll meet you up there." Then he walked around, squatted by Naomi's window and gave her a great big ole Nashville smile with his big ole white Newmarket teeth. "Howdy there, little lady. It's a real pleasure to meetcha."

Feet of clay or not, Naomi of course went all gooey. Oh brother.

33

Small World
Monday October 10, Thanksgiving Day

ONCE I GOT Naomi calmed down and settled in at the giant black marble kitchen island in Coop's upper-level party room—a room that rivalled the size of my entire condo—I stepped out onto the huge wrap-around porch. It was a beautiful evening and it had a dark quiet that you just can't get in the city anymore. A few amber lights glowed in a large barn below. Horses were being brushed down and led to stalls. So peaceful.

I decided to ruin it and dialled my new best friend, Royce Hughes, at 7:30 p.m. as promised. He answered on one ring.

"Royce, Andrew Bierce. I got your text."

"Yes, thanks for calling. I can only speak for a few minutes. I'm giving a seminar tomorrow morning to the first-year Criminal Law class at Osgoode Hall Law School. I try to do it every year. It's good to keep in touch with this younger generation."

Like I give a shit. "That's really admirable that you take time to do that. I bet they appreciate it. Would it be better if we spoke tomorrow? I'm actually with clients anyway. I just stepped out to make the call." It took everything I had to resist telling him I was standing on the porch of my famous client—*the* Coop.

"No, no, listen, I appreciate you calling. Just two developments. It looks like they are moving up the meeting date for us and the inquiry lawyers to deal with the scope of evidence. It's going to be with Justice Williams alone and with presenting counsel."

Shiiiit.

"Okay, great. I got a text from them. Sooner the better."

Sure, but it would take days to get ready. And with just a $5,000 retainer. That wouldn't even cover Lindsay's time. I'm an idiot.

"Wonderful. And on a without-prejudice basis I can tell you that I spoke to my client about your client's costs to date. I explained to him that you're senior counsel, that you had already put considerable effort into representing her and that she did not want to be left out of pocket. He understands the situation and is prepared to cover her legal fees in full, provided of course that they are reasonable. "

"I see."

"There is no need to tell me what those fees are right now, but if you're seeking instructions from Ms. Rimini you can assure her on that point, again provided the fees are reasonable."

"I appreciate you letting me know. I'll be meeting with her this week to prepare her evidence, review the twin myths," (might as well let him know that I am at least aware of them), "and the recent case law with her and hope to discuss your approach to resolution. I will let you go. I bet those law students will be on the edge of their seats."

"Thanks. As luck would have it the Hay decision is one of the cases I'm reviewing with students tomorrow morning. I argued it in the Supreme Court."

Holy shit. Why hadn't Lindsay mentioned that? He's going to be all over Williams with the law, explaining how the Glinka matter is *totally different* and how we need to hear *all about* the context of Francesca's history with Glinka.

"Yes, I saw that when I reviewed the reports. Good decision. Congratulations."

"Thanks. Anyway, I look forward to discussing the matter further. I should be in the office preparing tomorrow after the seminar, so feel free to call anytime. Oh, sorry, I'm being paged for our Thanksgiving dinner. Cheers." And the great man was off.

Well, it looked like I was going to have to share Hughes's proposal with Francesca and Lindsay.

I sent Lindsay and Bonnie a message. *Let's meet tomorrow morning at the office at 9 a.m. Get Francesca in. Major developments. And I just learned that Royce Hughes argued Hay in the Supreme Court. Would have been nice to know.*

Lindsay hit back immediately. *I thought you said you were VERY familiar with the case.*

My phone pulsed with a text.

Rick Z: *Andrew. Small world. I've been retained by Justice Singh. Time to chat?*

I hit back. *Welcome aboard. Interesting situation.*

Rick Z: *True. Very unfortunate. Seems straightforward. Marriage con. Had ILA. Best to discuss face to face. Keep things discreet. Coffee soon?*

I hit back. *You know me, nothing's straightforward. Maybe her legal advice was incompetent.* I threw a devil emoji on it. *Tomorrow afternoon works.*

Rick Z: *I will be at the cottage with the family—starting to close up—but I can make time for a call. And you know me. I don't like to make things harder than they need to be. She had ILA from your friend.* He threw a smiley-face emoji with a wink.

I sent a simple *?*

She didn't tell you? It was Dave Goodwin.

Shit.

34

FOMO

Monday October 10, Thanksgiving Day

WHEN I CAME back into the party room Coop was playing his guitar and singing to Naomi. Oh brother.

"Everything okay here?"

"Hey, Andrew, I brought Naomi up to speed on the Kayla situation."

I looked at Naomi and wondered what she thought of his feet of clay. "You okay?"

She shrugged and said, "She's an adult. She makes her own decisions."

Huh? I was a little surprised to hear that from the mother of two soon-to-be-teenaged boys. Was this the effect of Coop's country charm? I'd been gone only ten minutes and he's corrupted her?

"We need to be strategic about this."

"I like the sound of that but what the hell am I going to do? I'm not getting the band back together and giving Brent songwriting credits. Period."

"Naomi, have you talked about the Bow Valley Credit Union?"

"Not in detail."

"I haven't had a bank account there since my first marriage. It was a joint account and my ex took it over as part of the settlement. I was glad cuz it was overdrawn anyway." Coop looked at us with a big goofy smile. Naomi and I went to the same place fast.

"What was the outcome of your divorce?"

"Nothing but a D-I-V-O-R-C-E as Loretta Lynn would say. We just walked away from it after three years, most of it on the road. She was in the band too at that point. Played piano, organ, fiddle, hell she played just about anything. She'd been screwing around. Wouldn't say with who. It hurt. I just told her to hit the bricks. I kept the music portfolio and she took the truck. It was fast. She left for Tofino and Brent, Kim and I carried on with the band. Then Brent slid into the business side of things and it was just me."

"What was Brent's relationship with your ex like?"

"Good. They went back awhile. He had dated her before I came on the scene. He introduced us and brought her into the band. After they split, she and I kinda started up." He leaned forward conspiratorially and whispered, "Tell the truth we'd kinda started up before they split but Brent didn't know. Still doesn't to this day."

Naomi was hanging on his every word. "Your song 'The Road More Taken.' Is it about her?"

Coop put his head in his hands and whispered, "You know my music that well? Wow. It's a real honour. Yeah, I guess it's about her."

"The words are so sad and it has such a haunting guitar solo."

"Yeah, that's Brent. He came up with that. Very moving. Those were early days. Around the time we split."

"Where is she now?"

"Not sure. Still out west probably. Don't care."

I looked at my watch. It was 8:30 p.m. already.

"Okay. We have a lot to think about. And we need to know more about Bow Valley."

"What am I supposed to do in the meantime? Brent's waiting for an answer. I'm supposed to be listening to this." He tossed a device on the island.

"What's that?"

"The music we're supposed to record together." He said it as if it was preposterous. "Bunch of old horseshit rockabilly."

"Okay. Listen, as I said we have a lot to think about and I need to get Naomi back to her family in Toronto. She did me a big favour by coming out here on short notice. We have to hit the road."

Coop decided to turn on the cornpone. "Well I shore do appreciate you doin' that, Naomi. I hope you'll come out here an' visit with me again and not just for business. Do you like fine automobiles? I'd like to show you my collection."

I bet he would. I could see Naomi going all gooey again. "Gosh, that would be wonderful."

I'd heard enough and jumped in. "Maybe you can bring your kids along Naomi. They would enjoy the tour too. There are some beautiful vehicles." I started to steer the star-struck accountant to the door.

As we headed to my car, Willie the dog and Sarah Trager were making their way up the cobblestone path to the house. "Goodnight, Mr. Bierce."

Seeing her gave me an idea. "Naomi, do you mind waiting for me in the car?"

"Sure, I'm good. I'm going to pair my phone so we can listen to some Coop on the way home."

"Great idea." Kill me now if I have to hear "Love Poultice" again.

I walked over to Ms. Trager. "Sarah, got a minute to speak confidentially?"

"Sure. What's up?" She looked eager.

"It's about Patrick and Coop."

"He's doing his best to get something going with him."

"Are you helping him?" I raised my eyebrows. "Or yourself?"

She frowned at me as Willie tugged and pulled and tied himself up in her legs. I thought dogs were supposed to be smart. Not this one. "I know Coop and I looked pretty cozy earlier but I'm here for Pat. He knows what's going on. He's cool with it. This business works in different ways. I'm suggesting to Coop—gently, of course—that they look at working together."

"Pat's not just my client, he's a friend. The reason I'm even here is because of him. So, . . ." I looked around to make sure we were able to speak confidentially, "I want to help when I can. Are you in the loop on the new music direction Coop's looking at?"

She looked at me, puzzled. "He hasn't said anything to me."

"It's confidential. I was just discussing it with him. Can I share something with you? Just you. No one else."

She looked around. "Yes, of course. What's going on?" She was salivating.

"Coop's business manager, Brent, used to be in the band, the original band, when they wrote music together. Brent wrote a lot of the stuff that launched Coop."

"Right. I mean, I wasn't aware that Brent had such a prominent role in the writing. I knew about the band."

"But did you know that Brent's been sitting on a pile of original music?" I let that tidbit sink in. "I'm no music critic but I've heard some of it. It's got a sound that Patrick should be all over. I'm talking Eagles meet Kid Rock."

"Ouch! Willie!" The dog had bolted so hard he nearly pulled her arm out of the socket. "What are you saying?"

"You've heard the expression, 'Go to where the puck is going to be'?"

From the look on her face I could tell she was not following me, let alone the puck. "If I were Patrick I would try to get to Brent before Coop does. They're in preliminary talks now but . . . once it's gone, it's gone."

"I had no idea. Coop's said nothing like that to me. When can I share this with Patrick?"

"It's potentially huge so everyone is being very tight-lipped. Like, three people know. Can you sit on it for a couple of days? There are a few moving pieces. And please do not let Coop know that I told you. He would kill me."

The dog proceeded to wrap his leash around her legs again. "My lips are sealed."

I'm betting they aren't. "I'll keep you posted. Have a nice evening. That's a great dog by the way."

When I slid into the car Naomi was singing along to "The Road More Taken." She turned it down and gave me a look. "What was that all about?"

"One of the most powerful forces known to mankind, my dear: FOMO—Fear of Missing Out."

"You have that look on your face. I've seen it before."

"What look?"

"The look when you are about to pick someone's pocket and expect them to thank you for it."

"I have no idea what you're talking about." As we pulled out of Coop's drive and headed back to Toronto I asked Naomi, "Can we listen to some of that music Brent is pushing on Coop?"

"Sure. Give me a second to pair it."

Poor Brent's dream cache of future hits didn't even make it to the 401 before I was pleading with Naomi to put on "Love Poultice." When that final shot rang out at the end of the song, Naomi was crying but I envied the horse.

35

A Bone to Pick
Tuesday October 11

AS LATE AS the previous night was and as shitty as my sleep had been, I woke up early and headed out for a short run to burn off what had been a rather large nightcap when I got home. Big mistake, because honestly, I was cooked after a couple of Ks. I felt so out of shape I had to stop a half-dozen times as I headed down Bathurst to the lake. I was dying, gasping for air and sweating like a hog. A young woman stopped, bent over and asked me, in the most humiliating tone of voice, "Sir, are you okay? Should I call someone? Do you have a caregiver?"

I was so out of breath, all I could do was wave my hands, shake my head and grunt, "No. I'm fine. Fuck off."

Usually a run clears my head but all I could think about was Sean. He looked like shit yesterday. Was he actually going to die? Leave me with this shitstorm? Why does this always happen when I try to help Sean? Defrocked? His funeral arrangements? He was desperate to be buried as a priest and that prospect was looking very unlikely. Should I be looking at alternatives? Where? Should I prepare him for the worst? That little prick Shannon. Was he going to get away with this bullshit? He'd cleared the way for McKay in Parkdale–High Park and now Sean was being . . . *we* were being thrown under the bus. My mind was spinning. I didn't want to let Sean down. I could not.

When I reached Fort York, a thought stopped me dead in my tracks. It suddenly occurred to me, does Sean even have a will? Powers of attorney? Was I going to get stuck looking after his affairs? Does he even have property? He's a priest for Christsakes. A wave of pins and needles crawled over my shoulders as acid reflux bit into my jaw and chest. Exhausted, I gave up and half walked, half jogged back to my condo for a quick shower, some pain relievers and a few gulps of Gaviscon. And, to be totally honest, some hair of the dog.

Once downtown, I grabbed two tall lattes from Daphne at Starbucks and marched up to the office. There were a couple of very serious matters that needed immediate attention: the smell of the office and the so-called *dog* file.

As I entered my otherwise beautiful reception area I gave it a few good sniffs. It still smelled. Fucking Hopeless Helen and her toxic tea. I should sue her. Bonnie was setting out some new magazines and looked up at me, clearly puzzled by my loud sniffing and huffing.

"Bonnie, it stinks in here. What's the landlord doing about the smell and the carpets? And I mean today."

"Good morning to you too."

"Sorry, but it was a very late night and I'm not in the mood. I didn't get back from The Compound until after midnight and by the time I dropped Naomi at her place in Moore Park I was cooked. I tried to go for a run this morning but I just couldn't get going, I had no wind . . . fucking COVID."

"You are looking, shall we say, even more *prosperous* than when we met at the Vatican." She thought her smile would soften the blow.

I had noticed that my court pants were a little tight around the waist and when I tried on my expensive new court shirt, the sixteen-inch neck was also quite snug. I would need to get back into some kind of workout routine. But with everything piling up, now was not the time.

I was too tired to respond so I decided to ignore her comment about my weight and focus on the real problems at hand. "I want the smell in here addressed immediately. Get someone up here to deal with it. Today. And now, if you will excuse me, I need to have a very difficult discussion with Ms. Braun."

Bonnie knew that when I said "difficult discussion" it was bad. "Whoa, whoa, whoa, wait. Discussion about what? This is the first time you've ever had an associate. She's good. Don't blow this because you're tired, hungover and feeling tubby . . . I mean, out of shape. I still haven't figured out her office or furniture."

Well, look at Bonnie protecting her new best friend. And who said I was hungover? And tubby? Really?

"I'm not going to blow anything but I'm also not going to tolerate a junior associate judging the quality of files that are assigned to her. I asked her to look after Marrs and all I got was a bullshit text message . . ."

I headed for the boardroom with Bonnie on my heels.

"Andrew, . . . Andrew, . . ."

When I walked in Lindsay, as usual, had her nose in her laptop.

I decided to just say it. "Lindsay, I have a bone to pick with you. We have a lot of work ahead of us between the inquiry and all these new files . . . not to mention my brother being sick . . ."

"Good morning to you too. And let's not forget that you're supposedly running in a provincial election." She looked back at her laptop.

This was not a good time to be smart with me.

"I gave you a file to work on, the Marrs matter. The client is a referral from someone at the AGO. I'm in the . . ."

"Curators' Circle. I know. You've mentioned that before . . . several times." She did not even look up this time.

Oh, she was really poking the bear.

"On Marrs we have a solid ten grand in trust and in my opinion it's a quality file."

"I've read the file and . . ."

"Don't interrupt me."

"Andrew, . . ." Bonnie was getting worried.

"You say you read the file and yet last night when I was in a very important meeting with a very important client, what do I read on my phone?"

"Andrew, . . ." Bonnie actually pulled on my arm.

"I read a message in which you had the gall to characterize the Marrs matter as a *dog file . . . a dog file . . .*" I had not used that expression in years *because all my files were quality files.*

"Andrew, . . ." Bonnie would not let go. She knew I was getting a head of steam.

"You're a junior lawyer, out less than three years. You do not get to assess the quality of a file I assign to you. You can assume it's a good file, do the research required, meet with the client, prepare a memo and then meet with me. You do not tell me what is a *dog file* and what is not. There is no such thing as a *dog file* in this office. Am I clear?" My voice was rising with each declaration. And so was my headache.

She looked at me, stunned. She looked at Bonnie. She looked back at me. I looked at Bonnie. Bonnie looked at Lindsay. No one spoke.

I started to feel like maybe I had gone too far and hoped I was not about to witness a flood of tears just because I had spoken so firmly. I have no time for snowflakes.

Lindsay calmly closed her laptop, pursed her lips and folded her hands on the boardroom table. "Have you read the Marrs file?"

"Of course. I'm the one who attended and spoke quite passionately to have the matter adjourned." I recalled my speech to the judge that morning of the parking garage incident and how Justice Linton had been so moved by my words. One of my best adjournments.

"I wish I had been there to hear your submissions. Did you read Justice Linton's endorsement for the adjournment?"

I had not. I assumed it was a simple adjournment with costs. What was there to read?

"Have you ever met with the client?" Lindsay was surprisingly calm.

"No, as a matter of fact, I was expecting to do that today after being briefed by you."

"Do you know what the file is about?"

What a ridiculous question. "Of course I do. We are representing Ms. Marrs in a hotly contested dispute concerning custody of her twins."

Lindsay looked at Bonnie. Bonnie looked at me. I looked at Bonnie and then back at Lindsay. Something was off.

Lindsay screwed up her face in feigned puzzlement. "You're right. It is a hotly contested custody battle over twins . . . twin *dogs*."

Bonnie added softly, almost sadly, "Andrew, the client and her husband have no children, they're fighting over their two French Bulldogs."

Lindsay opened her laptop and went back to work, and without even looking up said, "*Ergo*, a dog file."

Shit.

My exhausted and hungover mind was suddenly swept back to a foggy recollection of my appearance before Justice Linton a few weeks ago. What nonsense had I spewed to the judge when seeking that adjournment? Snippets of my words, and those of Justice Linton, now rained down on me as clearly as if I had said them an hour ago.

***Idiot Lawyer (not having read file):** Your Honour, we are faced with a potentially tragic set of circumstances in this matter. Sadly, we all know that COVID has divided families in strange ways and this matter is no exception. But here we have a situation in which my client's response to the isolation caused by COVID, when forced to work from home, brought a semblance of peace, love and even sanity to her life. These twins have become the centre of her universe. They are her emotional support and she, theirs. The care, the treatment, the love shown for them by my client cannot go unrecognized by this court. Certainly, her husband cared for them from time to time when not at work, took them for medical appointments and prepared meals for them, but his love and affection for them is not on a scale comparable to my client's.*

***Justice Linton (who, having read the file, is clearly puzzled):** Mr. Bierce, I see your obvious passion for your client's position—frankly I'm a little surprised at the strength of your feelings given these unusual circumstances—but are you suggesting that the husband's love for Abby and Penny is somehow less than? . . ."*

***Idiot Lawyer (interrupting judge):** Your Honour, that is precisely what I am saying! And that is why an adjournment is necessary for a full answer by my client. I don't want to get into the merits, but I understand that the twins were endangered during recent travel with my friend's client. The court needs to err on the side of caution. It's an appropriate case to apply the classic but standard best-interest test in favour of Abby and Penny. The status quo should be maintained.*

(How many times I had uttered those words over the years, I know not.)

> *Lollipop Guild Lawyer (jumping out of chair): Your Honour! There is no evidence before you about the travel incident and I can assure this court that my client followed all airline travel protocols to ensure Abby and Penny's safety. There was a mix-up but they were all reunited within twenty-four hours.*
>
> *Idiot Lawyer (staring directly at Judge, shaking his uninformed head and pleading): Twenty-four hours, Your Honour? Twenty-four hours? It must have felt like a lifetime for Abby and Penny . . . It certainly was for my distraught client.*
>
> *Judge Linton (apparently an animal lover): Frankly, I am very moved by Mr. Bierce's submissions. I'm ordering that the status quo remain in place for ninety days. I will leave it to counsel to work out some visits with Abby and Penny in the interim. My full endorsement will follow by email. Costs will follow to Mr. Bierce's client.*
>
> *Blissfully Unaware Idiot Lawyer: Thank you, Your Honour.*

Oh. My. God. I thought Abby and Penny were children, not fucking dogs. No wonder Linton was shocked by my submissions. What had his endorsement said?

Lindsay and Bonnie were now staring at me, waiting for some kind of acknowledgement of my stupidity and, I assumed, an apology.

"Okay, look, I've been under a lot of pressure with my brother. I'm sorry . . . the office smells, . . ." I'm not sure why I added that. "I'm sorry. Really. Let me read Linton's endorsement and then let's sit down and discuss it." In fact, I felt like putting my head down and just having a deep sleep.

Lindsay slid a hard copy of the decision across the table. "Ms. Marrs can see us in an hour so you will get a chance to meet her . . . and maybe the *twins*." Sarcasm dripped from the word twins.

"What? Dogs in this office? In an hour? No, no, no. I don't think so. I'm not comfortable with that. We have enough problems with smells around here."

Bonnie tilted her head towards me and half whispered to Lindsay, "Not an animal person."

"Too late, anyway she says she needs to meet you at the AGO, someplace called the Norma Ridley Lounge."

"Oh great." I picked up the endorsement and headed to my office, shut the door, sat in the Egg and began to read.

Endorsement July 22, 2022
Marrs, John v. Marrs, Beatrix File # F - 12345-00
Counsel for Applicant: Lollipop Guild
Counsel for Respondent: Bierce A., Q.C.
This matter comes before me today on an urgent interim basis at the instance of the Applicant, Mr. Marrs. The matter was served properly in accordance with the Rules, notwithstanding Ms. Marrs's alleged attempts to evade service.

Oh-oh. Service evader? A clear sign of trouble ahead.

However, the Respondent has just retained new counsel, Mr. Bierce, Q.C. He seeks an adjournment and preservation of the status quo. Mr. Bierce is the Respondent's third lawyer of record . . .

I closed my eyes and let out a deep sigh. I had no idea she'd had two previous lawyers. That's a sure-fire sign of a problem client.

This is the Respondent's third request for an adjournment.

Oh God, problem client? No, definitely a psycho. What have I got myself into?

The Applicant and Respondent separated approximately three months ago. There is some dispute as to the actual date as Ms. Marrs insists the marriage is invalid and should be annulled.

Annulment? The refuge of a heartbroken dimwit in denial.

That issue I assume will be resolved later as a part of the larger question of equalization of their property.

What concerns the parties and the court today is the issue of their pet dogs, Abby and Penny. They are French Bulldogs that were adopted during COVID.

Bulldogs? Possibly the ugliest pets available. If they're not snorting, they're farting. A cruel joke by dog breeders.

Who did what for these dogs during the parties' cohabitation is in dispute and is not for me to determine as a part of terms of an adjournment.

What is not in dispute today is that on the day the Respondent says the separation occurred, she put both dogs into her vehicle and fled. Despite numerous requests the Applicant has not seen the dogs since that time. The Respondent wife has refused any contact, notwithstanding that it is not contested that she gave both dogs to the Applicant as a forty-fifth birthday present. According to Mr. Marrs's material, title to the dogs is in his name, as are the animal licenses and a bill of sale from Pooch Heaven Kennels Inc. These documents are annexed as Exhibits A, B and C to Mr. Marrs's affidavit. He is also the owner of a policy of pet health insurance with Fetch, at a cost of $109.00 per month. (See Exhibit D.)

He remains in the matrimonial home (see Exhibit E) which is the only home Abby and Penny have ever known. He seeks the return of the dogs and alleges great personal distress. The dogs both suffer from Degenerative Myelopathy and Brachycephalic Obstructive Airway Syndrome (BOAS) . . .

Barf.

. . . which he had been attending to by administering medication. (See Exhibit F.) The court has no assurance from Ms. Marrs that the dogs are receiving their medication.

Mr. Marrs seeks damages for psychological harm caused by the Respondent's actions. This is an issue for the trial judge to determine.

I will take a moment to consider the actions of the Respondent, Ms. Marrs, on the day in question back in April. These facts, to date, are not contested.

She was proceeding in an easterly direction on Bloor Street West between Avenue Road and Bay Street in the City of Toronto in her vehicle, a forest green Range Rover, licence DOG LVR, at approximately 2:30 p.m. It was a sunny, warm spring afternoon and people were out enjoying the good weather. As she passed the Louis Vuitton store situated on the north side of Bloor Street, she observed what she was certain were Abby and Penny. They apparently were clad in very recognizable red velvet dog jackets.

The dogs were exiting the Vuitton store in the company of a woman Ms. Marrs did not recognize. (Nothing turns on it but this woman is Mr. Marrs's new partner. She had lawful possession of the dogs.) The Respondent did an immediate U-turn (which I note is prohibited by clearly posted signage at that point on Bloor) and slowly drove in a westerly direction alongside the woman and the dogs. Immediately before Avenue Road, Ms. Marrs mounted the sidewalk on the north side of Bloor with her vehicle, exited it and confronted the woman. The dogs, recognizing her, leapt into her arms. Notwithstanding the shock and protests of the woman, Ms. Marrs then took the dogs from her forcibly, placed them in her vehicle and departed at a high rate of speed, nearly running over a group of school children from a nearby daycare.

In his material, Mr. Marrs alleges that there are numerous video clips of this quite foulmouthed confrontation posted on social media. There is a possibility the Respondent may be charged with a number of offences, traffic and otherwise. I offer no comment as that is for others to determine in the criminal process, should it proceed.

Mr. Marrs alleges that the Respondent refuses to disclose the dogs' whereabouts or even her own location. He reports that he has heard through mutual friends that the two dogs were returned to the Pooch Heaven kennel from which they were purchased. He has also been told variously that one dog, Penny, is very ill and then later that the dog had died. These rumours—which I note are hearsay—have understandably caused him great distress.

Ms. Marrs needs an opportunity to respond to these serious allegations.

I admit I was prepared to order the dogs returned immediately, until hearing Mr. Bierce's powerful submissions and his comparison of these two dogs to children, urging me to do not only what is best for the adults involved, but also to apply the classic best-interest test reserved for parenting issues to these animals. I know this is only an interim motion, but counsel's argument has persuaded me to at least consider at this point that these two dogs are sentient beings and we must act in their best interest.

I am granting the Respondent's request for an adjournment. Her responding materials must be filed in accordance with the Rules. I urge the parties to arrange interim without-prejudice visits, supervised if necessary. This matter should move forward expeditiously. It is in the interests of all concerned, including Abby and Penny.

Signed, Justice H. Linton

French bulldogs? Sentient beings? Sentient is from the Latin *sentire*, to feel.

I feel I have been an idiot.

36

AGO
Tuesday October 11

LINDSAY AND I made our way by Uber over to the art gallery to meet with Ms. Marrs. On the way I was appalled to learn that notwithstanding growing up in Toronto the lovely Ms. Braun had never been to the AGO. I assume this had something to do with living in *north* Toronto as opposed to the actual city, south of St. Clair Avenue.

My phone pulsed with a text from Daria. *Sean needs to meet with you. Soon. He's not doing well.*

Okay. I'll pop over later this afternoon.

"Everything okay?" I assume Lindsay heard my deep sigh.

"Yeah, my brother. He's not doing so good."

"I'm sorry. I hope I get to meet him."

I didn't know what to say. Meet him? Why?

The ride was also a good opportunity to lay out how we would complete the handoff of Ms. Marrs as a client. I was not accustomed to passing a client to an associate, so a plan was needed. Clients have come to me *for me*, not someone else. They are prepared to pay a thousand dollars an hour for personal carpet-bombing, not battlefield re-enactments. They want the real deal.

"Now, here is how we will handle this. As we get settled in at our meeting, I'm going to introduce you, lay out your credentials and ask you to provide an overview of the situation. She will then see that you have a firm grasp of the matter and relax, especially when I mention that your hourly rate is lower than mine."

"What is my hourly rate?"

Right, we had not discussed this or her office or her furniture for that matter. I prayed Bonnie was following up.

"I'm thinking six hundred. On Marrs's salary, which I'm guessing is less than a hundred thousand, that will still be dear for her."

Lindsay let out a low whistle. "Six hundred. With Williams I was billed at four hundred and fifty."

Whatever. You are in a different world now.

"Now, at some point she's going to ask if I will remain involved. I will assure her that you and I will review the matter daily. You jump in and say that no steps are taken without my authorization and all court appearances of any significance are handled by me. That may not be true but that's what she will want to hear. Good?"

"Good." There was a brief pause and then a loaded comment. "I understand from Bonnie that you are not an *animal person*?" She said it with the dreaded female uptalk tone that converts a statement into a question.

As we exited the Uber on Dundas West at the front doors of the AGO, I explained my high-level view on animals and humans. "Lindsay, people may be divided into two general groups: those who place themselves in the position of animals, and those who identify themselves with human beings. Based on my experience and observations, those who identify themselves with animals—and here I mean particularly those who are almost professional lovers of dogs—are capable of greater cruelty to human beings than those who do not identify themselves readily with animals."

She shook her head in feigned shock. "Wow, how profound. Should I write that down?" There was no uptalk now and her comment was dripping with sarcasm.

"No need. Hemingway already did." Now she just looked puzzled. Surely she has read Hemingway's *Death in the Afternoon*. I must get her a copy.

The Norma Ridley Members' Lounge was a little busier than I recall it ever being prior to COVID. There were usually never more than a half-dozen members in it (mostly retired cotton tops enjoying their pensions) but now that food service was back I guess there was pent up demand for cheese platters. It was packed with all kinds of people, old and young. I was surprised to see the ample black leather couches full and every table occupied but one.

Fortunately, Ms. Marrs had reserved a cozy corner spot for us by the window and old fireplace mantel. I had never met her face to face so, as we entered, I was glad she stood to greet us.

Sort of.

Now, of course, I never met the famous Mexican artist Frida Kahlo, who died in 1954. But I'm very familiar with her work. Over a decade ago, actually just after I became a member of the Curators' Circle, the AGO had an exhibition of her art alongside that of her partner, the rotund beast, Diego Rivera. And let me just say that when half of an artist's entire body of work is self-portraits, it says something about them. So, bottom line, not a fan. To me, Frida and Diego were one of those artsy couples whose otherwise obnoxious behaviour—which included fighting, extramarital affairs, abortions, marriage, divorce and remarriage, not to mention her fatal drug overdose—is ignored by aesthetes because, well, it's art after all. But I digress.

What is important, though, is that, if Frida Kahlo had had an older, taller, uglier sister, then she now stood before me, unibrow and all. (I confess upon seeing her I had a brief flashback to my client, the awful Drago Markovic, and his fierce eyes smouldering below a solid thick hairy mantel.)

She reached to shake my hand. "Mr. Bierce, I'm so glad to meet you at last. You have been a godsend."

I kept my eyes fixed firmly on hers so they would dart to neither her furry brow nor her now visible wispy moustache. "The pleasure is all mine. I would like you to meet my associate, Lindsay Braun."

She barely acknowledged Lindsay with a nod and simple, "Hello." Not even a handshake. Odd.

"Mr. Bierce, I know you're very busy. Shall we get down to business?"

"That would be wonderful. Things have become quite urgent with a pending motion. I want Ms. Braun to walk you through . . ."

Ms. Marrs cut me off. "But before we do anything I want you to meet some of the people who have gathered here today."

Huh?

She turned to the busy lounge that was now quieting to her large outstretched arms. "Everyone, can I have your attention? Quiet please. Thank you, and thank you for coming. I want to introduce Mr. Andrew Bierce, K.C." Before she could finish the introduction everyone in the room stood and began to applaud.

What the F.

I looked at Lindsay. She simply shrugged, as puzzled as I was.

Surely this wasn't because of my work with the Curators' Circle.

Ms. Marrs waved over a tiny young Asian woman in a black and white flannel shirt, black jeans ripped at the knees and Doc Martens boots with bright red laces. On her head sat the ubiquitous wool toque that signalled membership in the exhausting Worldwide Society of Hipsters. (Will this fad never die the death it deserved so long ago?) I smiled as I assumed she was going to take my order for a coffee.

"Mr. Bierce, I would like you to meet one of your colleagues. This is April Chu. I assume you've heard of her and her law practice devoted exclusively to animal law."

I reached to shake her hand and tried to introduce her to Lindsay, but before I could so much as say *latte please* Ms. Marrs had another hand for me to shake.

"This is Claire Kinsella. She's just finished organizing the very successful Charity Dog Walk sponsored by MyPetsTheBestCo!" The young woman, an unfortunate-looking shrinking violet with a devastated complexion, was dressed in baggy beige overalls covered in *I Heart Dog* buttons and something about *Save the Pigs*. From the look on her face, you would think she was meeting Brad Pitt. She kept repeating nervously what a pleasure it was to say hello, thanking me and then backing away in awe. Poor thing.

Another hand reached out. "This is Andrew Kuznick, President of Justice for Animals." Here stood an older man, dressed in a very dated brown double-breasted suit, an ancient yellowing white shirt and a purple paisley ascot. His shoulders carried a considerable dusting of what was either soap flakes or dandruff. He wore a stained white mask that said, "Home is where dog hair sticks to everything but the dog." He did not appear to be the least bit in awe of me. I leaned in to try to make out what he was mumbling into his mask. It came out grumpily, "We have a lot to talk about." I hoped not.

Then another hand. "This is Becky Brooker. She is a lawyer who specializes in defending claims against owners of so called 'dangerous dogs.'" Everyone within earshot laughed at that notion, as if such a thing was pure fantasy. Of course, they don't bite, all dogs go to heaven.

Another hand. "This is Jonah Tripe. He ran for mayor in the last election along with Hercules, a dog he *rescued* from Russia." She said rescue as if he had crawled under live gunfire with the mutt. How heroic. I'm sure someone will get a government grant to make a documentary about your perilous journey.

"Pleasure to meet you."

"Mayor Tripe" was clearly primed to talk. "We have got to get salt off our streets. It's killing our pets. This past winter Hercules's feet were burned by the salt! Salt has to go!" I wished I was wearing a mask as he sprayed that plank of his platform across my face. "And we've got to expand public transit hours so it's safer for pets." I took a step back before he launched another volley of spittle. Someone pulled him aside as he started to expound excitedly about making Toronto the capital of the world for pet-friendly patios. What a kook.

I don't know why but I smiled, thinking, *Why not just change the name of the city to Animal Farm while we're at it?* Honestly, how do these people survive?

Then another hand appeared. "This is Alix Roster, the head of the HPDOCFOLS—High Park Dog Owners' Coalition for Off-Leash Spaces. She has been working tirelessly to expand dog access to off-leash spaces in city parks but especially in High Park."

A bright pink pamphlet—"PARKS ARE FOR PETS!"—was thrust at me. A sixtyish grey-haired woman scowled at me through those weird red plastic-rimmed glasses older women wear to serious "No Oprah" book clubs. This was not a happy woman, and I assumed it was in part because she may be starving. She could not have weighed more than eighty pounds. No wonder she wanted more off-leash space, she couldn't have the strength to restrain more than a cat on a leash. "It's a pleasure to meet you, Ms. Roster."

"Do you know what the fine is for having a dog off leash?"

"I . . ."

"It's three hundred dollars plus a sixty-dollar victim surcharge and five-dollar admin fee! That's three hundred and sixty-five dollars! For a dog off leash!"

"I . . ."

"Are you prepared to support the NDP private members' bill to repeal the DOLA?"

Dola. Dola. Hmmm. I thought doulas had something to do with midwives and babies.

"I . . ."

Lindsay finally jumped in. "The Dog Owners' Liability Act is . . ."

Ms. Red Specs, blinking wildly, was not here for any two-way conversations and began to rant about commercial dog-walker licensing and the two-million-dollar insurance policy they must carry.

Thank God Ms. Shrinking Violet took her by the arm and began to compare notes about the harsh rules of procedure at the Dangerous Dog Review Tribunal, the upcoming protest to save pigs from a slaughterhouse and about how our *fascist* city state monitors pets.

What a collection of nutbars.

Another hand. "Hello again, Mr. Bierce."

Well, well, well. It was none other than Ms. Art School, the icy but pretty receptionist from Williams's firm. She reached over for Lindsay's hand and pulled her into a deep embrace. I could tell they had something in common, unfortunately it was that creep Williams's paws.

She turned back to me. "I'm glad I have an opportunity to thank you. When I heard from Ms. Marrs that you would be here today I just had to say . . . well, thank you."

"For?"

"For the wake-up call during those two encounters we had in reception at Randall Williams's firm. Your comments about art, about Kim Dorland and Dean Drever, about me being there, wasting my talents. It made me realize that I had to get busy doing what I love. I'm working here at the AGO now. So, thank you."

I didn't know what to say but hoped Lindsay was catching this praise for my sage advice.

"Are you a part of this . . . this, . . ." I drew a small circle with my finger, ". . . group as well?" I prayed she was not.

She raised her perfectly groomed eyebrows (two, regular issue), pursed her soft pink lips and shook her head slowly as if to say, *Not likely*. "No, I just wanted to say hello and good luck with your crusade. And by the way, my name is Heidi. Let's stay in touch." And with that she stepped aside to commiserate with Lindsay about Williams's appointment to the bench.

My heart gave a little flutter, but crusade? What crusade?

Another hand reached out, but not to shake mine, as it was holding a phone to record my every word. It was attached to a young man with a well-groomed lumberjack beard (a clear contradiction in terms).

"Mr. Bierce, I'm with *Now* magazine. I've been trying to reach you through your office. I'm doing a story about your animal rights case. Do you have any comments? Would you be willing to sit for an interview? I assume this will form a key part of your campaign for election in Parkdale."

"First, it is not *my* case. It is my *client's* case and I have no comment at this point. This is a private matter."

He looked around the room and gestured with his phone. "Private matter? You have mobilized the animal rights community with your passionate plea for all animals to be treated as sentient beings."

All animals to be treated as sentient beings? He'd obviously never seen me at a ribfest. "Perhaps we can speak another time. I have to meet with my client right now." I turned to Lindsay and whispered, "What the hell is going on?"

"Apparently Judge Linton's endorsement has gone viral on Twitter . . . They've all seen it. You've become a sort of pet folk hero . . . by accident, of course." She seemed very amused by the whole idea.

I was finally able to steer Ms. Marrs to the table. "Ms. Marrs, we need to talk."

"Yes, yes, let's. But I need to order some lunch. I've become a little peckish in all the excitement. Will you have something? Lunch? The steak tartar is really quite good. Tea? Coffee?" She still had not even looked at Lindsay.

"No, I'm fine. I would like to review your situation and consider how we might move forward."

Ignoring me, she motioned for a waiter with a hand and her eyebrow aloft.

I added, "In a cost-effective way. I need you to be aware of the potential costs of this litigation. There is a motion pending and we need to take it seriously. I can get things adjourned only once and I've already done that. Your husband seems quite determined. Your initial ten-thousand-dollar retainer is almost gone," there had been my one adjournment and Lindsay's review, after all, "and we need to discuss a further retainer before we proceed with next steps."

The waiter, a young person of indeterminate gender, arrived at our table. He/she clearly knew Ms. Marrs and did not so much as take a note as she reeled off her lunch order without even looking at a menu.

"I'll have the Pickles and Such to start, along with the sourdough bread and butter—but make sure it's fresh. The last time the bread was dried out and felt like it had been cut hours previous. Plus four pats of butter, unsalted, then I'll have the *lapin à la crème* appetizer—warm, not too hot—and for a main the braised Ontario beef—tell the chef who it's for. He knows how I like it. For dessert bring the charcuterie platter with cheese. I'll have a glass of white wine—Chardonnay—as well. Did you get that? Do I need to have you repeat it to me like I should have had you do the last time?"

"No, Ms. Marrs, that won't be necessary. I've got it."

"Good. Let's hope so. And oh, you might as well bring the bottle of wine and one extra glass."

Finally she turned to me. "Since COVID it has been impossible to hire competent staff. It's like no one wants to work. They take everything for granted. So entitled this generation. Always complaining about being 'anxious.' We pay them handsomely too."

"Ms. Marrs, . . ."

"Please call me Beatrix."

"Beatrix, your husband has hired a lawyer, Mr. Fernstein. I know him very well and have crossed swords with him before. I don't think it would be unfair if I said that he has little common sense and will pursue every avenue at great expense. Hence this upcoming motion. I shudder to think what your husband has spent on this to date. He has prepared and filed extensive materials, there have been multiple adjournments already and . . ."

Lindsay jumped in. "We need to get your comments on all of the attachments to his recent affidavit . . ."

She turned to Lindsay, coldly, bent her eyebrow into a frown. "I would prefer if you did not interrupt Mr. Bierce."

Oh-oh.

I jumped in. "I want to be clear, Ms. Braun and I will be working together on this matter. She is fully briefed and I need her to be involved, especially if we are to keep your costs reasonable. As I mentioned your retainer . . ."

"Ohhh, Mr. Bierce, nooo. Noooo. I hired *you* to look after this matter. You have been excellent to date, you understand how important it is to see animals as living beings, beings endowed with sensitivity, with their own interests and ultimately as beings with dignity."

Dignity? I guess those qualities didn't apply to the rabbit, the cow and whatever other animal sacrificed itself for her charcuterie board.

"I will do whatever I have to for the protection of Abby and Penny." Tears began to flow. "They are my everything and money is no object. I need you *and you alone* to handle the matter."

I looked at Lindsay. I could read her thoughts as she smiled back at me. *So money is no object? How do you feel about the so-called dog file now, Mr. Not an Animal Person, K.C.?*

"Ms. Marrs, Beatrix, I know this can be very difficult. Abby and Penny are our primary concern but when I say the costs can be very high . . ."

"How much do you need, Mr. Bierce?" She dabbed her eyes with the linen napkin that had arrived with her Pickles and Such.

"Well, Mr. Fernstein has a penchant for making things difficult. I think you should anticipate spending as much as a hundred thousand dollars on this matter." Lindsay's delicately shaped eyebrows (two, also regulation issue) perked up. Was this an attempt at a fuck-off fee?

Ms. Marrs, who was clearly not familiar with the term bitesize, put an entire large gherkin in her mouth, and through noisy crunches said, "That will not be an issue. I will transfer the funds in the morning." And without missing a beat—or a bite—she chewed out, "Are you sure you won't have something?"

"Well, perhaps a glass of wine." After all, I still had a hangover and a little hair of the dog wouldn't hurt. "For a toast to Abby and Penny's good health. And may I ask, where are Abby and Penny now?"

She leaned into me, held a large breadstick to her chapped lips and hairy chin and whispered, "Downstairs. In my workspace. Safe and sound." She seemed absolutely thrilled. You would think she had Anne Frank down there.

After our session with Ms. Marrs—during which Lindsay might as well have been invisible—we Ubered back to the office in silence until my phone pulsed with a text message. It was Naomi.

Got a minute?

What's up? More on The Coop's situation?

No, It's about the election. Your fundraising.

Oh God, the election. The pointless election. The thought of being outmanoeuvred by that little prick Shannon put my stomach in a knot. I needed to have a heart to heart with Sean about the situation and the dreaded *alternatives.*

I do not intend to spend any time or money fundraising.

Who's looking after it?

Some guy Dikoobe hired.

It's Dikembe. Have you seen your numbers?

Nope

Do you know how much you are entitled to spend?

Nope

For Parkdale–High Park your estimated FEC is about 85,000.

FEC?

Final Elector Count, number of voters

And why do I care?

It drives your spending limit.

Spending limit? Why would I spend a dime now? I bite. How much can I spend? LOL

About $120,000

Right now I intend to spend $0—max. Why would I spend a nickel? The church is screwing Sean over, McKay doesn't need us. Sean's likely being defrocked as we speak.

So you haven't seen your numbers?

Nope

Do you want to know how much you have raised so far?

Don't care.

$157,235—in one day.

What the F?

I'm not looking for extra work but how would you feel if I took over the CFO/campaign manager roles for your campaign?

You're hired.

I looked out the window, shook my head and gave what must have been a huge sigh because Lindsay put her hand on my leg and said, "Your brother?"

"Yeah, my brother."

37

A Way Out?

Thursday October 13

I WAS TRYING to find a good time to break it to Lindsay that His Majesty Royce Hughes, K.C., had proposed a possible way out, a way that would spare Francesca humiliation, would allow Glinka to retire with an apology for the *misunderstanding* and that would get us paid handsomely. Unfortunately, it would also allow that creep Randall Williams to wrap up the inquiry, if not highly praised as a hero for his deft mediation skills in reaching a settlement, at least with an unscathed reputation. Lindsay would not be happy. If we took the deal, there would be no inquiry and that was the sole reason she had agreed to come and work with me. Would she quit? Maybe. And don't misunderstand this, I was feeling pissed too because I was looking forward to torturing him as much as she was. Maybe more.

At around 5 p.m. I found her in the boardroom hovering over her laptop. "Hey, got a minute to throw around some ideas?"

She looked up with a smile. "Sure, especially if it's about sentient beings." Her beautiful eyes lit up. "I've been doing a lot of research about the progress of this sentient animal movement worldwide. Did you know that in Canberra, Australia, you can be fined $2,500 US if you don't walk your dog every twenty-four hours? Quebec, British Columbia, France, New Zealand, Brussels, Australia have all got laws recognizing . . ." She was gushing with love, a love of the law. Wow.

"Lindsay, thanks. That sounds great but we need to discuss Francesca and the inquiry. There may be a way out."

"What do you mean a *way out*?" The enthusiasm drained from her face.

I walked her through what Royce had suggested, the upsides and the downside. When I wrapped up I couldn't tell if she was angry or sad, or if she even understood the practicality of the settlement. She just sat there looking at me.

Thankfully Bonnie knocked and stuck her head in the boardroom. "Andrew, a couple of things: I have an update from the landlord on the smell situation, a reminder that you have invitations to several all-candidates meetings and I printed a copy of an online article from the *Toronto Star*. You should see it. We also received a $100,000 deposit from Beatrix Marrs. I put it in trust."

"Not a good time, Bonnie. Give us a minute." The last thing on my mind was an all-candidates meeting or a news article. The smell issue, however, that needed addressing. But not now. "Whoa, whoa. Wait. Did you say we got $100,000 from Marrs?"

"Yes. Money order."

"Wow. I did not see that coming. I wonder where she got the money. I can't wait to see her financial statement."

"We have it. It's in the file. She really hasn't got much. No savings to speak of." Lindsay was clearly pissed.

And Bonnie could see it. She looked at Lindsay. "What's up?"

I explained the situation again, step by step. Still nothing from Lindsay although her tongue did a few quick flicks to the spot of the long-gone cold sore.

Bonnie simply said, "Wow, Royce Hughes is something else."

I wasn't sure what she meant by that. Was it a compliment? Was the deal too good for Glinka? Was he getting let off the hook too easily? Was I missing something? Was everyone missing the point that we were going to get paid very well on behalf of a client who had no money?

Lindsay sat back in her chair and finally spoke. She was equal parts pissed, disgusted and disillusioned. "I thought something like this might happen. This is how it works. I suppose Francesca is supposed to sign an

NDA? Everyone signs NDAs and we all go on with our lives as if nothing happened? Except Francesca, of course."

"Not *quite*, let's not forget . . ." I thought she needed to be reminded that we were essentially working for free on Francesca's case and our client faced a potential privacy buzzsaw at a hearing.

"Oh no, that is *quite* what happens. I know. I know where Francesca is headed. I've been there. What happened to *tortura legum pessima*?"

Bonnie looked puzzled at the Latin.

"You know *patient torture*?"

Bonnie weighed in. "Andrew, what have you been teaching her?"

"Nothing."

"Nothing?" Lindsay retorted. "What happened to all that brave talk when you hired me? Or was that the whisky talking?"

Wow. She was angry, and pushing her luck with that comment.

Thankfully Bonnie stepped in. "So if she accepts the deal, what will happen to Francesca?"

"First," I looked directly at Lindsay, "she has no legal fees to pay. Second, she keeps her job. The attorney general will accommodate her request to work in a court of her choice."

"Where she will be shunned. Everyone knows what's been going on. Even with NDAs," Lindsay said matter-of-factly.

I'd forgotten about the shunning. "Yes, she likely will not be very popular. It'll take time." But frankly, not our problem.

"Time?" Lindsay snorted at my understatement. "And Justice Singh?"

"He and Glinka drop everything and he gets assigned where he chooses, obviously a different courthouse than Francesca."

"And because they signed a marriage contract, he keeps everything? His pension. Pays no support. Moves on to Ms. French Teacher. He comes out very nicely, doesn't he?"

"It's not my fault she signed a marriage contract. She obviously saw an upside in the marriage."

"Worst of all, Mr. Justice Randall Williams walks away the hero. Well done. I hope someone tortures me like that some day."

"What's with all this talk of torture?" Bonnie looked back and forth between us.

I pondered Lindsay's comment for a moment. She was right. It was true. Why was I passing on an opportunity to torture that SOB Williams? For the money? And Singh too. For a judge who had surrendered to his appetites in his judicial chambers—screwing an employee no less—a man who had assaulted another judge, an older man to boot, and who had not even given his wife the benefit of the doubt, he was also coming out very well. I let it roll around in my mind a bit more. If the inquiry went forward, he had as much to lose as anyone. Even Ms. Hébert would have trouble keeping her job after that news came out. She was getting paid to *parlez-vous* not *avoir des rapports*.

"Do we have the Singh-Rimini marriage contract handy?"

Lindsay hit a few strokes on her keyboard and it was displayed on the monitor. (I was still in awe of this new technological wonder.)

"Scroll to the ILA certificate."

The certificate did indeed show Dave Goodwin's signature. He had sworn that he had reviewed the contract with her and that she had signed voluntarily on the very eve of the wedding. She had received independent *family law* advice from an avowed expert in *personal injury law*, and a man with whom she had a past intimate relationship. On the face of it the contract was legit, but the circumstances of the advice were not pretty and certainly not what I would consider bulletproof by any stretch.

I grabbed my cell and dialled. "Francesca, Andrew Bierce. I have a couple of quick questions. Your ILA from Dave Goodwin. Did he open a file? Would he have notes from your meeting? Did he get you to sign a retainer? How did you pay for it? Cash? E-transfer? Would there be a credit ca . . . What? Sorry, what? Can you speak up? There was no charge *sort of*? What does that mean, *sort of*? Yes, I need to know. I don't care. It's a little late for embarrassment." I imagined her shrugging her way through her clarification. "Really? I see. Okay. Does Jay know that? Calm down. I'm just asking. No, no it's confidential. Okay. Thank you. I'll keep you posted." I put my phone on the boardroom table.

"What did she say?" Lindsay and Bonnie were on the edge of their seats.

I let out what must have been the longest sigh of my life. "She says there was a *quid pro quo*."

"What do you mean?"

I looked at Bonnie. "There was an *oral* agreement—so to speak."

Bonnie understood immediately and looked at the floor. "Oh no."

Lindsay was still baffled. "What do you mean? An *oral quid pro quo?*" Then the penny dropped. "Oh no." Her innocence was being shredded day by day.

I needed to speak with The Major asap.

38

A Major Disappointment
Thursday October 13

I STEPPED AWAY to my office to call Dave. I was torn. A part of me prayed it was untrue—the part that remembered The Major as a classmate from law school. Imagine that, I was praying that a client was lying to me. However, the part of me that saw the distinct possibility of setting aside the Rimini-Singh marriage contract and extracting a settlement from the naughty judge, not to mention the smug Rick Z, well that part of me was absolutely salivating.

I'd not forgotten that Rick Z had steered Francesca my way to begin with. Was he betting that I was desperate enough, fool enough, to take her on, that I would be desperate to settle? That I would fold? What was he thinking? So he'd won a hundred bucks in The Major's pool? We'll see how smart he thinks that was if I take the equivalent of one of Drever's chrome bats to his client. Judge or no judge, Singh could be in for Total War over that contract if Dave had misstepped on the ILA.

If.

I mulled it over a bit as I searched his number. Dave and Francesca had a history of intimacy so a little ongoing hanky-panky would not be a shocker. They are adults after all. Lawyer or not, these things happen. I could hardly cast the first stone given my Ms. Lululemon and Muskoka client romps. Mind you I never discounted fees for sex. That's just crazy. Hell, I charged them more.

Maybe it didn't even happen. Maybe it did but was totally unrelated to the agreement getting signed. Maybe his advice was *pro bono*. Maybe. However, if Dave had made his so-called independent legal advice conditional on the receipt of her sexual favours (i.e., pro boner), well that was a whole other matter. I recalled that lawyer up in Ottawa who'd set his career on fire doing that kind of *quid pro quo*. It could end up in a disaster for Dave but a jackpot for Francesca. There was a lot to mull.

As Dave's number rang Bonnie slid a paper in front of me. It was a printout of a *Toronto Star* article about the election.

Headline, **Your Provincial Election Primer: The Highs. And the Lows.** The byline said simply, Your Election Team.

"You should take a look at this."

"Maybe later. I need to speak to Dave. This could get even messier than it already is."

"Well, I think you need to read it soon. You're mentioned." She said *mentioned* as if it were not in a good way. "Fifth paragraph, under the Lows. And I'm off to work on the Reyes campaign. I'll see you in the morning."

Shit. I need her to stay tonight. We have work to do. Coop's matter is also in serious play. There are a lot of moving parts.

I scanned down to a heading.

West End Head Scratcher
One has to wonder what the devil is going on in Parkdale–High Park. Traditionally an NDP or Liberal stronghold, the PC's McKay, polling at 37%, has taken a commanding lead over A. Bierce and A. Bierce. You read that correctly, there are two A. Bierces running, one for the NDP and one for, well, no one is sure. He says he's an Independent but word from the Liberal spokesperson for Kaminski (currently polling at 10%) is that the second A. Bierce is none other than the fire-breathing lawyer Andrew Bierce, K.C., with a reputation for making nasty divorces even worse. Sources say he's apparently getting into politics now, after being suspended from his practice for getting too cozy with his clients.

Readers may recall that name as a key figure in a shooting three years ago in which a senior lawyer was gunned down in a Toronto

*courtroom with a weapon unwittingly smuggled into the courtroom by
his law partner, none other than A. Bierce, K.C.*

*It is a curious campaign. He does not live in the riding. He has
no political affiliations. He has no campaign to speak of but he can be
seen driving around the riding in his new Porsche Taycan. He does not
respond to requests for interviews and yet recent polls have him at 5%.
Dikembe, McKay's campaign manager, professed to be just as mystified by the oddball campaign and denied vehemently that it was a
political ploy to split the vote of McKay's likely challenger, the NDP's
Aaron Bierce (now polling at 17%) by confusing voters. "We live in a
robust democracy. Anyone can run. I assume he has his reasons. Who
knows, maybe comic relief? Career change? We are focussed on getting
McKay elected so he—as a part of a PC majority government—can
start addressing some of the issues that plague this neglected part of
the city, issues such as guns and the murder rate. Just last week there
was a drug-related murder of a homeless man on Queen Street at
Dunn Avenue. This has to stop and only Progressive Conservatives
have the answers."*

I don't know why, but the thought of that recent drug-turf-war murder on Queen near Dr. Shelia's office made me feel nauseous. That
homeless guy had been right. The shoes hanging on the telephone line
had actually been a warning about coming violence. Who knows these
things? Street people. Rain dogs. Little did he know that it was his life
that would end.

My stomach growled as I realized that I had not eaten all day. And
oddball campaign? Comic relief? What the F. That fucking liar set the
whole thing up. It was the typical political BS I hated so much.

It was a good thing my call flipped to Dave's voicemail.

*This is Dave Goodwin. I will be in trial for the next two weeks in Toronto
and unable to respond to messages in a timely way. I will do my best to return calls
within twenty-four hours. If you need immediate assistance . . .* The message
ended with his tag line, *You want tough? You called the right number.*

That's right. I forgot, he's in a trial. Suddenly feeling like I might
throw up, I hesitated for a minute and then left a short, benign message.
"Dave, Bierce. I need some advice. Call when you get a minute. Thanks."

A drink might help but *the AA police* were still in the office so I shut my door, poured a half tumbler of Irish and set the glass on the floor out of sight in case Bonnie hadn't left and poked her head in unannounced.

My phone pulsed and my already upset stomach twisted into a knot as I dreaded speaking with Dave. I wasn't ready. How could I put the question of an oral *quid pro quo* diplomatically?

I took a gulp of Irish, crossed my fingers and answered. "Andrew Bierce."

"Mr. Bierce. It's Gavin McPhellan. I've been asked to take on the Justice Glinka Inquiry as presenting counsel. I thought it might be helpful to touch base with you."

It's about time. "Yes, yes. No worries. Thanks for calling."

"Look, I want to say that I feel bad that Royce and I have spoken without you being involved."

Oh, so you're on a first-name basis with His Majesty.

"We just happened to cross paths at Osgoode Hall Law School a few days ago. I'm a sessional lecturer there. He was a guest speaker for my Criminal Law class."

Well, isn't that cozy.

"Not a problem. I have nothing but the utmost respect for Royce," *my new best friend.* "I've been pretty busy lately but it's nice of you to reach out. How can I help?"

"Royce mentioned—very briefly, nothing in detail of course—that there might be a resolution?"

Nothing in detail? Right. Of course not. Sure. You guys are as thick as thieves. And to make matters even worse, here was a grown man who had just used the dreaded uptalk reserved for teenage girls. "There might be a resolution?"

"Yes, Royce raised a couple of options. One could lead to a full resolution." I paused for effect. "The other, to a rather intense *conflagratio.*" A little Latin between lawyers never hurts. "I think a pivot point will be the outcome of our deliberations with respect to the scope of evidence. Twin myths." *I would need to look those up again. I'd already forgotten the second one.* "I assume you as presenting counsel have views on just how much the panel needs to hear. Are we talking about just a Christmas party? Or more?"

Pretty clear choice. Would he take the bait?

There was a long pause. "While I don't have any settled views, . . ." *right, sure you don't,* ". . . in any review of judicial conduct, it seems that a *broad* net should be cast so the panel has a *full* understanding of the relationship between the parties."

I said nothing and let him fill the silence.

"I'm of course speaking generally here as I don't know the full details about this particular situation involving Ms. Rimini and Justice Glinka. That's what we need to discuss with Justice Williams . . . again, if the matter proceeds."

"Yes, of course. We're just speaking generally."

"If there is a history of similar intimacy between the parties then it may be relevant."

Excellent. Bait taken.

"I see, so you would agree that casting a *broad* net for a *full understanding* could be best and would include not just these two individuals but evidence from others as well. For example, and I'm just speaking off the top of my head here, in this case that might include Justice Singh, his French teacher, Ms. Hébert, the paramedics and police who responded to 1000 Finch to attend to Justice Glinka after the assault, sorry *alleged* assault, the court reporter who in the past made a complaint about Judge Glinka's penis light switch, the female Crown attorneys who elected not to attend this particular Christmas party because they felt uncomfortable, other judges and lawyers at Finch. And so on. That would permit a *full* understanding. Generally speaking, of course."

I think he may have been *mutus* because all I could hear was his breathing. But then, quietly, he said, "That would be the *conflagratio* option."

"Indeed."

Perhaps coincidentally, the thought of *conflagratio* immediately made me think of a rhyming word when a text from Dave popped up on my phone. *Calling in 2 min.*

"Listen, Gavin, I'm sorry but I have another call scheduled in a couple of minutes. Let's touch base again before our meeting if we have a chance."

"Sounds good."

Within seconds Dave was calling. "Hey, Bierce, what's up?"

I decided the bandage should just come off. "Dave, Francesca says you gave her ILA on her prenup in exchange for a blowjob."

"What?!"

"That's what she says."

"And you believe her?"

"I didn't say I believe her. I said that's what she says. And before we get to whether it's true or not, why the fuck are you giving ILA on marriage contracts? Weren't you the guy who told me at Barb's that he *sticks to his knitting in PI?*"

"Okay, whoa, back up. First, she begged me—*literally begged me*—to give her ILA. She didn't want to pay a lawyer. She was going to sign anything Singh presented to her anyway, legal advice or not. She wanted to get married to the judge, full stop. Singh wouldn't go ahead with the wedding—it was less than a week away—unless an actual lawyer signed off. That's the honest truth."

"And the oral *ooh-la-las?*"

"I'm not going to shit you. Yeah, it happened but it had nothing to do with the advice. We'd been on and off for years."

"She says it was a *quid pro quo.* She released everything under that contract. In a divorce she gets diddly."

"I know that. I reviewed it with her line by line. I even told her not to sign it. This is deep shit . . . If this went public . . . I just plunked down a million-dollar commitment on a TV, radio, and social media campaign. I'd be fucked."

"I'm thinking about taking a run at the contract. Inadequate ILA. If I can set it aside . . ."

"Oh shit. Bierce, come on."

"I know."

"Bierce, buddy, I need you to have my back on this. It's fucked up. She's full of shit. I swear. Maybe she saw it that way but I sure didn't."

Well, that's an interesting comment. *She saw it that way?* He's dead if he ever says that out loud.

"I know, it's fucked up. I know. Let me think about it. I won't do anything without giving you a heads-up. To be honest I'm not sure how anxious she should be to tell anyone she was fooling around a week before she got married."

"That doesn't help me if this becomes public."

"I know."

A swarm of texts pulsed on my phone. The first one was Dikoombe.

Then Naomi.

Then Daria.

Then Bonnie.

Then Coop.

They all said the same thing. *We need to talk.*

"Dave, I gotta go. Something's up."

What fresh hell is this?

39

Priorities
Thursday October 13

I KEPT MY priorities straight and called Bonnie first.

She answered on one ring. "Thanks for calling me back, Andrew. Did you reach Dave Goodwin?"

"Yes. Not pretty. What's up?"

"Andrew, I'm going to need some extra time off during the next few weeks . . ."

"Whoa, whoa, whoa. We have a lot going on right now. I need you. Coop's got problems, Marrs . . ."

"When I took the job I told you that I was going to be working on this campaign and you said . . ."

"Yes, I know what I said, but there was no campaign at that time. I didn't know this was going to happen."

"Oh, so you said yes because you never thought I would actually take the time off? Just like the offer of extra vacation because you know I never use it?" She was getting hot.

"Okay, look, calm down . . ."

"Don't tell me to calm down."

Oh brother. The temperature was rising. "Okay. Sorry, you're right. What has changed? Why the sudden need to take more time off?"

"I know you're not paying any attention to the campaign but the ground has been moving already in this election. The NDP are looking very strong. Their leader, Madeleine Franks, was awesome on the campaign trail. So was our leader. You should have seen him. PCs are not connecting. Did you hear that their leader is stepping down? Health reasons or something. He has a press conference tomorrow . . ." She was babbling on excitedly about the usual election rumours and unsubstantiated gossip that so enthralls people involved in politics.

Judas hole time: I didn't think this was the best time to tell her that not only had I known when we had dinner at the Vatican that there was going to be an election, but I also knew why Gord Moore, the PC leader, was going to be stepping down. It had to do with his health alright—the possibility that his wife would murder him. He had recently disappeared for a week claiming to have gone "off the grid" for an extended hike, alone, on the Bruce Trail. The public would soon learn that he was neither on the Bruce Trail nor alone, but rather meeting with a very junior member of his staff for a sexual getaway at an Airbnb cabin outside Tobermory.

That revelation would be bad enough, but put alongside the fact that this so-called family man's wife was in hospital recovering from breast cancer *and* that he had also been caught sexting with a fifteen-year-old girl (a regular Carlos Danger) *and* that the teenager was now apparently selling her story to the *Toronto Sun*, well, he was about to be political toast. Burnt toast. An interim leader, a Mr. Roger Brazeau, a francophone MPP from Eastern Ontario, would be stepping up to manage the party through the election as best he could.

Bonnie was clearly enthralled by her new-found political work. "But the best news is in Scarborough. Reyes is surging in the polls. He is really connecting over some of the local environmental issues, transit, bike lanes and . . . he's running third now but . . ." She kept rattling on about her hero.

Surging? Oh God, she had really swallowed the Green Kool-Aid. Her candidate's surging? Please. People tell Green candidates they're going to vote for them and then mark the ballot for a PC or Lib or worse, a Dipper. She was setting herself up for political heartbreak.

"That's great he's connecting but I really need you, the inquiry . . ." Her mention of the PC leader stepping down reminded me that I should look at the package of stuff that Sean had given me. It was still sitting on my office windowsill, unopened.

"Andrew, I'm not asking."

Oh-oh. I knew that tone of voice. "What're we talking about? What do you need? How much time?"

"I will be in the office as much as I can, but I will not be in on Mondays and Fridays until E-day and evenings are going to be busy. If we can push him over the top, we will have the second Green member ever elected in Ontario."

Push him over the top? From third place to winning? In less than two weeks? Oh, that will be just great for the province. He can sit in the corner of the Legislative Chamber and beg for time to ask a question once a year, draft useless private members' bills, attend protests and environmental roundtables for the next four years. "No, I get it. It's a big deal. Good luck. Really. I hope he does well."

Jesus Christ, what a fucking waste of her time. And when I need her most.

"Thank you. It means a lot to me. You won't regret it. I'll do my best to make up for the time. I'll see you tomorrow . . . a little late actually because we're doing some subway canvassing early on . . . It's going great. He's really connecting."

"Okay. Okay. Have fun. I know it means a lot. See you tomorrow or whenever, I have some calls to make."

I shuddered to think about her feelings when her hero comes in fourth, right after the People's Party whack job. It would take a long time for her to recover from this.

Next up. Naomi.

I dialled. When she answered I could barely hear a word she was saying. "Naomi, I can't hear you."

"Hang on. I'll step outside." I could hear people yelling, doors slamming, banging and then cheering. "Okay, sorry. This is better. I'm at my son's hockey game up in Thornhill. You'd think it was the Stanley Cup the way some parents up here carry on. They're nuts. The kids are ten years old. Novice for Christsakes. The GTHL circus."

"Hey, it's Toronto hockey. It's twisted. I got your message. What's up?"

"I can only talk for a minute but you remember that cash I was following, the small withdrawals that ended up in a credit union in Banff?"

"Yeah, a lot, over time."

"Yeah, that. I found out who was on the receiving end."

"Okay. The suspense is killing me . . ."

"It's a joint account. Two names on it. Brent and one Caroline Burgess."

"Okay, who dat?"

"Coop's first wife."

"Hello. Why would she be getting a stream of cash? When he divorced her she signed a release, no support. It was quick. Over and done. She moved on."

"That's right. She walked away. She got nothing except that truck. I had someone pull the divorce file in Alberta."

"Wow. You're good."

"It gets better."

"Okay . . ."

"In the proceedings, she never revealed who her secret love interest was, the one who supposedly broke up the marriage. She signed the release to end it without ever getting into the who-did-what-with-whom."

"Okay. But why?"

"Do I need to connect all the dots? She kept a secret and now she's getting support through the back door. And it's not even covered up with any kind of fancy scheme. Brent deposits money into an account in his name and she has access to it as a joint account holder."

"Do we know what's in the account?"

"I don't know the balance but she must be living well because monthly withdrawals top eight grand. That's $96,000 a year, tax free."

This is why I love her. "This is a major fraud. Have you said anything to Coop?"

"No, I never even told him about the transfers. I wanted to get the full picture before I said anything. I thought you needed to know first given what's going on. I'm trying to get an address for her. She's still in Alberta. I've got a guy following up. I should know soon."

"Okay, good. This is very helpful. Coop's going to be very grateful. I just need to find a way to position this."

"Well, that is your specialty, isn't it? Holy shit! I gotta go . . ."

"What's up? What?"

"My husband's in a fight in the stands. I gotta go."

And with that she was gone.

Next call. The Coop.

Before I could even dial, my phone pulsed with a call from the man himself. "Andrew Bierce."

"Andrew, it's Coop. We have a problem." Surely he hadn't heard about Naomi's digging into his divorce out west.

"What's up?"

"Your friend Patrick."

"*Your* friend Patrick, my *client* Patrick."

"He's your buddy too. Don't deny it. Look, his girlfriend, the one you met . . ."

"Yes, the image consultant, Sarah."

Coop snorted. "Yeah, she was *supposed* to be looking after my image, you know. Give me some new ideas. Take things in a fresh direction."

"I thought it looked more like a *romantic* direction when I saw you two."

"Yeah, well, she's hard to resist, if you know what I mean . . . but I think it was a mistake."

"Does Patrick know you've been giving her a tour of the backseats of some of those vintage automobiles?"

"I don't know, but he'd have to be blind not to see the way she carries on around me. But here's the problem."

"What's that?"

"I don't think she knows fuck all about image consulting. She's made some real shitty moves, trying to get me into some crazy-ass country-rock album with Patrick. Come on man, that's bullshit. If he's country, I'm Frank Sinatra. I think I'm gonna have to let her go but Pat's not gonna be happy."

Oh shit. No, no, no. We need her.

"And now she's poking around asking questions about Brent, his music, his song writing and genre choices. Where did she get that idea?"

Perfect. *My lips are sealed.* Right.

"She got that from me."

"Shit, man, what're you doing? You're gonna make matters worse. She's a loose cannon."

"Look, Coop, do you trust me?"

"Yeah, I guess."

"Do you want me to deal with this Brent issue?"

"Of course, but I think I'm fucked, man."

"Not if you do what I tell you to do."

"Okay, I'm desperate, man. What should I do?"

"First, don't fire her, at least not right now. We have to sort this Brent stuff out first and she's going to help us, so sit tight. Keep her busy on something. If she mentions Brent's music again just say it's very confidential and you're not at liberty to speak about it. Let her think something big is brewing, though, with you and Brent. Be vague. Can you do that? Don't nix any album ideas. I'm working on something. If Brent asks to meet with you, tell him you have turned the deal over to me."

"Okay. Have you got this?"

"Yes, and here comes the hard part."

"This can't get any harder right now. Kayla's packing. She'll be gone in a day or so. She's asking questions."

"Okay. But do this. Around your place, start listening to a lot of Eagles and Kid Rock."

There was a long pause. "Are you shitting me?"

"No, trust me. Make sure Sarah hears you listening to it."

"I haven't had that stuff on in years."

"One more thing."

"Shoot."

"Stop fucking her. Tell her it's out of respect for your fellow musician, Pat. Let her down easy. Keep it businesslike."

"Oh man, that's some smooth bullshit." He just laughed. "Yeah, I'll tell her it's out of respect for Patrick. Oh man, you're good."

"Deal?"

"Deal. Hey, while I got ya, how's that campaign of yours coming along? Where do you find the time, man? You really into that shit? I saw an article about you in *Horse Canada*."

"*Horse Canada*?"

"Yeah, some case you did, some speech you gave at a museum. I didn't know you were such an animal lover, man. That's great. I sent along a donation to your campaign. Keep the faith, brother. I'm tweeting about you, man. I got a million followers. Hey, let's go riding the next time you're out here. Deal?"

"Deal. And thanks for the donation." *There's no fucking way I'm getting on a horse.* "Listen, I gotta make a few more calls before I call it a day. Go write a song."

"Right on. Man, I don't know how you do it." He was laughing as he hung up.

Next up. Daria.

It was late in the day but I called anyway.

"Andrew, thanks for getting back to me."

"I haven't got a lot of time. What's up?"

There was a long pause and I could hear her sigh. "Well then, you're not going to like this. I need you to be more involved right now. I'm at my limit."

"*You're* at your limit? You're at your *limit?* I'm juggling a half-dozen cases, Bonnie just told me she's taking time off to chase an election Green pipe dream, I've got a client who's into me for tens of thousands of dollars and there is no way out, I'm supposed to be running for office, Sean's getting defrocked unless I can pull a rabbit out of a hat . . ."

"You can add one more thing to the list."

"What now?"

"Sean needs to move to a hospice. I cannot justify to the hospital keeping him here any longer. We've done all that we can. We're looking at just a few weeks, maybe a month. Maybe. It's palliative care he needs now, Andrew, maybe even closer to end-of-life care. I don't have any authority to make those decisions. Do you hold his power of attorney?"

I didn't know what to say. Hospice? Power of attorney? End of life? My chest tightened up and I recalled my excruciating run a week ago when I realized that I might be stuck with Sean's care, even his funeral.

"Andrew? Are you there?" Daria's voice was a million miles away.

Then Burdettes flashed through my mind along with memories of Lester's funeral and the drunken blowout at Keg's service.

"Fucking Burdettes."

"What? Andrew. You need to get involved. Decisions have to be made. I've tracked down some options for you. But that's the best I can do. You need to take over. He needs you right now. Andrew?"

I felt like throwing up.

40

What Comes after Reality?
Wednesday October 19

AFTER DARIA WALKED me through the various hospice options, I could see that there was no real choice, especially on such short notice. No reputable hospice takes someone on twenty-four hours' notice. So I made a decision, Sean should live out his final days with me. My condo has a never-used spacious spare bedroom with its own ensuite, high-def TV, internet and a nice view west down College, especially when the sun sets. It had to be more comfortable than any hospice bed and I'm pretty sure it smells a hell of a lot better.

Daria booked a rotation of PSWs and nurses to come in to look after Sean while I attended to business. And she had the gall to ask for the code to be able to look in from time to time. Seriously? Sean's needs or not, she was not setting foot in my home. I told her she was welcome to Zoom him. That didn't go over very well with Sean. Too bad. My house, my rules.

Notwithstanding all the carping, I thought it was working well with just the two of us. For the first few days I was up early and out the door as soon as the nurse arrived and home after he was asleep. We barely had a chance to speak, but really, what was there to say at this point?

One night I came in late after having dinner and a few drinks down the street at Café Diplomatico. The evening PSW shift had just left and even though he had taken his meds for the night Sean was still up, on his computer and wanting to talk.

He called to me from his bed. "Hey, buddy boy. You have a few minutes to chat? You can't avoid me forever."

I stuck my head in. "What do you mean, avoid you? We're living together, you asshole."

"Yeah, right. I've barely seen you. Listen, I know you're busy and probably wondering if I have my things in order, you know, a will, POAs. There's nothing to be afraid of."

"Afraid? I'm not worried about that shit. Let's work on it maybe this weekend. It's been a long day. Work's been brutal. The so-called campaign trail is rough."

"I just want you to know there's nothing to work on. Everything's looked after. There's a file over there on the dresser with my will and POAs. I hope you don't mind but I named you estate trustee and attorney. Okay?"

"Sean, if we're going to talk about shit like that, I'll need a drink."

"Sounds good. What's the bar's best?"

"I'm pretty sure you aren't allowed to drink."

"A taste of something quality can't hurt at this point."

"Quality? You want quality? I have your favourite."

"If you insist."

I cracked a bottle of JW Blue and poured two glasses, one tiny, one very large. And we sat and had a talk that lasted into the wee hours. There were a few memories and no laughs. It was a talk about reality and what comes after reality.

41

A Trap for Brent
Thursday October 20

WHEN I WOKE up in the morning, head hurting from all that whisky and post-reality talk, I realized that I needed to see this McKay character up close. What was he all about? Why was the archdiocese so committed to him? Why should his election affect Sean getting a proper burial? So, against my better judgment, I decided to check out the Parkdale–High Park all-candidates meeting being held at the Mechanics Hall on Keele Street the following Monday evening. This likely snooze fest was being sponsored by the local BIA and what harm could there be in going to have a discreet listen to the candidates answer a few questions about the neighbourhood's issues? Maybe that prick Shannon would be around and I could get a straight answer about Sean. Do we have a deal or not?

But first I needed to head to the office to deal with Coop's matter. Brent had agreed to come into town to talk about "the new arrangement." I had Naomi's full report now and all the numbers on the fraud he had been perpetrating on Coop. She was still tracking down his partner in crime, Ms. Caroline Burgess, and had a very good lead. Any day now we would have Coop's ex and Brent facing a repayment schedule that could last the rest of their lives. I had Brent in the crosshairs. He wants a deal with Coop? He'll get a deal.

When he arrived in my boardroom Brent was not at all the reformed pothead I expected. In his early forties like Coop, he had none of the faux-country look. There was no remaining evidence of the former musician in his well-styled hair, his fashionable upscale clothing or his confident manner. This guy was all business. He had clearly gone to the other side and looked more like a junior accountant than the business manager for one of the biggest acts in Canadian music. Well dressed and comfortable in expensive black jeans, a tailored white dress shirt and an olive-green linen vest, he knew what suited him. I could tell by the way he moved that he was fit and looked like he worked out. He settled in at my boardroom table with a large Starbucks and flipped open his laptop. I tried to make a little small talk but he would have none of it.

"I have a tee time at Glen Abbey at noon so let's get down to business. Coop says you're authorized to make a deal. Is that true, because I don't want to waste my time?"

"It's true. I have complete authority."

"I don't know how much you know but I've been after Coop for years to deal with the matter of proper songwriting credits on *our* music. It shouldn't be this hard. I shouldn't have to force him to the table to discuss this. This shit with Kayla was needed to just make this discussion happen? I didn't want it this way. This isn't the first time these issues have come up in bands. It could have been a lot easier." He seemed almost apologetic.

"You mean like Robbie and The Band? Burton Cummings and Randy?" I knew I would need to sound like I knew a bit about the business of fighting over music rights, so I'd done some research about the animosity some of these artists had suffered through. Pat gave me a little insight too with the problems he had in the early years of his career. There's always someone waiting to screw over a musician and it's often his best friend.

"Okay, so you know what I'm talking about. It's a simple matter of amending the publishing rights. We can work out some retroactive comp calculation. I'm willing to be paid by taking a larger share going forward."

"Anything else?"

"The album. I have over twenty songs in the bank. I think we should pick the best twelve and record them. I would welcome Coop's input on the twelve. I'm thinking we do four songs together, he does four on his own and I do four. But we each play instruments on all twelve. We will use studio musicians, not his usual band. I will have the songwriting credits—100 percent. Coop can either take points on sales or a lump sum up front, which can be deducted from the compensation he owes me. I would prefer the latter because it's cleaner. I have some Excel spreadsheets that set out some scenarios. We can look at them."

"Sure. If we get to that part of the discussion."

"If?"

He wanted to be all business so let's be all business. "I have some spreadsheets too. Let me throw them up on the flatscreen." I'd had Lindsay show me how to do it so, with a few well practiced keystrokes, I had them on the monitor.

"What's this? What's that got to do with me?"

"You can see from the left-hand side the amounts that flowed out of CME . . . that's Cooper Music . . ."

"I know what CME stands for. I incorporated it."

"Good, so you see the funds then flow through a couple of accounts and then into an account held at the Bow Valley Credit Union in Banff."

"Where did you get this? This is totally unauthorized access to our corporate accounts."

"No, it was authorized by Coop. A team of forensic auditors put it together on his okay. Those same auditors have transferred all corporate control to a new set of accountants. You are locked out, effective . . ." I looked at my watch, "two hours ago." (That wasn't quite accurate but it served my purpose for the moment.)

"This is illegal."

"No, it's quite legal. The account into which the money flows is in your name jointly with a Ms. Caroline Burgess, Coop's first wife."

"You don't know what you are getting into. You're going to regret this big time. Coop too."

"The auditors called it fraud. I didn't want to be that hasty so we have not discussed any of this with the police. That can wait until Monday, if it has to go that route."

He smiled. "What do you think you've found?"

"There is no think, I know what we found: a fraudulent transfer of over a half-million dollars, by you, to an account shared with Ms. Burgess. I assume you two planned this some time ago since it has been going on for years. She walked away from her divorce from Coop with nothing but a truck. She released any entitlement to support from him. I assume she did that to keep secret the fact that she had a lover whose name she did not wish to disclose. I also assume that person was you, because you two had a prior relationship before she met Coop."

He sat there smiling.

"You think this is funny?" I decided to drop the hammer. "And I assure you of this. Every single penny is going to be paid back. I'm waiting for a call from my investigator about the whereabouts of Ms. Burgess. I assume that you and she have probably built yourselves a nice big lodge somewhere out in the Alberta Foothills where you can live out your days. That will not happen. I will find it and force a sale if I have to."

"You sound like a hard man. A bit of a bastard actually."

"You have no idea."

"Does Coop know about this situation with the money?"

"No, and he doesn't have to know. Just like Kim doesn't need to know about Coop's inappropriate moments with Kayla."

"Oh, it was an inappropriate moment? And just like I'm not supposed to know that Coop and Kim have been carrying on for the last two years and are getting ready to tell me something I already know?"

I was not surprised that he knew. People who screw around want to get caught. They want to be discovered. "Yeah, just like that." I suddenly felt sorry for him. It must have been tough knowing that their screwing around was going on right under his nose. No one likes to be the cuckold. "You know, a big part of my professional life is dealing with this kind of shit. People fucking around. Getting caught. Doing stupid things. Blowing up marriages. It happens a lot." I almost told him that it happened to me. Almost.

"I feel sorry for you." He sat back in his chair and seemed oddly at peace. "Why wouldn't I tell Kim about Kayla and him now? Fuck it. If there is no deal on music rights and an album, I might as well blow the whole thing up."

"I didn't say no to a deal."

"You don't really understand the situation. You think you know. But you don't."

"I think I do, but fill me in if you think it will help."

He filled me in alright. Just when you think you know what's going on, something like this comes along.

42

Four Strong Winds That Blow Lonely
Thursday October 20

I GUESS THERE'S a certain peace that arrives with coming clean because Brent made himself very comfortable. He pulled out his phone and made a call. "Geddy? Yeah, it's Brent. Look I'm not gonna make the tee time. I know, I know. I'll make it up to you. Great. Thanks."

"So fill me in."

"Okay, first on the songwriting and publishing rights . . ."

"Not gonna happen."

"No, I'm talking about where the songs came from. Has Coop told you his tall tale about sitting in vintage cars and being inspired to write his songs?"

"That sounds familiar." I think he said he got the idea from Neil Young.

"It's BS. Truth is I sat in the front seat of some old beat-up cars in the early days and wrote songs while he screwed any groupies he could get his hands on in the back seat. The hearts he broke along the way provided a lot of inspiration . . ."

"Like 'Love Poultice'?"

"Ha! Not one of mine. He can keep all the credit for that dog." He had a good laugh before carrying on. "That shot at the end? Kill me now." He put a finger to his head and mimed pulling a trigger. "It actually worked like this: I would write the music because I can read and write music. He can't. He plays by ear. It's a talent and he has a good ear and a great voice. I would play a basic version on acoustic guitar or piano for him. He would then take the music and lyrics into a little studio we had, do a rough recording—by ear—and send it to our recording company—with just his name on it. That's how almost all the music was written and eventually recorded. Every year I would ask him to make sure the song-writing credits were fixed and every year there would be an excuse. He would try throwing money, cars, bags of pot and stuff at me to make up for it but he never fixed the credits."

"Sounds familiar."

"Tell me about it. Randy and I have commiserated over the years because he was going through the same shit with you-know-who. They still haven't figured it out and look where they are. Miserable when they should be buddies. We were successful, toured a lot. Coop got the attention being up front. And, of course, it doesn't hurt that he looks country, at least when he's all dressed up. Not too many cowboys came out of Newmarket looking like that."

I was starting to like this guy. "So it never got fixed. It's a little late now."

"After he promised me that he would fix the credits for, like, the hundredth time, I stopped asking. Instead, I moved more into the business side of things and set up an account to transfer an amount equal to about 50 percent of what I would have been entitled to in royalties. It was a backstop for when we eventually got around to fixing it. So I really see the money as mine. I have absolutely no guilty feelings about taking it."

"I'm not saying I buy any of this and don't get me wrong, it has what lawyers and judges call the ring of truth, but it doesn't explain one thing."

"Why transfer to an account with Caroline Burgess?"

He was one step ahead of me. "Exactly."

My phone rang. It was Naomi. "Sorry, Brent, I have to take this."

"Not a problem."

"Hey, Naomi. You have it. Great. I'm meeting with Brent right now. Text it to me. Thanks."

"Anything interesting?"

"Ms. Burgess's address. Does Okotoks, Alberta, sound familiar? Remote, but I knew it wouldn't take long to track her down."

"I hope you're not bothering her with this. I set it all up. It wouldn't be fair to her."

"Not yet but we need to see where it ends. And not fair to her? First thing Monday morning I'm going to retain lawyers in Calgary," *not really,* "to put a *lis pendens* on this home you two bought and paid for with Coop's money, that's a lien to make sure it doesn't get sold before we work this out. Preventative medicine, so to speak. You've been draining eight thousand dollars a month. That must be a sweet life she's living."

"I wish you good luck with any sale." He was practically laughing. They must have changed title somehow to make it judgment-proof.

"I'm pretty good at forcing the sale of homes, even if they're in Alberta."

"Can you google the address and put it up on the screen? Let's take a look at the home we bought."

Thank God Lindsay had run me through this a few times. I plugged in the address and searched. A bunch of websites popped up about skiing in Alberta, sponsored by the tourist association. Useless garbage.

Brent could see my frustration as I tried again. "Go to Google Earth. We can do a tour."

I tapped a few more keys but got nothing. Fucking technology.

Brent leaned over and spun my laptop around. "Here, let me do it." Why was he helping me? He hit a few keys and bingo, an image appeared on the screen. He zoomed in. "There you go, counsel."

"No, that's not it. What's that? Go over to the left."

"That's her home. Right there."

He zoomed in again on a large sign in front of the building, "Foothills Country Hospice. Okotoks, Alberta."

Shiiit.

43

Credit, Where Credit Is Due
Thursday October 20

I STARED AT the screen. Brent stared at me. Caroline Burgess was living in a hospice.

"What's going on?"

"She's been a guest there for several years. She has amyotrophic lateral sclerosis. It's . . ."

"ALS. Lou Gehrig's, I've seen it."

"Yup. She is pretty much near the end of the line. Maybe a couple of years. If she wasn't such a tough son of a bitch she would have been gone long ago."

"Does Coop not know about this?"

"No, and she does not want him to know. She has been very clear on that."

"He could help her. I'm sure he would help her. I saw him get all teared up playing a song about her . . ."

"'Road More Taken'?"

"Yes, 'Road More Taken.' He played that one evening at his place."

"I wrote that about their breakup. He really screwed her over."

"He said you did the guitar solo on it."

"Well, at least he gave me credit for something."

"The money you have been taking covers her care?"

"Yup, and a few other things for her."

"I don't get it. Why did she walk away? Why keep your relationship a secret? She would have got spousal support regardless. It would have been indefinite and, based on Coop's earnings, it would have been a lot. More than eight thousand a month." I would have loved taking on a case like that. Easy money.

"The only secret she kept from him in their divorce was that she had just been diagnosed with the disease. There was no lover. That's what he assumed because she was being so secretive and because that's what he was doing, screwing around with a different woman every night. She knew the marriage couldn't last and she didn't want him to stay in it because she was sick. So she took the truck and left. She's a gutsy woman. Pretty good fiddle player too in her day."

"But you knew?"

"Of course. We've been friends since childhood. I always wanted to marry her but Coop came along. That was that."

"He got your girl and your music."

"Hey, that sounds like a pretty good country song, don't it? I don't like to think of it that way, but yeah. Hence my power play around his trying to screw Kayla—or what you called an *inappropriate moment*. That's BS lawyer talk. But you kinda fucked up my move now."

I needed to digest this. Coop's feet were made of something worse than clay if all of this was true. It sure sounded true.

"What if we can work something out?"

"What are you proposing?"

"Is it too early for a drink?"

"Not at all."

It turned into a good afternoon. Better than any round of golf.

44

All-Candidates Meeting
Monday October 24

AFTER TWO FULL days at the office working on Brent and Francesca's matters, and before heading out to High Park for a riveting evening of political debate, I reviewed (with a sturdy tumbler of recovery bourbon in hand) the file Sean had given me at the hospital a couple of months ago. The thick manila envelope had been on my windowsill gathering dust along with a few of the new files that were being neglected because of all this nonsense with Sean and the election. Once I'd spread the envelope's contents out on my boardroom table, I'd treated these documents as if I was prepping for trial. In other words, I inhaled them, every last page. How Sean had come to be in possession of this information, I dared not ask.

It was a rainy evening, so I parked the Porsche close by on a side street just off Annette Street, took a few long sips from my emergency flask, popped a handful of breath mints and slipped in the front door of the hall a little after 7:30 p.m. To my surprise it was packed, easily three hundred people had turned out to hear the usual political nonsense.

McKay was up on the stage, with his wife Pam no less, reaching down into the crowd, double-glad-handing, *polipointing* at people he recognized, giving them the standard politician's thumbs up and absolutely beaming. He looked confident, like a man who stood at 37 percent and headed for victory. Across from him sat the Liberal candidate, Kaminski, studying a fistful of index cards like he was getting ready to defend a PhD dissertation. His leg was jumping nervously, and I had a brief flashback to Paul's electrified leg in the courtroom that day as Judge Harold prepared to sentence Chloe for killing Angie. My stomach tightened and I wished I had eaten something before leaving the office. Next to him on the stage sat a young blond-haired woman, and when I say young I mean, honestly, she looked like she should be on *Reach for the Top* not seeking election as an MPP. A gaggle of barista-like hipsters buzzed around her so I assumed she was the Green candidate. I had to laugh at the thought of the debate that was about to unfold. What a joke. McKay would likely mop the floor with these two.

The moderator, president of the local BIA, was a very pretty middle-aged Asian woman in a standard issue black business suit with a large colourful red and yellow scarf draped over her shoulders and hanging down to her hips. She was all business, calling the meeting to order and urging the candidates to take their seats on stage. A young man scurried across the stage with three microphones checking the audio and repeatedly saying, "Check 1, check 2, check 3." Clearly, they were working just fine but he seemed to be enjoying his time on stage, in the political limelight.

As people noisily settled down, I tucked into a spot at the back of the hall beside the tech booth and did my best to blend in. Granted this was a challenge because I was wearing a $3,000 charcoal grey bespoke three-piece suit, an immaculate white shirt and a gorgeous new red and blue tie. I have to admit I looked good, and it felt great getting back into my upscale clothes—even if my pants were a little snug. I vowed, as I tugged at my belt, that when this election was over I was going to start working out again. Seriously. Or even maybe try this Ozempic craze. How bad can it be?

The moderator cracked a gentle whip to get things rolling. "Thank you, thank you everyone for coming out on such a dreary night. This promises to be a great evening for democracy with our local candidates debating the key issues in this election and answering your questions. There are just over ten days to go, so we're coming down to the wire. Let's get started, shall we? . . . Quiet please. Thank you." She turned to the young man with the microphones, who was still relishing his moment on stage, "Max, are we ready to go?" He gave her a concerned look and decided to give them all one more *check 1, check 2, check 3* for good measure.

I saw him give a thumbs-up to her and then wink at a beaming, cute teen-age girl in the front row. *Atta boy, Max. Milk it, buddy.*

The moderator then removed a card from her pocket, lifted her reading glasses to her nose and solemnly began. "Before we begin our debate tonight we would like to acknowledge that we are on the territorial lands of . . ."

Oh boy, here we go. If more than one person in that room listened to a word she said it would have been a miracle. As she read from the card, stumbling over the pronunciation of First Nations names, the audience unwrapped candies, cracked water bottles, read brochures that had been left on chairs and checked their watches. Basically, virtue signal received, move on. I wondered if the First Nations mentioned would prefer clean drinking water to these much less expensive pronouncements.

Clearly relieved to have that task out of the way, she announced that, although the NDP candidate Aaron Bierce had registered to be on the ballot for the election, he would not be attending any debates, having withdrawn to take a very important policy position at the United Nations. She then added, "In New York City," in case anyone didn't know where the UN had been located since 1948. This sent a buzz through the crowd as apparently at least half the room had not heard the big news. McKay looked like he could hardly keep a straight face. He glanced down from the stage at someone and gave a subtle little thumbs-up. I leaned forward and could see Dikoombe, his campaign manager, in the front row scowling at him as if to say, *Be cool. We're supposed to be as surprised as anyone at this news.*

That son of a bitch had not returned any of my calls over the last month. Once he had my name on a ballot it was radio silence. Sitting there, I remembered his words, *It's good to be needed.* Well, I didn't feel very needed right now. It looked like Sean was halfway under the bus and that little prick Shannon had his consent to laicization in his hip pocket. We were screwed. I was suddenly furious with myself for ever agreeing to get into this mess. It had all been for nothing. What was I even doing here?

I felt a hand on my shoulder and turned to see none other than Dr. Sheila Rubin. Her puffy grinning face was perched above her standard massive wool cowl. For some reason she was also wearing a long green plaid cape and matching tweed cap. She looked like an overweight Agatha

Christie. I had not seen or spoken to her since our last session months ago. So much for promising to stay in touch.

"I'm so glad you made it, Andrew. I've been looking forward to hearing your thoughts in this election and what you have in store for our riding if you win."

Win? Is she crazy? "Hi, Sheila, I'm so sorry I haven't been in touch. It's been very busy . . . The inquiry . . . I'm just . . . My brother . . . Working hard, though. Change is possible but it isn't always easy. But I'm doing the work." *Blah blah blah.* Surely this was enough of what she needed to hear.

"Oh, no need to apologize. I know what you've been up to. I follow you on Twitter . . ." Then, with a stage whisper, "You're my star client."

Whoa. What the F? Star client? Isn't that supposed to be confidential? And I'm on Twitter? "I . . . I . . ." I didn't know what to say.

As usual she carried on talking, oblivious to anything I might want to add. "Don't be so hard on yourself. You can't make it to every all-candidates debate. I'm just so glad you've taken such a strong position on animal rights."

Whoa, whoa, whoa. Oh God. No. Not another animaltarian. "Thanks, Sheila. I appreciate it, but tonight I'm just here to . . ."

Without missing a beat, she talked right over me. "I let Ms. Chang, the moderator, know you're here." She leaned in to whisper, "She's a patient of mine too. She didn't even know that you had arrived." As she said these words the woman in the black suit and massive scarf smiled, waved and gestured for me to come forward to the stage. *Shit.* I knew it was a mistake coming. I could hear her calling to Audio Max, "We need another microphone for Mr. Bierce." He fairly leapt from his girlfriend's side. *This is an audio emergency!*

A few heads strained to see me as I walked along the edge of the crowd toward the stage. I heard an old man turn to his wife and yell in her ear, "I thought she said he was in New York at the UN?" Someone called out, "Animal rights, not wrongs!" to strong supporting applause. And then, "Being cruel isn't cool."

Through the buzz Ms. Chang tried to explain to the audience that *this* Mr. Bierce was the *Independent* candidate, not the NDP candidate. Mass confusion followed, of course. Dozens of NDP supporters, clad in orange scarves, were thrown into a desperate tizzy. What?! No NDP social warrior? I guessed that later, when they got home to their apartments in Parkdale, they would console themselves with some Bruce Cockburn music, from the period during which he wished he had a rocket launcher and some son of a bitch would die. There's an answer to our problems.

I could see a puzzled-looking Dikoombe in the audience, whispering something up to McKay on stage. So I walked over to him and grabbed his hand, making sure everyone saw my enthusiastic handshake. He hissed at me. "We shouldn't be seen looking so cozy. Get away from me."

Really? For good measure I threw my arms around him in a bear hug that suggested not only friendship but my personal commitment to good race relations. I leaned in, smiling broadly, and whispered, "You should return my fucking calls. Where is that little prick Shannon? What about our arrangement? My brother?"

He struggled to get out of my warm embrace. "You'll need to take that up with Father Shannon, it's in his hands . . . Unfortunately, he's in Haiti now dealing with another matter. I think he feels—we feel—the election of Mr. McKay is well in hand, so to speak. I'm not sure what I can add."

"In other words, we're not needed. Sean's to be defrocked?"

"That's up to Father Shannon." He looked at the floor, too cowardly to admit that Sean and I were totally fucked.

Nonetheless, I smiled broadly for the crowd, released him and headed to climb the steps to the stage. Before I could move, I was suddenly surrounded by a dozen or more familiar faces. It was the animal rights cabal from my meeting at the AGO. The barista–animal rights lawyer still in torn black jeans and Doc Martens, the elderly man in his dated double-breasted suit (were those the very same flakes on his shoulders?) and soiled dog mask, the lady in the red plastic-rimmed glasses scowling at me, still blinking madly and carrying a small dog, all of them patted my back and struggled to shake my hand.

The barista-lawyer stepped forward from the clutch. "Oh, Mr. Bierce, we are so glad you're here to speak for us."

For us? Uh, not really. "Thank you. I'm so glad you came. I really wanted to come to the other debates but," *I have a life,* "I appreciate your support tonight. Financial and otherwise . . . You guys are the best."

They were clearly thrilled to hear that. "Oh, it doesn't matter. You're here now. It's wonderful! We can't wait to hear you speak."

I looked around at their excited eyes and noticed that the young woman in the overalls covered with *I Heart Dog* buttons, and *Save the Pigs* pins, the one with the devastated complexion, was not there. "Where's . . ." I had no idea what her name was, ". . . the young lady from the MyPetsTheBestCo! Charity Dog Walk?"

Their faces turned sullen. "I guess you've been so busy you haven't heard."

"Heard what?" Surely she wasn't at another dog walk fundraiser this very night.

"Claire was killed two days ago. She was run over by a transport truck near the slaughterhouse."

"What?" I heard the older fellow mutter through his dirty mask that it was "more like *murder*."

"We were protesting at the corner of Lakeshore and Strachan, where the transport trucks turn and bring pigs to the slaughterhouse. One of the trucks took the corner too fast, too tight, and she fell under the wheels . . . it was horrible."

"Oh my God." The poor truck driver must feel terrible.

The moderator called again for us to begin. Stunned by the news, I made my way to the stage. McKay stepped forward and shook my hand solemnly and whispered, "Welcome aboard. And nice suit." I wish I could have said the same about his. For one thing it was olive-green and he was wearing a light-green shirt with it. And the suit was double-breasted for heaven's sake. His ensemble was topped off with a blue and black bowtie. I assumed he must be colour blind.

Max set up a chair, gave my microphone three *check, check, checks* for good measure, handed it to me with a smile and whispered, "Go get 'em. It's not cool to be cruel." *Oh God, these people are everywhere.*

The moderator introduced us and explained that each candidate would remain seated for the evening and had the option of giving a maximum three-minute opening overview of their platform.

McKay decided to kick things off with a list of key issues followed by a generic *only we can solve all of the above problems* platform. It was a low-risk, nothing controversial, *I'm in the lead so stick to the plan* speech. Having heard nothing of substance, the crowd gave polite applause.

His remarks were followed by three very nervous minutes of the Liberal candidate, Kaminski, reading—from index cards piled on his jumping leg—statistics about the cost of living. He had to conclude his economics lecture when his electrified knee fired all the remaining cards onto the stage floor. Well done, professor.

We were then treated to five excruciating minutes of the *Reach for the Top* girl haranguing us about oil, climate change, composting and how everyone in the room was responsible for some melting ice shelf and the impending global collapse. I shuddered at the thought of her poor parents being subjected to composting speeches at the dinner table every night, or recycling lectures when they arrive home from Costco with piles of plastic packaging and a pallet of bottled water.

The moderator finally got her to stop by getting Max to kill her microphone, but her team of a dozen or so supporters were ecstatic with her performance and carried on for another few minutes with a standing ovation. It was by far the most entertaining thing to happen so far. I gave her two thumbs up and a wink.

In response she scowled at me and mouthed, *Phoney*.

Okay, so it's like that. I smiled, gave her another thumbs-up and mouthed, *Fuck off*. She looked shocked and like she was going to cry.

The moderator turned to me. "Mr. Bierce, would you like to make an opening statement?"

What could I say? I had not prepared anything. "No, I'm fine. I'll just wait for the questions. Thank you."

I could see despairing looks of disappointment from the animal rights trolls in the front row and even Max. *Reach for the Top* muttered "Phoney" again. Then, I swear, out of the corner of my eye I saw McKay roll his eyes and Dikoombe shake his head in disgust. Was he laughing at me?

Hmm.

"Madam Chair, you know, on second thought, I think I will make a few remarks."

After that, the evening didn't really go as everyone might have expected.

45

I Could Get a Taste for This

Monday October 24

THE MODERATOR SEEMED pleasantly surprised that I would speak, especially after that Green doom tirade had bummed everyone out. I'd noticed people hiding their water bottles as she hectored us about recycling. "That's wonderful, Mr. Bierce. You have three minutes."

I'm more comfortable speaking while standing so I rose from my chair, microphone in hand, walked to the middle of the stage and looked down at eager faces yearning for enlightenment, waiting for wise words from the candidate.

I'd seen this movie before. Too many times. Suckers.

"First, let me thank you folks," *political word designed to convey humble solidarity with everyday people,* "for coming tonight." I pointed at the front row of my admirers. *Identifying them conveys to the larger audience the presence of existing support and acknowledges them as significant supporters, personal friends perhaps.* They were thrilled, of course. "It's important to be here," *reassures crowd that they are not wasting an evening missing* The Voice *or* Dancing with the Stars, "to hear candidates, actually eyeball them. See what you're buying, so to speak. But before going any further, maybe we should give a shout-out to Max," *gesture toward young man in front row,* "who has been working hard up here with the audio." *Conveys solidarity with little people working behind the scenes.* This triggered a hearty round of cheering for Max, who actually stood and acknowledged the applause with a huge smile. *Generates warmth with crowd by sharing the limelight.* I'm pretty sure the two people I saw punching the air with both arms were his parents. Two votes right there probably, and Max already in the bag.

I gave Max a firm thumbs-up and carried on. *If that doesn't get you laid Max, nothing will.*

"I was especially moved by Mr. McKay's remarks." *Suggests civil camaraderie with other candidates.* He was a little surprised as I turned to him, but he nodded and smiled as if to say, *I appreciate your support.* "If I could summarize his policies, they seem to be basically . . . blah blah blah housing, blah blah blah health care, blah blah blah cost of living, blah blah blah crime, blah blah blah mental health, blah blah blah homelessness." As I carried on reciting his list, emphasizing each topic with my fingers held aloft, counting them off, the audience shifted from stunned silence to a puzzled buzz and finally to outright laughter. "Blah blah blah traffic congestion, blah blah blah subways, blah blah blah environment. Did I miss anything, Mr. McKay?" *Draw audience's eyes to puzzled-looking opponent.*

He sat *mutus. What is going on?*

"Oh right, sorry, I forgot, blah blah blah bike lanes." There was another wave of laughter. "I've been a lawyer for a long time," *indicates professional credibility,* "and in my line of work, blah blah blah isn't worth the paper it's not written on." *A chestnut that never gets tired.* "Let's take some questions." *Leave audience wanting more.*

I returned to my seat, sat down and looked at my watch. Three minutes pretty much to the second.

The room suddenly burst into applause.

McKay was furious, leaping to his feet, waving his arms. "That is a gross misrepresentation of what I said."

The moderator stepped in, "Well, let's move to the question-and-answer part of the evening and you can address Mr. Bierce's comments at that time."

McKay would have none of it. "I should be able to rebut his comments now! This is totally unfair. He didn't talk about what he would do. He only criticized me."

"Well, as I said, we are moving on to the question-and-answer part . . ."

"I demand an opportunity to respond."

A few audience members started to boo and chirp, some yelling, "Move on. Move on. Take questions." And I heard an "It's not cool to be cruel," for good measure.

McKay headed back to his chair, furious. I could see Dikoombe gesturing for him to settle down. I'm sure he thought, *Hey, we're at 37 percent. Relax*.

From a battered wooden podium the moderator turned to the audience, "I have a series of questions. Some have been submitted by people in attendance tonight and a few from those watching online. We are randomly selecting the order in which the answers will be given. First question is for . . ." Ms. Chang turned to Ms. Reach for the Top.

McKay was out of his seat again. "Why is she getting the first question? You said I could respond."

"No, I said we were doing the questions randomly. We are drawing from a hat, Mr. McKay. You will get your turn. Please. Now, Rebecca Hatfield, here is your question: There was a murder recently at the corner of Dunn Avenue and Queen Street. Drug related. Gang related. What is your party's position on the increased level of crime in Toronto?"

Five minutes later Ms. Reach for the Top was still trying to explain with some kind of cat's cradle logic that environmental problems create refugees which in turn contribute to homelessness which adds to mental health problems and therefore drug use and finally crime. So, to solve the problem of murders in Parkdale we need to do more about that ice shelf—three thousand miles away. She sat down to dead silence until her cohorts leapt to their feet chanting, "No more oil, no more oil!"

I turned to her and mouthed, *Great answer.* She sneered at me.

The moderator reached into the hat and then turned to me. "Mr. Bierce, same question."

"Thank you, . . ."

Before I could get a word out McKay was on his feet. "I have been sitting here waiting for a question and an opportunity to respond to his . . . his . . . accusations . . . and now he's going again?"

"Mr. McKay, your turn will come. These are being drawn randomly. Please. Mr. Bierce, carry on."

I saw Dr. Rubin in the front row. She was beaming, no doubt at the thought that her handiwork had molded this new dynamic moral character, her star client. I could not let her down.

"Thank you for the question. I think we were all taken aback by the random tragic violence that occurred on Queen near Dunn." *Acknowledge solidarity with community.* "And I know everyone here sends their thoughts and prayers to the family of that poor man." *Thoughts and prayers, while having no monetary value, are given great weight at such times.* "He was homeless, the man who was murdered there was homeless." *Stress pre-existing tragic state of victim.* I thought a little extra emphasis was needed. "Oh, and Dunn Avenue, for anyone who doesn't know, is basically the opposite side of the riding from Mr. McKay's residence way up on Riverside Drive." I pointed to the heavens as if McKay lived in Forest Hill. *Make comment and gesture that separate opponent from larger community based on perceived wealth and, therefore, insensitivity to plight of others. Added humour a bonus.*

There were some ohhs from the audience and a few laughs. But McKay was livid. "I know where Dunn Street is . . ."

"*Avenue*. Dunn *Avenue*." *Stress lack of familiarity with disadvantaged section of riding.*

"Whatever," he sputtered. "At least I live in the riding. And you, Mr. Bierce, are no . . ."

I looked to the moderator and held up my hands in feigned exasperation, imploring her to exercise some control over McKay.

"Mr. McKay, you'll have your chance. It's Mr. Bierce's opportunity to speak. Mr. Bierce, please. Continue."

"This is unbelievable." McKay fell onto his chair.

"As I was saying, everyone who *knows that area of the riding* was taken aback by this violence. My colleague and, dare I say my friend, Dr. Sheila Rubin, is here this evening." I polipointed her out in the front row for good measure. *Clear indication to mob that I have connections to the riding.* "That murder occurred just steps from her home and her practice so I can tell you that it really hit home for both of us." *Indicates personal devastation at the murder of a total stranger.* I saw a few nods of approval from the crowd and some friends on either side of Dr. Rubin patting her plaid cape, comforting her. "These issues—homelessness, drugs, mental health and crime—are linked." I knit my fingers together for emphasis. *Indicates that I know that these problems, while fully understood by me, are nonetheless complex.* "Trying to solve them in isolation will not work. I would like to say more on this but I'm out of time." *Deflect to avoid having to go into more detail but also indicate I follow the debate rules, unlike others.*

I could see that McKay was out of his seat again, microphone in hand, pacing around behind me. The moderator looked at him, alarmed, and said, "Mr. McKay, same question to you. You have two minutes."

"Two minutes? Everyone else has had more than that." He was in attack mode. Not a good look at 37 percent.

"You have two minutes. Crime."

"First, Mr. Andrew Bierce does not even live in the riding. Second, let's talk about how you're friends with this . . . this psychiatrist . . . and talk about violence, were you not involved in a deadly shooting in the court a few years ago? Were you not suspended by the Law Society? You . . . you . . ." Exasperated, he turned to the crowd for some kind of validation. It was not there.

"Mr. McKay, is that your response to the question about crime?" The moderator was confused. "If so, we will move on to the next question."

I raised my hand politely and said, "Madam Chair, I don't want to interfere with your agenda. I know you run a tight ship." *Praise moderator for difficult job.* "Please, may I reserve a little time at some point to respond to those unfair accusations? If there's time." *Suggests there is more to the story. Leave audience curious.*

"Certainly, if we have time." She reached into the hat. "Our next question is for Mr. McKay . . ."

"Finally!" McKay threw his hands up in the air.

Someone at the back of the room shouted, "No! Let Bierce answer now. Is it true?"

A group started to chant, "Let him speak. Let him speak." My front row cheering section joined in enthusiastically by stomping their feet.

I held up my hands in feigned protest. "It's okay. It's okay. If there's time . . . Later." *Indicates that I'm the victim here but I'll manage.*

But they would not stop. The moderator turned to me, realizing it was not going to end unless she gave me a chance. "Mr. Bierce, quickly. One minute response."

McKay would have none of it. "Why does he get to respond when I couldn't respond to his attack?"

A new chant started. "Sit down. Sit down. Sit down." And again, a wit yelled for good measure, "It's not cool to be cruel."

I could see Dikoombe waving his arms to get McKay to cool down. His candidate was losing his composure and the room along with it.

The moderator turned to me. "Mr. Bierce. One minute."

"Thank you for the opportunity. I'm sorry, but I really need to correct the record and answer that shabby attempt to smear me. That's old-style politics." *Suggests I would not stoop to such tactics. After all, I'm not a politician.* "We need to change." *Suggests I offer a fresh approach.* I looked at the crowd and then McKay. "We're better than that." *We are better, but not you McKay!* "But, briefly, it's true." *Disarming admission generates curiosity.* "My client smuggled a gun into a courtroom and used it to kill a senior member of our legal community, a man who was my close friend, my valued colleague, his name was Lester Donald." There was dead silence as I spoke. "Actually, . . ." I waited a couple of beats and put a closed fist to my mouth as if composing myself, "he died saving my life." A woman in the front row burst into tears. *I looked at her and nodded, then held up a hand to her as if to say. It's okay to cry. It was a tragedy, after all.*

"It's also true that I did take a *pause*," *alternative fact to suspension,* "from my law practice after that happened. It was at the *recommendation,*" a*lright, granted, it was a compulsory recommendation,* "of the Law Society. I'm not ashamed to say I sought counselling." *What?! Who admits that?! Only the strong, that's who.* "That's what mental health is all about, isn't it? Reaching out when you need it?"

I could see Dr. Rubin standing and applauding and Red Spectacles, blinking madly, nodding and patting the little dog that sat in her lap barking.

"And now, as a candidate, I feel I've been given a second chance." *Redemption is possible.* "People can change." *That one's for you, Dr. Rubin!* "I'm asking to be given a chance to do something about it." *It's called public service for a reason!* "But I need more than your vote. I need your help—everyone's help—as a community." *I can't do it alone after all!* "We," *point around room,* "are all in this together." *While a meaningless statement, it typically generates nods of agreement. I mean, we're not in this together?* "Thank you."

I sat down slowly, clearly moved by my own words and thought, *Dear God, someone open a window.*

Instead, the room burst into applause.

I glanced at Dikoombe and smiled. *Oh, I'm not finished with you yet, not by a long shot.*

"Thank you, Mr. Bierce. That was . . . well . . . very powerful . . ." The moderator was actually choked up.

I had a thought. "If I might also just add a further word? Since we are on the topic of violence . . ."

McKay was on his feet. "You gave him one minute and he has gone well past that. This is totally unfair."

"Let Bierce speak. Let Bierce speak." The chant went up again.

"Mr. Bierce, I'm really bending the rules this evening, but briefly, just on the issue of violence. One minute." I could see McKay gesturing to Dikoombe to do something.

I looked directly at my cheering section. "On the issue of violence in our society, we should pause for a moment to think about a young woman, Claire, who was tragically killed recently while supporting the rights of animals. She was run over—crushed—by a transport truck down by the Lakeshore at Strachan." *Pause. Allow buzz to sweep through the crowd. Did he say crushed?* "It was terrible." *I made it sound like I might have actually been there at her side.* "When a person cares about something so passionately," *as I clearly do,* "and they put their life on the line, well," *it was for pigs, after all,* "we need to acknowledge that sacrifice."

The entire room, led by the cheering front row, stood and gave a solemn round of applause for a young woman they had never met and who had been fighting for a cause they probably thought was a little crazy, especially with pork shoulders on special this week at Costco.

Once things settled down, the moderator took us through a few more questions about bike lanes and the teen mental health clinic at the local hospital but it was obvious that people were getting restless. It was almost 9 p.m. More index cards were read. More angry accusations were hurled. More alarm bells were rung about the coming climate catastrophe. At one point McKay struggled to recover the room by telling a sappy story about his supportive wife and his kids and how well they were doing at their local high schools but there was no traction with the crowd now. Minds were being made up.

Ms. Chang steered a tight ship and asked for quiet. "Finally, it is getting late but I am going to turn now to a question that was just submitted by someone watching online. I'm addressing it to you, Mr. McKay: *COVID devastated many small businesses, many restaurants in this very riding, for example. What are your views on the federal and provincial responses to COVID? What if anything would you do differently?*"

My phone pulsed. I took a quick look at it as McKay began to pace in front of the crowd like a game-show host. He was recounting how the government supports had saved businesses and families. The text was from Sean. *Watching online. Quite the show. Missed your calling. I just teed it up for you with that question. Go get him.*

McKay had no idea what was coming.

46

Noses in the Trough?
Monday October 24

ONCE MCKAY HAD finished his spiel about how successful he had been as a local businessman and how great COVID supports were for people in need and how lucky his entire family had been to never get COVID, the moderator turned to me. "Mr. Bierce, two minutes. Same question. Did COVID supports work?"

"First, let me thank the person watching online for the very good question." *Always acknowledge source of question and tell them it is a very good question regardless of how stupid.* "Technology is allowing us to reach more voters. That's a good thing and I support getting our young people, like Ms. Hatfield here, involved in politics." *Double points for expressing—at the same time—support for technology and the only people who understand it. Well done.*

I turned to her scowling face and, with both hands, gave her two thumbs up. "I applaud your efforts, putting yourself out there. Well done." There was a wave of applause for my magnanimous comments and, if her parents were in the audience, I might very well have landed their votes as well.

"This issue is very important. Especially now that the leader of Mr. McKay's party has been forced to step aside . . ." *Intriguing salacious tidbit for audience.*

McKay shouted over me. "He wasn't forced, it was his health . . ."

"Sure, it was, but now that he has stepped aside—*whatever his reasons*—your name, Mr. McKay, is being touted as a potential leader so your views on many matters are becoming of greater interest. So, it's about your character too." *Character? What has that got to do with anything? This is politics.*

Uninvited, McKay decided to clarify his status. "I'm not the leader of my party but it's flattering to have my name even being mentioned. I'll serve in any capacity the party or the province needs me. Certainly as premier I would be in a better position to serve this riding, my home."

Oh-oh, he went too far. There were some ohhs and ahhs after that proclamation. "Premier!?" Someone in an orange scarf called out, "Win a seat first!"

Surprised by the crowd's sour reaction, he added, "I just mean I'm ready to serve."

"Sure you do. But about COVID supports. I can tell that you were a big fan of the COVID financial supports. Although lawyers and law firms could not benefit from CERB or any of the other COVID supports, I followed the use of these benefits closely. For many of my needy clients it was a godsend." *Hypothetical because, frankly, I cannot recall ever having a needy client, financially at least.* "But some people milked a cash cow." *Plain talk never disappoints.* "Fraud ran rampant."

I turned to the crowd. "I'm sure we all agree that anyone who took CERB money fraudulently should be held to account." *Who could disagree?* A murmur spread through the audience as people looked at each other and nodded.

"That was not free money. It was taxpayer money. Your money." More nodding and buzzing. "Did you know, Mr. McKay, that there were 7.8 million CERB claims paid out, but for some reason Canada only recorded five million jobs lost through COVID." *Pause to allow audience to perform simple mental math.* "That's a lot of money to people as COVID support, but to people who hadn't lost jobs. What happened to our tax dollars?" *Pour foundation, then patiently erect scaffold.*

I saw McKay look at Dikoombe. He was worried. Dikoombe looked puzzled. *Where was this going?*

"Neither I nor any member of my family benefited from the COVID supports." I turned and pointed at McKay. "Can you say the same, Mr. McKay? Yes or no?"

He was stunned. "I think people's confidential tax information is their own business, besides that's federal jurisdiction, federal tax dollars . . . What has it got to do with this provincial election?" *Weak ineffective flat-footed deflection.*

"There's only one taxpayer, Mr. McKay." The crowd loved that one. *Who doesn't love an old reheated political chestnut?*

"It's irrelevant."

I launched a rocket. "So, it's not true that your son Marcus, who lives at home, applied for and received CERB benefits?"

"Leave my children out of this." That came out a little angry.

Another rocket. "And your daughter Haley, who also lives at home, she applied for and received CERB benefits?"

"Mr. Bierce, you are dragging my children into this . . . that's unfair." Now angry and defensive.

"Well, you were the one telling us how well they are doing in local high schools?"

He was livid.

"If your children were in school, not in the workforce, and living at home, COVID-free, why were they applying for and receiving CERB benefits?"

That's when I saw McKay's wife elbowing through the crowd and coming at the stage. She was a ball of parental fury. Dikoombe managed to intercept and restrain her before she climbed up the steps to get at me. Unfortunately, the moderator's microphone picked up some of her salty language.

I pointed to her at the front of the stage and launched another rocket. "I see your wife, Pam, is here this evening. I understand she filed as well to get a CRCB grant. Those grants were designed to assist people who needed to stay at home and care for a child under twelve or a family member sick with COVID. You had neither. Correct? Is that because your wife wasn't at home caring for anyone? She works for Canada Revenue Agency." I heard a few gasps.

McKay turned to the moderator. "His two minutes are up."

It didn't matter because before Ms. Chang could cut me off, I unleashed another missile. "Did your family then use that CERB money—taxpayer money—to finance a series of cannabis shops around the riding, on Bloor, on Roncesvalles and on Queen Street . . . near Dunn Avenue?"

There was now another audible gasp and then silence as people awaited his answer. "I think people here want to know the answers to these questions. They deserve answers."

"You said he had two minutes and now he's dragging my family into this."

The moderator stared at him. Someone called out, "Answer the questions!"

Desperate, McKay looked at Dikoombe. There was no lifesaver there.

I hated to let a fully armed bomb sit unused, so I carried on. "Mr. McKay, the Glenforest Ski Club, near Collingwood."

He looked at the floor, despondent.

"It's a private club. I'm told it costs thirty thousand to join. You and your family are members." I turned to the crowd. "Too rich for my blood." *Not really, but I don't ski.* "I understand you used your position as chair of their board to apply for and receive CERB grants. The club then used that money, taxpayer money, to replace their chairlifts. Is that true? I guess your wife helped with that application? Have you and your family been enjoying those nice new chairlifts?"

McKay stared at the crowd.

And then it was time for the mother of all bombs, the *coup de grâce.* "Mr. McKay, your brother-in-law, the one who's in prison for fraud, I understand he filed successfully for CERB as well. From prison. And invested the taxpayer money he received in your chain of cannabis shops?"

McKay had heard enough. "This is an outrageous attack on my family. I won't stand for it. You will hear from my lawyers." McKay stormed off the stage to boos and chants of "Answer the questions!" while the Liberal candidate searched through his index cards for the party's suggested answers to questions about CERB.

The moderator, having lost control of the meeting, wisely decided to call it quits and adjourned with a loud "Thank you and don't forget to vote!" Various groups began to chant, "Answer the question," and, "It's not cool to be cruel," and, "No more oil, no more oil."

Satisfied with a job well done, I turned to Ms. Reach for the Top, gave her another double thumbs-up and said, "Compost that." She just stared at me, I assume in awe of my decimation of McKay. But then somehow inspired, she leapt to her feet and tried to link CERB with the amount of fuel burned by the private jets of Canadian celebrities. Clearly not a straight line. As she shouted over the noise of people packing up to leave, I decided to leave well enough alone and started to slip through a sudden wellspring of supporters and a couple of reporters. I desperately wanted to get out to my car and enjoy a well-earned drink.

Suddenly, the old man I'd overheard earlier yelling at his wife grabbed my hand and gave it a firm shake. "Don't go to New York. The UN is a bunch of communists! Stay here."

I took his hand and gave it the patented political double-handed grasp and shake. "Only if I can count on your vote."

"You've got it and my wife's too."

"God bless you."

Politics, insufferable.

However, being realistic, I knew my bullshit dance in front of a couple hundred people wasn't going to be nearly enough to dislodge McKay's considerable lead. But at least he would have some explaining to do over the next couple of days. And my attack certainly wasn't going to help stop Sean's defrocking, that's for sure. Dikoombe was probably on the phone to Shannon as I sat there, telling him to process the paperwork from Haiti out of pure revenge for that public roasting of his anointed man.

When I slid into the comfort of my car I fired up a cigar, poured another generous shot from my flask and watched people leaving the Mechanics Hall, going to their cars, waiting for buses and even some brave ones climbing on to bikes. I had to smile as Max emerged holding hands with that cute young lady from the front row. But then, dear God, no. I watched as he strapped on a helmet that had small horns on it, climbed aboard a unicycle and pedalled off into the night, leaving her to catch a bus home alone. Oh, Max. No.

Suddenly, there was a crisp tap at my car window. Shit, surely a cop wasn't out prowling side streets for people drinking and driving at this hour. I threw a coat over my flask and lowered the window.

It was Dikoombe. "That was quite a show you put on."

"Oh that? It was nothing really."

"I've heard of opposition research but that was good. Well done. Won't ask how you came by that."

"Anything else? I'm a little busy."

"I can see you are. Just wanted to say that I wasn't aware of any of the CERB stuff . . ."

"Sure you weren't. Just like you weren't aware of why I'm in this election as a candidate. I think you called it comic relief. Funny, eh?"

"That was different. I could hardly admit that we brought you into the race to make mischief with the NDP, could I?"

"Anything else?"

"No, but I hope we can stay in touch."

My phone rang. I said nothing as my window scrolled up.

"Andrew Bierce."

"It's me, Bonnie. I hear you killed tonight."

"Ha, word travels fast."

"It's called Twitter. Naomi had someone post your entire opening remarks and then your CERB fraud attack. You're a sensation."

"Wow. It's a new world. I hope your fellow Reyo is stronger than the teenager they're running in Parkdale–High Park. She was awful."

"I don't know her. Candidate *Mateo Reyes* is doing well, but that's not why I'm calling. I'm back at the office trying to catch up."

I looked at my watch. It was nearly 10 p.m. God bless you, Bonnie. "I don't know what I would do without you."

"Well, hold your praise cuz you're not going to like this."

Oh shit, what now?

"What's up?"

"We've been served with a stack of paperwork by the Public Guardian and Trustee."

"PGT? What file have we got with them?"

"Marrs."

"Marrs, the dog file?"

"They obtained an *ex parte* order freezing our trust account. I took a quick look at the affidavits in support and it looks like the $100,000 she gave us is not actually hers, it's money she is supposed to be managing for her mom, a mom who's in long-term care."

"Does Marrs have a POA?"

"Not for long, the PGT is moving to have her removed for misuse of her mother's accounts. She hasn't been paying the long-term care home or any of Mom's personal needs, glasses, hairdressing and so on. The home was threatening to kick the mom out. PGT is looking for her to reimburse her mom's accounts about $300,000."

"Does the mom have a will?"

"Yup, looks like it leaves everything to our client."

"So, it's going to be her money . . . eventually."

"Eventually, but not yet."

"How old's Mom?"

"Hang on." I could hear Bonnie flipping through paperwork. "In her nineties."

"Does Marrs know about the motion to remove her as POA?"

"Yes, she was served today, around the time when we were served."

"She wasn't with the usual animal-lover clutch at the all-candidates meeting tonight. Did they get an order keeping her away from her mom?"

"I don't see one . . . Andrew, you don't think she'd hurt her mom?"

Hemingway came to mind.

47

The Good, the Bad, the Ugly
Friday October 28

I HAD TO put the nonsense of the election aside and focus on two matters: Marrs and The Coop. Sure, all-candidates meetings could be fun but attending them was a waste of time and, therefore, money. After the horsewhipping Monday evening, McKay decided he would skip the remaining debates, I assume out of fear that I would show up with more dirt. I heard from Naomi that the meetings in Parkdale–High Park turned into shouting matches between Reach for the Top Girl and the Liberal Index Card guy. Can democracy survive this nonsense?

My phone pulsed. It was Patrick. "Hey, Pat, what's up?"

"I'm a little disappointed that my lawyer—and friend, I thought—was not prepared to share a little music intel with me."

Okay. Good. I guess Sarah had finally blabbed about Brent. I was surprised it took her so long. "What do you mean? Intel? On what?"

"A little birdie told me that Brent's sitting on a busload of new music and he's after Coop to record with him. I would like to have known about that. I've got no music, you know, except for 'Hockeytonkin'' and a few others. I was counting on Coop to have some ideas."

"What can I say? I was sworn to secrecy by Coop. It could be a pretty big deal if they do it. They see it as a kind of reunion, like Bachman and Cummings getting back together. I'm not so sure about that direction but I'm not a music person."

"You know they say you should skate to where the puck is going to be, not where it is."

That sounded familiar. "What are you saying, Pat?"

"Should I be chasing Brent instead of Coop?"

"Oh wow, that is pretty big advice for a lawyer to be giving but . . ."

"But what?"

"If I were you, with your sound and what I've heard of Brent's music . . ."

"Whoa. You've actually heard some of it?"

"Yes, but no one's supposed to know. I think he's more in your music lane."

"I heard it's kinda Eagles meets Kid Rock."

"Yeah, I heard that characterization too." *Because it was me who said it.*

"That's where I think I should be headed. This pure country stuff is not really my . . . you know . . ."

"It's not you. You're rock, man. With maybe an alt country feel. Almost retro rockabilly."

"Yes, yes. Exactly."

"So, what are you saying? What can I do?"

"If you've heard the music, can you speak to Brent? Get me into a conversation with him. Without Coop knowing I'm trying to scoop him. I don't want to piss him off. He's powerful in the biz."

"I could make a few calls if you think it would help."

"Andy, you are the man. Can't thank you enough."

"Listen, I'm here to help my clients, my friends."

I dialled Coop. He had been on standby and answered on one ring. "What's up, counsel?"

"I think I can put something together for you and Brent."

"I'm listening."

"We had a long meeting on Thursday. There could be a win-win. He'll keep the peace on Kayla. He will not pursue the songwriting credits. You will not have to record an album with him."

"Holy shit! Man, this is golden. Pat was right. You're a fucking wizard."

"Thanks, but let's wait until all the pieces are in place first. I'm going to need a couple of things from you."

"Say the word."

"Brent's going to have to stay on as your business manager for three more years and then step aside to pursue his own career."

"Done."

"Naomi's going to phase in over that time to take over your accounting."

"Absolutely done."

"You will keep your hands off her."

"You're no fun but done."

"Patrick McGovern, instead of you, is going to record an album with Brent. Brent is going to use some of Patrick's music."

"Hell ya, done!"

"You're going to be executive producer and provide advance reviews for their new album."

I could feel him hesitating.

"Remember the fucking wizard part?"

"Okay. Okay. Done."

"You're going to *reluctantly* allow Sarah to transition to a full-time job promoting Pat and Brent's new project."

"No problem but can I still, you know, . . . with her?"

"No."

"You really are no fun but done."

"Here comes the hard part."

"I knew there would be a catch."

"I need you to be mildly pissed with Pat but not ruin the relationship."

"Why? I love the fact that he is going over to work with Brent on a project."

"He needs to feel that he scooped you on the album with Brent. Can you play it out like that? Let me lay it out for him first. And then I'll give you some lines to say. Sound good?"

"Fucking awesome. Can I ask you a question?"

"Sure. Fire away."

"How did you get Brent to back off on the credits and the album? He had some serious leverage on me with this Kayla shit."

"It wasn't easy. It took the whole day. He had to cancel his golf game with Geddy."

"Oh, he wouldn't have liked that. He's a golf fanatic."

"But we hammered it out. I think we understood each other. I want to button the whole thing down with Brent and Patrick, and an NDA too."

"Sounds good to me. Nobody needs to know our business."

"By the way, I'm sending you a bill. It's a big one."

"Hey man, just send it to Brent and tell him to pay it. You're worth every penny."

"Can I ask you one last favour? It's a personal one."

"Sure."

I explained the situation.

"Not a problem. Happy to do it."

"You are the man. Thanks."

Now I needed to deal with Marrs.

Ms. Marrs was not returning Bonnie's calls. Never a good sign. She needed to explain what the hell was going on with the PGT and my now frozen retainer. I was certainly not going to waste time preparing for any dog hearing nor would I spend a nickel of my time trying to unfreeze the account until I heard from her.

She had absolutely refused to arrange any visits between her ex and the dogs, so I could hardly blame Fernstein when he arranged an expedited hearing to have her found in contempt and to turn over the dogs forthwith. Frankly, I was dreading the embarrassment of re-attending in front of Judge Linton to deal with dogs instead of children. What was I supposed to say when he asked where the dogs were? *The artful dodger has them hidden in the basement of the AGO, Your Honour.*

I spread the file out on the boardroom table and read the materials the PGT had filed. Affidavits from nurses, police officers, neighbours and an investigator. In a word? Brutal.

Marrs and her two little bulldogs were living the good life on her mother's money rather than her modest salary at the AGO. An affidavit from the nurse at the long-term care home was enough to bring any normal person to tears. The mother had not had a single visitor since admission. None of her personal needs, whether so much as a haircut, a fresh set of clothes or replacement of her broken prescription glasses, were being met. She was essentially abandoned and when the monthly bill for her care was missed a third time, they called the authorities.

Once engaged, the PGT investigator found a litany of not just physical neglect but financial abuse as well.

Rewind a few months back to June, around the time Ms. Marrs started leaving messages with Hopeless Helen. It turns out that she had her mom put in the home after the police found her wandering around the neighbourhood, half naked, in soiled clothes and emaciated. The third time the police officer picked her up, he asked when she had last eaten. She told him that her daughter had "given her an apple the day before."

The neighbours felt the mom had developed dementia over the last couple of years. They had been feeding her off and on and keeping an eye on her for months since her daughter, Ms. Marrs, had pulled into the driveway in her Range Rover and moved in with the dogs. Soon after, they were witnessing her abusive yelling at the mother whenever she managed to slip out of the locked house.

When the cops took Mom home again, they saw that her once beautiful single-family home in the Kingsway—bought and paid for by her and her long-deceased husband—had recently been roughly divided up into three units. Mom was confined to the main floor. The door to the second floor was blocked. The kitchen was unusable because part of the ceiling had caved in from crappy renos done above. The bathroom, they said, was "not fit for a human." There was an old TV and a radio. Fast food bags were piled in a corner. The basement was being used as a place for dogs to crap and was filled with dog feces.

With a little creativity (leaning heavily on the blocked door), they managed to access the second floor which was now being used by Ms. Marrs and her dogs since her marital separation. It had a new kitchen, a spa-like bathroom that included a shower stall for the dogs (which now leaked into the kitchen below), two large well-furnished bedrooms, an entertainment area and a well-stocked wine fridge.

The third floor was allegedly being used as an "office" by Ms. Marrs to carry on her art conservation work from home during COVID. The officer's affidavit explained that it was in fact being rented out for cash to a young woman who used it as an artist's studio and who walked the dogs from time to time for an offset on her rent. No conservation work was being done there. (Notwithstanding Marrs's assurance that she could not come to the gallery out of concern for COVID and was accomplishing just as much at home, if not more, than she did at the AGO.) It turns out that the only time she made an appearance at the AGO was to dine there regularly, because of the employee discount and to hide the dogs from time to time when her husband was looking for them.

After I'd read the first few affidavits I'd had enough—I dialled her. I needed to hear her explanation for this crap. Was it true? Any of it? There was no response to voice messages. I texted. No response. So I poured a drink and read on.

It got worse.

The PGT investigator had determined that by using a questionable power of attorney Marrs had transferred the mom's home to her name alone. She then put on a HELOC and transferred all of Mom's accounts into her name alone—except the one that received her OAS, CPP and a pension benefit deposit. Those deposits were immediately transferred to Marrs's personal account each month. The PGT had it all, chapter and verse, from the bank. Thousands of dollars flowing from Mom's savings and assets to her daughter's account.

My phone rang. Distracted, I answered. "Andrew Bierce."

"Mr. Bierce. Ms. Marrs." I could hear barking in the background.

Well, well. Finally. "Ms. Marrs, I have been trying to reach you for days. My assistant, Bonnie, has been trying to reach you. We have a very big problem. The Public Guardian . . ."

"I have the materials from them. All lies."

I didn't know where to start. "Does your mother have dementia?"

"She's old but she is very independent. She won't be told what to do. I've tried but she just won't listen."

"They have affidavits from her neighbours saying . . ."

"What do they know? Liars. They all hated me, growing up in that neighbourhood. They are just vengeful. Envious of my inheritance. Envious of my career."

I don't think I've ever heard of anyone being envious of someone restoring art in the basement of a museum. "They have evidence of significant financial misconduct by you with your mother's finances. Alleged."

"My mother wants me to have that money. It's my inheritance. She doesn't need it anymore. She said I should have it for looking after her."

"But the long-term care bills remain unpaid, three months' worth. And that is not your money. It's not an inheritance until your mother passes. You have very strict rules to follow while you're her POA. You have to account for all this money."

"Mr. Bierce, you of all people should understand that I have been dealing with the trauma of my separation and the care of two very sick dogs. Abby and Penny are not well. They need constant attention. Or have you forgotten, being so busy with your political career?"

The part about the dogs needing constant attention sounded about right because I could hear constant barking and yapping in the background. Was she running a kennel?

"Ms. Marrs, with the funds in my trust account frozen I have no retainer. We cannot do any work for you. Mr. Fernstein has this matter back in court. A judge is going to order those dogs returned to your husband. There's nothing I can do."

Her voice turned mean. "So you are abandoning me and Abby and Penny? Is that it? I knew it. If you weren't so busy running for office, you could help me."

Oh boy. Here we go. "Ms. Marrs, my political candidacy has nothing to do with . . ."

"What if I get the money?" She suddenly sounded desperate.

"Ms. Marrs, at this stage, I cannot imagine you coming up with enough of a retainer before the hearing. Every account, including your own, is frozen and will be for months. This is serious. You need to think about returning those dogs before any hearing. And this PGT application, it's very damaging. I will not be able to represent you."

All I heard was an angry anguished scream. And a lot more barking.

48

Hockeytonkin'!
Friday October 28

I DECIDED I should get back to Patrick sooner rather than later. If there was a deal to be made that satisfied everyone, then we should strike while the iron was hot.

I dialled. Pat must have been waiting for my call because I didn't even hear it ring.

"Hey, Andy. What's up? Any news for me?"

"There's news. Good and bad."

"Gimme the bad news first."

"Really?"

"I can take it."

"Okay. Coop's pissed at you."

"Oh shiiit. Oh man, that's exactly what I didn't want . . . oh man . . . wait . . . but why is he pissed?"

"That's the good news. Brent and you are going to be working together and Coop's a little pissed that you scooped him."

"What?! Are you serious? That's awesome!"

"It looks like 'Hockeytonkin'' is going to be shared with the world."

"Brent's okay with me contributing songs?"

"Yup. I think he sees a bigger upside working with you and your sound. It was a slight change in direction but he's totally on board."

"How can I smooth things over with Coop? I don't want any bad blood after this."

"Can I make a suggestion?"

"Sure."

"If I were you and Brent, I would find a role for Coop. Could you imagine him being, say, executive producer? Maybe ask him to do some advance reviews? Help pump interest?"

"Totally. Would he do it?"

"I think so. One other thing. Coop seems to have liked working with Sarah. Given her work behind the scenes," *and under the sheets*, "you are obviously going to want her on board to work with you and Brent. So I would bring her along but don't make a big deal of it. Tell her to be cool and have her just say that given her relationship and history with you and her respect for you as an artist, it would be best. Do you think she can be cool?"

"Totally. I will speak with her. I'm confident she'll be on board."

"Do you want me to stickhandle this a bit? I can talk to Coop about all this stuff, the EP role, advance reviews. I think you guys may want to button the whole thing down with a non-disclosure agreement too. Keep the process under wraps. No one needs to know that you scooped The Coop."

"Agreed. No way I want to embarrass him."

"Good. Let me talk to him and put the whole thing into a package. I'll get back to you. And I wouldn't press Coop just yet. Let him cool down."

"Andy, I don't know how to thank you. This is awesome, man."

"Well, I am sending you a rather large bill for all the time I've spent on this. Sound good?"

"Absolutely. Send it along. You are worth every penny."

Excellent. Nothing like a little double billing at a time like this.

49

E-Day, at Last
Monday November 7, 9 p.m.

BY THE TIME I got back to my condo it was almost 9 p.m. I was beat from putting the Brent-Coop-Patrick deal together and needed a drink—bad. It had taken the entire week to button down the details and get it signed. But it was done. And it was beautiful. As I punched in my security code, I could hear noises from inside, children shouting and a woman's voice. I even stepped back and looked at the door to make sure I was trying to get into the right condo. I was so tired I could have got off on the wrong floor. As the door swung open and I stepped in, there were a half-dozen people—more people than had ever been in my condo in all the time I'd owned it. What the hell.

Two PSWs slipped by me with a quick good night. They looked like they couldn't get out of there fast enough. Naomi was perched on the edge of my couch with a laptop balanced on her knees and a phone tucked between her ear and shoulder. She gave me a wave and turned back to her screen.

A young man wearing headphones and staring at two laptops was calling out results from different ridings, and what I assumed were polls from across Parkdale–High Park. I had never seen him before. He was surrounded by cans of Coke and his hand alternated between his laptops and a huge bag of popcorn beside his chair.

Two children now sat like zombies in a corner on my two beautiful Stockholm knot cushions. They were also under headphones and playing what appeared to be a video game. Occasionally one of them would yell *Yes!*, laugh and then punch the other. Brothers, I assumed.

Sean was stretched out on the couch wrapped from head to toe in a cocoon of blankets. The only reason I knew it was him was the grey face peering out, smiling weakly, and the whispered, "Hey, buddy boy. We've been waiting for you."

"What's going on here?"

"It's E-day. This is your campaign team."

"Campaign team? You mean gluttons for punishment. This is hopeless. I'm not even going to give a concession speech. I have bigger problems to solve."

"Naomi and I called in some troops to help track the results as they come in. Grab a drink. The polls are closing. It'll be fun. *'Fasten your seat belts. It's going to be a bumpy night.'*"

As sick as he was, there was now just a touch of excitement in his voice. Oh, how he loved an election. It would be his last. "Of all your attempts, that was the worst Bette Davis impersonation I've ever heard."

Undeterred, he carried on. "*I'd like to kiss ya but I just washed my hair.*"

Naomi giggled at another of his infamous terrible impersonations. She clearly had a soft spot for him. "Do that Pacino one. From *Scarface*? Or De Niro. The one from *Raging Bull.*"

"Oh God, no, please stop."

Giggling or not, Naomi was still glued to her phone. "Yes. Okay. Okay. Who knew?" She turned to me, "Hey, Andrew. If you're making a drink, I'll have one too. Scotch and soda if you have it."

I looked at Sean. "If I have it. She has no idea."

My sixty-inch flat-screen TV was tuned to CP24 and three monitors had been set up at my dining room table tuned in to CBC, CTV and Global.

That's when Daria came out of the bedroom.

"What the fuck are you doing here? And in my bedroom?"

Sean struggled to sit up. "Andrew, Andrew, easy, she came to help me get settled here. The PSWs had to leave. Naomi can't do it. She's busy with the campaign. Please. Daria's been a huge help."

"I'm not staying anyway. I have to get back to the hospital."

"Daria, stay to see the results. They'll be coming in any minute," Sean was pleading.

She stood by the door with her coat over her arm. No sooner had he said it than Naomi called out, "Hush up. Here we go." She stared at the TV as the numbers rolled up from the first round of results. "Turn it up."

The TV host turned to the political panel for comment but they were all looking at their phones. Clearly something was up.

"Colin, can we start with you? Based on these preliminary results I have to think that Liberals are very disappointed. Palmer called this election hoping to catch the PC leaderless."

"No, no, Vanessa, that's not fair. He called the election because it was a good time to seek a fresh mandate for important reforms."

Important reforms? They're going to need to open a window in that TV studio.

"Can you believe this crap? Fresh mandate. Jesus Christ, what horseshit." I poured a large scotch for myself and took a big sip. Ohh, that felt good going down. I mixed a scotch and soda for Naomi and set it down beside her. "Naomi, I appreciate the valiant effort. Are these your kids?"

"Yup, they're missing hockey. My husband is banned from the arena for the rest of the year because of that brawl. It was a condition of having the charges withdrawn."

"They look happy." I needed to make sure that no food got near those expensive cushions they were rolling around on.

"Just wait. It'll get worse as the evening goes on. Trust me. Brothers."

Sean called out to Daria, "Are you sure we can't get you a drink before you go?"

"No, I'm good. I'm leaving as soon as they give the first round of results."

The host pressed on. "Colin, leaving the spin aside, are you not surprised? Liberals trailing in fifty ridings? Looks serious."

"These are preliminary results, Vanessa. It's early going. We have a long night ahead of us. Things will turn around with the next batch of polls." He didn't look like he meant it, though.

She turned to a man wearing a turban and dressed in orange from head to toe, even his running shoes were orange. Dipper. "Jag, you look like you are about to burst out cheering. Thoughts?"

"Our leader, Madeleine Franks, has been outstanding in this election. Since the debates—both the French and the English—she has distinguished herself. The NDP have shown that we have the right policies for these times. Homelessness must be addressed. Support for refugees and new immigrants, housing, health care. Help for seniors and of course more rights for tenants."

"I'm going to throw up if he keeps going on like this. Is he reading from a prompter? What about free ice cream for everyone?"

Naomi looked concerned. "Shhh. Easy there, partner. The NDP is surging. Look at those results. They are now declared or leading in thirty-five ridings. PCs are taking a beating. Libs too. They'll be lucky to hold their majority. I was just talking to a friend at NDP headquarters, they are looking at up to forty seats. That's crazy."

"Crazy is one word for it. This province is going to hell if they become official opposition. I'm getting another drink." I looked over and saw Daria still standing by the door. "I thought you had to get to the hospital?"

"In a minute." She curled a lip at me. I'd seen that look before.

The young popcorn-eater threw off his headphones and snapped another can of Coke. "This is BS. None of the polls saw this. The NDP is declared in thirty-seven ridings now. Disaster."

"Arlo! Stop hitting your brother. How are we doing in Parkdale?" Naomi walked over to her sons and gave one a swat. No sooner had she turned back to look at her laptop than the other one delivered a kick to his brother's shins and they fell to the floor wrestling. I had to smile. Good times.

Popcorn Boy was dead serious. "Parkdale's tight. They had to keep a few polls open past the deadline because of some incident, not enough workers showed up at one poll so they opened late. Some results are delayed. The Lib Kaminski has been stronger than expected."

I had to laugh. "Which just goes to show you that what people see at all-candidates meetings is meaningless. That guy was scared shitless the night at the Mechanics Hall."

He ignored me and my statement of the obvious "But we only have half the polls reporting. McKay must be sweating bullets. Hang on. Here are more numbers now. Hello! Look at Mr. Andrew Bierce! Right behind McKay. Liberals are running third! The Greens are fourth but they are eating into Lib support."

I pictured Ms. Reach for the Top in a friend's basement watching results, forecasting environmental doom and praying, *Forgive them, Father, for they know not what they do.*

"Andrew, at least you're making it a horse race. Atta boy." Sean was ecstatic.

I'm not sure why anybody thought this was news to celebrate. McKay was going to win and either way the whole process had virtually guaranteed Sean's defrocking. It had probably already happened. This called for a fresh bottle of bourbon.

When I turned to head to my liquor cabinet, Daria was gone. Good. That alone called for a toast.

50

E-Day Takes a Turn
Monday November 7, 11 p.m.

BY 11 P.M. and with no final results I was very hungry, tired and frankly a little bit drunk.

As usual Naomi came to the rescue. I could see her tapping away on a food app. "Guys. It looks like we're going to be here for a while. I'm ordering food. Choices are pizza or pizza." There were no objections but lots of suggestions for toppings. Satisfied that she had looked after her people, but before she could get back to work, she turned to me. "Andrew, my husband says he's on his way to get my boys but for now they're asleep in your bedroom. I hope that's okay."

"Not a problem. I really appreciate you hanging in like this but at what point do we get realistic and just call it a night? McKay is going to win this thing. I've got a big meeting tomorrow morning on this inquiry and I have to get some sleep. I'm thinking maybe I'll just head down to the office and work. Then I can sleep there for a while. It wouldn't be the first time. You can lock the door on the way out. PSWs will be arriving to look after Sean early tomorrow." I looked over at Sean. Sound asleep.

"Daria was doing quite the job looking after him. You're still not past that?"

"Naomi, let's not go there. I will never be past that. I detest the woman."

"Wow. I'll mind my business. I'm just saying that she really cares for Sean."

"Naomi, . . ."

"Okay, message received."

I looked over at Sean. Still sound asleep. But then a phone began to ring with an *Ave Maria* ring tone. It sure wasn't mine, Naomi knew it was not hers and Popcorn Boy had not moved. Sean woke, fumbled through his blankets and pulled out his phone.

"Sorry, I need to take this." He turned his head away and spoke softly. "Hey, yeah. I'm hanging in. Thanks. You're too kind. I know. Looks like you're having quite the night. Good for you. Yeah. I know. Crazy. Hard to say. But let's stay in touch. Let's not get ahead of ourselves. Okay. Thanks. Talk later."

"Who was that?"

"Oh, just a friend from one of the campaigns. Having a good night. Just wanted to say hi and see how I was doing."

Popcorn Boy hushed us. "More results from Parkdale–High Park coming up. Stand by. The polls didn't close until ten o'clock at 75 through 80. That's down in the southwest corner of the riding. Turn it up."

Naomi turned to watch the TV announcer just as I received an email from none other than Royce Hughes. He had copied Gavin, the presenting counsel for the inquiry.

Andrew, looks like you are having a busy evening. I hope you won't object if we move our meeting scheduled for tomorrow for a day. I'm faced with an emergency conflict that should be resolved quickly. Gavin, I assume you are able to accommodate me. Look forward to hearing from you both. Good luck this evening.

Given how much I'd had to drink, moving this meeting twenty-four hours was a good idea. I hit back. *Happy to accommodate if Gavin's on board.*

I sent a text to Lindsay to give her a heads-up. Knowing her, she was still in the office preparing to face Williams for the first time in nearly a year. She would probably be a little relieved that we would have another day. We had no idea how it was going to go. Conflagration or fizzle? I loathed the idea of sitting with Williams and being under his thumb, but if Total War was the only way through this, then so be it. Francesca must be dreading the experience and would bear most of the scars. Lindsay hit back in minutes with a sad-face emoji, followed with, *Looks like you are doing well in PHP. My friend Rebecca was the Green candidate. She is disappointed but vowing to fight on.*

Good for her. She ran a good campaign. Maybe she could run for class president next time. Or go back to spray painting boxcars with clever Green slogans.

Thoughts of the upcoming meeting with Hughes and Gavin also made me think of that pile of files on my windowsill. Once this election nonsense was over I would have my work cut out for me. Thank God Lindsay was on board. She could handle the Bay Street fellow for a few weeks. I could deal somehow with the inquiry and Marrs. Oh God, Marrs, my chest tightened just thinking about it. And my pants suddenly felt very tight too. I'm getting fatter by the minute. No pizza tonight.

Naomi's voice brought me back to the unreality of the election. "Andrew, are you following this? Listen to this." She turned up the volume again.

"Well folks, it's been a long evening in some parts of the province but the picture is becoming clearer. We are able to say with confidence that based on the results we can declare those elected in 120 of 124 ridings. That leaves four ridings to be called and there are some nail biters. You can see from the crawl across the bottom of your screen the results from individual ridings in your area, but here is the big picture: Ontario will have a minority government . . ."

"Oh my God, Palmer will have to resign after this fiasco." Naomi just shook her head. "What a fool. This rivals Peterson in 1990. The hubris of these politicians. It's never enough." She was furious. I'd never seen her like that.

"Just to remind viewers that when this election was called the Liberals had a majority government with 68 seats, the PCs held 40, the NDP held 15 and the Green Party held one for a total of 124 seats. Those standings have been turned upside down with Liberals holding onto just 35 seats, the NDP rising to 58, the PCs are declared winners in 26 and the Greens have held one seat. The PCs seem to be holding all their incumbent ridings notwithstanding the loss of their leader just as the campaign began.

We are waiting on results in . . . sorry . . . wait . . . there are more ridings reporting. We can now declare based on all polls reporting in those ridings that the NDP have picked up two more seats and are now within two seats of a majority. What a turn of events."

"This is unbelievable." Popcorn Boy was aghast. It was not serious enough, though, to stop him eating an entire butter-chicken pizza.

The political TV host continued, "So, to recap, we have Liberals reduced to 35, the NDP now with 60, PCs reduced to 26, and Greens have held their one seat, for a total of 122 ridings. We are waiting on two more ridings: Scarborough, where the Green candidate Reyes has given the incumbent Liberal a run for her money, and Parkdale–High Park, a riding that has seen one of the stranger races between the PCs, Liberals and an Independent. Let's go to our panel for reaction."

Naomi closed her laptop, shook her head and smiled at me. "You, Andrew, are unbelievable. You scared the hell out of McKay and the PCs." Her phone rang. "Hello, yes. Ha, no kidding. It's been quite a night. I'll tell him. He's here if you want to speak with him. No, he's right beside me. Okay. Okay. If you insist. Thank you. You too."

"Who was that?"

"Dikembe."

"What did he want?" Snivelling piece of shit.

"Well, part of it was telling me that I ran a hell of a campaign." She was clearly pleased with herself.

"You did. I appreciate everything you did. Not that it will make any difference for Sean. What was the other part?"

"That Father Shannon fellow is coming back from somewhere and he wants to meet with you."

"He couldn't call me directly? Coward."

Naomi just shrugged and went back to her laptop.

Sean's phone sang out *Ave Maria* again. He turned away from us and huddled in his blankets but I could hear him. "Yes. Of course, I'm still up. I wouldn't miss this for the world. I know. Unbelievable. Of course. I can speak with him. Leave it with me. Let's see how things turn out. Okay. Really? Interesting. Okay. Good to know. You too. I will, I will. You're too sweet."

"Who was that? Sounded pretty cozy." Sean had a way of summoning a hidden reserve of strength when a woman was involved.

"Just a friend who has better information than what's on the TV right now. Reyes has just won in Scarborough. Greens will have a second MPP. Palmer is going to make a statement in about thirty minutes."

OMG. I suddenly remembered Bonnie's campaign. How could I have forgotten about her? I'm such an idiot. I dialled her but when she answered I could barely hear her voice. It sounded like a victory party was in full swing. As she yelled into the phone, "I have to go," I could see the TV coverage shift to the celebration at Reyes's campaign headquarters. There stood Bonnie on stage with her hero. Hands held aloft, green ribbons, confetti and balloons falling from the ceiling, with music blaring. I had never seen her happier. "Well done, Bonnie." At least she would be back at the office full-time once the political dopamine was weaned out of her veins. Granted there would be a hard withdrawal period, cold turkey— like coming down from a big trial—but eventually we could get back to the business at hand. And start making some money. My subsidizing of the firm could not go on forever. Not one bill had been sent in months. Not even the bills to Coop and Patrick. Unprecedented.

Sean tucked his phone back under the blankets. "Andrew, can we chat for a second? Naomi, you too."

"Look at Bonnie. I've never seen her so happy." There she was, dancing for heavens sake, on stage with the candidate and his supporters.

"Andrew, . . ." Sean struggled to sit up.

"I'm going to pour us drinks just to toast her victory. She worked hard for that . . ."

"Andrew, . . ."

Naomi looked at Sean with a grimace. She could tell it was serious. "Andrew, I think Sean needs us."

51

Did Not See That Coming
Monday November 7, Midnight

NAOMI, HAVING SEEN the writing on the wall, turned to her loyal assistant and suggested he call it a night. It was nearly midnight. They had survived on popcorn, pizza and Cokes for eight straight hours.

He turned to her. "Not a chance. We're going to win this thing. I'm here until the bitter end."

Oh boy. Talk about the political delusion drug in full force. Bitter was going to be the operative word. Poor Popcorn Boy. For all my cynicism about politics, I'm also a realist. The likelihood of flipping a thirty-seven-point lead in ten days is virtually nil. I had attended one all-candidates meeting, done no door-to-door and given no speeches or interviews. Naomi had worked hard to spend every nickel that had been donated by delusional supporters, but you can't really buy votes with just ads on social media and a few hundred lawn signs. But Naomi and her faithful drone had taken the usual election narcotic. You have to in order to do this nonsense. You have to *believe* you can win against all odds. I just hoped they weren't too disappointed when we got the final results.

Perched on the edge of my couch, Naomi turned the TV down and looked at Sean. "What's up? Sean, are you okay?"

My phone pulsed with an email. It was Royce Hughes again. "Hang on guys, I need to deal with this."

Sean was sitting up now. "Andrew, I need you . . ."

"This is important. It's about the supposed inquiry." I looked at Royce's message. *Thanks to both of you. Can we reschedule to Thursday at 10 a.m.?*

Gavin responded within seconds. *Good by me.*

I jumped in. *Good by me. What about His Honour?*

Royce responded to all of us. *He's good but wants to press ahead aggressively now that the election is done. Let's just say he is keen to move back to TO from Barrie for this thing.*

I texted Francesca to let her know of the delay. She responded with a simple *Whatever.* Great, very enthusiastic for someone getting free representation for the biggest event in her life. Nothing about the election. She was probably shrugging and texting while watching *The Golden Bachelor.*

It seemed like a good time to text Bonnie, so I sent her a quick *Well done! You called it. Greens have doubled their contingent at QP.*

Within seconds a text popped up. *Thanks, Andrew. It's been a ride. For the first time I feel like I made a difference. Mateo's a good man. I can share with you now that we're also kinda involved.* This was followed by a smiling emoji and floating hearts.

"Dear. God. No." Bonnie's in love! With a politician! "This is terrible."

"What? What happened?" Naomi was alarmed.

"Bonnie's fallen in love with her candidate Mr. Reyo . . . Redo."

"I think you mean, Mateo Reyes, the new MPP from Scarborough? That's wonderful for her. She deserves it." Naomi was thrilled. (I don't even know what that means, some one *deserves* love. Why? It's a mystery.) Sean, as exhausted as he looked, was beaming too and obviously agreed wholeheartedly. He's always loved Bonnie.

"No, this is terrible." All I could think of was her now needing more time off. I would insist she have a marriage contract or cohab at the least. This was terrible if we were supposed to get back to work.

"Sorry guys, can we leave Bonnie's happy news for a moment and deal with something?" Sean was serious again.

"Hang on. They have more results." Naomi turned the TV back up.

"Naomi, let's talk first . . ."

"Well folks, thanks for hanging in with us. The final results are in from all ridings and we have a final count. Here we go . . ."

With flashy graphics and blaring some kind of election night theme music the scoreboard appeared on the screen:

ELECTION RESULTS
NDP 60
Liberals 35
PC 26
Green 2
Independent 1
Total 124

"Before we go to our panel, the big picture is, just as our election desk called it at 10:14 p.m., Ontario will have a minority government for the first time since 1985. Premier Palmer is scheduled to speak shortly and we will take you there live when it happens, but for now back to our panel. Colin, your thoughts . . ."

We all stared at the screen. It had not sunk in. Then Popcorn Boy said in disbelief, "We won. We won Parkdale–High Park."

I laughed. Idiot. "No, there were other Independents running. It can't be. It's another riding."

Naomi was laughing now too. "No, there it is, on the crawl. Look! You beat McKay by fifty votes. We won. We won! Aaron Bierce withdrew too late to have his name removed from the ballot. He got 1,500 votes. He split the Liberal votes. Aaron Bierce helped you win! And that's enough of a margin that there is no automatic recount." They were dancing around the living room, laughing. "We won. We won. Do you have any champagne? We won, we won."

The irony was too much. Having an A. Bierce on the ballot split votes, just not the A. Bierce intended, and as it turns out not for the benefit of McKay. Shannon must be losing his mind. Had I not run, McKay might have won.

As Naomi and Popcorn Boy danced, I thought about the fifty votes that delivered my so-called victory. Dog lovers? Claire's pig-saving cadre?

Homeless advocates? Audio Max's parents? The old man who was sure I was Aaron Bierce? Dr. Rubin and her neighbours? A few of Coop's Twitter followers? Democracy is head-spinning.

I looked over at Sean. I was not smiling. He was not smiling. We said it at the same time. "We need to talk."

Noticing our mutual grimace, it suddenly sank in for Naomi. My victory was going to guarantee that Sean was defrocked—if it hadn't already been done. "Oh shit. Sean. I'm so sorry. We got caught up in the campaign. It just feels like a big win."

"I get it. You ran a great guerrilla campaign. They'll be talking about this one for years."

"Talk about it? Yeah, let's talk about it. I don't know what you've got me into, Sean. MPP? I have a law practice to run. Clients. I can't be an MPP. Plus they don't make any money!"

As I struggled to digest this disaster, texts began to pop up on my phone.

Daria: *Congrats. What now? How is Sean?*

Bonnie: *Whaaaat?! Congrats! What about Sean?*

Royce: *Congratulations. Will you need a little more time before we meet?*

Lindsay: *We need to talk.* There was some kind of brown emoji beside it.

Hopeless Helen: *Congratulations. End mask mandates!*

Ms. Marrs: *This is why you abandoned me!*

McKay: *You f'n sleazebag.*

Dikoombe: *Shannon wants to speak with you.*

Popcorn Boy looked at me in shock. "What do you mean you can't be an MPP? What did we do this for? You have to be the MPP." He turned to Naomi. "Why did he say that?"

"Ben, I told you this was a long shot. We didn't think we could win." She turned to me. "I didn't tell him."

I looked at poor Ben. As I said, you have to believe you can win to waste your time on this bullshit.

"Yeah, well I played to win. All that social media we bought. It was genius stuff I did. All that stuff on Twitter . . . the animal rights, the homelessness crusade . . . Why?" He was despondent.

Sean finally piped up. "Okay. It's unexpected. We all get it, but can we speak confidentially here for a minute? Everyone?"

Naomi looked at Ben. "Can we?"

He nodded. "I guess."

We sat in a half-circle in front of Sean.

Sean pulled himself up a little and turned back his blankets. "That call I got a few minutes ago. There may be, I say may be, a silk purse to be made from this sow's ear."

Ben looked confused. "A sow's ear?"

"Let me explain."

He did. It wasn't a sow's ear, it was the rabbit that only Sean could pull out of a hat.

52

The Lord's Mysterious Ways
Tuesday November 8

I PULLED UP a chair and Ben grabbed one of my knot stools.

"Who was that?"

"That call I got a little while ago was from Madeleine Franks."

"The leader of the NDP called you? Why is she calling you?" Ben was mystified. Naomi put a hand on his knee to settle him down and indicate he should just listen.

"We're friends from way back. I like her and have a lot of time for her." I had never heard Sean utter such words about a member of the NDP. "Anyway, her team had a better read on the results long before anyone else. Their polling was showing a very strong surge after her debate performances."

"Surely, they didn't know they would win sixty seats." Naomi was surprised.

"No, they did not. They were seeing the Liberals' support fall but were only expecting to be asked to form a minority government with them, like back in 1985 with Peterson and Rae."

"That didn't work out very well for the Dippers back then." I recalled that they were later wiped out by a Liberal majority for Peterson. Typical NDP had botched their so-called Accord.

"I know. This is a fresh NDP crew but a few of them recall that time. Anyway. It's very different now."

Naomi was curious. "How different?"

"They are three seats from a working majority . . ."

"What are you thinking?" Naomi was now more than just curious.

"Sean, Naomi, . . . no offence, Ben, . . . maybe I've had too much to drink but I'm not following . . . I won as an Independent. That is, a back-bench loser. Tits on a bull."

Ben looked puzzled again at yet another reference to animal parts.

Sean gazed at Madeleine Franks as she now appeared on the muted TV. "Madeleine is more *practical* than previous leaders . . ."

Naomi was clearly following. "*Practical* meaning she would rather have a majority than some type of Accord with the Libs . . ."

"Exactly."

"Meaning?"

"She needs three MPPs to work with her reliably in order to have a majority."

"Oh, oh, oh. I get it. If you think I'm joining the NDP, you're crazier than I thought. I don't even want to be an MPP."

"Stop saying that!" Popcorn Boy was getting angry.

"What if it was not *join* but *work co-operatively with*?"

"Why would I do that, why prop up Dippers?"

"She's open to suggestions about your role now that you're elected."

"Suggestions like what?"

Sean raised his eyebrows in a knowing way. "Andrew, you were the only lawyer elected among sixty NDP and two Greens."

"So?"

Naomi smiled. "Andrew, didn't you say, *it's good to be needed*?"

It took a few seconds but then it wasn't a penny that dropped. It wasn't a silver dollar. It was a gold doubloon, and when it dropped I saw the promised land. That's right. *It's good to be needed.*

"Can I call Madeleine and let her know you are open to some confidential discussions?"

"You can do that, Sean, and while you do, I think I might have a bottle of well-chilled champagne in the fridge. Maybe two."

As I slipped into the kitchen Sean called out, his voice hadn't sounded so strong in weeks, "The Lord works in mysterious ways."

Indeed He does.

It took until the wee hours, but by 2 a.m. He had possibly delivered the means of my revenge . . . of our revenge.

53

Act Fast, Think Slow
Tuesday November 8

WHEN I AWOKE the next morning I needed to do three things immediately (right after I had a drink—too much champagne on top of scotch and bourbon was having revenge on my head). First, I needed to lock in any potential deal with the NDP leader and then, second, I had to see Lindsay. I dreaded meeting with her. With my unexpected election her worst fears were being realized. I would need to step aside from my law practice, leaving her in precisely the caretaker role she did not want. And finally, above all else, I needed to conclude the Glinka Inquiry before any word leaked about co-operation with the new government. There were a few moving parts that weren't yet in position.

On the way to the office, I called Bonnie to congratulate her personally. I assumed I would get her voicemail but she answered on one ring, hoarse from celebrating.

"You have a lot to be proud of. You called it. I'll give you credit for that. Your new fellow will make a great addition to Queen's Park. And did I detect love is in the air?"

"Thanks, Andrew. It has been quite a journey we've shared. Fingers crossed it works out. He's just such a lovely man. Never felt like this before. How are you feeling? I assume the win was not what you expected and Sean must be very disappointed. Do you know what you'll do?"

"Not really." I was giving nothing away at this stage. "Does Mr. Reyes know what he will be doing?" A little political fishing wouldn't hurt.

"Oh, so you remember his name now. I guess you're becoming a politician."

"Ouch, I deserve that. I would like to meet him. Let's try to get together for lunch soon." *Oh God, listen to me. Lunch?*

"Sounds good but it may be a while. Can you keep a secret?"

"Of course." I'm a professional and she's my friend after all.

"Mateo is meeting with Madeleine Franks tomorrow to discuss working with her to form a majority. He won't leave the Green Party but he and the leader, Neil Gruber, may be able to work out a deal that could deliver the two seats she needs for a majority. It's all very hush-hush. Mateo says they would do it only in exchange for a seat at the Cabinet table. He thinks he could be Minister of the Environment. Imagine that?" She was thrilled.

Shiiiit. Imagine that indeed. "Wow. Exciting. Good luck to him. Listen, I'll let you go. And again, congrats."

"Same to you. Please give Sean my best. He was a steady supporter throughout the campaign. Tell him I really appreciated his advice. It paid off. And remember that Reyes/Gruber meeting with Franks is on the Q.T."

"Of course. Will do. My lips are sealed."

Oh, Bonnie. What have you done?

If the Greens gave Ms. Franks two seats, she would have her majority and then she wouldn't need me. *And I was just beginning to enjoy being needed again.* I had to act fast and lock in my role today, before she met with the Greens.

Franks and Palmer were meeting later with the lieutenant-governor about options for forming a government, so Sean arranged for me to connect with her secretly late that morning at the Gardiner Museum, a stone's throw from Queen's Park. Mid-week, it's quiet there except for senior-citizen pottery classes and I was pretty confident no one would be interested in a couple of people wandering through the European ceramic collection.

Ms. Franks didn't arrive until nearly noon but I didn't waste my time while waiting for her. I find the Gardiner's non-ceramic collections more interesting than the actual ceramics and asked the curator if I could see their rare print of Benjamin West's painting, *The Death of General Wolfe*. They even have a ceramic plate depicting the tragic scene. Those items are not on public display but when I insisted that I should be given a special showing because I'm in the Curators' Circle at the AGO, she relented. Nice to have clout.

I was surprised when I finally met Ms. Franks. Easily six feet tall, she was dressed impeccably in a beige cashmere jacket, black gaucho pants and high-heeled leather boots. She looked like the CEO of a tech company, not the leader of a lefty political party. I have to say, she was very attractive in a strange, exotic way. She had long dark hair, pulled back, sultry eyes, full lips and a beautiful roman nose. Her appearances on TV did not do her justice. She reminded me of someone famous, Sofia Coppola? Amal Clooney? Beautiful. Sean's friendship with her suddenly made a lot more sense. He told me she was actually a member of the Mohawk First Nation. But how did this woman come to lead the party of hand-spun wool toques, wide-wale corduroy pants and keffiyehs? This was not some local political hack who used to be a school board trustee. She was all business. And she smelled great.

"Good morning. I'm so glad we could connect. How was your meeting this morning?"

"I think we understand each other." Interesting non-statement.

"You and my brother go back a few years."

She smiled as if recalling some fond memory. "Yes, back to a time when neither of us was quite sure of our career choices. We took different paths."

"His was a bit bumpy from time to time. He's not doing well right now. The prostate cancer is taking its toll."

She just frowned knowingly. "I've been chatting with him these last few months. He hasn't lost his naughty sense of humour."

"He's special that way." I shudder to think what the incorrigible flirt had been saying to her.

We walked a bit into the collections. I wasn't sure if she had been to the museum before. "So, what are your thoughts on forming a government?"

"Do you mean, how much am I prepared to give you in exchange for your support?"

"I see we can be direct."

"Yes, can I call you Andrew?"

"Of course. And feel free to ask me anything. I'm an open book." *New edition, heavily redacted.*

"Good. That's my style too. I hope we can speak confidentially. I would like to have your help to form a government but there are limits. I have a large caucus of excited and ambitious MPPs who want to be involved. I'm going to be very open with you now . . ."

I cut her off gently. "You're meeting with Mr. Reyes and Mr. Gruber tomorrow afternoon about the Green Party supporting you."

She smiled and took a step back from me. "I'm impressed. My office has been very tight-lipped. No one is supposed to know about that."

Forgive me, Bonnie, but these are desperate times.

"I assure you that information did not come from your office, your team is fine, but I think you'll find the Greens have a leaky ship. Which is not good at this early stage." I turned and we walked more deeply into the quiet of the collections. "With my background as a lawyer for over four decades I know how important it is to be discreet. And it's critical right now. I think those two gentlemen may be in a bit over their heads, over-anxious—perhaps ambitious is a better word—trying to elbow their way into seats at your Cabinet table. Reyes, Minister of the Environment? Really?"

I could see her weighing those comments. "I spoke with Sean early this morning and he sowed a few seeds. But what do you have in mind?"

I needed to play hard to get.

"There are a few things you need to know about me. First, I fought hard to win that seat." *Okay, slight exaggeration, in fact quite the opposite.* "My victory over McKay was unexpected." *That's true.* "Someone," *me,* "used the term, *giant killer.* I wouldn't, but the media gets carried away." *Even if false, demonstrates my humility.* "Second, I have no long-term political ambitions." *Again, true.* "I ran as an Independent for a reason." *Vague, but surely she knew what went down in Parkdale–High Park with her candidate being poached off to the UN.* "I don't covet leadership of any party." *Good God, who would?* "I am a one-term MPP." *Less if possible.* "I will not run again." *Guaranteed.* "That gives me total freedom from the influence of voter passions. I'm a neutral, truly independent. And I'm the only lawyer elected among sixty NDP and two Greens."

"Meaning?"

As we leaned into the glass case to look at a beautiful bowl, she was so close I had to struggle not to be distracted by her subtle perfume and the smell of her body. I could tell she had been sweating at that earlier meeting. It lit a fire in me.

"Meaning, you'll need an independent attorney general." I swear a ray of sunshine broke through a window and illuminated the very spot where we stood as I uttered those words.

She gave not a hint of surprise. "I see. Attorney general. Is that all?"

"Do you mind if we walk over and see the European earthenware? There are some plates there that are really wonderful. And, yes, there is something else. Some commitments."

She unleashed her beautiful smile. Intoxicating. "I'm curious." I wasn't sure if her curiosity was about the plates or the commitments.

We walked a bit until we stood before a series of brilliantly coloured plates by Francesco Xanto Avelli da Rovigo. "Here we are."

"Oh, they *are* beautiful."

"Each tells a story. I love this one. It depicts the story of Icarus, who flew too close to the sun . . ."

"I know the tale."

"Like Mr. Reyes pressing for a Cabinet portfolio?" I laughed.

"A little dramatic." She frowned.

"Not as much as this one, though." We stood before Avelli's *Shooting at Father's Corpse*.

"I'm not sure I know this story."

"It's an old moralizing tale about deciding succession after the death of the king. In the story a judge told the king's three sons to fetch his corpse and tie it to a tree. The son who could shoot an arrow closest to his father's heart would win."

"Gruesome."

"The two eldest sons shot at the corpse but the youngest refused. And the judge decided he should be the heir. I think it's a story about respect for what has gone before. Respect for family. I'm big on those things."

"Very interesting. Oh, I love this one." She pointed to a nearby display. "It's beautiful. A bourdaloue. It looks like a gravy boat."

"Yes, it's beautiful. German." I didn't have the heart to tell her it was a lady's chamber pot, so I turned the discussion back to the business at hand.

"So, these other commitments. Can we discuss them?"

"Of course."

"These are critical. I would need your government's confidential commitment on three things. And it's not that I don't trust you, but I would need that commitment in writing, ideally today."

"I see. Go on."

"If you cannot commit, I will understand and leave you to haggling at the power bazaar with Mr. Reyes and his leader. Based on what I've heard I think you will find that they're ambitious politicians who will demand action on unpopular environmental laws as a condition of support and you will need a firm hand to control them at the Cabinet table."

"I see and what do you suggest I do with Mr. Reyes and Mr. Gruber?"

"An alternative might be to agree to work with them, but not at the Cabinet table. Offer a junior position, perhaps as a parliamentary assistant. As your attorney general I would be in a position to screen any of their proposed environmental laws, laws that might cause trouble for your government with the business community, intercept them before they even got to Cabinet. You will have your hands full enough with the business groups. You won't need green problems. The only environmental issue I want to make a priority is clean drinking water on Northern reserves. It's a passion of mine." *Well, I have thought about it from time to time.*

"I see, interesting. That's a priority for me as well. And what are those three *commitments* you require in writing today?"

I laid them out for her.

She listened thoughtfully. "You have surprised me, Mr. Bierce. You're not at all what I expected. I'd heard about your history with the Law Society, your colleague being killed. Sean said the stories weren't fair to you, I believed him. Everything you've said today? It's wise, like your brother. Your insight on Mr. Reyes and the Greens is helpful too. I thought I could have more confidence in them to keep matters confidential."

"And ..."

"And I will make those commitments. I will send you an email summarizing our arrangement. I look forward to working with you, Attorney General." She reached out an elegant hand.

I took her soft warm hand and gazed into those sultry eyes. "I look forward to working with you too." *You have no idea how much.*

"And, Andrew, ..."

"Yes?" I prayed she wasn't going to suddenly start adding some conditions.

She had a mischievous smile on her face. "I was joking about the gravy boat. A bourdaloue is a chamber pot. They're named after the Jesuit priest Louis Bourdaloue, I believe. Hence the term 'going to the loo.' But I appreciate your diplomacy."

My heart skipped a beat. I think I'm falling in love.

54

Dear Lindsay
Wednesday November 9

LINDSAY AND I agreed to meet at the office. It had been less than forty-eight hours since the polls closed and I was exhausted. Sean suggested I lay off the booze for a few days and keep a clear head. It wasn't easy but I took his advice. I think it paid dividends in my meeting with Ms. Franks. I couldn't get her out of my mind. I should be able to go a few days without a drink. I think.

When I arrived Lindsay was already there. No office of her own, of course (gulp), so she was parked at the boardroom table. The room had a very bad vibe.

"So, not quite what I expected in Parkdale–High Park the other night." It was an understatement, as if I had accidentally won a game of poker.

She stared at me and looked like she might have been crying. Dear Lord, could I see the impending birth of a large cold sore on her upper lip? Stress was eating her alive.

"Look, I'm as surprised as you. I wasn't supposed to win. Vote splitting ended up putting me over the top. What can I say? First past the post. It's not like I'm happy about this, you know, there was my brother to consider . . ."

She looked at me, puzzled. "Your brother? You're playing the cancer card again?"

Right, I had never explained that aspect of the deal to her, why I was being recruited to split votes and help McKay win. I think she assumed I wanted to win. Little did she know.

She said nothing, simply looked at me and chewed her lip.

"You're just going to sit there stewing?"

Wrong approach and the floodgates opened.

"*Stewing? Stewing?* No, *suing*, I'm thinking about *suing* you. You hired me under false pretences. You told me that the election was nothing to worry about, that the Glinka Inquiry was our priority, which was the only reason I came here; that we would go forward, even with no retainer; give 'em hell you said, get some justice for Francesca. I said I was worried about ending up babysitting your practice, you said 'Oh, there's nothing to worry about.' Now what do I do? I gave up the practice that I spent a year building."

"Look . . ."

"Then you said I could have the Marrs matter. But I immediately get reamed out for calling it a dog file . . ."

"I apologized for that."

"Of course, it actually *is* a dog file. I know it is because I read it. You went to court and you had not even read the file. I get introduced to the client but she will have nothing to do with me, so you take over."

"Plus, her retainer turns out to be no good."

"What?!" That stopped her rant dead in its tracks.

"PGT froze it. It was her mom's money. I'll explain later."

"Oh, that's great, now we won't get paid? And speaking about being paid, you asked me to do all kinds of research on Christian Brothers and the archdiocese. So I did it. When I went to record my time, it turns out there's no file. There's no one to bill. Is that time and work just written off?" She was getting a full head of steam again.

"I'm going to need that research."

"And I seem to recall you saying I would get an office, with furniture . . . oh, and fancy business cards too . . . even though I said I don't need business cards but, oh no, you say, I'll get them anyway. Really? Where are those precious bone-white linen-embossed business cards? Nothing."

"They're on order, so is the furniture . . . COVID delays." *Not really but, you know.*

"I offered to work on the Cody Cooper file but, no, you handle it alone. I get nothing even though I told you how much I wanted to meet him and work on his case. You even dragged Naomi off the file to work on your campaign."

"She volunteered. There were good reasons . . ."

"And you know what?" She turned and looked at me, her face contorted in anger. "This office smells. It smelled the first time I set foot in it and it still smells today. You blame tea, tea of all things? What a bunch of BS."

She was right on that. The office does still smell! Fucking Hopeless Helen.

"Are you done?"

She started to cry. "I made a huge mistake coming here. My father told me not to do it . . . but . . . but . . . I trusted you. I'm so stupid."

"Lindsay, listen to me. There's more you need to know but it can't leave this room."

Through her tears she screamed at me. "Why would I trust anything you say?!"

Wow. If there's one thing I cannot stand, it's a woman yelling at me. I had a flashback to my ugly fights with Daria.

"Well, you're going to have to trust me on this. Can you stop crying for a minute? Please . . . can you just stop?"

She stared at her hands for a few minutes and then looked up. "What? What now?"

"There are a few things that have happened since election night. We need to be strategic but work fast. There is a meeting tomorrow at ten o'clock with Williams, Hughes, Gavin McPhellan. We're going to talk about the scope of evidence for the inquiry."

She sneered at me. "I know all that. What's your point? How can you even go forward as Francesca's lawyer with your new job?"

My God, she was pissy.

"Let me finish. If everything goes according to plan, we will settle the entire case tomorrow . . ."

"Ohhhh, I get it. Now that you're going off to be an MPP she gets thrown under the bus for a settlement. That's just great. Nothing changes. This is how it works. I know, I've been there."

"Are you going to let me finish? The plan comes in three parts."

"Oh, a three-part plan? Genius." She looked skeptical. "Fine. Tell me *your plan*."

It took a few minutes but I walked her through Part 1 and the approach to the meeting the next day. If it went as planned, it would render an outcome that would satisfy Glinka, Francesca and Singh in every respect and get us handsomely paid to boot.

"Good so far?"

She scowled at me. (And her tongue shot up to lick her upper lip. Oh boy. Here we go.) "Duh, isn't *Part 1* pretty much what Royce Hughes was proposing a few weeks ago? What's so great about that?"

"Yes, it's similar. But there are a few tweaks. There was some research you did a while ago that we'll need for the next part." I explained Parts 2 and 3, her role and the expected outcome.

When I was done she stared at me in disbelief. Her BS detector was on high alert.

"Can you handle it?" She looked on the verge of tears.

"Can I handle it? Can you do it? You can do that?" She was skeptical.

"Yes, and if I can, are you in?"

"One thousand percent."

I could hardly ask for more. I would have settled for 100 percent.

55

Sweet Simony
Wednesday November 9

ONCE I HAD Lindsay on board I needed to make another very important call—to that little prick Shannon. I relished the prospect of seeing him face to face but this couldn't wait, it had to happen before any news broke about the new government. A phone call would have to do.

I poured myself a drink (hey, it had been nearly forty-eight hours dry) and climbed into the comfort of my Egg chair. I'd sent him a text telling him he was welcome to call me anytime after 7 p.m. The phone rang at 7:01.

"Andrew Bierce."

"Father Shannon."

"We find ourselves in an unexpected situation, Father."

"You might call it that." His venom poured through the phone. "If you're going to plead with me not to defrock your disgraceful brother, then please don't waste your breath and my time, *Mr. Independent MPP*." Sarcasm was dripping from his voice. "The paperwork will be processed as soon as I return to the archdiocese from New York City on Friday."

"I heard you're just back from Haiti?"

"Yes, and it was a very successful trip if I do say so myself. More than this fiasco with Mr. McKay." Arrogant little prick couldn't help but toot his own horn.

"Wonderful. Was the work in Haiti along the lines of what you were doing here in Ontario? Getting victims of clerical sexual abuse to confidentially settle claims for peanuts? Was that keeping you from finishing up Sean's defrocking? I assumed that you had already pushed Sean's paperwork through."

If a thought transmitted through a telephone line could kill, I would have been dead in my Egg. I'd hit a nerve and his loathing flowed silently toward me. "You can be an irritating man, Mr. Bierce. I have no idea what you are talking about, just as you have no idea what you are talking about. For your information, I tried repeatedly to have the paperwork processed from Haiti but their so-called communications system leaves a lot to be desired. Laicization will be a *fait accompli* by five o'clock on Friday. Rest assured. Your just reward is coming soon."

"Well, I'm glad that it hasn't been done yet. I was hoping we could discuss the arrangements for Sean's funeral and burial."

I heard him half laugh and snort. "Those two matters are now completely in your hands, Mr. Bierce. You had your fun in the election. You embarrassed me and Mr. McKay. I'll give you that. I know your brother had his hand in the matter too. Well, laugh all you want while looking for a place in this archdiocese that will even perform a Funeral Mass for him, let alone find a plot at a Catholic cemetery. I have put the word out, so good luck."

I pretended to ignore him. "I'm now thinking on a somewhat grander scale than originally planned. First, I would like a priest to attend Sean within the next twenty-four hours so he may receive the Sacrament of the Anointing of the Sick . . ."

"You are such a fool." There was disbelief in his voice.

"And in terms of the actual funeral, if we are going to use St. Michael's Cathedral Basilica for the Funeral Mass we will need to schedule something now. I've looked into the times but, of course, we need to be flexible."

"Mr. Bierce, I think you have been into your drink. I've heard you are wont to over-indulge. If you're not mad, then you are drunk. There will be no Funeral Mass at any church. Your brother is to be defrocked! Period." He was getting angry now. Good.

"No, I haven't had anything to drink—yet. But perhaps later, when I tell Sean about our plans for his receiving the sacrament, the mass and burial, then it will be a good time to toast his life as a priest."

"I suppose you expect the archbishop himself to perform your fantasy mass." He was laughing now. "You are a drunken fool. And a stupid man."

"Now that is an excellent suggestion. Can I ask you to prevail upon him to perform the mass? Sean would be touched if he knew that before he passed."

"Actually, my next call is to the archbishop. I'm to report to him on my travels, so I will tell him of your requests for the sacrament, the mass and burial, and especially that you would prefer that he himself perform the mass. He enjoys a good laugh as much as the next man. We will both enjoy that laugh."

"Excellent. Please do. And don't forget a priest will need to come to see Sean for the sacrament within the next twenty-four hours. I'll send you an email setting this out, if that's alright?"

"Oh, of course. Please do. I'll get right on it." He was laughing as he hung up.

It was nearly 8 p.m. and Lindsay was still in the boardroom preparing for the next day. There had been no sign of Bonnie around the office since the election, so I texted her.

Hey, what's up? Ready to come back to work?

I may need a few more days. Can I share something confidential?

Of course. Is everything okay?

Can I call?

Of course. The phone rang within seconds.

"Mateo's meeting with Ms. Franks didn't go as well as we had hoped. I'm not sure she takes him very seriously. I don't get it. A day ago she was very eager to meet with him and then she changed. Very distant. I thought she needed us to form a government, but she would not commit to anything for him in Cabinet. Something changed. Mateo's very upset. I'm going to reach out to Sean for advice on this. It doesn't make sense."

Shiiiit.

"Uhhh, Bonnie, . . . I wouldn't bother him right now. He hasn't been up to it. Let me touch base with him when I get home tonight. If he's okay with it, I'll get him to text you."

"Okay, thanks. I—we—really appreciate the help."

"It's the least I can do."

56

The Scope of the Evidence

Thursday November 10, 10 a.m.

OUR MEETING TO discuss the scope of evidence at the inquiry was booked at 100 Dundas Street West in a drab eleventh-floor conference room used for administrative hearings by tribunals like the Labour Relations Board. When I arrived, Royce Hughes, K.C., Gavin McPhellan and His Honour Justice Randall Williams were gathered around a table with coffees, shooting the shit like old friends. I felt like I was interrupting a class reunion. A young woman court reporter sat to the side quietly, ready to take notes of our meeting and doing everything in her power to avoid my eyes.

"Good morning, gentlemen, sorry I'm a little late. I hope we can get started as I have a meeting this afternoon."

Royce and Gavin both stepped forward and shook my hand to congratulate me on my victory at the polls. Both seemed to exude genuine respect for my accomplishment. It felt good, if unexpected.

Justice Randall Williams? Not so much. "You're late, Mr. Bierce. Are your new duties as the *Independent* MPP from Parkdale–High Park already interfering with your client commitments?" Williams was practically sneering through his phoney smile. "I was worried you might not have time to carry on with your representation of Ms. Rimini. I am not sure how you can even continue your sole practice and be a competent representative for such a needy part of the city."

"I'll try to do my best, Your Honour." Translation: Fuck off.

"This inquiry is very, very important and it will require 100 percent of your attention. Should I assume new counsel will be coming on board? Is there really anything we can accomplish today? I have a busy court calendar waiting for me, so I am not in a position to waste time."

He was really lording it over me as if, as a Superior Court Justice, he had descended from the mountain top of serious matters to dabble with the inquiry.

I was tempted to ask how the court lists were moving in Barrie these days but resisted the bait. More important matters were afoot. "No, Your Honour, I will remain her counsel and I'm hoping to move the matter forward today. I have an associate now, who should be joining me shortly, but we might as well begin. How would you like to proceed?"

Williams rolled his eyes as if he felt we were indeed wasting his valuable time.

"Very well. Gavin," *oh, we're on a first-name basis with presenting counsel,* "would you like to begin? *I* need an agreement on the scope of the evidence for the inquiry, which in turn will drive the witness list and the number of days *I* will need to sit. Have *I* got that right?" It was all about Williams already.

"Yes, you are quite correct, Your Honour. However, as presenting counsel I feel that we're in the hands of Mr. Royce and Mr. Bierce. We all know the basis of the allegation by Ms. Rimini against Justice Glinka at the party." *Did I just see Williams smirk?* "The question is: do we need to know more than just what happened that day?"

Gavin was being very diplomatic. What he really meant was how deep were we prepared to go into Francesca's history with the judge and others, and into her own history? Would there be a conflagration or a simple bonfire? Were we going to be *Ghomeshied?*

"Maybe I can be of assistance . . ." Hughes leaned forward, presumably to make some suggestions, but he couldn't get a word out before Williams was fawning all over him.

"Yes, Royce, please. What do you think? How do you see this unfolding? You probably have more experience than all of us added up when it comes to such matters. Didn't you argue the *Hay* matter in the Supreme

Court? You, more than anyone, understand the operation of the twin myths in such circumstances."

"He did argue the case, Your Honour, and I can tell you that Mr. Hughes thrilled my class with a guest lecture on the matter a few weeks ago. It was a master class in evidence. He was wonderful." I wanted to check to see if Gavin had a boner after that little interjection.

"That's great. Good of you to do that, Royce. Gavin, if you're looking for guest lecturers this fall, please keep me in mind. I would be happy to assist those coming up the ladder in our profession. Give them the *view from the bench* perspective." *Oh God, please. Make him stop.*

"Thank you, Your Honour. That's very generous of you." The three lawyers sitting there knew that Gavin had absolutely no intention of inviting this judge to speak on anything, given his burgeoning reputation as an unmanageable a-hole on the bench.

Royce began again. "The circumstances we face here call for an inquiry into the evening, the party and the specific allegations. What happened at the party? We should listen to the witnesses who were there. Judges, lawyers, police. There is no need to have Your Honour spend weeks listening to evidence from people who were not there at the time this alleged incident happened."

Interesting tack. Royce was hoping a narrow inquiry would mean it would boil down to Francesca's word against Glinka and the other judges and lawyers. *He said, she said.* No need to get into what happened before and after.

It was a trap, of course. His position would leave it to me to insist that the inquiry open the can of worms of evidence about Glinka and Francesca having a pre-party history, about Singh confronting Glinka the next day, about Pauline Hébert and her French lessons. It would be up to me to strike the match and begin the conflagration that might include Francesca's troubled upbringing. When they started to probe her life, I would not be able to object because I was the one who had opened that door.

Williams looked at me as if to say, "I assume you agree with Mr. Hughes."

The door at the back of the room opened and in stepped Rick Zanutto, King of the Bs and Justice Singh's divorce lawyer.

Williams recognized him immediately. "Good morning, Mr. Zanutto. I think you're in the wrong room. Check with admin and they can steer you where you need to go."

"Good morning, Your Honour. I'm looking for the Glinka Inquiry. Mr. Bierce said I might find the discussion interesting as Justice Singh is a potential witness. May I listen in?"

"Well, this is a little unusual but if Mr. Hughes and Mr. McPhellan have no objection."

Royce and Gavin looked at each other, nodded and assumed I was plodding headlong into the trap. "We have no objection, Your Honour."

My phone pulsed with a text from Lindsay. *Now?*

I tapped a quick response. *Hold for a minute.*

Another text popped up, this one from Sean. *Deal with MF is locked in, and in writing as requested. She needs you to meet with her caucus asap, though. Today 4 p.m. Followed by a press conference tomorrow at 10 a.m.*

I tapped in a quick thumbs-up.

Williams saw me typing into my phone. "Mr. Bierce, if you're too busy for this discussion because of your new duties . . ."

"No, Your Honour, but thank you for your concern." *And fuck off.* "I'm just making sure my associate is on the way. I also want to welcome Mr. Zanutto."

Rick Z reached out to shake my hand. "Congrats on your election. Well done."

I could tell that Williams was getting irritated. He was not happy seeing everyone congratulating me. "Very well, Mr. Bierce. Let's move forward. What's your view of the scope of evidence, that is, if it's any different than Royce's, er, Mr. Hughes's?"

I tapped out a message to Lindsay. *Now, and remember*, tortura legum pessima. *Patient torture.*

"Mr. Bierce. Really? On your phone again? Can we focus?"

"Sorry, Your Honour, my associate is just about to arrive."

And with that the door opened and in strode the beautiful, confident Ms. Lindsay Braun, long auburn hair to her shoulders, dressed in her unforgettable tangerine suit with the off-white piping, pulling my large black briefcase on wheels. She looked magnificent. Hughes, McPhellan and Zanutto all stood to shake hands with her, and frankly looked delight-ed to have this beautiful young lawyer as part of our discussions.

"Your Honour, I believe you know Ms. Braun."

Justice Randall Williams? He looked like someone had suddenly put a finger in his anus.

57

Lindsay's Day
Thursday November 10, 11 a.m.

ONCE EVERYONE HAD settled in, I invited Lindsay to walk the group of four men through the Glinka *conflagratio* evidence options. In preparation she and I had discussed a couple approaches to her presentation, but I left it to her to put the final touches on it. As I had never really seen her in action, I was a little nervous that she might fold under the pressure of appearing before her former tormentor, so I silently willed her some patience and crossed my fingers.

She began slowly, dealing with the need for evidence of the history of the relationship between Francesca and Glinka. Royce looked satisfied that I was prepared to open that door. I smiled at Williams squirming, while she patiently drew an invisible parallel between the mentoring role Glinka played in writing a reference letter for Francesca, getting her the job, commenting on their friendship, and Williams's slimy mentoring of Lindsay as an associate. It was crystal clear.

Then, in a delightful twist, she turned the question of the parties' sexual history upside down and drew another silent but powerful parallel between Glinka's history of alleged past misdeeds and Williams's history of harassment in his law firm. Nicely done, Lindsay.

Royce and Gavin were deferential to her as a young woman lawyer, allowing her to proceed uninterrupted through to the Glinka assault itself.

I knew as she described Glinka's grubby fingers penetrating Francesca's vagina on the dance floor that she was drawing on the panic she must have felt as Williams tore off her bra in the boardroom that night. It was raw, passionate. Royce and Gavin looked down at their shoes, embarrassed that such a thing could have happened among members of the Bar, between a judge and a young woman.

Even I was surprised at how Lindsay then deftly turned Justice Singh's initial lack of support and ultimately his assault on Glinka into a damnation of him morally. She made it equivalent to the fact-finder hired by Williams's firm and her abandonment of all the women who had been assaulted and harassed in exchange for more money and an NDA.

As a calm aside she mentioned Justice Singh's relationship with Ms. Hébert and underscored that, while not directly relevant to the alleged assault on Francesca by Glinka, it certainly gave colour to the culture among judges, who apparently enforced one law in their courtrooms but practiced another for themselves in their chambers. Williams shifted very uncomfortably at that dagger and then glanced at the court reporter. Interesting.

And to Lindsay's eternal credit, she did it all with such patience that she would have made an excellent serial killer. Never a smile, a smirk or a frown. She simply laid it out for all to see and the beauty of it was that only Lindsay, Williams and I knew what she was really talking about.

This torture of Williams had gone on for sixty full minutes, uninterrupted. Finally, Williams, ashen, thanked her for her presentation, and suggested we take a break and reconvene in fifteen minutes.

Before he left I suggested that perhaps the time could be put to use by counsel to discuss a narrowing of the issues. "It's always worth a discussion."

"I think that's a wonderful suggestion, Mr. Bierce." Williams left looking like he needed a drink or a plane ticket out of the country.

The court reporter decided to stay put until a staff person stuck her head into the hearing room and called, "Amber, Justice Williams needs you in chambers." She looked like she wanted to throw up.

Royce and Gavin headed to the men's room and I turned to Rick Z. "I'm glad you heard that depiction of Justice Singh. When we resume, I will be reviewing the pending divorce situation between Francesca and

His Honour, Ms. Hébert's role, the intercourse taking place in his chambers, the assault on Glinka, the draconian marriage contract that purports to give Ms. Rimini nothing, . . ."

"Purports? You know very well that she had ILA from your buddy, The Major, I think you call him? He called me. He said *you have his back*. You're not going to fry him in public for Ms. Rimini's sake, not with her history. He has too much to lose. It could ruin his practice. Do you want that on your head?" Rick sounded very confident.

"Rick, you sent Francesca to me. I heard you even made a few bucks in a pool thinking I would be fool enough to take it on."

"That was a joke. We were just having some fun."

I stared at him. A rage was starting to surface. "You told her how I operate. You know me. What do you expect? Buddy or not, I'll be moving to set aside the marriage contract. There are some 'complications,' shall we say, around the way in which the ILA was given, and on the eve of the wedding too. Courts don't like that, especially when the bride gets nothing for her signature other than a ring."

"Bierce, . . ."

"The role of Ms. Hébert will be especially interesting. A married judge sleeping with an employee. Aren't there rules around that? I will make certain that she is out of work as a French teacher pretty fast. And don't think I will be consenting to any private arbitrations for this husband and wife." I knew Rick Z was always ready to settle. Never prepared to get down and dirty, to wage war, go *à l'outrance*. "This divorce is going to be front-page news. You remember that hockey player a few years ago on the front page of the *Sun*? The one fucking around with the uptown girl? I can see the headline now, *Busted!* The next judicial inquiry will be the Singh Inquiry."

"Bierce, . . ."

"I don't give a shit. I'll burn the whole fucking thing down."

I could see Lindsay out of the corner of my eye, watching me as I promised to do what I do best. It was the threat of Total War. Did she understand now? *Maligno?* No, a path to justice.

Standing there, seeing my rage, Rick knew I would do it too. "So, you'll burn it all down?"

"All of it and everything within ten miles."

"Then what's the alternative?"

"Off the top of my head?" *I know.* "Assuming we wrap up the need for this inquiry today? Singh agrees to toss out the marriage contract. Shares his pension. Shares the value of the home. Pays Francesca support for ten years. She'll give him a release at that time. I will do an uncontested divorce. He pays her legals. Thirty grand."

Rick Z considered my alternative. "I'll recommend the pension and the home. But it was a short marriage, so support for five years, then a full release. Twenty grand for legals because you don't have that much time in it. And I'll need something else."

"What?"

"NDA. Full. Total settlement is private. No mention of Ms. Hébert. Singh wants her left out of this. They have plans. Your client breaches it, and she repays everything in damages—the support, the pension and the home. And the costs."

Lindsay jumped in. "Andrew, you can't let him have an NDA . . ."

"Lindsay, please. Leave this to me." I waved her off.

"Andrew, . . ." She was pleading.

"Okay. NDA. I'll get Bonnie to write up the minutes." We shook. His handshake was one I trusted but I would send him a confirming letter nonetheless.

"Oh yes, Bonnie. Give her my regards. You're lucky to have her. She's a gem."

My gut tightened at the thought that I had probably cost her and her new lover boy a spot in Cabinet. She could never know.

Lindsay stormed over to her files and began dramatically throwing them into her briefcase. Rick nodded toward her and whispered to me, "She'll get over it."

"We'll see."

Hughes and Gavin returned, deep in conversation about problems with the students at Osgoode Hall Law School and their obsession with leftist causes. The last thing I heard Royce say was, "Honestly, as articling students they're useless. All they talk about is what's wrong with the system, protesting everything. Free speech is great as long as it's their speech, they never know how to make the existing system work for clients. You should hear them lecturing our clients about how racist the colonial justice system is. And then the client asks me, 'Colonialism? Am I paying for this?'" They both started to laugh.

I turned to Rick. "Stick around for a few minutes. There could be fireworks. Royce, can I have a word before His Honour returns?"

"Sure."

"That offer you proposed a few weeks ago. Is it still on the table?"

"It could be. I would need to get instructions."

He turned to Gavin. "Are you on board if we can resolve this?"

"Hey, whatever you guys come up with I'll support. This shitshow needs to end."

I summarized what I needed. "Parties walk away. They agree there was a misunderstanding. Glinka apologizes for his role in that misunderstanding. No criminal charges proceed. He retires, full pension. Justice Singh is moved to a new court. Francesca gets her job back and her pick of courthouses to work at . . ."

"Okay, so far."

". . . but only after she has a six-month paid sabbatical and completes her law clerk courses at community college. Her legals are covered. Williams writes up a report and he gets to give himself credit for negotiating the settlement."

"Williams will love the last part but what are we talking about for costs? How much?"

"A hundred thousand."

"My eyes are watering. No. I already had instructions for $75,000. I could probably get him to $85,000. But there is one other thing that Glinka needs."

"Done on the costs at eighty-five but what's the other thing?"

"NDA. Full. The usual."

Lindsay was at my elbow again. She was sounding angry. "Andrew, you can't include an NDA. Please."

Royce looked at me and raised his eyebrows as if to say, *She's young. She'll get used to it.* "Sorry, NDA is mandatory. It's how we get these deals done, Ms. Braun."

Lindsay piped up thoughtfully, "What if we ask His Honour to opine on the NDA and include something in his written reasons?"

"Okay, but regardless, I'm going to need an NDA. I don't have an issue with Justice Williams adding some thoughts about an NDA. He gets it."

Gavin piped in, "I'm good with that."

No sooner had he said those words than His Honour walked into the courtroom with a smirk on his face. The young woman reporter followed behind him, totally flustered. What just happened? Royce looked at me, concerned, as if to say, *She looks upset.* No doubt he'd heard the rumours about Williams in the Barrie courthouse.

"Well, gentlemen . . . and Ms. Braun. Are we ready to proceed?"

Royce stood and said, "Your Honour, I am pleased to report that we have a potential settlement of all issues but we're hoping to have your thoughts on one important aspect." He then spelled out the terms to which we had notionally agreed.

"That sounds like a reasonable outcome for everyone involved, particularly Mr. Bierce and his usual fees." He was smirking again.

"Those are the client's fees, Your Honour."

"Of course they are, Mr. Bierce. Royce, on which aspect do you require my thoughts?" He sat back in his chair and said *my thoughts* as if any of his musing would be of almost biblical proportions.

"We are discussing whether there should be an NDA signed by the parties. My client requires one in order to settle. What are your thoughts about the role of an NDA here?"

Williams unconsciously shot a look at Lindsay before he raised his fingers together in a pyramid of wisdom and proceeded to hold forth on the incredible value of NDAs in resolving difficult matters such as this, stressing how important it was to maintain privacy for litigants. He was praising the role of NDAs and their value to settlements as if they were equivalent to the presumption of innocence. The reporter could barely keep up.

I rose for a moment. "Your Honour, I'm sorry to interrupt but I see that the court reporter is having trouble keeping up and seems to be crying. I wonder if she is alright and if she feels able to record your comments or requires a break. Your comments on this issue are very important and I assume they will form a part of your final report in this matter."

Williams looked at her with a frown. "Amber, are you alright? This is very important. Are you able to continue? Or shall I get another reporter to complete the work? You're booked for the full week are you not?"

Ahh, she was an independent contract reporter. Needs the work.

Her back stiffened as she sniffed out, "I'm fine," and continued to type.

"Very well, . . . where was I?"

"You were describing the value of NDAs to settlements."

"Yes, right . . ." His Honour continued for a few more minutes expounding on the value of NDAs and then concluded by congratulating counsel on a job well done.

"I know I speak on behalf of Mr. Hughes, Mr. McPhellan, myself and Ms. Braun when I say that your management of this difficult matter today has helped move the parties to a fair resolution that is in everyone's interest. Thank you. When does Your Honour expect to release his report that the matter has been settled, that it is confidential and that it will be subject to an NDA?"

No doubt Williams, sitting there, thought that the sooner the world learned of his deft handling of this controversial matter, the better for his career aspirations. Surely, his role in bringing the matter to a wise, confidential conclusion would stand him in good stead with the chief justice and the attorney general. It would thereby grease the wheels to a new, more prominent, judicial placement for him, ideally in downtown Toronto, where he should have been all along. Perhaps the Court of Appeal? After all, a man can dream.

Williams smiled. "I will get to work immediately and release my report this afternoon. Amber, I will need you to stay and work for a couple of extra hours." Her shoulders slumped. "Thank you, gentlemen, and Ms. Braun."

I turned to Lindsay and winked. Part 1 was done.

58

Caucus

Thursday November 10, 4 p.m.

LINDSAY HEADED BACK to the office to await Williams's report and I Uberred up to Queen's Park for God knows what was going to happen next. I arrived at security at the East entrance at 3:50 p.m. and was stunned when the guard recognized me.

"Welcome to Queen's Park, Mr. Bierce. I have a security badge ready for you. You will be heading to the Ninoododaiwin Room on the second floor."

"I beg your pardon? The nindoobiewhaat?"

He smiled and said, "Committee Room 228. Elevators are straight ahead on the right." And then he whispered and winked, "It's not cool to be cruel."

Oh my God. They're everywhere.

When I pulled open the worn wooden door to Room 228 there must have been two hundred people crammed into a space designed to hold no more than ninety. It seemed that every one of the sixty elected NDP MPPs had decided to bring two staff members, their wives, husbands and friends. There were even a handful of kids running around. It was chaos. I made my way through the crowd toward Madeleine, who was surrounded by well wishers. I could tell the gathering was high and getting higher as they whiffed the rarified air of imminent political power—along with the smoke from some members of a First Nation who were chanting and drumming in a corner. Her people?

A large fellow with a thick grey ponytail and dressed in an ill-fitting brown corduroy sports jacket, black T-shirt with a wolf's face on it, green corduroy pants (I know) and battered Blundstone boots called everyone to order and asked that anyone who was not an MPP-elect or member of the leader's staff please leave. There were groans and pleading to stay but he cracked the whip. "Out if you are not an MPP or on the leader's staff! Now! We have work to do. No media. Out!"

It took a few minutes but that reduced the room to about eighty people.

Madeleine sat at the centre of one of several long wooden tables that had been arranged in a huge square with MPPs-elect spread out around it. She motioned for me to sit at one corner of the square, a couple of members over from her. It was clear that not everyone in the room knew everyone else. These people were from all over the province.

A young Black woman of maybe twenty-five with a heavy French accent sat next to me and explained that she was a physiotherapist from Timmins. Her name was Chantelle and it turned out that this was the first time she had been to Toronto. How exciting for her. Maybe she will be Minister of Northern Ontario and Mining. I noticed as I looked around the table that of the sixty MPPs-elect, easily forty-five of them were women, six of whom were wearing keffiyehs, and a few others I could not be certain of their gender. I was the only person wearing a suit. This should be interesting.

The big fellow with the ponytail called the meeting to order. "Dylan is handing out an agenda. Dylan uses the pronoun they, and they are new to the leader's staff so please say hello. Please sit tight for a few minutes while we get organized. And please turn off your phones. I'm asking that there be no tweeting, emailing, texting or anything for the next hour. We have work to do today." Someone's phone immediately rang.

"We're going to start with a few words from our leader but first, . . ." The land acknowledgement that he then read solemnly was drowned out by cheering, hooting and hollering. The First Nations folks in the corner and Madeleine looked dismayed. I banged the table with my hand and called out, "Quiet! Show some respect, for heaven's sake."

Madeleine thanked everyone and asked that we get down to business. She was warm but serious. "I want to congratulate everyone around this table on their election. You have done something amazing." She laid the charm on them for a few more minutes, to more cheering and laughing, but then brought matters down to reality. I liked her style. A lot. "We need to talk about what happens next. I've been forced to keep my cards close to my vest these last couple of days. As many of you know there have been some discussions underway."

That set the room abuzz. Someone's phone rang. Really?

"I'm very pleased to report that I've met with the LG, the leaders of the other parties and, as a result of some agreements that will be shared over the next few days, we, the New Democratic Party, will be forming the next government of the Province of Ontario."

There was stunned silence and then pandemonium. Some people even cried. They had returned from the wilderness. Now every wrong in the world could be righted. The meek had truly inherited the earth. Well, sort of.

Big Ponytail got matters back under control and Madeleine continued, "We are able to form a government for one reason and one reason only, it is because we have developed a working arrangement with three MPPs who were not elected as NDP members. This will give us sixty-three members and a working majority."

The room erupted in conversation. A phone rang. I'm not kidding.

I had to admit I was curious now. Three members? Given my comments to Madeleine, who were the other two? Had things worked out with the Greens?

"I would like to start by introducing Mr. Andrew Bierce, K.C. He was elected in Parkdale–High Park as an Independent. Mr. Bierce has been a lawyer in Ontario for over forty years. He is the only lawyer elected among this group. I'm pleased to announce that he has agreed to take on a Cabinet position."

There was an audible gasp and a buzz of astonishment. But, but, but . . . he's not an NDPer. How can this be?!

"Please, settle down. He has agreed to take on a Cabinet position as attorney general. In such position he will not only be independent, but he has committed to support our government for a minimum period of two years and to support our agenda." There was more grumbling and muttering. Not everyone was happy.

"The other two MPPs who have agreed to work with us are Mr. Gruber and Mr. Reyes, the two elected members of the Green Party."

There were more gasps and a buzz of conversations.

"However, unlike Mr. Bierce, they will not be taking positions in Cabinet at this time but rather will support us issue by issue." This element was met with approving nods and table-banging.

"This next part gives me great pleasure, but it has been a difficult task to select a few individuals from our elected MPPs to join my Cabinet. A press release is being sent out as we speak, announcing the members of my Cabinet." She then introduced the remaining Cabinet members and their portfolios and announced that she intended to recall the Legislature immediately.

My seatmate, Chantelle, was thrilled to learn that she would be Minister of Citizenship and Multiculturalism. She leaned over to me and said, "When I get my first paycheque I'm going to buy a car."

I see. How wonderful.

My phone pulsed and I saw a text from Lindsay. *Williams's report is in hand. He has released it to the press. He really thinks NDAs are invaluable. Copy attached.* Beside it was a thumbs-up emoji.

I texted back. *Beautiful. Let Francesca know. Bonnie too.*

Will do. Part 2 was complete.

59

The Noose
Thursday November 10, 4:30 p.m.

AS THE MEETING broke up I slipped over to a corner of the room, away from the grousing of the MPPs who had not been selected for Cabinet and the glad-handing of those who had been elevated to the status of the angels. I needed to see just how far Williams had gone in his report. I opened the attachment to Lindsay's text and read.

> ***In the Matter of Certain Allegations Concerning Justice Glinka, Judge of the Ontario Court of Justice***
> *Presenting Counsel: Gavin McPhellan*
> *Counsel for Justice Glinka: Royce Hughes, K.C.*
> *Counsel for the Complainant: Andrew Bierce, K.C.*
> *(and Associate Lindsay Braun)*
> *Court Reporter: Amber Irwin*
>
> *The Chief Justice of the Ontario Superior Court recently tasked me with this very important matter. Initially, there was to be participation by other judges and a layperson. However, at an early stage, during preliminary discussions about evidence, I met with the above noted counsel to consider the matter in question. The issues they confronted were very complex and involved difficult questions of substantive law, new aspects*

of evidentiary law and very real practical matters of procedure. I was able to address them all alone.

Counsel made presentations to me which were helpful. I delved into the issues in great detail. However, drawing on my own considerable experience as a member of the Bar and now as a member of the bench as a Justice of the Superior Court, I was able to assist counsel in resolving this matter, not only in a way that meets the interests of all concerned, but also in a way that conserves the increasingly scarce resources of our justice system for matters of genuine importance. The settlement is confidential and subject to non-disclosure agreements signed by all parties.

I feel it is necessary to add a few words of explanation about the use of the non-disclosure agreements. Some will no doubt question this aspect of the resolution and insist that the details of the allegations be made public, that transparency is needed for any settlement and that this is particularly so when it involves members of the justice system.

I must respectfully disagree. Non-disclosure agreements allow matters to be settled. They allow parties to a dispute to make binding arrangements, arrangements that protect their privacy, their reputations, their employment, their families and their conscience. Without non-disclosure agreements the circumstances faced by parties would be forced into the light, causing potential embarrassment. It would leave complainants with a stark choice: go forward and face a public hearing and all that it entails, or abandon their claims altogether. This is particularly so in the case of complaints of harassment, sexual and otherwise. Non-disclosure agreements allow for a third option: a private settlement. These private settlements benefit everyone involved and I support them wholeheartedly and especially so in this matter.

Signed this 10th day of November . . .
Justice Randall Williams

Perfect. Foundation poured. Scaffold erected. Noose ready.

"Judging by the smile on your face that must be good news." It was Madeleine (and her perfume). If I wasn't smiling enough already, her arrival at my elbow certainly gave me a reason to.

There was just something about her and I suddenly felt a goofy little flutter in my stomach. "Yes, it's good news. A difficult matter has been wrapped up quite nicely."

"Are you going to be okay working with this group? It's diverse."

Diverse? That was one word for this collection of poorly dressed social workers who were about to earn more as MPPs than they had ever earned in their lives. "Yes, I think you have some real quality people to work with. I've already met Chantelle, your Minister of Citizenship and Multiculturalism."

"Good. She has a remarkable background in immigration, PhD in international affairs focussed on refugee claims. She was working as a physiotherapist to pay the bills. Supports a family of six. I took your advice about Mr. Reyes and Mr. Gruber. I think that arrangement will work but I may need your help keeping them onside, especially Reyes. He's ambitious. Pushy. He was in my office again today trying to wangle something from me. And I can tell you this, also a bit of a flirt."

I'll murder him.

"I hope I can come to you for input on things, not just legal matters."

Oh my. I felt dizzy. "Of course. I'm at your disposal. Just call."

Still a little under her spell, I made my way out into the hall and to the elevator. I needed to get back to the office. Attorney general or not, I still had a law practice to run before I was actually sworn in. I had no idea what would happen next with my firm. I couldn't appear in court or negotiate files once sworn in, but I could sure as hell bill them. With a cool $85,000 coming in from Glinka and another $20,000 from Singh and big bills going out to Coop and Pat, I could at least cover Lindsay and Bonnie's salaries and some office expenses. I just hoped Bonnie was recovering from her political delusions and could get down to business. I was going to need her now more than ever.

My phone pulsed with a text. It was from Daria. *I think you should get home. Sean's not good.*

Okay.

You're welcome.

Whatever.

Another from Bonnie. *I need to speak with you. When are you coming back to the office?*

Oh-oh. I hope she hasn't got wind of my blocking Reyes from Cabinet. Maybe I was reading too much into it.

Another from The Major. *Thanks. Read Williams's report. I owe you one.* Yes, you do.

I guess the press release about my Cabinet position had hit the news because a stream of congratulations began to flow in. Royce Hughes, Gavin McPhellan, Rick Z, Dr. Rubin, Alvin, Coop, Patrick, Dikoobe, Fernstein of all people, Naomi, even Heidi the Art Girl. I scanned down a stream of names, many I didn't recognize.

Then one from Father Shannon. *We will need to meet.*

I hit back. *Certainly, how is Sean's anointing coming along?*

As I waited for the elevator, texts and emails continued to pour in.

I punched the down button a few times and muttered to myself, "Where is this fucking elevator?"

The ornate doors suddenly opened to reveal an embarrassed young couple who looked like they had been making out in the corner. She couldn't have been more than a university student and looked a little distraught. The man turned to me and reluctantly extended his right hand as he pulled up his zipper with his left.

I reached out and grabbed his hand firmly. "I'm Andrew Bierce, Attorney General Bierce. Everything alright here?"

He sputtered, "Yes, I'm . . . I'm . . ."

"I know who you are."

It was Mateo Reyes.

60

Oh, Bonnie

Thursday November 10, evening

AS I MADE my way back to the office after the Queen's Park meeting, exhaustion sank in.

No wonder I was tired. I'd almost forgotten that my day had started at 5 a.m., helping Sean make a trip to and from the bathroom before the PSWs arrived. That felt like days ago. It had been an *emergency* and I could tell he was embarrassed. I think we both suddenly had an appreciation for what our father had gone through during those last few weeks with Mom. There had been no PSWs to help him. We certainly were no help. It was just him doing it all, followed by a bottle of JW at the end of the day.

Election night and the days that followed seemed to have drained every last ounce of energy out of Sean. But when I finally got him back in bed this morning, he had been full of questions. Things from our childhood. Questions about Madeleine. Questions about the new government. And then questions about whether Shannon had been in touch. Where were we at with the paperwork? The funeral? Had I looked at his paperwork, his will, his POA?

And then out of the blue he had dropped a bomb.

"You never told me the results of the DNA for Angie."

"What?" Oh God, where was this coming from? His meds were too strong. Or not strong enough.

"You know what I'm talking about. I haven't forgotten. I've been thinking about it a lot lately. You know, I'm trying to make peace with some things. Angie and Paul. What did his DNA test say?"

"Sean, I haven't got time for this right now. I have to get to the office and then over to the meeting with Williams, Royce and McPhellan about the inquiry and then I'm supposed to be at Queen's Park later for the first caucus meeting. It's going to be a hell of a day."

"Did you open the envelope Paul gave you from the lab?"

"The envelope?" I had a flashback to those awful moments at SickKids when we learned about Angie's poisoning and Paul's disgust with me when I asked him for the DNA results. He had been poisoned as much as anyone that day.

"Don't screw around, Andrew. I haven't got the energy to argue with you. What did it say?"

"Do you mean to tell me that for the last three years you've been wondering if you were Angie's father?"

"Yes, that's exactly what I have been worried about. Did Chloe murder my daughter?" Wow, that was blunt. "I need to confess these things before I go." He was on the verge of tears.

"Confess? Surely you don't believe in that nonsense anymore, do you?"

"I do. And right now I'm not taking any chances. Tell me."

"Sean, I wish I'd known sooner this was still so much on your mind. I could have saved you a lot of useless worrying. Not your baby. You were not the father, Father. Relieved?"

Then the tears came and he managed to blubber out, "Thank you. That means a lot to me."

"Hey, no big deal. I wish we'd talked about this sooner. Look, I have to get to the office before I head up to meet Williams. The PSWs will be here any minute. I'll call or text you later."

As I left, I seemed to recall that the penance for lying was a pile of Hail Marys and a couple of Our Fathers. It's a good thing I don't believe in confessing anymore. Plus, I really didn't have the time for all that nonsense.

It had been quite a day. When I got back to the office after the big announcements, it was nearly 6:30 p.m. I couldn't get the image of that snake Reyes out of my mind. Bonnie was head over heels for this guy and here he's grabbing some intern in the elevator within days of being elected. She would be devastated.

Usually when I step through the front door of my office into that beautiful reception, I feel a sense of coming home. Not today. The office still smells!

I wasn't even through reception before Bonnie was coming down the hall. "Where have you been? I heard the news about the Cabinet. Congratulations but . . ."

"Congratulations . . . but? Is that all you've got? But? But what? It's been a long day and I need a drink. Why don't you join me? We can catch up. And by the way, is it just me or does this office still smell?" I had absolutely no idea what to say about Mr. Reyes.

"I know it stinks. I work here. More than you most days. The landlord says they can't do anything more. Anyway, we need to talk." She was dead serious. Yikes.

"Okay. Let's crash in my office. Is Lindsay around?"

"No. I'm not sure where she is." Bonnie fell into the Egg as I slipped off my suit jacket and poured two tall whiskies. She was down and I wondered if she already knew about her Romeo.

"Lindsay's supposed to be putting the finishing touches on the Glinka Inquiry settlement. We put a bow on that this morning. We need to bill that thing."

She was not the least bit interested. "Andrew, if you're going to be attorney general, what will happen to your practice? You can't keep it. What about the clients?" She hesitated. "What about me? Lindsay?"

"First, can we say cheers to the election? You ran a great campaign. And personally, for me? I'm still in shock."

"Thanks, but that's over." Oh, I see, the political fever had broken. "I need to know what's next. I came back to work with you based on that generous offer you made." It sounded like Bonnie had forgotten that it was she who wanted to return to my office.

"I have been wondering if Mateo is planning to offer you a job in his office at Queen's Park. You seemed to be his right arm." I was fishing.

"He says he has to follow some kind of protocol at Queen's Park before he hires. He was interviewing some potential staff today."

I think I saw the little weasel interviewing someone in the elevator. He'd used Bonnie to get elected and now Mr. Rising Green Star was moving on to younger pastures. He was going to break Bonnie's heart.

Not on my watch.

"Bonnie, if you haven't accepted a job with Mateo would you consider coming to Queen's Park and working for me? I'll need an executive assistant. You could even get involved in some policy." *Anything but Green policy, of course.* "I have some matters that the premier says will be given priority. Clean water up north, for one."

"Are you serious?" She looked half shocked and half thrilled.

"I think there are a few upsides. Aside from our history together you would be able to get experience working for an actual minister. Then if Mateo ever joins Cabinet as a minister," *over my dead body*, "you'll be ready."

"Oh, it sounds wonderful, but I would want to run it by Mateo first." God, she said his name like he was the premier. "He told me he really needs me as part of his team going forward . . . just to be patient. He wants to keep our relationship confidential for a bit."

I bet he does. "I'm confident he'll support the move. I'll speak to him and explain how it's actually in his long-term interest."

"You would do that?"

"Of course. It's a win-win-win." I raised my glass to hers. "To our future together at Queen's Park."

"I can't wait to tell Mateo."

"Me too."

61

Lindsay's Future
Friday November 11, Remembrance Day

I HAD NO idea what I would tell Lindsay. My practice was going to end. It was a fact. Clients would need to be reassigned. I couldn't carry on as a lawyer in private practice and be attorney general at the same time. She had been quite clear about not being a babysitter. Who could blame her? How long could she be expected to babysit a law practice? Years? Forever? Not realistic at all.

I recalled the chewing out she had given me when she learned of my election. Was I going to be in for another one of those sessions? Probably. But I felt strangely calm about everything that was developing. Part 1 and 2 of the plan had unfolded as designed. Lindsay had to be pleased with that. My goal—our goal—of revenge on Randall Williams was within reach. I was about to give Father Shannon a royal roasting. Sean's wishes would be attended to as he had hoped. The only downside of this whole turn of events was the money. I was about to take a huge hit in the earnings department. This new job couldn't pay more than a couple of hundred thousand. Who can live on that? I would need to take a serious look at my finances.

Although I had been texting her late last night and all morning, Lindsay was nowhere to be found. That was not a good sign. I needed her. Our work was not finished.

At 10 a.m. I got a text from her. *Time for a coffee?*

Sure, I'm at the office. Where you been?

Meet at Osgoode Hall? Dining Room? Does 11 a.m. work?

Sure, but Osgoode?

I'm here doing some research and working on a couple of other things.

Okay. See you at 11. Could use a walk.

The last time I'd been at Osgoode was when I had first called Daria and learned about Sean. It seemed like a thousand years ago, but it had only been a few months.

Solvitur ambulando is good for the soul, so I set out walking up York Street to Osgoode Hall and braced myself for a heart-to-heart with Lindsay. In the distance, I could hear the trumpet from the Remembrance Day ceremony by Old City Hall. But I was still stuck in the problems of the here and now. Maybe I could find Lindsay a job at the AG. I'd already been told that a full staff awaited me at 720 Bay Street. Bunch of bureaucrats. Maybe I could find her a spot. Could she go back to her own practice? It had only been a couple of months. I could transfer the remaining clients to her. Maybe. There had to be options.

As I went through security at the Queen Street entrance, I fumbled through my pocket for my lawyer's ID. Before I could pull it out a voice called out, "There's no need for that anymore Mr. Attorney General." There stood a young woman who clearly knew who I was. I had never seen her before. "I assume you are here for the Law Society Bencher's monthly meeting. We're having a special one, marking Remembrance Day. As attorney general you are automatically a lifetime member. They will be thrilled that you have made coming to one of the meetings a high priority."

Bencher? The Law Society? I was now a member of the very organization that—at the insistence of Randall Williams—had suspended me for ten months, ordered me into counselling with Dr. Rubin and made my life miserable? And for life?

I could get used to this.

"Thank you for intercepting me. Although I was planning to attend the Bencher's meeting—it's one of my priorities—I've just received an urgent message that I must meet counsel in the dining room. Please give

my regrets to the other Benchers. If my meeting finishes early I will be
sure to drop by."

"Of course. I will pass on the message. And good luck with your term.
It's very exciting, the possibility of, you know, better protection for animals." Her face lit up at the possibility.

Oh, dear God. No.

"Yes, of course. Another top priority."

I made my way upstairs to the beautiful dining room and found
Lindsay tucked in a corner at a table by herself.

"Hey, how have you been? What brings you up here?"

Before she could answer, a waitress was at my arm asking if "the new
attorney general" would like a coffee or tea. Well, la-di-da. "A coffee
would be wonderful, thank you."

Lindsay looked totally nonplussed by the attention. She had that
look, the look of serious matters needing to be discussed. I decided to
head her off at the pass. "Lindsay, I'm glad we have a chance to meet pri-
vately. I've been thinking for days about the firm, your role, your career
now that I've been elected . . ."

A lawyer I had never met suddenly stood at my elbow. "Mr. Attorney
General. I just want to introduce myself and congratulate you on your
appointment." He handed me his card. It was okay. Pretty standard stuff.
I recognized the firm. Bay Street. "There is so much to be done. If I can
ever be of assistance, please don't hesitate." He backed away as if from
royalty.

"Thank you." I held the card up to Lindsay. "See. These are still in use."

"Yeah, I wish I had one." Riiiight. I never got her those business cards.

"So back to your career . . ."

"I've accepted a position with Royce Hughes."

I was *mutus*.

"After we wrapped up with Williams yesterday, Hughes approached
me to go for a coffee. We chatted a bit. He said he was impressed with my
presentation to Williams."

"You didn't tell him about your NDA?" Please Lindsay, tell me you
didn't.

"Of course not. But, you know . . . Anyway, he offered me a position
with his firm and I said yes. Actually, Gavin McPhellan approached me

too, but Hughes seemed a stronger choice. I hope you're okay with my decision."

I looked into her beautiful eyes. How could I not be okay with it? My worries about her were solved in an instant. "That's a good call. Are you giving me two weeks' notice?"

"Uh, I think when you were elected you gave me two weeks' notice."

"When does he want you to start?"

"Soon, but I told him I needed to finish off a couple of things for you. Ms. Marrs has decided to represent herself. So I packed up the physical file and put everything else on a USB. She says you failed her and she can do a better job herself. She wants her first retainer back."

"Not gonna happen."

"When she picked up the file she was pretty angry and looked a little crazy, to be honest."

"I think you mean crazier. Bonnie would never have let her in the door. Good that she's gone. I guess I'll have to eat the fees on that one. Lesson relearned. Get a retainer or get screwed. I bet Hughes doesn't make that kind of mistake."

"Speaking of fees and settlements. Francesca."

"I've got Bonnie doing the accounts as we speak. Those may be some of the only fees we collect from the last few months."

"Well, you remember the Graph of Gratitude you so carefully explained?"

"No. No. No."

"Yes, yes, yes. She thinks she should have got more. More support, more paid leave, a longer period of time to go back to school. She actually said that you should have asked that she be allowed to go to law school."

"Law school?"

"Yes. And there's more. Why does her husband get to keep his job? What about Pauline? Why didn't Glinka apologize? Why does she have to sign an NDA?"

"Did you explain everything to her? What follows?"

"I couldn't get a word in edgewise."

"I better speak with her."

"And she thinks you charged too much for your fees."

"But she was represented for free. It didn't cost her anything."

"She thinks you should refund some of your fees to her."

I didn't know what to say. It was classic. The Graph never fails. If I hadn't been so busy with the election, I could have sat her down and explained it to her.

"Lindsay, I appreciate you wrapping matters up. I know it hasn't been what you expected. There was some research you did for me about Christian Brothers settlements. I'm sorry it wasn't billable. Is that available for me?"

"Of course. It's in the system under the file *CB/Cath research/Comp Claims*. I included some other information in there that you will find interesting. Look under *Charity Can/Intel*. I think you'll find it helpful." She said *helpful* as if that file contained clues to solving the Kennedy assassination. The first one.

"Okay, thanks. More reading materials. Just what I need."

My phone rang. "Bierce."

"It's Daria. You better get home asap. The PSWs are calling me. I'm headed over there now. An ambulance is on the way."

"Oh." I felt the blood leave my face.

Lindsay looked at me. "Is everything okay?"

"No. I have to go."

"Is it your brother?"

"I have to go. Can you email me those files?"

"Sure, I'll put them in your Dropbox. I hope he is okay, I'm still looking forward to meeting him."

Why? Her wish is an abiding mystery.

62

Death in the Afternoon
Friday November 11, midday

I HAD TO practically fight my way out of Osgoode Hall to get an Uber. I needed to go no more than twenty blocks to my condo but it was taking forever just to get out of the building. The Benchers monthly meeting had just finished and forty lawyers and staff discharged into the hallway in front of me. Suddenly, I was the star of the show. Everyone needed to congratulate me personally and remind me that they had always been pulling for me during those challenging times after the unfortunate incident at court and poor Lester's death. Of course you were pulling for me. Fucking hypocrites.

"I'm sorry, there's an emergency. I need to get to a meeting."

"Oh, get used to it!" one wit called out. "This is the life of an attorney general."

As I made my way outside and down the steps, a reporter stepped forward. Someone had tipped him that I was at Osgoode. "Mr. Bierce, any thoughts on how you will handle conflicts that arise from your previous practice now that you are attorney general?"

What on earth was he talking about? And where was that Uber? I looked at my phone. The car was coming south on University. I needed to go north to College. He would need to make a U-turn. In midday traffic. And the construction. Idiot. Four minutes away.

The reporter persisted. "Any thoughts on this new potential conflict?"

"What are you talking about?" I looked at my phone. Still four minutes away.

"As attorney general you are now responsible for Crown attorneys and prosecutions."

"Yes, I'm aware." I looked at my phone. The Uber was not moving.

"Will you be able to remain objective when those prosecutions involve your former clients?"

I looked at him like he was crazy. "My practice was confined primarily to family law, so I don't foresee any issues." Where was that Uber? I could see that it had passed Queen Street going south. Now he was five minutes away. Idiot.

"I assume, then, that you are not aware of what has been all over Twitter today."

"I don't follow Twitter . . . It's toxic."

Lindsay was suddenly at my elbow. "Andrew, it's Marrs. He's talking about Marrs. It just hit the news."

"What hit the news?"

She fumbled with her phone to show me. "Her mother died yesterday during one of her visits. She's been arrested and charged with manslaughter, failing to provide necessities of life, fraud and more. She killed the twins too."

Hemingway came to mind.

63

Remembrance Day, Indeed
Friday November 11

IT TOOK NEARLY forty minutes to get from Queen and University to College and Bathurst. If I hadn't been so distracted trying to figure out what a Dropbox is, I would have murdered the driver before we pulled up in front of my condo, never mind give him a good review. I could've run there faster if I wasn't so out of shape.

When I finally got to Sean's bedside it was dire. The PSWs were crying in the kitchen. Daria was at his side holding his hand. Two paramedics stood looking at their phones, not sure what to do next. I heard them whispering, "Should we move him? Pointless. Might make matters worse. There's another call. Homeless guy again, same one, at Bloor and Spadina. Should we take it? This guy's not going to a hospital."

Sean was a shade of grey I had never seen, like wet ashes.

"Is he conscious? Can he hear us?" I pulled up a stool and sat close to him.

"It's hard to tell. He has been in and out. I think he's been waiting for you. A priest just left. He did some special thing . . ."

"Anointing the sick." Good, clearly someone at the archdiocese got at least part of my request. "Sean, buddy. Stay with us. You got this." I'm not sure what I was hoping for. "I think his eyes just moved."

Daria looked exhausted and let out a long, sad sigh. "I'm going to leave you two alone." She motioned for everyone to get out of the bedroom. "Give these brothers some privacy."

He wasn't gone but he was going. I was worried. I hadn't heard from Shannon or the archdiocese about my demands. It was a good sign that the anointing had happened but what about the rest? Had I asked for too much? Were they laughing about it? Had the papers been processed? Shannon said he would have it done by end of day Friday. Today was Friday.

My phone pulsed with a text. It was Shannon. *Time for a call?*

Did I have any choice? *Yes. Now is good.* I stepped away from Sean to the window and looked west down College. It was a drab grey afternoon. A suitable day for solemn remembrance, but never a good look for Toronto.

My phone rang. "Bierce."

"Father Shannon."

I decided to push. "I see that a priest was here. I assume Sean's papers have not been processed and that you are meeting my requests."

"The papers have not been processed. You'll be happy to know that the laicization has been canceled. But there is a matter on which I need clarification."

"I'm listening."

"The archdiocese needs your assistance as attorney general on certain matters. Matters with this new government. Relations are strained."

"I see. First, thank you for your non-congratulations. Madeleine—I mean, the premier—has made me aware of her concerns." *She had not told me anything but I could well imagine her feelings about the church, given what they had done during the campaign and the candidates they had supported.*

"I'm in a position to facilitate your wishes for Sean . . ."

"All of them?"

"It wasn't easy but yes, all of them."

"Including the archbishop performing the Funeral Mass?"

"That was the biggest challenge of all, but yes. That can be arranged too."

"And what do you need from the attorney general and this government?"

"Can we meet to discuss this?"

"Certainly, right after the Mass and the funeral. I will tell my assistant to make your meeting the first one on my agenda. It will be unofficial, of course."

"Notwithstanding the need for confidentiality, can I ask that you send me a memo confirming that? I'll need to show the archbishop something."

"Father, you of all people understand that this is something that cannot be reduced to writing. It will be done based on trust and faith. I know you are a big supporter of those two things."

"Indeed." I hoped he recalled our meeting at the Blue Jays game.

"I think a Mass possibly next week sometime would be best."

"I see. That is the situation?"

"Yes, that is the situation."

"Thank you."

"And, Father, I will give the premier your regards. She will be attending Sean's funeral, of course. I don't know if you are aware, but they are quite close."

"I did not know that, but thank you for letting me know now."

"Unfortunately, I had to make her aware of the situation in Parkdale–High Park, the reasons behind my candidacy and your threat to defrock him as leverage." *Not really but, you know.* "She was distressed to say the least. Once I relay your commitments around Sean's funeral to her, I'm sure she will be relieved to know that her dear friend will get a proper send-off. I will do my best to smooth things over going forward." *Not really.*

"I see."

"It's going to be quite a Funeral Mass, isn't it Father?"

"We will do our best."

I looked over at Sean and I swore I saw his lips curl into a little smile.

I turned to the window and, as corny as it sounds, the sun blazed through the clouds and down College Street. People were out and the street suddenly seemed to come alive.

"I expect no less, Father."

I looked back at Sean. He was gone.

64

The Snares of the Devil
Monday November 21, 10 a.m.

ST. MICHAEL'S CATHEDRAL Basilica can accommodate the rear ends of 1,600 souls, and on this sunny Monday morning every one of its solid oak pews was filled to the brim for Father Sean's glorious send-off. They had come from all across the province, men, women (lots of women, some with children in tow), dozens of priests and clergy and a surprising mix of Sean's friends, businesspeople, politicians, the people who gather around politicians (fart catchers, as they are known), professional athletes, entertainers, artists and musicians. It had become a must-attend event, opening with the St. Michael's boys' choir and followed by the archbishop himself giving the Funeral Mass.

I insisted Premier Franks join me in the front row to let the archbishop and Father Shannon see what they were dealing with now. Sitting as close to her as possible, I found her perfume a tonic to the stifling air of the church and the so-called *ambience of incense* being burned. I pray that heaven doesn't actually smell like that.

As I scanned the crowd during the service I recognized many of the faces. Standing tall among them was none other than The Coop, dressed in full cowboy gear and with Kim on his arm. That was a good sign. With Kayla packed off to university in B.C. and Brent having taken a vow of silence, maybe they could settle down. Maybe. But people do not change, so it was a big maybe.

Alongside him stood my rockstar client and now close friend, Patrick McGovern, struggling to fashion a new look based on a blend of the Eagles and Kid Rock. It was not quite coming together and I wished I had never suggested that odd musical fusion to him. On Patrick's arm was his wife Laurie, but I could also see Ms. Sarah Trager hovering just one pew behind them, waving and smiling at their kids. Not a good sign. The former nanny was taking her life in her hands sitting so close to her former employer, particularly Laurie and her cubs.

On the other side of Patrick sat his new musical partner, Brent, dressed as if he was transitioning back to the creative side of life, in a black tuxedo jacket over a black T-shirt with a Nirvana image and topped with a Jagger-like scarf around his neck. It probably looked better in *Guitar* magazine. Oh well.

They had all somehow made the peace that would be needed to forge their new musical sounds. Each was happy in his own way with the settlement I had fashioned, never knowing how it had really come together. I would certainly never tell. Bills had been rendered and were paid.

A few pews over sat Bonnie, sobbing onto the shoulder of that weasel Mateo Reyes. I could not help but throw eye daggers at him. There were well-founded rumours that he was already becoming a notorious hound at Queen's Park, chasing everyone from interns to young staff in the Legislative Library. Bonnie was in for a big disappointment any day now. How could she not see through his smarmy facade? From the sour look on his face I could tell that we were on a collision course, as word had filtered down that I'd nixed him from any Cabinet posts. I would need to ensure that his reach always exceeds his grasp.

Lindsay sat next to them, no doubt still regretting that she had never had a chance to meet Sean. He would have loved her. Beside her sat Royce Hughes, K.C., in a magnificent charcoal three-piece suit. I made a note to find out who he uses for his tailoring, but then on second thought I will be facing some belt-tightening on a public servant's salary. I would stick with Manny for now.

Naomi, looking perfectly put together as the pretty upscale soccer mom, sat quietly with her husband who still had a cast on his arm from his brawl in the hockey stands a month ago. Their two sons sat on either side of them, separated I assume to keep the peace until the end of the Mass. I had to smile. Brothers.

At the very back of the church I could make out a row of familiar oddballs and their smiling faces. It was the animal rights crew in full force, waving to me as if at a concert. How do they survive in this world? Nearby sat the beautiful Art School Girl, Heidi. She smiled and nodded and I wondered if there might be something there in future. I was touched, though, that they had all come to my brother's funeral. But thank God churches don't allow pets. Yet.

In one packed row sat Dr. Rubin, beaming, and Francesca, scowling. She still had no idea what was going on. She would find out soon enough and no doubt be thrilled. There was Alvin, balls still firmly in the grip of Lorelei, and both of them no doubt wondering how on earth this startling turn of events had come about. Dave Goodwin was squeezed in there too, and likely had come early to light a candle in gratitude for his salvation from professional destruction. He owed me one.

Oh brother, that Pudgy Red fellow was with him, the button on his tight sports jacket in imminent peril of popping off. At least he'd put on a tie for the occasion, even if it wasn't done up properly. Christ, Fernstein was there as well, wedged in beside Rick Z. Even now, when I looked at Rick, I could not get his Peanuts–character boxers out of my mind. Hard to take a man seriously when you know such unfortunate particulars. With the Singh separation agreement details pinned down I'm sure he thought it was safe to relax, having protected the judge from scandal. Dream on my friend, you have no idea what's coming.

A huge contingent of lawyers was packed into a series of pews at the back, lawyers I had never met from the Law Society, from big Bay Street firms, from the government, corporate lawyers and even policy lobbyists, all there to be seen, to make a connection of some kind. I would need to get used to these types clamouring for my attention. Little did they know how impervious I would be to their influence. I had my own plans and they didn't involve favours, deals or positioning for re-election. No, there would be no such distractions. I had plans for one thing, and one thing only—revenge.

My discreet scan continued but I could find no trace of Father Shannon. I assumed he was ensconced in the corner of a side chapel conspiring on church business like some small-time Medici plotter.

And then my eyes landed on Daria. She was alone at the end of a pew up in the balcony of all places. Good. Keep her as far away from me as possible. I didn't need any unpleasant distractions. This was Sean's day and I needed to stay focussed on my eulogy. I wanted to do him justice. No sooner had Daria and I locked eyes, we exchanged sneers and I was up.

Show time.

When I reflected back on our late-night discussions of reality and what comes after, I got a few ideas about what Sean might want said at his funeral. But it wasn't until I cracked the file he had left for me that I really understood a very big part of my brother, something at his core. He had kept his secrets right to the last. Along with his power of attorney, his will, a sheaf of banking information and his childhood St. John's Sunday Missal, was a journal and a surprising collection of poetry, his own words achingly expressing the pain he carried alone.

The St. Michael's lectern is made of white marble and it was so cold to the touch that I pulled my hands away when I laid my notes down. Madeleine looked up at me, so serious, so sad, and yet as beautiful as the icon of the Madonna behind me. She touched a hanky to her eyes and nodded to me as if to say, tell them.

My Eulogy

I want to begin by thanking everyone for coming today to join me in bidding farewell to my brother, Sean. I recognize so many faces, faces of people who had met him, who knew him, who loved him, who were loved by him.

And there are faces here that I don't recognize. These are people who unfortunately did not have that opportunity. They probably heard stories and came out of curiosity or perhaps as a favour to me. Whatever your reasons for coming, thank you for being here, I appreciate it and I'm confident Sean knows. He always knew what was going on, didn't he?

That drew a round of murmurs and knowing nods.

> *Now, I want to begin by getting out of the way some of the terrible things about Sean.*

There was dead silence as I'm sure those who truly knew of some of his antics over the years were concerned about what I might say next. Was I about to become a loose cannon?

> *First, Sean did some of the worst impersonations I have ever heard.*

Those who knew him burst out laughing.

> *I think his Bette Davis was perhaps the worst.*

More laughter.

> *He would deliver her classic line, "Fasten your seatbelts, it's going to be a bumpy night," as if he had studied under Lee Strasberg in New York City. It was more Second City than anything, and he may have missed a career in stand-up comedy.*

A woman in the second row began sobbing through her laughter as she no doubt recalled him saying that line many times over the years.

> *God forbid you ever heard him do his Al Pacino Scarface routine, which came off more Speedy-Gonzales Mexican than anything Cuban. He sounded like he wanted you to actually pet a little friend, perhaps a small animal.*

It took a few seconds for the laughing to stop.

> *Or, I pray you never had to endure his De Niro Taxi Driver performance, "Are you talking to me? Well, I'm the only one here." He always sounded as if he was genuinely confused about whether someone was speaking to him.*

People were in hysterics, including Madeleine, who looked at me and simply shook with laughter.

It was criminal what he did with those impersonations.

I took a moment before carrying on.

Sean loved Toronto but . . . but . . . he also let this city down when he decided to join the priesthood instead of playing for the Toronto Maple Leafs.

A few people looked at each other and called out, "What?"

For those who didn't know, he had an offer in hand and said no. It's true. He had an offer from the Leafs, and said no. I said, "Sean, Jesus Christ!" and he turned to me and said, "Exactly."

More laughter, even from a few of the priests.

And he thereby made a choice that put him on a path away from professional sports but towards all of you. No offence to the hockey players in the crowd today, but had he merely played hockey many of you wouldn't be here.

I heard some of his Leaf drinking buddies call out, "Here, here."

Sean drank. He drank too much. He tried to stop. He would fail. He would try again. He would fail. Repeat. It took prostate cancer to make him stop. I never understood it. Why it always went too far. But I have a better idea now.

I let that hang out there and gave people a chance to digest their own memories of Sean's struggles with alcohol.

In our family there were only so many good looks to go around. My father was a handsome man. Sean was a very handsome man. And unfortunately for me, that was it. Those looks, that Paul Newman smile and his natural charm made him a formidable force. He was hard to resist. That was sometimes not for the best.

That sent a buzz through those in crowd who knew what it meant, especially after the Thornbird-Three catastrophe at St Joseph's High School a few years back.

But my God, when he turned those powers to help someone, there was no force that could stop him. I stand here today as living proof of his power. I would not have run in the election had it not been for Sean. I would not have had such a capable campaign team without the help of people like Naomi Smart, who helped me. Why? Because she knew Sean.

I nodded a thank-you to her and her family.

And I would not be the attorney general of Ontario right now had it not been for the friendship Sean shared with Premier Franks.

I turned to her.

Thank you, Premier, for having confidence in me and I will not let you down.

She gave me a gracious nod and a beautiful smile.

But today is not about me. I only mention my recent success as an example of Sean's influence—influence which I intend to carry forward after his passing. This is not the time or the place but soon you will know what I mean by that. That time and place will be in the Ontario legislature.

That sent an electric buzz through the crowd.

In closing, I would like to share a few words that I found in Sean's journal.

We think we are moving in a straight line
Toward some end
But yesterday stole tomorrow
And then tomorrow stole today
So there is no end
Just a painful curiosity
And a wondering, why?

My words sent an uncomfortable charge through the crowd, and had a few priests shifting awkwardly in their pew. I could see puzzled heads turning, people asking each other, "Did something happen to Sean?"

As strong as Sean was, he had been hurt. I think going forward we need to do everything in our power to make sure that doesn't happen to others, whether it be our children, our young women and young men, our elderly or anyone vulnerable in our society.

I struggled not to sound angry.

Mark these words, my words. Tomorrow will deliver justice for those painful yesterdays.

I could hear a crackling puzzlement. *What does he mean?*

I'm leaving here with my brother in a few minutes and we are heading to St. Augustine's for a private burial service. Before we go, please join me in a prayer that I think is appropriate. It's on the back page of your program. Fittingly, it is the prayer to St. Michael.

St. Michael the Archangel, defend us in battle. Be our protection against the wickedness and snares of the Devil. May God rebuke him we humbly pray; and do thou O Prince of the Heavenly Hosts, by the power of God, thrust into hell Satan, and all the evil spirits, who prowl about the world seeking the ruin of souls. Amen.

After a few more words from the archbishop, I accompanied Sean's casket, a white pall draped over it, down the main aisle as 1,600 people stood in his honour. When I reached the outer doors and prepared to help lift him into the waiting hearse, there stood the fierce little Father Shannon. He was not happy. Furious, actually. It was the fury that comes from being beaten—horsewhipped, in fact—at one's own game.

And I wasn't done yet.

65

Bankrupt, Indeed
Wednesday December 14 and Thursday December 15

IT TOOK A couple of weeks to settle into my new office at 720 Bay Street. In the early days of practice, I had imagined someday being one of the infamous "Bay Street lawyers." Those dreams never included this address, though. Instead of meeting with clients about real-life problems, my days were now filled with non-stop rounds of briefings about everything from court reform to the appointment of new judges to courthouse renovations to budget concerns over court delays. Criminal charges were being thrown out left and right by judges because they had taken too long to get to trial. COVID had only made a terrible situation worse. Many a guilty person walked free. It was disgusting.

I had good reason for deferring as long as possible any meeting with Father Shannon. I needed time to work with staff lawyers and legislative counsel on my own ideas about how to handle the plague of abuse by clergy. Lindsay's work had been invaluable, but the bureaucrats had tried to delay me by putting my legislation through some kind of sausage factory of interministerial committees and so-called stakeholder task forces. I finally put my foot down and told them to have it on my desk within twenty-four hours or look for work in the private sector. Thank God, Bonnie was there to run interference for me most days as I stepped on toes throughout the government. But it had worked.

I was keeping her busy and away from her beloved Mateo as much as possible for her own good, but she still found time to sneak away for midday *tête-à-têtes*. She was actually getting a little pushy with me and suggested more than once that I let him sit in on briefings and even my upcoming meeting with Father Shannon. Not gonna happen. Besides, he probably appreciates the free time to hound around the Main Legislative Building, flaunting his new celebrity status with the media and junior staffers as the "I Can Save the Planet" MPP.

Madeleine—er, Premier Franks—called me one morning about my projects. "I hear they're issuing boot casts and splints at the AG for all the broken toes you're causing over there."

"To make things happen, I need to break a few eggs."

"Fine. But just remember, you don't have to break *all* the eggs."

Hearing her warm voice was a balm. "Thanks. I appreciate the advice. I'll be ready next week to address my issues in the House. I think you'll approve."

"I'm sure I will. Good luck. And, just a tip, lighten your step, we're going to be here for a while, I hope."

"Understood." Hearing her voice gave me a thought. "Any chance you would be free for dinner sometime this week?" I tried not to sound like a teenager asking a girl to a movie.

There was a long pause. "I have my hands full so perhaps some other time." Shiiit. I had pushed too soon. Then she added, "But that would be nice, sometime soon."

My heart nearly leapt out of my chest. "Awesome."

Really? I had just said awesome? To the premier? About having dinner? Adolescent idiot.

"Right, *awesome*." I thought I heard her giggle. "By the way I heard that you are meeting with some folks from the archdiocese tomorrow."

"Father Shannon. I mentioned him before. He's the priest from Ireland. The one they sent over to . . ."

"I remember. Step carefully there. Remember we have a majority but it's slim right now. I'm dealing with a lot of carping. Mr. Reyes is not happy and he's stirring up grumbling among my caucus—after just two weeks in power we're not pursuing a *green agenda fast enough*. He's also a very big supporter of the Catholic Filipino community. He called me about your meeting tomorrow. He wants to sit in. I need to keep him busy. I fear he has too much time on his hands."

Oh-oh. Where are Bonnie's loyalties right now? Was Mateo using her to push his personal agenda? Was she supporting mine? What had he told her about his missed Cabinet opportunity? What was Bonnie telling him about the goings-on in my office and my carefully laid plans?

"Premier, I was thinking the other day, you're from Northern Ontario. I seem to recall that there are a number of pressing environmental issues that reach across several ridings, the most *northerly* ridings. It's not for me as AG to say but, if the Minister of the Environment should propose that an all-party committee—a task force, if you will, that includes a Green MPP—should undertake a tour of the North for the next few months to meet with stakeholders and prepare a report on the issues—clean water, for example—I, for one, would heartily support the proposal."

"You sound just like Sean."

"I will take that as a compliment." I felt a pang, realizing that he was indeed gone forever.

"That's how it was intended. Leave it with me. Good luck with your meeting."

The next morning Shannon arrived with four lawyers in tow. I left them waiting for thirty minutes in my main eleventh-floor boardroom, looking out over possibly the most boring stretch of Bay Street.

When I walked in with Bonnie, they all stood to shake hands and congratulate me on my election and appointment. Shannon looked like he could barely be civil. I was surprised to see Steve Larson, Randall Williams's protégé, among the group. I guess Shannon thought he needed some big-firm firepower to make his pitch for whatever he had in mind for the church. I wonder if Shannon knew about my Novak file with Williams. No, probably not. Larson wouldn't be bragging about that settlement.

"Father Shannon, can I start by thanking you so much for the way in which you organized and facilitated my brother Sean's Funeral Mass and burial service? And for the archbishop himself to perform the service? It was really something. I couldn't be happier."

The lawyers looked like they thought this was setting a great tone to the meeting, the attorney general thanking their client—and profusely. Beautiful. Shannon? Not so much. His face burned. I could feel the heat coming off him and all he could manage was, "I'm glad it met your expectations."

"It did. Father, you mentioned that the archdiocese had some requests or proposals for justice reform. I promised you a meeting and I'm a man of my word. I think we should get underway."

Larson jumped in. "Attorney General, would you prefer to wait for the Ministry staff lawyers to join you? Some of the proposals are quite technical."

"No, I think we can proceed. If I get in over my head, we can always pause and call for reinforcements."

A lawyer introduced himself as senior partner with the biggest firm, not just in Toronto, but in Canada. "We have eight hundred lawyers and offices in every province."

"Impressive."

"You may not be aware of it, but we have been in negotiations with the federal department of justice and your federal counterpart, the attorney general of Canada, over a number of issues."

"Great to have all your experience at our disposal. Please continue."

"May I put some information up on your monitor?"

"Please, I'm a big supporter of technology in law."

Thank God I got Bonnie to explain what a Dropbox was and had her make hard copies of all of Lindsay's research. I had worked into the wee hours inhaling it just last night.

On the first slide appeared the words "Confidential and Without Prejudice."

The next three slides set out a series of columns containing dates, dollar values, names of institutions, parishes and claimants identified by colour codes and numbers. Another lawyer, a very serious young woman, walked me through what we were looking at. It was a detailed estimation of claims faced by the Christian Brothers and Ontario Catholic clergy for the period 1950 to present. There were hundreds of claimants. "Names have been removed to protect claimants' privacy."

"I see."

The third set of slides set out similar information but confined to schools for the deaf and the blind operated by Catholic charities. Again, there were hundreds of names.

"Can we go back to the first set of slides?"

"Certainly." The lawyer clicked back a slide. Then another. I felt Shannon watching me closely.

"One more."

She clicked again.

"That's it. Good. Thanks. Carry on."

I felt my blood start to boil. In the middle of the second page sat the name of a parish I knew too well. It was our childhood parish, St. Gertrude's, in Toronto. There were a dozen claimant numbers in the column beside it.

"Was there anything in particular you needed to ask about those first slides, Attorney General?"

"No. Carry on." I'm sure they thought I was simply overwhelmed by the volume of information.

More slides followed for the category of provincial residential schools. There were dozens of claimants. The humourless young lawyer explained, "These claimants were not captured in the settlement of the residential claims against the federal government. Their claims are still live."

I looked at Bonnie. She looked unnerved and upset. We were looking at a social catastrophe spread over generations. I leaned over and whispered in her ear, "Are you going to be okay?"

"Yes, but I wish you had included Mateo in this briefing. I think he could help with this. He has a strong relationship with the church."

I'm sure he does. I could see now why she was upset. It wasn't the horror we were looking at, it was the fact that her hero was not present. My heart sank. I knew looking into Bonnie's eyes that I could no longer count on her. I needed to get her out of this meeting.

"Oh shit."

"What?"

"Bonnie, I just remembered that I forgot to deal with that report on the issue of Crown attorney compensation. They need an answer this afternoon."

"Are you sure?"

"Yes, I got so distracted last night. Can you shoot up to the Main Leg and get it for me?"

"Can't they courier it?"

"No, it's too confidential they said."

Father Shannon interrupted our whispering. "Do you need to take a break? Get your legal team in here now?"

"No, thank you, it concerns another urgent matter." I think Bonnie suddenly realized that she could probably pop in to see Mateo, so she agreed and promised to be back "after lunch." Whatever.

"Please, carry on. Where do you think this situation leaves your client?"

A third lawyer—a corporate type, numbers guy—stepped in, presumably to give me the sad news. "The archdiocese would essentially be bankrupt and could not meet this volume of claims. Lawsuits, class actions—if successful—would destroy the church as we know it in Ontario. The litigation costs alone would be in the millions of dollars."

"I see. Is there a slide for that? It sounds dire."

"Exactly." He seemed relieved that I understood so quickly but produced no further slide on the church's financial situation.

"What do you propose?"

"Father Shannon and his team of lawyers have been travelling the province and negotiating settlements with many of the claimants, especially the deaf and blind communities. He has made considerable progress. Those have been dealt with conclusively. But the balance of the claims cannot be funded."

"I see. What do you estimate the value of those claims to be?"

They looked at each other and then Father Shannon. "It's hard to put an exact number on it."

"Try."

"Well, it depends on a few variables . . ."

"Try harder."

Larson jumped in. "Approximately $257 million."

I didn't even blink. "That's a lot of money."

"As my colleague says, it is money the church doesn't have."

"What are you proposing?"

It was the fourth lawyer's turn to earn his fat hourly rate. He was the closer. "We are proposing to do two things: (1) through Catholic charities and our parishes we are going to run a campaign, a challenge to members of the church, to donate what they can through fundraisers, charitable walks, bake sales and so on . . ."

"Like crowdfunding."

"Yes, in a way . . . but then, (2) whatever they raise, the church will match dollar for dollar. That money will be put in a fund called the Provincial Catholic Compensation Fund, and used to pay claims." He made this sound downright exciting, like a Terry Fox run.

"Well, that sounds like a plan. How much do you expect to raise and then match?"

"We think we can raise five million."

"And with the church matching you would have ten million."

There was an awkward pause. "No, actually, that would be the total after matching. We think we can create a five-million-dollar compensation fund."

"That would leave you about $252 million short, though."

"Yes, that's where the provincial government can help."

"I see. How would we do that?"

"We are hoping that the government would enter into an agreement, supported with a very brief piece of legislation, that would insulate the church from the balance of the claims—once the commitment to create the Provincial Catholic Compensation Fund, PCCF, is met."

"I see. How would that be achieved?"

"Can I put some wording up on the monitor? Our lawyers have been doing the drafting. It is the same wording we agreed to with your federal counterparts, with the necessary changes, *mutatis mutandis*."

Ahh, Latin. This is getting good. "Please."

A new slide appeared with two paragraphs:

Ontario does hereby remise, release and forever discharge, the Catholic entities, its directors, officers, shareholders, agents, lawyers, and em-ployees, of and from all manner of actions, causes of actions, suits, debts, dues, accounts, bonds whatsoever against the releasees.

Ontario further covenants and agrees not to directly or indirectly join, assist, aid or act in concert in any manner whatsoever with any person or entity in making any financial claim or demand whatsoever against the releasees and further indemnifies the releasees for any claims made over and above the amount contained in the PCCF.

"That's very dense language."

Larson, thinking I may not have understood such complicated language drafted by *Bay Street lawyers*, decided to explain: "Bottom line, once you cut through the legalese, this would protect the church from bankruptcy. It should be incorporated into a very short act called something like, *An Act to Protect the Financial Integrity of the Catholic Church and Its Entities in Ontario*. Of course, your legislative draft people can make other suggestions for a title. Our concern is the content."

"I see. Thank you. I think I understand. The provincial government would then be responsible for any claims made successfully over and above your five-million-dollar fund—the PCCF."

"Yes, that is assuming our parishioners were able to raise $2.5 million and we matched it. The government would cover the balance. Obviously, the government would be free to litigate and defend those claims as you have considerably more resources to do so."

"I see. We could defend against the claims made by victims? If we wanted to? Do you mind if we take a short break and let me pop out for some help?"

I heard Shannon mutter, "I knew this would happen if he didn't have his team in here to explain it to him."

Larson placed a hand on his arm and apologized. "Take whatever time you need. We can wait while you get your team together."

"I'll just be a minute. I'll have some coffee and cookies sent in. We may be here a while."

Shannon let out a sigh of exasperation.

Oh, if you're exasperated now, you had better brace yourself, Father. I smiled thinking of Sean doing his terrible impersonation of Pacino in *Scarface*. "Say hello to my little friend."

66

Reality Check
Thursday December 15

"SORRY ABOUT THAT, gentlemen." I slid back into my chair and opened my laptop.

Larson saw me close the door. "Will they—the lawyers—be joining us?"

"No. I just needed my laptop. I want to understand this financial predicament in which the church finds itself. Do you have some slides for that?"

"Sorry, we don't but you can take our client's word for it that . . ."

"We don't have to take anyone's word for this. Let's use my slides." Actually, Lindsay had prepared them, and thoroughly.

I hit a few keystrokes (as rehearsed with Lindsay over the phone last night) and threw a slide up on the monitor: Archdiocese of Greater Toronto Area (AOGTA).

Five chairs turned in unison to look closely at a spreadsheet.

"It was a little tricky understanding the AOGTA charitable reporting because it doesn't use the accepted non-profit accounting standards. That's highly unusual, isn't it?"

"Well, let me try to explain. As a charity . . ."

"That wasn't really a question. It's highly unusual. Let's look, for example, at how the AOGTA handles the value of all its lands and buildings.

Each year it writes down all spending on its properties and then reports the value of those lands and buildings as $2.00."

"Yes, but . . ."

"What have your own auditors estimated the book value of those properties at?"

"We don't have that information available."

"I do. They estimated the value to be $973.8 million."

"Where is he getting these figures?" Shannon looked hopeless. This was not his area. He was relying on the lawyers to pitch his solution and answer these questions.

"Can we look at the Good Faith Capital Campaign? Would that be called the GFCC? It had a goal of raising $125 million. How much did it actually raise?"

Nothing but blank stares.

"It raised $144.8 million. About $20 million of that money is for parish and diocese priorities. Correct?"

More blank stares.

"I see the AOGTA reserve fund in 2021 was $51.1 million."

Blank stares and now mouths open.

"It's probably not fair to look at just the AOGTA in isolation."

"I agree, we should look at the big picture, which is different when you account for all the variables, unaccounted-for variances and unknowables . . ." A word salad was coming out of Larson. Even his colleagues looked at him with serious doubts about where he was headed. Maybe he is paid by the word, like the old days.

"Let's look at the Catholic Church nationally." I threw up a new slide. "Okay, so it looks like aside from being the biggest and most successful charity in Canada, it received $986 million in donations last year and had a profit of $201 million. It has $1.2 billion in investments, stocks and bonds and $3.3 billion in property. Its wealth is on par with the Vatican itself. Am I reading that correctly?"

Father Shannon glared at me. "Mr. Bierce, . . ."

"Attorney General Bierce."

"Attorney General Bierce, if you insist. I'm not sure what your game is today. We had an understanding that if I accommodated your request with respect to your brother's funeral," his team of lawyers was now looking at him puzzled, "you would meet with me and accommodate the church's requests on a number of issues."

"Father Shannon, I said I would meet with you and consider your proposals. You have come here today and asked me to consent on behalf of the taxpayers of this province—a place where you do not live—to pick up the tab for abuse by your employees over five decades—an estimated $257 million. You have made that request on the basis that, if the church is called upon to meet its obligations, it will go bankrupt. Your lawyers have told me that point blank. Yet when I look at financial records—the ones that are actually available to the public—I see something quite different." I turned to the lawyer, the numbers guy, "Counsel, do you see any errors in my math?"

He looked stunned. "Not on the basis of the numbers you have presented. I'm not in a position to contradict those calculations."

"Thank you. I could go on. I have a very sound grasp of these financial statements and more. I don't need four Bay Street lawyers to execute grade two math for me. If there's nothing else, I suggest you leave before I really get up a head of steam and start talking about the Christian Brothers."

Larson finally spoke. "I think we're done here."

"Oh, you're done." *Please exit through the gift shop.*

As I stood to leave, Larson and two lawyers had to physically restrain Father Shannon. I kind of hoped he might get loose. That would be a great headline in the *Sun*—PRIEST ATTACKS GRIEVING ATTORNEY GENERAL.

67

A Dish Best Served Cold
Monday December 19

THINGS MOVED QUICKLY for the new government after the swearing in of the new Speaker. I had prevailed upon Madeleine not to give away too much in the throne speech and she acquiesced by including a one-liner about justice reform. An afternoon had been set aside for the introduction of new bills and I was first up.

Show time.

As members returned from the lunch recess, the legislative chamber was a place to behold. It was a cacophony of conversation between MPPs on the floor and political staff crowded in behind the Speaker's chair. Young pages in their black uniforms, having memorized the new seating plan, scooted about delivering messages to the all-important politicians. The re-elected were still getting caught up with friends from opposing parties and sizing up the new arrivals. And speaking of new arrivals, you would think Mateo Reyes was still running for election based on the glad-handing and back-slapping he was doing as he made his way to his seat in the far corner of the chamber. I would need to keep my eye on this troublemaker.

The public gallery was gradually filling up with noisy classes of high school kids, political science students and a few tourists intrigued by what actually happens at Queen's Park, and my special guests.

It hadn't been easy but I made sure Bonnie was kept far away from the announcements I was about to make. Keeping her busy on admin tasks and setting up my new constituency office in grim Parkdale (apparently I have to be in the riding from time to time) was a challenge, but I think she was none the wiser. I had told her that I would share drafts with her when the time was right. It just never felt right. I guess I had lost confidence in her. It happened so quickly.

I was lucky to discover on my staff at the Ministry a young cracker-jack expert on legislative procedures. I kept him close at hand to ensure there were no missteps.

As I settled into my seat on the front bench, Bonnie appeared behind the Speaker's chair. She looked angry as she snapped her fingers at a page and scribbled out a note to be delivered to me. I opened it and read, *Have you heard about Mateo?*

I looked over at her, shrugged and shook my head. I did, however, know what was coming. Mateo was headed for the chillier parts of Ontario.

The Speaker recognized the Member from Ingersoll and Minister of the Environment who first wished to make a statement to the House. A former Iranian pharmacist but now a barber from Ingersoll, he was settling nicely into his new position. However, unfortunately for his role as a politician, he did not relish the prospect of speaking in public. His staff had handed him a typed statement with specific instructions about where he should add emphasis, telling him to read it word for word.

The Speaker called for order and the Minister began.

"Mr. Speaker, I am very pleased to rise this afternoon and make an announcement that will benefit the people of Ontario for generations to come. Before I do so, I would like to take a minute to acknowledge some special visitors in the gallery . . ."

He then rhymed off the names of a half-dozen environmental, farming, forestry and mining group representatives. When I looked up, I saw none other than Ms. Reach for the Top in the mix. I assume she had been invited to witness this glorious green announcement. She was smiling and waving a little too much at Mateo for my liking, and I wondered if Bonnie was picking up on the vibe being exchanged between them.

I saw too that my fan club of animal lovers had come to see me table legislation in the House for the first time. I waved and tried to think of a way I might take some credit for my colleague's upcoming bill, An Act for the Prevention of Unethical Puppy Farms.

"Mr. Speaker, I am very pleased to announce the establishment of the Northern Ontario Environment Policy Futures Task Force. This task force will undertake add emphasis very important meetings with stakeholders." The room slowly rolled into laughter as he carried on. "These stakeholders are among our add emphasis most active environmental citizens." The Speaker called for order as the place erupted into laughter. A page arrived at the Minister's side with a note. He read it and turned beet red. After a few deep breaths and the Speaker restoring order, he carried on bravely to announce that Mateo Reyes and a merry band of MPPs would be touring Northern Ontario for the next three months, meeting with stakeholders. He concluded by advising the House that the task force report would be tabled once their work was complete. When he sat down, the members rose for a standing ovation—with added emphasis.

I glanced at Madeleine who raised her eyebrows and winked. The troublemaker would be on the road for the foreseeable future during the dead of winter in Northern Ontario. Sweet Justice.

I looked at Bonnie. She was distraught. Clearly Mateo had not said anything to her about being recruited by the premier herself to lead this important committee, a committee whose report would be read in six months by a handful of bureaucrats and set aside unused as another "important consultation with incredibly valuable stakeholders."

I had made provision for Lindsay to get a special pass that would allow her to join Bonnie behind the Speaker's chair and then sit in the members' guest gallery so she could hear Part 3 of my plan. She arrived just in time to console Bonnie and hear my statement. After all her work, I knew she wouldn't want to miss it. (Plus, I hadn't said anything to either of them, but I had asked Coop to get them and Naomi backstage passes for his upcoming show at Scotiabank Arena.)

The Speaker called for the introduction of new bills.

"The Speaker recognizes the Honourable Member for Parkdale–High Park and Attorney General . . ."

There was a thunderous round of table-thumping from my new-found caucus colleagues, who had absolutely no idea what I was about to say. I glanced into the gallery to see Father Shannon and his law suits, apprehensive about what they were going to hear.

"Thank you, Mr. Speaker, I am very pleased to rise today to introduce Bill 1, my first bill as attorney general, and to make a related announcement.

"Mr. Speaker, I would ask that first reading be given to An Act to Revoke the Effect of Non-Disclosure Agreements in Cases of Sexual Harassment, Sexual Assault or Threats. The short-form title will be An Act to Allow Victims of Harassment to Speak Up."

There was stunned silence.

"Mr. Speaker, it has come to my attention that in Ontario, individuals who have been subjected to sexual harassment, assault and threats face very high hurdles in seeking redress and compensation for their injuries. A terrible situation involving sexual assaults by hockey players has recently been in the news. Even when victims advance their well-founded claims, they face the prospect of slow and expensive hearings, not to mention personal embarrassment. I have been told, Mr. Speaker, that many such claims are concluded with settlements for the victim but a key part of the settlement requires the victim to sign an NDA, a Non-Disclosure Agreement."

Some members called out "Shame, shame."

"Mr. Speaker, some would have us believe that these NDAs are for the benefit of the victim, to protect their privacy. But, Mr. Speaker, they in fact protect the person who has perpetrated this harassment, these assaults, these threats."

There were more shouts of "Shame! Shame!"

"Mr. Speaker, this legislation will give any victim who has been required to sign an NDA in order to receive a settlement, the option of setting aside that agreement, publicizing their situation and, if they wish, re-opening their claim in a confidential process established by the regulations under this Act. They will be able to do so without penalty. They will have a two-year period from royal assent of this legislation within which to commence action."

There was thunderous applause from nearly every member. I saw from the corner of my eye that three members immediately stood and walked out of the chamber. I also noticed that my friend Mr. Reyes looked a little shell-shocked. He was probably wondering why Bonnie couldn't get him in on this legislative blockbuster.

"Mr. Speaker, importantly, this Act will have retrospective and retroactive enforcement provisions. Any NDA signed between the years 1975 and today, the day of first reading, will be subject to its provisions."

Well, Father Shannon, you can wave goodbye to all the NDAs you gathered on behalf of the Christian Brothers, priests and clergy.

"Mr. Speaker, the legislation will apply to any person, entity, corporation—non-profit or for-profit, charitable or non-charitable—doing business in the Province of Ontario and will apply to NDAs entered into by the entities or person worldwide. If an Ontario-based entity, for example, has employees in other countries who made claims for abuse or harassment and their matters were settled with an NDA, then that NDA, too, is subject to being set aside."

Goodbye to the Haiti NDAs, Father Shannon. That's when he and his law suits, now aghast, headed for the exits under a full head of steam. Too bad they were going to miss the good part.

"Mr. Speaker, this legislation is needed, and it is needed sooner rather than later. I am therefore asking for unanimous consent to give the bill first and second reading today and to send it straight to the Standing Committee on Justice for public hearings."

The Speaker called out, "All those in favour, say *Aye*."

A roar went up in favour of my proposal. I turned and smiled at Lindsay. She was standing and applauding. So were students in the gallery. Even Ms. Reach for the Top. We had done it. Part 3 of my plan was now going to be law. We had poured the foundation and built the scaffold. All Lindsay's research had paid off. Not only was her NDA with Williams toast, she had also led him down the garden path into writing a defence of NDAs in his recent report. His words would form the noose around his neck. Francesca's NDA with Singh and Glinka was also now null and void. So was every NDA signed by lawyers, staff and clients who suffered harassment at Williams's firm, and every NDA signed for Father Shannon by victims of abuse around the province. We were throwing open the doors.

Lindsay sent me a text. *I'm going to draw out Williams's torture as long as possible. I'm waiting the full two years from royal assent.* Good, she was learning.

I turned from Lindsay to Bonnie. She was not smiling. She just shook her head in disbelief. A flurry of angry texts lit up my phone. Why had I kept this blockbuster announcement from her? Why had I not found a way to include her precious Mateo in the process of drafting this landmark bill? Why had I shut her out?

As the applause continued, I turned to Madeleine and hoped she was impressed with this show of force. She had picked the right person to be AG. We were doing good work, and at the same time I was reeking revenge on my enemies, Justice Randall Williams and Father Shannon. The torture of laws. It was perfect as I stood there soaking it in. I prayed Sean was looking down on this scene. Who could have imagined this just a few months ago?

Instead of joining the standing ovation, Madeleine looked up from her phone, alarmed. What had just happened?

The Speaker announced the result of the vote. "Hearing that the matter is unanimous, the bill is referred to committee as requested."

He then turned to me again. "The Speaker recognizes the attorney general for an announcement."

I wasn't done yet.

Before I could begin, I saw Madeleine rise from her seat and hurry behind the Speaker's chair. Ponytail man, now her chief of staff, was waving his arms around, clearly upset about something. *She has a tough job and can't even enjoy this moment of doing good.* I decided to press on.

"Mr. Speaker, I am rising to inform the House that as attorney general I will be establishing a commission to investigate historic sexual and physical abuse in the Province of Ontario, in its educational institutions, schools, churches, parishes and any related entities. Its mandate will be broad. It will have subpoena powers. It will have the authority to open the financial records of any institution in its sights. It will have the authority to assess the value of claims made by victims of abuse. It will have the authority to order assets be frozen and to preserve those assets for any needed compensation of victims. It will, in short, Mr. Speaker, address a long-neglected injustice in this province.

"In the upcoming week, I will be announcing the members of this commission and unveiling its formal mandate. Thank you, Mr. Speaker."

I sat and enjoyed the applause and the fact that Father Shannon must be losing his mind. The church was not going to dodge any more claims. Above all, St. Gertrude's Parish's sins would be laid out for all to see. I hope you're watching, Sean.

Members were clearly onboard with the new bill and the commission. I just wished Madeleine could stand there beside me to enjoy it as well. But she was gone. So was Bonnie. I looked over to the back of the chamber to see Mateo's seat empty. I would need to have a heart-to-heart with Bonnie. If I laid it out for her plainly, I think she would see the light with this character Mateo. Eventually the gossip would get to her. I needed to cut it off at the pass and save her a lot of embarrassment. She would get over it.

As my father would say, *Tempora Tempore Tempera—Time alleviates all troubles*.

68

The Torture of Laws
Monday December 19

WHEN I ARRIVED back at my office at 720 Bay, I expected a hero's welcome after that performance in the House. It was my first time and I'd come off the bench a rookie and immediately hit a grand slam. It would be hard to top that. In fact, now that my two biggest enemies—Father Shannon and His Honour Randall Williams—had been vanquished I wondered what I would do for an encore. The only upside of staying on as an MPP I could think of was to be near Madeleine. There was something there. I hadn't felt this way in years. In fact, I couldn't remember ever feeling quite like this.

I decided to have a very generous celebratory drink the minute I sat down in my office. I had slipped a good bottle of single malt into the drawer for just such an occasion. And perhaps I could sneak a cigar. I wished Sean was here to enjoy it with me.

But when I arrived on the eleventh floor there was no hero's welcome—it was like a funeral. Everyone just stood and watched as I made my way down the hall to my office. Wow, these bureaucrats are a drag. Don't they know a win when they see one? I guess they weren't accustomed to such sweeping action, such total legislative progress. Well, watch and learn.

When I got to my door, Bonnie was sitting at her desk. She did not look up. Not a good sign.

"Okay, what's your problem? You can't enjoy these two big wins with me? This is what I came here for. Justice."

She swivelled around and glared at me. "Justice? You came here for revenge, plain and simple. I don't know where to begin. You can't allow Mateo even a small part of the limelight? Or me? You kept it all to yourself. And don't think I haven't heard the rumours that you blocked him from Cabinet. You'd better call the premier's office. They have lost their minds over the proposed legislation. They have been calling here looking for you."

This didn't seem like a good time to mention the backstage passes, so I went into my office and called Madeleine. Her chief of staff answered with a brusque, "I've been looking for you."

"I understand the premier would like to speak with me. Is she available?"

"Attorney General, we have a major problem. I'm assembling a team to discuss this on a high priority basis. I'll need you for a meeting at the Main Legislative Building at seven o'clock this evening. Premier's boardroom."

"Will the premier be there?" I looked at my watch. It was nearly 6:30 p.m. The drink and cigar would need to wait.

"She's dealing with another crisis. She may try to join us later."

"I'll be there but what's this all about?"

"I'll explain when you get here. I have to reach a few more people. See you at seven o'clock."

At 6:45 p.m. I walked into the East entrance of the Main Leg and made my way to the massive central staircase. When I got to the foot of it, I caught a glimpse of the Lothario Mateo Reyes slipping into the Amethyst Room, a large meeting room reserved for committee hearings. But no hearings were scheduled. What was this hound up to? He'd left the door open a crack, so I walked over and glanced in.

Around the table sat a collection of familiar people. Father Shannon was at the head with Steve Larson by his side. The Bay Street lawyers from our meeting at my office were there as well, setting up a screen for a presentation of some kind. I recognized three male members of the NDP caucus sitting together. Across from them sat Mr. I Like CERB McKay and his wife Pam along with the ruthless Dikombee and Brazeau, the interim leader of the Conservatives, as well as Green Leader Neil Gruber and the weasel Mateo Reyes. Behind them sat none other than Hopeless Helen and her red-checkered-shirt husband. They were engrossed in a conversation with the unmistakable Lorelei Novak. It was a rogues' gallery of malcontents. What were they up to? I leaned in a little further to see who else was at the table and my heart sank. There beside Mateo, preparing to circulate a sheaf of documents, stood Bonnie. A bright purple file wrapped in duct tape—my Law Society discipline file—was tucked under her arm. My beloved Bonnie had gone to the dark side.

I slipped away and made it to the premier's boardroom a few minutes late. A dozen people sat around the table. Mr. Ponytail was at the head but I did not recognize any of the other staff.

"Sorry I'm late."

"Ah, Attorney General. I'm glad you're here. Let's get started." He went around the table introducing people, giving their titles and responsibilities. Based on what I was hearing this was a high-level damage control group. He had Dylan pass around packages of materials that included the bill I had just introduced and the announcement of the commission.

"Okay, so here is where we are at. The two items in front of you may bring this government down in the very near future." That sent a buzz around the group.

"Forgive me for jumping in but why on earth would you say that? You saw the reaction in that chamber today. Members love this package. It went through first and second reading in one fell swoop. It's going to Justice Committee for public hearings."

"Maybe not."

"I beg your pardon? Maybe not? I don't think so. That's my legislation. I cleared it with the premier. She was totally on board with it. There is no way I'm withdrawing that bill or that commission." I looked around at their stony faces.

"Wait, . . . did the archdiocese get to you? Is that what's going on? You're caving to the archdiocese? I thought you people were brave reformers."

"Andrew, we are reformers or at least we hope to be reformers." It was Madeleine's calm voice. "Listen everybody, why don't you carry on with this meeting, look at some options, think of interim damage control, while Andrew and I speak in my office for a few minutes?"

We slipped through double wooden doors to her office and sat in chairs near the windows that look down University Avenue. The streetlights were on, and the year's first snowfall was just beginning. It's a pretty view at that time of day, even if a lot of it is just the lights of cars sitting in the usual traffic gridlock.

"Damage control? Madeleine, what happened? One minute you were sitting there happy and then I saw you. You looked terrified. What happened?"

"First, Andrew, there's nothing wrong with the bill or the commission. They are good pieces of work. But . . ." She was trying to find the right words. "When you made your statement explaining how the bill will reopen NDAs, I got four messages within two minutes. Three of our MPPs cannot vote for the bill. The opposition knows it and they see an opportunity. They will try to make it a matter of confidence in the government. They could bring us down. We've been in power less than a month."

I recalled seeing some members walk out while I spoke, but I assumed it was other business. "Can't you crack the so-called whip? Make them vote for the bill?"

"I would love to but . . ."

"But what?"

"But—I was not made aware of this until this afternoon—three members of our caucus have signed NDAs within the last two years."

"I see."

"The NDAs concern incidents here at Queen's Park. Harassment of pages, interns, staff in the library and others. A couple of these members have been involved in more than one incident. If they vote for this bill, they will be effectively ending their careers. One phoned me, despondent, and said that disclosure of the NDA would end his marriage. I know him, his wife and their kids very well."

"You said there were four messages. Who is the fourth?"

"Our friend Mr. Reyes cannot support the bill due to NDAs concerning his conduct in the Catholic Filipino community."

"That little asshole. I knew he was trouble."

"And speaking of trouble. You must be learning that at Queen's Park secrets have a short shelf life. I heard through the grapevine that Mr. Reyes has formed quite a bond with your executive assistant. Do you have confidence in her? There are already rumours of some report that may be used to smear you. You're going to find they play rough around here."

Play rough? They have no idea. Based on what I had just seen downstairs, after all these years Bonnie and I had come to the end of our time together. I wondered if I should tell Madeleine what I had seen. It would bury Bonnie as a staff person. I would have to fire her for her duplicity. My God, people fall in love and are instantly blind.

"I can do the math. If the bill comes forward for a vote, these four members are in trouble. The bill would not pass."

"Correct. And these members couldn't sit on the Justice Committee to hear the public submissions. They would be in conflict. In fact, it would raise a few eyebrows even if these particular men were not on that committee. All four will actively campaign against the bill. They're drumming up support to kill it as we speak."

I should tell her what I saw. I could see that she was in a jam.

"There may be even more NDAs involving other members for their conduct out there in the real world . . ."

Ironically, she pointed down University Avenue toward the corporate towers that housed Williams's old law firm and the courts. She had no idea the havoc and accountability the bill was designed to create out there in the so-called "real world."

"What are you thinking?" I asked.

"I know what I'm being told. Kill the bill. Kill the commission. Never let it get to committee. Make up some excuse and delay the whole thing. Hope it disappears. Andrew, to be frank, I have bigger fish to fry than NDAs. I have a budget to present. I had no idea we might lose the government over what sounded like a wonderful and just idea. Is it worth losing power?"

She didn't need to know that above and beyond the wonderful and just idea, my sweet revenge would be denied if the bill and commission were flushed. Father Shannon and Justice Williams would be laughing at me if my handiwork was killed by the very people it was designed to out. It would be sinful if those two bastards brought down her government.

"When do you need to make a decision?"

"You saw what's going on in the other room. They want it killed tomorrow."

Exhaustion swept over me and I really needed a drink. "It's funny, but twice today my father's words have come back to me."

"Sean used to quote your father a lot. Was he some kind of minister?"

"Ha! He could have been. No, he sold cars. He was just a good-looking charmer who could sell you any car he decided needed to be sold. But he was a wise man."

She frowned. "I wonder what he would say about this situation?"

"*Tempora Tempore Tempera.*"

"Time alleviates all troubles."

"Yes, you know Latin?" Was she the perfect woman?

"Only what Sean used to quote. That was one of his favourites."

I don't know why, but all of a sudden my eyes welled up at the thought of Sean saying those words. I choked and suddenly had a hard time swallowing.

"Are you okay? It's a lot to give up."

"Oh, I'm not giving up. I was just thinking about Sean. A few weeks ago, the archdiocese was in my boardroom asking me to get you—this government—to cover the cost of all the abuse claims they had caused over the last five decades, a couple of hundred million dollars' worth. They said they would go bankrupt if they had to pay. Instead, these billionaires offered to do a few bake sales and then get taxpayers to cover the rest. When they made their presentation I saw our parish, Sean's and my parish, St. Gertrude's, on their spreadsheet. There were a dozen claims associated with our parish. No names, they were just dollar estimates on a slide." I choked back some tears. "Sean was one of them. I never knew. It was in his journal. Sorry."

I felt her arm around my shoulders. I could smell her body, her perfume. "I know," she said softly, "Sean told me years ago."

"Why didn't he tell me?"

"Shame."

When she said it, I thought my heart would break and the tears came again. "Sorry, I . . . I . . ."

"Andrew, don't be sorry. They hate the idea of not having power, of being held accountable. I've been up against this my whole life. My grandparents went to residential schools. I know what it feels like to be told that I can't do something that would be good for my people because someone in power will be made uncomfortable. That's why I ran."

Her motives were so much more honourable than mine, but it made no difference.

Dylan stuck their head into the premier's office. "They want to know if you're coming back. They've run out of ideas."

"We'll be there in a minute." She turned back to me. "What's that?" She pointed to a gift-wrapped box I had under my arm. In the furor over the bill, I'd forgotten that I had brought her a gift.

"It's for you. It was supposed to be in celebration of today . . . of beginning together . . . you know, beginning . . . to work together." That came out a bit awkwardly.

She unwrapped it, opened the box and lifted from the tissue paper an exact replica of the ceramic bourdaloue we had seen at the Gardiner Museum that day we first met. "It's beautiful." And then she giggled. "I will keep it on my desk as a reminder . . ."

"Of what you have to deal with?"

She sighed. "Sometimes actions with good intentions have bad consequences."

I had to laugh. "It's usually the other way around for me. My methods have always been quite nasty at times, but in order to obtain good consequences. Ironic."

"Sean mentioned something about your practice, your skills. Total War he called it? Nasty, but effective."

I explained what I was trying to do for Lindsay, Francesca and dozens of other young women at Williams's firm, how I built the scaffolds for Father Shannon, Justice Williams and Judge Glinka, and how they would now answer for their behaviour. I told her about *tortura legum pessima*— the torture of laws is the worst kind of torture.

She was intrigued. "Could something like that . . . would something like that apply to this situation?"

I thought for a minute. She needed to know. So I told her what I had seen in the Amethyst Room: her disloyal caucus members; the grasping hound Mateo Reyes; Mr. Brazeau, hoping to be more than merely an interim Conservative leader, the likes of the grifters McKay and his wife Pam; the cold, mean-spirited Father Shannon and his team of soulless Bay Street lawyers; the anti-vaxxers along for the ride; the slippery Lorelei Novak, looking for a way to be relevant again; and even Bonnie, my once-devoted assistant now in Mateo's thrall, betraying me. Madeleine would need to face this budding cabal. These disgruntled people could bring her down.

As her beautiful face drained of colour, I suddenly saw vulnerability and a flicker of fear.

Pondering the awful possibilities, she turned to me, for a moment, lost.

"There is an alternative," I ventured. "*Conflagratio.*"

As she stared at me, I slowly conjured for her a nasty, cunning plan of attack that could deliver her from those bastards, save her government, and even deliver sweet justice—not to mention my revenge.

Or would it burn everything she had worked for to the ground?

Her eyes met mine. I couldn't read her face now. Was she abhorred by my thoughts? The ease with which my *maligno* had poured forth?

She stood, walked across her office and placed my gift in the middle of her desk. Without looking at me, her voice barely a whisper, she said, "Let's join the others."

Had I gone too far? I wished Sean was here now to guide me.

When we entered the premier's boardroom Mr. Ponytail slid away from the centre of the table to make room for Madeleine. "Premier, we can walk you through some options to gracefully withdraw the bill and deep-six the commission. It's not pretty but then we can forget about it and live to fight another day."

Madeleine looked across the long table at me. Was she thinking of Sean? Me? Francesca and Lindsay? Her grandparents?

"That won't be necessary. I don't want to fight another day. We'll fight today. Attorney General Bierce has a proposed plan of attack. I'm going to ask him to walk us through it."

Our eyes locked and I smiled. "Thank you, Premier Franks."

We would charge through the Gates of Hell. Total War was coming to Queen's Park.

ABOUT THE AUTHOR

Michael Cochrane is a Toronto author and lawyer. He has published a number of bestselling books about Canadian law, including *Surviving Your Divorce* (now in its sixth edition). He is also the author of *Olympic Lyon: The Untold Story of the First Gold Medal for Golf*, the only book ever written about Canada's forgotten Olympic golf legend, George Lyon.

He is frequently featured on television and radio as an expert in a number of areas of Canadian law, including people who fight over lottery winnings. In over forty-four years of practice, he has been an advocate for a more humane system for separating and divorcing families. He was the host of BNN television's national legal affairs program, *Strictly Legal*, for three seasons.

He has lectured in law at Osgoode Hall Law School, Ryerson University (now Toronto Metropolitan University), the University of Ottawa, Common Law, and at Carleton University Department of Law.

He is Counsel to the firm of Brauti Thorning LLP in Toronto, Ontario (www.btlegal.ca), and can be reached at www.michaelcochrane.ca and mcochranellb@me.com.

www.ingramcontent.com/pod-product-compliance
Lightning Source LLC
Chambersburg PA
CBHW020349010826
48973CB00005B/1335